The Girl Who Wants

Shee McQueen Mystery-Thrillers
Book One

Amy Vansant

Vansant Creations, LLC / Amy Vansant
Jupiter, FL
http://www.AmyVansant.com

Copy editing by Carolyn Steele.
Proofreading by Effrosyni Moschoudi, Meg Bernhart

CHAPTER ONE

Three Weeks Ago, Nashua, New Hampshire.

Shee realized her mistake the moment her feet left the grass.

He's enormous.

She'd watched him drop from the side window of the house. He landed four feet from where she stood—still, her brain refused to register the warning signs. The nose, big and lumpy as breadfruit, the forehead some beach town could use as a jetty if they buried him to his neck...

His knees bent to absorb his weight, and *her* brain thought *got you.*

Her brain couldn't be bothered with simple math: *Giant, plus Shee, equals Pain.*

Instead, she jumped to tackle him, dangling airborne as his knees straightened and the *pet the rabbit* bastard stood to his full height.

Crap.

The math added up pretty quickly after that.

Hovering like Superman mid-flight, she couldn't do much to change her disastrous trajectory. She'd *felt* like a superhero when she left the ground. Now, she felt more like a Canada goose staring into the propellers of Captain Sully's Airbus A320.

She might take down the plane, but it was going to *hurt.*

Frankenjerk turned toward her at the exact moment she plowed into him. She clamped her arms around his waist like a little girl hugging a redwood. Lurch returned the embrace, twisting her to the ground. Her back hit the dirt, and air burst from her lungs like a double shotgun blast.

Ow.

Wheezing, she punched upward, striking Beardless Hagrid in the throat.

That didn't go over well.

Grabbing her shoulder with one hand, Dickasaurus flipped her on her stomach like a sausage link, slipped his hand under her chin, and pressed his forearm against her windpipe.

The only air she'd gulped before he cut her supply stank of damp armpit. He'd tucked her skull in his arm crotch, much like the famous noggin-less horseman once held his severed head. Fireworks exploded in the dark behind her eyes.

That's when a thought occurred to her.

I haven't been home in fifteen years.

What if she died in Gigantor's armpit? Would her father even know?

Has it been that long?

Flopping like a landed fish, she forced her assailant to adjust his hold and sucked a breath as she flipped on her back. Spittle glistened on his lips, and his brow furrowed as if she'd asked him to read a paragraph of big-boy words.

His nostrils flared like the Holland Tunnel.

There's an idea.

Making a V with her fingers, Shee thrust upward, stabbing into his nose, straining to reach his tiny brain.

Goliath roared. Jerking back, he grabbed her arm to unplug her fingers from his nose socket. She whipped away her limb before he had a good grip, fearing he'd snap her bones with his Godzilla paws.

Kneeling before her, he clamped both hands over his face, cursing as blood seeped from behind his fingers.

Shee's gaze didn't linger on that mess. Her focus fell to his crotch, hovering a foot above her feet, protected by nothing but a thin pair of oversized sweatpants.

Scrambled eggs, sir?

She kicked.

He howled.

Shee scuttled back like a crab, found her feet, and snatched her gun from her side. The gun she should have pulled *before* trying to tackle the Empire State Building.

"Move a muscle, and I'll aerate you," she said. She always liked that line.

The golem growled but remained on the ground like a good dog, cradling his family jewels.

Shee's partner in this manhunt, a local cop easier on the eyes than he was useful, rounded the corner and drew his weapon.

She smiled and holstered the gun he'd lent her...without *knowing* he'd lent it.

"Glad you could make it."

Her portion of the operation accomplished, she headed toward the car as more officers swarmed the scene.

"Shee, where are you going?" called the cop.

She stopped and turned.

"Home, I think."

His gaze dropped to her hip.

"Is that my gun?"

CHAPTER TWO

One Week Ago, Miami, Florida

"He isn't dead."

Tyler Vale stopped toweling his wet hair and scowled at the mirror, his cell phone pressed against his ear.

Something about his eyes...

I'm starting to look like my father. I'm not sure how I feel about that.

"Who is this?" he asked.

"You know who it is," said the unfamiliar voice.

This caught his attention. Tyler lowered the towel and turned away from his image as if it were spying on him. He glanced at the closed bathroom door and lowered his voice.

"No, I *don't* know who this is. And I *don't* know what you're talking about."

The voice on the opposite end of the line continued in its steady deadpan. "Yes, you do. I wanted to give you a heads-up about why the package didn't show."

"The package—"

"Consider your services terminated. Goodbye."

"Wait—"

He looked at his phone.

Disconnected.

Dialing back, he heard a single ring before the call ended. He tried again with the same result.

Blocked.

Dread dumped into Tyler's veins. He dropped the towel and strode naked into his bedroom.

"Where's my laptop?"

A girl with a nose too large for even *her* cherub face looked up from where she lay sprawled like an abandoned off-brand Barbie. Her thumb twitched, swiping across the screen of her phone.

"Huh?" she asked, eyelids at half-mast, mascara smeared on her cheeks.

Tyler's lip curled.

I should maybe try harder.

He had a nasty habit of picking girls who didn't turn heads in the bar. They were more responsive to his charms, rarely inspired competition, and in the end, provided what he needed the same as prettier girls. Often more enthusiastically and with less chatter about themselves and their boring, ridiculous lives.

Still, there was something to be said for *pretty*.

He sighed.

No time for soul-searching now.

Jerking open the door to leave his bedroom, he moved into the main section of his tiny apartment. Contract-killing was lucrative, but he didn't spend enough time in Miami to rent a more expensive place. He preferred seeing the numbers in his bank account and stock portfolio.

His ancient laptop sat perched on the kitchen counter, plugged into the same loose socket powering his coffee maker. Flipping it open, he typed in his password and navigated to his offshore online banking account to type in yet another.

He'd been expecting payment for killing the old dude for *weeks*. He scanned his totals.

Nothing new.

Shit.

Tyler grabbed his cell and dialed his handler.

"Casey Plumbing Supply," answered a gruff-voiced man, though no plumbing supply in the world kept hours after midnight.

"It's Deathshot."

Tyler winced. He'd chosen his codename during a different time in his life—the cheesy ramblings of an over-enthusiastic baby assassin.

Brett sighed. "It ain't here yet."

"No, I *know*. Someone just called to tell me the job wasn't finished."

"Called *you*?"

"Yes. Me. *Directly*."

"Well, was it?"

Tyler scowled. "Was *what*?"

"Was the job finished?"

"Of *course* it was." Creeping doubt crawled around the base of Tyler's skull.

I didn't check.

The guy accompanying his target was so *big*. He'd seen the old man drop. Knew he'd scored the headshot. Hadn't been paid for two dead old men. He'd packed up his stuff and headed home.

Dammit. Rookie mistake.

"You want me to check on it?" asked Brett.

"*Yes*, I want you to check on it." Tyler tried to mask his misgivings with anger, as much for himself as his handler. "And tell me how the *hell* the client got my number."

Brett's voice lowered to a growl. "Not from *me*. And

you better watch your tone, *Deathshot*. This means I'm out a piece, too, y'know."

Tyler huffed. "I know."

"I'll call you back."

Brett hung up.

Tyler raised his hand, preparing to dash his phone to the ground. He thought better of it and instead shook it in his fist, as if trying to choke the life out of it, before collapsing into a kitchen chair.

"Whachu screamin' about?"

Tyler looked up. The girl stood in the bedroom doorway, squinting at him, scratching her beak.

"Get out of here," he muttered.

She laughed. "Yer naked."

He tried again, this time with an expression he hoped would convey just how serious he was.

"Get. Out. *Now*."

Her dopey grin dropped.

The cell in his hand rang, and before she could protest, he put his finger over his lips and pointed to the exit with as much venom as he could muster.

Her eyes flashed with anger. She whirled on her heel, lost her balance, and smacked the side of her face against the wall.

Tyler rolled his eyes.

Great. Just what that face needed.

He would have laughed if he hadn't been so pissed.

Using the door frame for support, the girl righted herself and stormed into the bedroom.

Tyler answered the phone. "Yeah?"

"Sink's still leaking."

"What? They're *lying*."

"They're not. Not the type of client who lies to save a couple of bucks. You *missed*."

"I didn't *miss*."

"I don't know what to tell you. The sink's still leaking."

Tyler ran a hand through his thinning hair. "I'll handle it."

"Nope. They're getting a new plumber. And you're not gonna see any jobs from me for a while."

"What? Wait—"

The line went dead.

No second thoughts this time. Tyler hurled his phone at the far wall, chasing it with a string of profanities. The cell shattered, peppering the girl with bits of plastic as she returned to the bedroom doorway.

She yelped and covered her head with her purse.

The largest chunk of the phone clattered to the ground. The girl glared at him.

"You're an *asshole*."

Tyler sniffed. "Really? And I had such *promise*."

She huffed and left the apartment without another word.

Tyler dropped back into his kitchen chair.

Well, thank God for little favors.

Alone again, he had nothing left to do but obsess, Brett's words echoing in his skull.

You missed.

How was that possible?

He couldn't leave this black mark on his resume, but he didn't even know the name of his target. The client had provided Brett with the old man's location and description. Nothing more.

How could he find the target before the new shooter?

He straightened.

The big guy.

Certainly, the old man had been at his buddy's house before heading out to lunch? They'd arrived in the big man's truck. The target's friend was *local*.

Tyler smiled.

Last-minute airplane tickets back to Minneapolis wouldn't be hard to score in March.

CHAPTER THREE

Monday is red.

Wednesday is green, and it sits in the center of the row of boxes Shee saw in her mind's eye whenever someone mentioned a day of the week.

If someone said, "Show up on Wednesday," seven imaginary boxes appeared, like the row of a calendar grid, starting with Monday and ending with Sunday. Wednesday occupied the dead center, which was impossible. Its center position was as much a trick of her mind as the row of calendar boxes itself because to the left of Wednesday sat only Monday and Tuesday, while Thursday, Friday, Saturday, *and* Sunday all fell to the right. If her mental calendar's row was a seesaw with Wednesday as its fulcrum, there'd be a little girl with bones like a bird's sitting high in the air on the left and a football squad's offensive lineman squatting on the dirt to the right.

Still, Wednesday *felt* in the middle.

Maybe because Wednesday sat in the middle of the workweek. The theory made sense, except Shee had never held a Monday-to-Friday job in her life. Maybe the thing that centered Wednesday in *her* mind was the same thing that made her confuse her left and right.

That mental block had nearly gotten her killed more than once.

When it came to direction, she preferred military parlance.

"Check your nine!"

Left. Duh.

If someone screamed *left!* more often than not, she looked *right*. That's usually when something clobbered the left side of her skull.

Negative feedback didn't prevent her from making the same blunder the next time, though.

Even rats change their behavior if shocked often enough.

Not me. Ole 'dumber than a rat' Shee.

She fared better with time than direction. Time was a *thing*. A clock. She *saw* her internal clockface, white with bronze serif-font numbers. She faced toward the twelve, and she could *see* nine to her left and move without hesitation.

On your nine!

No problem.

Unfortunately, the rest of the world hadn't received the memo. Joggers approaching from behind who barked *on your left!* a moment before collision usually ended up on the ground in a tangled ball of limbs.

It didn't matter. And luckily for the joggers of the world, Shee was in a restaurant booth in Jupiter Beach, Florida.

Very few joggers in the booth.

"Sigh-oh-fra?" asked the server with *Alyssa* on her nametag, squinting at Shee's credit card. The girl's nose wrinkled as if she smelled something off. Something like the seafood at the next table, for example. One of the oysters had a bad attitude. Shee had smelled it as the platter passed by.

I should say something.

"Shee-fra," she corrected the server, the sound of her full name, Siofra, jarring to her ear. She hadn't used it for fifteen years. Most recently, she'd been *Hunter*. Before that, she'd picked *Charity* to see if men treated women with stripper names differently.

They did.

The waitress appeared dubious about Shee's real name. "Really?" she asked.

Shee dabbed her mouth with her napkin. "Pretty sure."

"What kind of name is that?" The girl's tone suggested Shee should pass a quiz to claim her own name. Maybe after fifteen years, she did.

"Irish. Siofra was my grandmother's name on my father's side."

"Oh, neat. Are you Irish?"

Shee blinked at her.

Does she not know how grandmothers work?

She couldn't help herself. "Nope, One hundred percent Mexican."

"*Really?*"

"No. I'm Irish. Grandma was from *Ireland,* Irish. I'm plain-old American Irish."

"Oh. Cool. I'm part Irish on my mom's side."

Shee nodded and cocked an ear toward the slurping behind her.

Uh oh.

She flashed Alyssa a smile, hoping the girl would sense the end of their conversation, but the server's hip cocked, and Shee knew she was in it for the long haul.

Alyssa pointed at her with the credit card. "You were here last week, weren't you? Maybe Saturday? I work Saturdays."

Blue.

Saturdays are royal blue. Sundays are *light* blue because they're gentler than Saturdays.

Orange rose like a sunrise in her mind. "Thursday."

Alyssa nodded. "Cool. Brunch here is awesome. Okay. I'll go run this for you."

"Thanks, Ally-Sah."

The girl stopped and pointed at her name tag. *"Alyssa."* She took another step and then spun on her heel, an open-mouthed grin on her face. "Oh, I get it. Like I said *your* name wrong." Laughing, she rolled her eyes and headed off again.

Shee's attention locked onto the credit card swinging in the girl's hand as she walked toward the bar. Alyssa's stride bounced like the floor was made of a gym mat. The young didn't know what to do with *all that energy.* Shee looked at the back of her right—no, *left*—hand and followed the network of lines ridging around her knuckles, the flesh spotted with what she liked to think of as hefty freckles.

The wrong side of forty didn't *bounce.*

In *so* many ways.

She sniffed as the perfume of the woman sitting behind her visited her booth. It hadn't smelled floral a moment ago. It had smelled like—

Oh right. Oysters.

She twisted to see her neighbors.

"Hi, I'm sorry, I think one of your—"

Her attention dropped to the plate of oysters positioned between the couple. The oyster shells remained resting in the silver serving tray's divots, glistening and *empty.*

The couple had unwittingly played oyster Russian roulette.

Who ate Stinky?

The man looked at her expectantly, and Shee smiled.

Ah well. I tried.

She pulled the napkin from her lap and dipped as if plucking it from the ground. The action happened too low for the man to see from his angle.

"I think you dropped one of your napkins," she said, handing it to them.

Oh, and by the way, you might want to shove your fingers down your throat.

The woman's mouth pinched into an exaggerated 'o' of surprise as she accepted the napkin. The lipstick smudge across the center wasn't her color. She didn't notice.

"Oh, thank you."

Shee turned back to her table, confident the couple would check their laps to find their napkins where they'd left them, but they wouldn't say anything. They'd confirm with each other, shrug, and then stuff the spare napkin aside somewhere. Shee guessed only one in ten would insist she take *back* the napkin. Most people avoided useless interaction unless they were *desperate* to talk and the couple had each other for conversation. Thank goodness because she'd overheard enough of their conversation to know all she ever needed about the pros and cons of the Keto diet.

Shee left her table and caught the attention of the bartender to whom Alyssa had handed her credit card.

"Hey, can I pay cash instead?" she asked, motioning to the credit card about to be plunged into a card reader.

The bartender nodded and returned her card without confirming it belonged to her.

Shee pulled a hundred-dollar bill from her shorts pocket and handed it to him.

"Can you add two pineapple ginger martinis to my bill and send them to that couple over there?"

She motioned to the couple. They were busy looking

for a spot to stow a spare napkin they didn't want to touch now that they knew it wasn't theirs.

The bartender appeared surprised but amenable. "Sure."

"Give the change to Alyssa."

He nodded—the twitch of one eyebrow the only evidence of surprise at her generosity.

Shee left the restaurant and stepped into the Florida sun. She'd done all she could for The Oyster People. Both pineapple and ginger helped digestion *and* the symptoms of food poisoning.

Maybe they'd get lucky. The oyster didn't smell *that* bad.

She looked at her credit card and frowned.

Siofra McQueen.

Running the card would have put her on the grid for the first time in over a decade.

She'd wimped out.

Again.

CHAPTER FOUR

Five weeks ago.

"I appreciate the catch-up Viggo, but you didn't call me to Minnesota to buy me a burger."

Mick McQueen shivered and wrapped himself like a burrito in his inadequate twill jacket. The elevator doors opened, and fingers of frost pinched his cheeks. As an ex-Navy SEAL with almost seventy years of life experience, he thought he could withstand anything, but the icy blast of a Minnesota winter had him ready to reel off his name, rank, serial number, and location of ally command.

"Damn. I forgot it could get this cold. Florida's made me soft."

Viggo acknowledged his distress with a tight smile and thrust a hand into his khakis to the tune of jangling keys.

Mick studied him as he looked away.

Viggo seems off.

Could be a lot of reasons why. They hadn't seen each other in years. Now they were old men. There'd been times he couldn't have dreamed they'd live so long. Viggo by his side used to mean they were in some foreign land doing

God-knows-what.

Now, where blond Viggo once strode into battle like avenging Odin, a paunchy, hunch-shouldered giant in khakis walked with the hint of a limp thanks to a recent hip replacement. With the addition of kinky gray hairs, his once-golden locks looked more like a sun-bleached pile of straw tangled on his thick skull.

They were near Viggo's car when Mick's musing ended, and he realized his friend hadn't said a word since they left the restaurant.

Maybe his lips froze together.

"Veeg?"

Viggo stopped and looked down at him.

A sour taste struck Mick's pallet.

I know that look.

His friend took a subtle step backward, the wrinkle between his eyebrows telegraphing *sorry.*

Mick's brain screamed its own word.

Move.

He pushed off his left toe.

"What have you *done*?"

His words were eaten by the blast of a rifle. Something struck the right side of his head. Force spun his body, and Mick collapsed against a car.

He could still see.

He could still breathe.

I'm here.

The shot hadn't killed him.

I have to move—

His elbow cracked against the paved floor of the garage.

When did I fall?

Betrayed by his limbs, he remained motionless, the wounded side of his skull pressed against the pavement.

He watched as Viggo's feet shuffled toward him. Heard a voice.

Veeg, help me—

The garage disappeared, replaced by the flickering image of a little girl playing in the sand by the water's edge. He smiled.

Shee.

The sun dimmed. Darkness oozed across the beach scene as if it were a jammed filmstrip frame, burning beneath the heat of the projector's lamp.

The girl turned to look at him as the world around her melted.

No, no, no—

CHAPTER FIVE

Present Day

Shee opened the box and wrestled foam away from the treasure nestled inside—a DJI Mavic video drone. Quadcopter, to be specific. She'd bought it using the *other* credit card, the one embossed with the name *Hunter Byrne.*

Her cheesiest alias to date.

She'd picked *Hunter* because she'd been in a bar plotting how to *hunt* her latest quarry when a chatty bartender asked her name. New town, new target—it had been time for a change.

With the Talking Heads' *Girlfriend* playing over the embedded ceiling speakers, she'd blurted *Hunter Byrne*, guessing the young bartender wouldn't know David Byrne from a rack of oversized jackets.

He definitely didn't know she hunted men.

Well, *usually* men. Not sexist, just a fact.

She'd been a skip tracer-slash-bounty hunter since she was eight years old. Over the years, she'd had a thousand names. Most of them she made up on the spot—a talent more difficult than the average person would imagine.

In a panic, names like *Foghorn Quackenbush* jumped to mind, but she'd learned to resist the urge to blurt nonsense. She didn't want to end up in a conversation about her silly name or, worse, inspire a mark to doubt her. Tell someone your name is Cockney Schnizzlefritz, and they'll blow you off on the spot.

Shee's *Hunter Byrne* credit card sat tucked in her phone case next to a driver's license boasting the same name. Back at her hotel, locked in the safe, sat five others featuring various other monikers, most pretty common.

Siofra was weird enough.

Her Gaelic name meant *fairy* or *changeling*, hailing from a time in Ireland's history when superstitious parents feared fairies might replace their babies with changeling twins.

She supposed the name fit. She'd lost track of whether she was herself or a changeling twin a long time ago.

Either way, now she had a drone to play with.

She'd charged the drone in her hotel room and scoped the perfect place to use as a launch and landing area—an unoccupied mansion not far up the river from The Loggerhead Inn. She'd borrowed the owner's paddleboard a week earlier for another mission. In towns like Jupiter Beach, it wasn't difficult to find empty vacation homes, even if the owners *alleged* to live there for six months and a day to claim Florida residency and avoid state taxes.

Sitting on the tax-dodgers' dock, she plugged her phone into the controller, and the drone sprang to life, an angry buzzing wasp rising into the air.

She touched the controller's forward arrow, and the drone shot away from her toward the trees lining the opposite bank.

Too fast.

She acclimated to the controls and video feed before

pushing the mechanical bird toward The Loggerhead.

Shee perched in the mansion's waterside lounge chair, her knee bouncing at the sight of the familiar hotel on her phone's screen.

There it is.

On her command, the drone ascended until it hovered parallel to the uppermost windows of the building. She buzzed closer. The sun's angle against the southern-facing windows sent light streaming through the impact-resistant glass, illuminating the face of a man lying in bed.

Dad?

Shee glanced at her watch to find it nearly ten-thirty.

Mick McQueen hadn't slept past six a.m. a day in his life.

What's wrong with him?

Through the drone's eye, she scanned the room. A chair and a pair of side tables clustered around the centerpiece of the room—a silver-edged hospital bed. Shee noted the matching Tetons of Mick's feet beneath the covers before turning the drone to its nine until the camera focused on her father's face.

Mick's eyes were shut. Zooming in, she spotted tubes of various sizes and colors leading into his forearm.

A lemon rolled from somewhere in her chest and lodged itself in her throat, lumpy and sour.

What have I done?

She let the drone hover there, hands frozen on the controls.

I waited too long—

The camera shook, waking Shee from her building panic. Her fingers scrambled to keep the drone from dropping. Steady once more, she wiped her eyes and studied the screen.

What was that?

It was as if something had struck the drone.

A bird?

A large insect?

She left the device hovering, hoping her father would open his eyes or move—anything that made him look less *dead*.

Squinting, she wished she'd brought her peepers from the car. Her forties had played hell with her reading eyesight.

Did his chest rise and fall?

No one had done her the favor of scrawling his diagnosis on the wall above his head. Moving her focus to the end of the bed, she searched for a chart that might reveal his illness. Her angle kept that area hidden.

She panned the room, zooming in on anything she thought might interest her.

Nothing.

She forced herself to guide the drone to the next window.

The rest of her father's apartment appeared empty and hadn't changed since the last time she'd been in it, over a dozen years earlier.

Dad still isn't a decorator.

Snorting a little laugh, she wiped away a wet bubble ballooning from her nose.

Get hold of yourself, Shee.

Something moved near the bottom of the screen, and she focused on it, hoping to identify what had hit the camera.

Not a bird.

The movement came from someone *in the room*, sitting with their back to the window, the back of their head visible above the sofa cushions.

The person twisted to peer at the drone. A woman in

nurse's scrubs.

The buzzing of the drone. She'd heard it.

Shee watched the woman scowl.

Time to go.

She jerked the drone away from the window and retraced the Intracoastal Waterway back to her dockside perch. The contraption hummed into view and landed beside her.

That's something, anyway.

She'd confirmed her father still resided at The Loggerhead Inn. She wasn't *positive* she'd seen him breathe but felt ninety-nine percent sure he was alive.

No reason to hire a nurse to watch a dead man.

He had all his limbs. She didn't notice any marks on his body. *Flu?* No. A hospital bed implied something more long-term. *Cancer?*

Am I too late?

She swallowed and popped her phone from the controller cradle. Time to get some lunch and review the video.

Time to think.

She dropped the drone into its packaging and paused to check its body for a sign of what had knocked it off course. A smooshed bug, a feather or—

Hold on.

Shee fingered a small black disk stuck to the side of the drone.

That's new.

Plucking at it, she peeled it from the 'copter's exoskeleton.

Hm.

Shee awakened her phone and reviewed the drone footage as it approached her father's window.

There it is.

Tucked in the corner where one angle of The Loggerhead's roof met another nestled what looked like a gun. Her imaginary clock told her the drone had dipped toward its nine as if hit from its three.

That has to be it.

She studied the disc in her palm.

A GPS tracker.

Smaller than a quarter, the device wasn't over-the-counter spy fun—this was military-grade. Cutting edge.

Why had her father set up a drone tracking gun?

He'd given her the all-clear nearly two years ago. She'd delayed returning for—well, she wasn't sure why. That was something between her and the imaginary therapist living in her head with the colors, calendars, and clocks.

Had the situation changed?

Shee packed up the drone and left the dock with the tracker still in her hand. She knew she needed to toss the GPS, but she carried it almost back to her car instead.

Maybe I want to be found.

As she opened her trunk, a motion in the underbrush caught her eye. She spotted the familiar outline of a gopher tortoise munching away at a patch of grass with its trademark grumpy mug. Every gopher tortoise looked like a ninety-year-old man told to eat his creamed carrots.

"Hey you, come here..."

She jogged toward the tortoise. The creature noticed her approach and scrambled away as if it had remembered it was late for a meeting.

"Fast little bugger."

She caught it easily enough and stuck the sticky tracker to its shell. It wouldn't hurt the tortoise. It would probably scrape off the next time the critter crawled into its hole, but the idea of her father tracking a turtle made her laugh.

"As you were."

She released the gopher, and it sprinted toward its hole to disappear inside.

Shee headed to her car, chuckling, trying hard to keep her mind on the tortoise.

CHAPTER SIX

Thirty-seven years ago

Shee's mind drifted to *syrup* as her father fussed with her dress.

Blueberry syrup.

"I want pancakes."

Mick rolled his eyes. "It's four o'clock in the afternoon."

"I don't care—*Ow!*" A bobby pin pinched in her father's clumsy fingers scratched across her scalp. She thought she'd *like* wearing a wig, but it felt like chimps were hanging from her hair, yanking as they clambered around her skull.

Her father grimaced and held out a photo for them both to study. "Sorry. I think I have it. What do you think?"

Shee looked at the photo, then in the motel mirror, and back again. The girl in the photo had blonde hair, long and curly. Shee's hair, dark and short, sat hidden somewhere beneath her blonde wig. Admiring herself, she tilted her head to one side. She enjoyed the length of the soft curls but decided she didn't like being blonde. Blonde made her look like an angel.

I'm not an angel.

I'm a tracker.

Her gaze tripped over a dot on the photo.

"The freckle," she said, pointing.

"What?"

"She has a freckle."

"No, she doesn't."

"Yes, she does. There, above her eyebrow."

Mick plucked the photo from her hand and squinted at it.

"Sonuva—"

Shee pointed at him. "You owe me a cursing quarter."

"No, I don't. I didn't finish saying it."

"But my *mind* did, and that's what counts."

Mick laughed and lifted her in the air by her armpits. "Sounds like your mind owes *me* a quarter."

He dangled her in front of him, his massive biceps bulging. She could barely contain her joy. Nothing made her happier than making her father laugh.

"Put me down." She said the words, but she didn't mean them. Her father picked her up less and less as she grew. His attention beamed like the sun on her face. Having her feet hovering three feet off the floor was a treat.

Mick sat her on the bed and fished his pockets for change. "I'm short on change. How about twelve and a half cents? We'll split the difference."

"Deal."

A dime and two pennies sat in his palm, but as she reached for them, he closed his fist and held it to his chest. "Whoa. You can't give in that fast. You need to counter with another option."

"Like what?"

"Like *twenty* cents. See?" He pulled another dime from his pocket, the jingle of more change alerting her to the depth of his deception.

"You said you didn't have enough."

He cocked an eyebrow. "Do people always tell the truth?"

"No."

Mick opened his palm again and added the second dime to the collection. "This is my counteroffer."

Shee counted the money and took a moment to process it. "Somewhere between what you owe me and what you tried the first time?"

"Right. A counteroffer."

"Oh wait, wait." Shee waved her hand in front of her as if she were erasing the last few minutes. "I have an idea. Put all your change on the bed."

"Why?"

"You'll see."

Mick retrieved the remaining coins from his pocket and dropped them in a pile on the bed. "There."

Seventy-three cents. The number flashed in her head as soon as she saw the different shapes on the faded floral bedcover.

Shee scooped up the money and held it behind her back, staring at him, silent.

"So what's your idea?" he asked.

"The idea was I get *all* the money in your pockets."

Mick laughed *again.* Shee fought to remain straight-faced and smug.

"You think you're *so* smart, smarty-pants." Mick pinched the top of her knee until she squealed with laughter and struggled to get away.

"Stop!"

"Okay, sorry, sorry. Careful, you're going to mess up your costume. Come here."

With breathy laughter, Shee rolled off the bed to her

feet and returned to the spotty floor-length mirror. Her father searched through the black box that once served as his shoeshine kit. He called it *Prestidigitation Pete's Box of Pranks and Ploys.*

She hadn't found a dictionary to look up *prestidigitation* yet. She wished motels put dictionaries in the drawers instead of bibles. They were more useful in the short term.

Mick pulled a stick of brown eyeliner from the box and used it to add the freckle above her eyebrow.

"There. Perfect. Anything else?" he asked.

Shee compared herself in the mirror to the photo again.

"*Dead* ringer," she said, smirking.

Mick shook his head. "You've got a sick sense of humor, girl."

Her grin faded as she watched his expression growing serious. He leaned down to place a hand on each of her arms.

"You understand we're doing this for *her*, right?"

She nodded. "For Vicki and her mom."

He nodded. "Right. Good. You shouldn't laugh at people's pain."

Shee swallowed. She hadn't meant to be cruel.

Her father sniffed and clapped his hands together. "At least not if they can hear you. In private, humor isn't a bad way to make horrible things feel less horrible."

He grinned, and she felt better. She didn't even point out that he'd called a man burned to death in a car wreck a crispy critter the day before.

She admired herself in the mirror again.

I am a dead-ringer, though.

She turned to find her father gone.

"Dad?"

Shee scanned the room. There were only a few places he could hide.

She guessed the opposite side of the far single bed.

She jumped forward, fists up in a fighting stance, giving the furniture a wide berth.

"Hi-ya!"

The space behind the bed hid nothing but the hideous carpet.

Hm. Not there.

Shee heard something rustle behind her and spun as her father roared from the closet.

"Arrrrr!"

She blocked his attempt to grab her, punched him hard on the inner thigh, and ducked to slip from his grasp.

He dropped to one knee to pantomime how he would have reacted had she hit him in the groin as he'd taught her to hit a *real* attacker. Seeing her watching, he collapsed to his back, rolling on the floor, howling in mock pain.

She giggled. "It can't hurt that much."

He popped to his feet. "You have no idea."

Mick wrapped his arms around her and squeezed.

"I love you, Shee."

Shee's cheeks warmed.

"You better not embarrass me like this in public," she mumbled.

He held her at arm's length, squinting one eye, his mouth twisted like an angry pirate's. "Are you kidding? Hugs in *public*? My reputation as a cold stone killer would be *ruined*."

"*Exactly*. Yours and mine."

He chuckled and stood. "Deal. We'll never speak of this again. We'll get some chow and then our man."

Shee danced away as he released her, whooping. "Pancakes!"

Shee and Mick entered the diner to the sound of a tinkling bell and sat in a booth behind the stools lining the counter. Beneath the frilly dress Shee's father insisted she wear as her *Vicki* costume, the cracked leather of the seat scratched the back of her legs. She shifted to find a smoother perch.

Mick scanned the room before leaning forward to speak in a muted voice. "The guy we're looking for eats at the counter every day at thirteen hundred hours."

Shee checked her watch.

Five to one.

"Got it."

"You know what to do?"

She nodded. Her stomach tightened, but the sensation felt more like excitement than fear. She knew the difference. Her father had been MIA for twenty-four hours once when she was six. She'd sneaked downstairs and overheard the babysitter discussing her father's disappearance on the phone.

Shee remembered her stomach tightening then, too.

That had been *fear*.

Mick sat back and then leaned in again. He had a strange, strained look. "Remember to get out of there. Don't let him grab you."

"If he grabs me, you'll have to kill him."

Her father scowled. "Why would you say that?"

"Because that's what you told me when you got back from the bar last night."

Mick cocked an eyebrow. "What makes you think I was at a bar?"

Shee ticked off the reasons on her fingers. "You smelled even more like cigarettes than the motel room already does. You put a slip from The Buckhead Tavern on the nightstand. You had red marks on your forearms from leaning against the bar. Your breath smelled like—"

Mick held up a hand. "Okay. I get it." He shook his head. "I think I've created a monster."

"—and you said you'd have to kill the man if he hurt me, and you don't say things like that when you're not drinking."

Her father poked a finger in her direction, and she could tell she'd reached her favorite place—the fine line between amusing him and out-foxing him. "*I got it.* Now pay attention, or I'll have to kill *you.*"

She giggled.

That counted. She'd made him laugh *five times* already in one day. It might be a personal record.

The waitress arrived to hand them shiny, yellowing menus and place two red, plastic glasses of water on the table. Cracks spidered across the surface of the glasses, giving them a well-worn appearance. Shee imagined a million lips kissing their rims. Her lip curled.

Who drinks water, anyway?

"I'd like pancakes with blueberry syrup," she said without looking at the photos of food scattered across the menu.

The waitress grimaced. "We don't have blueberry syrup, just regular."

Shee glared at her father.

Really?

His eyes went dead, and she knew she needed to swallow her disappointment with *regular* syrup.

Shee answered with a tiny nod of resignation.

All the diners in the world and their mark had to come to

one without blueberry syrup?

The waitress smiled, her dark red lipstick feathering into the lines etched around her mouth. The wrinkles, the ashy smell enveloping her like a fog, and the yellowing of the gray hair around her temples told Shee the woman had spent most of her life smoking.

"You knew what you wanted before you got here," the waitress said in a scratchy baritone, pulling a pad from the big pocket stitched to the front of her apron. "You're one of those breakfast-for-dinner girls, huh?"

Shee nodded and looked away to end the chit-chat. She had nothing to say to a woman who didn't have blueberry syrup.

Mick glanced at the menu and then put it down. "I'll take a bowl of chili."

"Anything to drink?"

"Two cokes."

"I want a milkshake," piped Shee.

Mick frowned, but she held his gaze, hoping her expression said *maybe a milkshake will make up for the syrup.* When he didn't immediately respond, she scratched at her wig as if she were about to rip it off, which wasn't far from the truth.

His shoulders dropped a notch. "Fine. One Coke and a *milkshake.*"

Shee grinned at the waitress. "Chocolate."

The woman nodded and left.

"That was blackmail," said Mick.

"What?"

"Scratching at your wig like that. Don't think I don't know what you're doing when you're doing it."

Shee smirked.

The tarnished brass bell above the diner's door tinkled again, and a lone man entered. He carried himself as if tired;

black smears crisscrossed his blue t-shirt as if he'd been whipped with licorice.

"Is that him?" she whispered.

Mick put his finger over his lips and pretended he was rubbing them. His opposite hand hovered at the edge of the table. He rapped the top, motioning for her to slump down.

Shee stopped craning her neck to see and slouched to make herself small.

The man clomped in heavy work boots to the counter and sat directly across from them.

A different waitress, this one thinner and hawkish, approached the newcomer from the opposite side of the counter.

"Hey, Gerald."

Shee knew the name. It had been in the dossier she'd insisted her father make for her for the mission. He'd been right. The staff knew him here. *Gerald* was a regular.

Gerald muttered something she couldn't hear, and the waitress moved away.

"Now?" she whispered to her father.

She saw him reach down and knew he'd just unstrapped his service weapon with a flick of his thumb.

"Now. Just like we practiced, and then *get away*."

Shee nodded, her body alive with electricity. This was the first time her father had let her help with the *in-the-field* portion of his job. If she messed it up, she'd be relegated to his research department.

With the ragged leather biting at her flesh, she slid from the booth as smoothly as possible and stepped behind the man. With a measured inhale, she shaped her eyes wide and soft. She'd practiced the look in the mirror for an hour the day before, imagining sad puppies in her mind.

Here goes nothing.

She tapped Gerald on the spine.

He twisted to look down at her.

"Daddy?" she asked.

Shee had read the phrase *went white as a sheet* in books before, but this was the first time she'd seen it in practice.

"Vickie?" Gerald whispered the word.

He reached for her, his eyes glassing over, lower lip trembling.

Shee jumped back and caught motion at her nine. With one long stride, her father appeared between her and the man.

"Richard Chapman, you're AWOL and wanted for the murder of your wife and daughter."

The man didn't seem to register Mick's presence.

His gaze remained locked on *her*.

"Vickie?"

Shee's giddy delight over completing her mission suddenly felt like a ball of snakes in her chest. She didn't know what the man was thinking, but she could *feel* something had snapped in him. He vibrated, seemingly unbound by the laws of nature, as if he could *will* himself to her, over oceans and through mountains.

"Vickie?"

Richard dropped from his stool and struggled against her father as if Mick were a wall he needed to climb, straining, reaching for her.

"Vickie?"

Shee jerked at the pins holding the wig to her head. She knew her dark hair had escaped prison when the man's expression shifted from hope to horror.

He recoiled, seeming to notice her father for the first time.

"You *sonofabitch*. You—"

Mick jerked the man's hands behind his back and shoved Richard's hips against the table where they'd been sitting, bending him over it.

"Hold still. Don't make this worse than it is."

"You're a monster!" screamed Richard, his face red, spittle flying.

Mick pressed his prisoner's head against the table. "Right. *I'm* the monster."

The man broke into wracking sobs, looking very much human now. Shee found herself out of air and gulped a breath. Looking down at her side, she noticed her hand shaking and balled it into a fist.

"Outside," said her father.

She led the way out of the diner. Behind her, Mick alternated between pushing the man before him and holding him up when he threatened to collapse to his knees.

I did it.

Captured. Richard Chapman, alias Gerald Toomer. Fugitive. AWOL. While on leave, he'd killed his wife with a shotgun and accidentally killed his daughter with a second blast as the girl ran to intervene.

My first collar.

Her father pushed his captive outside, where shore patrol waited to take Richard Chapman to the Naval brig in Jacksonville, Florida.

The master-at-arms, a tall bald black man, glanced at Shee and did a double-take. His gaze shifted to Mick.

"Did you have *your* daughter dress up as his *dead* daughter?"

Mick shrugged. "Seemed the easiest way to make him show his hand."

The man chuckled, shaking his head. "Damn, Mick. That's *cold*."

Shore patrol led a raving Richard Chapman away. Mick smiled down at Shee, his hand outstretched to shake.

"Good job, sailor."

She reached out, her grin fading as she noticed her hand still shaking. She looked to see if her father noticed.

"It's adrenaline. It'll stop," he explained. His voice dropped to a mutter. "It's scarier when it *doesn't* happen anymore."

He squatted to pull her tight to him, and she threw her arms around his neck, suddenly unashamed to hug in public.

"You know I'd never let anything happen to you, right?" he asked.

"I know."

"Good."

He stood, and she glanced back at the diner.

"Can I go back in for my milkshake?"

He shrugged one shoulder. "How 'bout we find a place with blueberry syrup?"

She grinned. "That would be—"

Shee stopped, recalling the faces of the women in the restaurant as they walked out the prisoner. The male patrons had watched Richard. The women stared at *her* and then let their gaze drift to her father.

Disapproval.

She squinted at Mick. "You're afraid if we go back in, they'll yell at you for bringing your daughter to catch a bad guy."

Mick guided her toward the car. "Blueberry syrup it is, Seaman Recruit."

Shee frowned. "I want to be an *officer*. I deserve a higher rank."

He laughed. "You want pancakes. You want blueberry syrup. You want a promotion. You want *everything*."

"So?"

He shut the door, but she heard him laughing as he rounded the car to the driver's side.

Shee clicked in her seatbelt, flush with joy.

She'd made him laugh *six* times.

CHAPTER SEVEN

Present Day. Jupiter Beach, Florida

"We got a hit." Croix stumbled from the room behind The Loggerhead Inn's front desk, her shoulder clipping the door frame in her haste to deliver the news. Dark ringlets danced around her face like bouncing black springs.

Angelina looked up from her concierge desk. "Easy there, spaz."

Croix slapped her hands on the reception desk to stop her momentum. "We got a hit on the tracker."

"What tracker?"

Silent, the young woman squinted from beneath a lowered brow.

Angelina grimaced. "Don't look at me like you're crowning me Miss Slow-on-the-Uptake, missy. *Talk.*"

"The tracker in the gun *you* had me set up on the roof outside Mick's window. Something triggered it."

"You did that?" Angelina stopped petting the Yorkshire terrier curled in the fuzzy black dog bed sitting on her desk. The pup grunted her disapproval.

"*Yes.* We talked about it, remember?"

"Sure, but it sounded like Star Wars stuff to me. Pie in the sky. I didn't know you could *do* it."

"Pie in the—" Croix shook her head. "I don't even know what that means."

"So you're saying you hit something?"

"I'm saying the gun did. Yes. That's what *we got a hit* means."

Angelina raised a hand, pantomiming her intention to slap. "Don't think I can't reach you from here."

Croix grinned. "Oh, *please*. I'd break you into so many pieces Harley would eat for a year."

At the sound of her Yorkie's name, Angelina resumed petting. "My baby wouldn't gnaw my bones. Would you, baby?"

Harley licked her momma's fingers.

Croix pointed. "See? She's tasting you."

"She's *kissing* me. So your gadget is tracking her?"

"It's tracking a drone, anyway. *Has* to be her, right?"

"Nothing *has* to be anything around here. Might be some horny teenager down the street hoping to catch honeymooners going at it."

Croix looked at her phone, the device magically appearing in her hand as it was often wont to do. "It's pinging not far from here, on the other side of the river."

"Flying around?"

"No. I don't think so. It's only moving a few feet here and there. She must have it."

Nerves fluttered in Angelina's stomach.

Shee's near. She has to be.

A middle-aged man with a shock of bleach-blond hair and a matching goatee appeared from the back of the hotel.

Angelina motioned to him. "William, can you keep an eye on the fort? Croix and I have to run out."

He shrugged. "Sure."

"Thanks." Angelina stood and caught Croix's eye. "Let's go."

Harley jumped to her paws, standing bewildered in the center of her desktop nest, sleepy but too startled by her mother's urgency to nap. The hair framing her face shot in every direction like an explosion of muddy water frozen a millisecond after detonation. For a dog who acted like a princess, she more resembled a Dickensian orphan.

"Come here, you crazy little thing." Angelina scooped the dog into the crook of one arm and strode toward the exit, her long, thin legs outpacing the rest of her body. The front door opened as she approached, thanks to the oversized doorman standing outside in his tropical shirt and khaki shorts.

"Thank you, Bracco," she said, clicking by in her heels.

"Ticky tack," he said, smiling. Sunlight glinted off his gold-capped front tooth.

Croix followed so close behind Angelina had to shoo her ahead to end the threat of an imminent rear-ending. She pointed the girl toward her Land Rover.

"Get in. I'll drive, you navigate."

Croix did as she was told, an event that didn't go unnoticed. It hardly ever happened.

Angelina climbed into the driver's seat and held Harley in Croix's direction, the tiny dog's legs dangling on either side of her palm.

"Take."

Croix pulled the Yorkie into her lap, eyes never leaving her phone screen.

Angelina started the SUV and crunched through the parking lot rocks to pull onto the street, the fronds of roadside Christmas palms waving her on.

"You have to go over the bridge," said Croix.

On Jupiter Beach, lives danced to the beat of the rising

and lowering bridges at either end of the island. Angelina headed toward the north turn lane. She glanced at her watch to see if they'd be hitting the bridge when it opened on the hour and a half past. It was twenty minutes after ten, so it appeared they'd get lucky.

Croix waved a hand at the windshield. "Not *that* bridge, the other one."

Angelina jerked the wheel right. A car she hadn't noticed following behind her honked, and she held up a hand for them to see.

"Sorry."

Croix cleared her throat. "You know they have these things called directional signals, or, in your old-timey language, *blinkers*—"

"Shut it. I'll start using mine the day these snowbirds start using theirs." Angelina made a right and weaved around a car with Connecticut license plates. Another driver pulled from a shopping center in front of her, and she hit the brakes.

"I swear if I could mount a cannon to my hood—"

"It looks like she's in the Crow's Nest community," said Croix.

Angelina hit the gas to pass, scanning the roadside for police. One more speeding ticket, and she'd have to buy a bike. She shuddered at the thought of showing up everywhere *sweaty*.

She rechecked her watch. If it were July, she wouldn't worry about missing the bridge opening, but thanks to it being *January*, seasonal traffic stretched far ahead of her.

Angelina zipped in front of a landscaping truck and crested the bridge with time to spare.

"Where now?" she asked.

"Next right. Oh, shoot."

"What is it?"

"Crow's Nest is gated, isn't it?"

"No worries."

They pulled to the Crow's Nest gate, and Angelina handed her license to the man at the booth, rattling off the name and address of a community resident she'd once met at a party. They'd dated on and off for a few months.

The man handed back her license without looking at it.

"How you doin' today, Miss Angelina?"

"I'm good, Joseph. How's your boy?"

The attendant smiled. "He's real good. Thanks for askin'."

Angelina tucked her license back into her small black purse and rolled under the rising gate arm.

Croix looked at her. "Do you know *everyone*?"

"Yes. Where now?"

The girl returned her attention to her phone. "She's still here. Make a right."

Angelina turned, and they approached a large Miami-modern mansion tucked at the end of a cul-de-sac.

"Stop here. She's here."

Angelina hit the brakes so suddenly Harley rolled forward. Croix caught the dog before she tumbled off her lap.

"I can't believe this worked," said Angelina.

"Me neither."

They exited the car, and Angelina retrieved Harley before heading up the walkway toward the home's door.

"Not *there*, over here." Croix pointed to the left, where well-manicured grass ended at a low bronze fence. Beyond the barrier, an empty lot of scrub bushes and trees stretched for as far as Angelina could see.

She looked down at her Louboutins. She'd *just* bought them from the high-end consignment shop up the road. The rough terrain would eat her heel leather, and *anything* could be lurking in the grass.

"I can't walk through there in these heels."

Without hesitation, Croix moved to the fence, flush with the fearlessness of youth. She climbed over the fence as if she'd spent her life teaching inmates how to escape from honor-system prisons.

Croix studied her phone, took a few steps into the forest, and stopped.

"What is it?" asked Angelina.

"According to the tracker, she should be standing three feet in front of me."

"Well, is she?"

Croix looked back at Angelina, clearly exasperated.

"*No.*"

"Maybe she's behind that tree?"

Croix pointed at the skinny palm in front of her. "How thin *is* this chick?"

"I don't know. Maybe she's been on Weight Watchers since she left. Just go *look.*"

Croix took a few steps forward. Angelina spotted something moving on the ground near the girl's feet through the fence.

"Snake!"

Croix jumped at the shriek and then stood with her hand on her chest, staring daggers at Angelina.

"Over there," Angelina added, pointing.

Croix squatted to inspect something on the ground.

"I'm not sucking out the poison. It will ruin my lipstick," said Angelina.

"It's not a snake, freakshow."

"What is it? Is it the drone?"

"A gopher tortoise."

Angelina frowned. A tortoise wasn't useful. It wasn't even as exciting as a snake.

Croix lunged forward, disappearing behind a weedy bush.

Angelina shifted Harley to her other arm. "Careful. It'll *bite* you."

"They don't bite," Croix grunted in the underbrush.

"Isn't it illegal to touch them?"

Croix reappeared, studying something pinched between her fingers. "Yes. But not because they bite. Because they're endangered."

Angelina strained for a better view. "What's that?"

"The tracker. It was on the tortoise."

Angelina retracted her neck, scowling. "You're telling me you shot a flying turtle?"

"It's a *tortoise*."

"Okay, Jacque Cousteau, just tell me—"

Croix folded the tiny tracker in her hand and mounted the fence. "Why would Jacque Cousteau track a land tortoise? He's the ocean guy."

"*Whatever*. Just tell me how you shot a turtle from the roof."

Croix dropped to the ground and displayed the tracker in the center of her palm for Angelina to see. "I didn't shoot the turtle. I shot a *drone*. *She* stuck it to the turtle."

"*Tortoise*," corrected Angelina with a smirk, suffering a flash of jealousy over how easily the girl had hopped over a fence in flip-flops.

Croix tucked the tracker into her shorts' pocket. "You don't pay me enough."

Angelina sighed. It seemed Shee hadn't lost her sense of humor.

This had to be her, didn't it?

"Maybe the tracker dropped, and the turtle rolled on it," she mused.

Croix peered at her from beneath a lowered brow. "I

think they spend a big part of their life trying *not* to roll. It's kind of a *thing* with them."

"Tortoise. Maybe this one practices yoga—"

"*No.* She's messing with us. It was right in the center, on top of the shell. She knew exactly what she was doing. Why am I not surprised Mick's daughter is a smartass?"

Angelina frowned. "Now, how are we going to find her?"

The girl thought for a moment. "She must have seen Mick—wouldn't that make her come to us?"

Angelina pulled her ruby lips into a tight knot. "You'd think so."

CHAPTER EIGHT

Commander Mason Connelly lay on his back, staring at a nail pop in the ceiling. His right leg ached, and he wiggled his toes to release the strange pressure in his calf. It didn't occur to him until a moment later that he had no toes to wiggle at the end of that leg.

No toes, no foot, no ankle, no shin.

Kept the knee, though.

Lucky, lucky me.

He closed his eyes and pictured himself jogging on the beach, the dark-haired young woman by his side, smiling—

"Look alive, Commander." First Lieutenant Arturo Felix wheeled into the room and didn't stop until he'd punched Mason on the arm so hard the discomfort distracted from his other aches. Arturo had been greeting him that way since the kid joined his team. Normally, Mason would punch him back, but not today. After delivering his blow, Arturo jumped an arm's length from Mason's hospital bed. For now, it was all he had to do to snuff any chance of retaliation.

"That doesn't seem fair," said Mason.

"You gotta be fast." Arturo dragged a chair from the corner and sat, careful to remain an arm's length away.

"How you feelin' today, old man?"

Mason pushed himself to a sitting position, his expression frozen to mask the pain the movement caused. "Oh, you know, *trim*. About ten pounds lighter."

Arturo's gaze bounced toward Mason's left shin, a long cylindrical lump beneath his sheets. To the right, the sheets fell flat after the knob of his knee.

Arturo motioned to the space.

"Quit whinin'. It's below the knee. You're like, *golden,* dude. You can get one of those badass blades or something. Run sixty miles an hour."

"I'm not sure that's how it works."

"Yeah, it is."

Mason chuckled. "You always were a leg-half-full kind of guy."

"Yeah, well..." Arturo took a deep breath and looked at him with empathy.

Sympathy?

Mason looked away with a grunt.

"This is God's way of telling you it's time to retire," Arturo added.

Mason stared out the window and nodded. Compared to the kids they kept sending to fill his teams, he was an old man. He remembered the forty-something man *he'd* served under as a baby SEAL in his twenties. The man had seemed a million years old. And now here he was. *The old man.*

"You gonna be an instructor?" asked Arturo.

"Nah. Not for me."

"Gonna take that money and run?"

Mason laughed. "Right. Buy a yacht. Travel the world. Nothing makes you filthy rich like the service."

"Well, hurry up and get your bionic leg."

Arturo leaned in to smack his good leg.

Mistake.

Mason's hand shot out like a snake strike to catch his friend's wrist.

"Don't make me embarrass you in front of all these nurses," said Mason, smirking. He squeezed his friend's wrist just enough to prove it had been a clean capture and then released.

Arturo chuckled, rubbing his wrist. "I was about to say I'll buy you a shot at McP's."

Mason gasped. "A whole shot? Wow. If you told me sooner, I would have ditched the leg *years* ago."

Arturo offered some retort, and Mason nodded, but his mind had wandered.

What am I going to do?

He didn't want to be an instructor. He didn't want to watch wave after wave of healthy young men run circles around his gimpy ass. He didn't want to hear they'd been blown to bits. He'd been *moving* for so long—now life had taken the legs out from under him.

Well, the *leg.*

This time he couldn't just volunteer for another tour. Throw himself into the mission. Forget about—

"Did you hear we lost Mick?" asked Arturo.

The name caught Mason's attention. "What?"

"Mick McQueen. He's dead, dude."

Mason swallowed. "I thought he was retired?"

"He was, but I dunno. Heard he got killed."

"*Killed?* How?"

Arturo shrugged.

Mason wanted to reach out and shake the information out of his friend. "Accident? Health thing? Give me some *details*, man."

"I don't have any. Just heard he was dead, and the situation was sketchy." Arturo squinted an eye and pointed at him. "Hey, didn't you date Mick's daughter or something?"

"Me?"

"No, the other lopsided asshole in the bed. I heard—"

"I didn't think you could make up a rumor about me I haven't already heard."

"What can I say? You're the legend."

"Uh-huh."

Mason lifted the water on his bedside table and sipped to hide his thoughts from Arturo.

Mick McQueen dead.

Does she know? Jelly? I have to find out how he died. If he was killed—

Arturo poked him in the arm, and Mason's attention returned to the present.

"I'm keeping your hand next time I catch it."

His friend stood. "Right. Seems like you better start keeping spares. Hey, I have a present for you."

"Yeah? Is it my leg?"

"Nah. Better than that piece of hamburger. Hold on." Arturo turned his head and called into the hallway loud enough for patients three floors down to hear.

"Ensign Trevor!"

Arturo returned his chair to the corner as a man wearing the Navy's tan type II camouflage uniform entered with a curly-haired mutt beside him on a short, black nylon leash.

The pup had grown, but Mason recognized its white, gray, and black patchwork. It had belonged to the kids of their last target and been left behind. When his team breached the compound, the firefight put the Muppet in a panic. During a final sweep, Mason doubled back to grab the dog right as an overlooked combatant lurking in the home's ductwork dropped a grenade into the hall. He would have lost more than his leg if he hadn't turned back to save the dog.

"That's the puppy from—"

Arturo nodded. "Yep. Your lucky charm."

Mason swung his left leg over the edge of the bed, dragging what remained of the right one with it.

"Let him go."

Mason rested his foot on the ground and leaned his tush against the bed for balance. He slapped his thighs.

"Come on, boy."

The ensign unclipped the dog's leash from his harness and it bounded forward to put paws on the bed, craning its neck to lick his face.

He rubbed the dog's ears and bent to accept a wet kiss, puppy breath sharp in his nostrils.

Arturo grunted. "That's gross, man."

"Shut up. How'd you get him here?"

"I convinced the captain to let me bring him home."

Mason lifted the dog to his lap. "That's great, 'Turo. Your kids will love him."

Arturo poked his chest with his finger. "*My* kids? Naw, man. He's *yours*."

"What?"

"He's your lucky charm. He can be your, whaddya call it, *therapy dog*."

The pup opened his mouth, tongue lolling, squiggling as if he wanted to find a comfortable way to sit but couldn't hold still enough to settle. Mason didn't know how he'd take care of a dog. He didn't even know how he'd take care of *himself* yet in his new reality.

"Are you sure your kids don't want him?"

Arturo waved his hands in front of him as if warding off evil. "No dogs. You don't want him?"

The dog finally wore himself out and slid to the ground.

Mason chewed his lip, thinking. "No. I want him."

He said the words before he saw them coming.

Am I crazy? What am I going to do with a puppy?

Arturo elbowed the ensign. "Told ya. Big softie." He turned his attention back to Mason. "When you gettin' out?"

"Monday. Can you keep him until then?"

The grin on Arturo's face folded like a cheap tent. "Me? I dunno..."

"What's wrong?"

"Nothin'. I mean, ain't you got a girl or somethin' who could—"

"Oh, right. I've been dating up a storm here in recovery."

"I saw the way that nurse looked at you. She'd do anything—"

"'Turo..."

Arturo sighed. "My kids would love it. It's just Josefina's not a dog person..."

The ensign snickered, and Mason locked on him. "Something funny, Ensign?"

"Sorry, sir. It just seems big bad Arturo's scared of his wife."

Arturo's face flushed red. "I'm not *scared* of her. I'm *respectful*. You better learn the difference, or you'll be a lonely man."

The ensign laughed louder, defending against Arturo's attempt to swat him.

Mason stared at the stump of his leg. He needed to get skilled with his prosthesis *fast* if he was going to be running around after a puppy.

He also needed to find out what happened to Mick.

Jelly would have to go to his funeral, right? Stick around? Get his affairs in order, maybe?

He fingered a hard lump beneath the rugged skin on

his left bicep.

He'd been looking for Mick's daughter, on and off, for almost thirty years. He hadn't found her, yet somehow she'd been there, standing between him and every other woman in his life, walking through his dreams like she owned him...

Yeah. She'd have to come home if Mick was dead.

Suddenly, he felt better. *Lighter.*

A man with a plan.

He looked down at the dog.

Or maybe the puppy's a therapy dog, after all.

He looked at Arturo. "So you'll take him for the week for me?"

Arturo nodded his head from side to side. "Yeah, sure. I guess I can't dump the mutt on you and run. Josefina will deal." He flashed a warning glance at the ensign, who squelched a grin and looked away.

Mason started a checklist in his head. "Can you get some stuff for him, too? I need his crate for my truck."

Arturo's brow knitted. "Why? You takin' him to Disneyland?"

Mason smiled.

"Closer to Disney *World*."

CHAPTER NINE

Thirty-Five Years Ago

"Listen to me, baby. I need you to pack your things."

Mason rubbed his eyes and blinked at his mother. "What?"

Even in the dim light cast from the neighbor's porch light through the slats of his shutters, Mason could tell she'd been crying. Though, he hadn't heard the screaming that usually preceded her tears.

Something felt *different*.

She opened his closet. "Pack some clothes."

"Why?"

"Don't ask questions. Just do like you're told."

She pulled his backpack from the closet and put his favorite sneakers inside. He shook his head, pointing.

"I want to wear them."

"Wear your other pair."

"But—"

She put a hand on his cheek. "Mason, listen to me." Her eyes were wide and wild. She'd never looked like that before. Not when looking at *him*.

"Wear your other pair. Don't touch those."

Something about her tone made him stop arguing. "Okay."

"Pack. I'll be right back."

"Where are we going?"

"You'll see. It's a surprise."

"Is Daddy going?"

"No." Her answer was faint. She was already in her bedroom. He heard the sound of drawers opening and closing.

Mason scanned his tiny bedroom, the desaturated colors of his baseball posters making the players feel even less alive.

Sliding out of bed, he felt the clothes he'd worn the day before beneath his feet and put them back on. He packed his favorite pair of shorts, two t-shirts, and three pairs of underwear with the shoes his mother had put in his school backpack.

He hesitated when it came to slipping his feet into his old sneakers. Torn canvas and ragged threads spilled across grass stains and holes.

"I hate these," he muttered. He looked back at the pair in the suitcase. It didn't make any sense he couldn't wear his good pair.

Mason reached to pull the good pair from beneath his underwear. He jerked them to the surface as tires screeched in the driveway. Headlights glowed outside his window.

Daddy's home.

A familiar dread roiled in Mason's stomach. His father had pulled into the driveway too fast. His mother was acting crazy.

All bad signs.

His mother burst into the room.

"We have to go."

"But I'm not done packing—"

"It doesn't matter. I'll buy new things."

"But—"

His mother's eyes flashed when she spotted the sneakers in his hand.

Uh oh.

She snatched them from his grip, dropping one shoe and then the other from trembling fingers. Frantic, she tied them together, lifted the pair by the locked laces, and took his hand in hers.

"Grab your backpack."

Mason did as he was told.

"Charlotte!"

His father's roar bounced off the walls of their little house. His mother jerked him forward.

"This way."

She dragged him toward the back door.

"Charlotte!"

Mason heard his father's footsteps following, pounding through the living room.

"Charlotte!"

His mother ran around the side of the house to the front, her grip pinching his hand. She stopped at the curb. Tilting back her head, mouth agape, she stared skyward as if willing herself to fly into the night.

For a moment, Mason thought they might rocket upward.

He followed her gaze to the heavens, seeing nothing but blackness.

His mother stepped back and lowered her chin to stare at his good shoes dangling from her right hand. With one motion, she jerked her left hand from his, squatted, thrust upward, and flung his favorite sneakers skyward.

"No!"

Mason watched his sneakers twirl through the air until the laces caught on the telephone wire. The lower shoe arced in a loop to secure a hold on the lines. The pair remained there, swinging like a pendulum.

He gaped at his mother, his eyes so wide he could feel the skin around them stretching. He'd waited months for those shoes. She'd complained about their cost as if he'd asked her for a sports car.

"Why would you—"

"Don't tell Daddy they're yours."

"But why—"

She dipped and again grabbed his face, staring deep into his eyes. "Don't tell your daddy those are your shoes up there. No matter what."

He looked away. "He'll know."

"No, he won't. He don't pay attention to your stuff. Don't tell him."

She squeezed his cheeks with her thumbs, and he jerked from her grip. "I *won't.*"

Behind them, Mason heard the familiar sound of the back door screen slamming against its frame.

Daddy's coming.

His mother straightened and took his hand again. She turned to face their home.

"Where are they?" shouted his father, rounding the corner of the house and striding toward them, his white t-shirt glowing beneath the porch light.

"Hm?" asked his mother. She sounded calm. Almost *sweet.*

Mason could tell she was trying to smile, but her lips trembled, making it hard for her expression to hold its shape.

His father thrust his face inches from his mother's, screaming, spittle flying.

"Where are they?"

She shrugged. "I don't know what you're talking about."

His father grabbed his mother's arm and glared at Mason when he moved to stop him. Her hand tore from his grip. She whimpered.

Mason stood.

"Go inside," said his father.

Something hard rose in Mason's throat. "Don't hurt her."

"What you say to me?"

"Don't hurt—"

The slap came too fast for him to duck. He stumbled sideways, his head ringing. When he opened his eyes, he saw his father's finger pointing at him, nearly touching his nose. The man spoke through gritted teeth, his breath heavy with alcohol.

"Get in the house, and don't sass me again."

Mason looked at his mother.

She thrust out her chin, looking defiant. She looked beautiful, moonbeams glistening through the wisps of her hair around her head, creating a sort of golden halo.

His father raised his hand, but his mother stepped between them before he could slap again.

"Go to your room."

It took Mason a moment to register her command.

"Me?"

"Yes. Go to your room."

"But you said—"

"Go to your room!" She screamed so loud Mason stumbled back and bolted for the house. He ran through the kitchen to the living room and stationed himself at the window where he could watch his parents outside.

They screamed at one another. His father shook her.

Slapped her. The neighbor's front porch light sprang to life, and his father's head swiveled in that direction.

"You mind your business!" he roared at someone Mason couldn't see. He pulled his mother toward the side of the house to hide from the neighbor's meddling.

Mason ran back to his room to peer through the side window. His father pushed his mother into the passenger side of his truck and shut the door so fast he couldn't believe he didn't catch her leg.

From inside the Ford, his mother placed her open palm on the glass. She looked at his window.

He yanked open the shutters and put his own hands on the glass.

"Momma!"

She smiled.

The truck roared to life. Mason heard the gear pop out of park. His father rumbled from the driveway, the red rear lights growing smaller until they disappeared at the end of the block.

The house fell quiet, but for the steady ticking of the scratched grandfather clock in the hall.

Mason padded to the back door and pushed the hanging screen door open. He walked around the house and stared up at his favorite shoes dangling from the telephone lines in the moonlight.

Mason awoke in his bed, his eyelids stiff and swollen from crying. Licking his fingers, he pulled them across his long, salt-crusted lashes and glanced at the clock on his bedside table.

Three o'clock in the morning.

A fog of despair enveloped him. He hated three o'clock. Anytime he saw that number on his clock, trouble followed.

He listened for the argument he guessed had woken him.

Nothing.

The memory of his father roaring out of the driveway with his mother returned to him.

Did they come back?

Mason swung his legs over the bed, preparing to drop to the ground.

Heavy footsteps thumped in the hall outside his door.

He jerked his knees back and whipped the blanket over him, slamming his head to the pillow so hard it bounced. Turning his face away from the door, he stared at his clock, the glowing red *three* taunting him.

I hate three o'clock.

A sliver of light cut across his bed to the opposite wall as his door opened.

"Mason?" His father's voice sounded strange.

Tired? Usually, he barked every word like a drill sergeant, but tonight he sounded as if talking tapped the last of his energy.

Mason turned to his opposite side to face his father, trying to appear half-asleep.

"Huh?"

"Hey, buddy, I gotta tell you something." His father walked to the side of his bed and stood for a moment, looming over him. Sweat covered his neck. As he twisted to sit on the edge of the bed, Mason noticed dirt on his tan arms. Streaks of mud crisscrossed the t-shirt that had seemed so white a few hours before. The stink of *swamp* filled his nostrils.

Did they go frog giggin'?

Mason couldn't picture his momma agreeing to that.

"Where's Momma?"

His father slapped the bed with his palm as if calling over a dog. "That's what I gotta talk to you about. Sit up."

Mason scrooched against his pillow, distrustful of his old man's unusually gentle tone. He spoke, staring forward, his back turned to Mason.

"Your mama left us."

"What?"

"She left us. You ain't gonna see her no more."

"She wouldn't—"

"She told you she was goin', didn't she?"

Mason fell silent.

She did.

"But she told me to pack."

His father sniffed, and Mason thought he heard him mutter a single word.

"Yeah, well, she changed her mind 'bout you goin'. Thought you'd be better off with me."

Mason's chest constricted. "With you?"

"Yeah. A boy should be with his father."

"But—"

"Look, no buts. You're with me, and she's gone, and that's the way it is."

His father stood and headed toward the door.

Mason found it hard to breathe. Something was building inside of him. He felt like a shaken can of Coke.

His father turned.

"Did your momma give you anything?"

Mason gasped for breath like a landed fish, his mouth wide. He'd forgotten to breathe.

"What's wrong with you?" His father's familiar sharp tone returned as if he'd been released from whatever held him back before.

"Nothing."

"I asked if Momma gave you anythin'."

"Like what?"

"Like *anything*. Rocks?"

"Rocks? Why would Momma give me rocks?"

His father stepped toward him, and Mason recoiled on his bed.

"Are you sassin' me?"

"No."

"She didn't give you nothin'?"

"No."

"She didn't tell you to hide anythin'?"

Mason's eyes pulled toward the front of the house, where his sneakers hung from the telephone wire. He turned his face toward the back of the house to keep from exposing his thoughts, his mother's words echoing in his brain.

Don't tell your father those are yours.

"She said we were goin' to Disney World."

His father exploded with one loud, cannon-shot laugh. "She did, huh?"

Mason nodded.

"See? She was mean as a polecat. She wasn't takin' you to no Disney World, and now she left us."

Mason remained silent, watching the right corner of his father's mouth pinch up until it made his corresponding eye squint.

"Where was she right before I came home?"

Momma had been helping him pack, but Mason felt sure if he said that, his father would remain in his room looking for whatever he thought she'd taken.

"She was in her bedroom."

"You mean in *my* bedroom."

Mason nodded.

His father wiped his brow on the back of his forearm. "Okay. You go back to sleep."

Mason slid back under his sheets. His father left and closed the door.

He stared into the darkness of his room.

The clock glowed three-fifteen.

It had only taken fifteen minutes to lose his momma forever.

CHAPTER TEN

Mason sat in a hard wooden chair beside an unoccupied police station desk. He assumed it *looked* like him sitting in the chair. The body and the face resembled him down to the last freckle, but the *real* part of him, the part that felt like *Mason*, had gone somewhere else.

Maybe with Momma.

The remaining hard shell looked like him.

His center had gone hollow.

"You want a Coke, sweetie?" asked a pie-faced lady in the biggest police uniform Mason had ever seen.

He shook his head. He didn't know much about this new Mason but knew he didn't drink soda. Nothing sweet. Nothing that reminded him of before.

"Well, if you want anything, you let me know," said the lady.

He nodded and let his gaze bounce over desks, chairs, and trashcans until he spotted a girl about his age sitting on the opposite side of the room. She sat in a chair as scratched and rickety as his own. A man in a white uniform stood beside her, his hand resting on her shoulder. Her face turned to the man, and she smiled, but he could see her eyes pressed to the right, looking at him.

She didn't look scared.

The man in the white uniform patted her on her head before following a policeman to another part of the station. They entered a room and closed the door behind them.

The moment the door clicked shut, the girl jumped to her feet and walked to him as if she'd been waiting all day to do it. She wore red sneakers and shorts with orange flowers splashed across them.

"Hello," she said. Her dark hair stretched from her temples toward a ponytail tucked once so it made a loop hanging from the back of her head.

"Hi." Mason was glad his new self didn't cry. She didn't seem scared to be in the police station. He *would* have been, but he'd run out of fears and tears a day earlier.

"Did you rob a bank?" she asked.

He scowled. "No."

"Did you pull a museum heist?"

"No. You're stupid." Mason shifted and looked away.

"No, I'm not. I'm smarter than just about anybody I know."

"No, you're not. You're a *girl*." He didn't know why he'd said it. He didn't think girls were stupid. There were three girls smarter than the smartest boy in his class, and Momma had always been smarter than his old man.

Though not quite smart enough in the end.

Instead of being angry, the girl laughed. "Mick says that makes me *stealthy*. No one sees me coming."

Mason had never met anyone *stealthy* before. He liked the sound of it. He liked the way she said it. She didn't have an accent like his. She wasn't from South Carolina—if she was, it had to be some other part he didn't know.

"Why are you here?" she asked.

"I'm not."

"You are. I'm looking at you."

"My *father* is here. They don't know what else to do with me."

"Where's your mom?"

Mason's new tough exterior thickened another inch. "She left."

"Left where?"

"I don't know."

The girl took a deep breath and let it out. "I don't have a mom either."

"Did she leave?"

She shook her head. "I never had one."

"Everyone has a momma."

"Not me. I was born in a Naval laboratory." She spilled hellacious lies as if they bored her.

He rolled his eyes. "No, you weren't. What's your name?"

The girl's gaze darted down to the desk at which he sat. "Jelly."

He looked to where her attention had jumped and spotted a pack of grape jelly poking from beneath a sheet of paper.

"You just looked at that jelly."

"No, I didn't."

"Yes, you did."

She shrugged. "Coincidence. What's your name?"

He scowled. "Peanut Butter."

She thrust out a hand. "Nice to meet you, Peanut Butter."

Mason heard yelling from the back of the station and glanced toward the room the man in the white uniform had entered. It was the same room where they'd taken his old man. His cheeks grew hot.

Jelly turned to look, too. He didn't want her to see his

father come out of the room, so he asked the first question he could think of to draw her attention back to him.

"Who's that man you're with?"

"My dad."

"What is he?"

"Huh?"

"The uniform."

"He's Navy."

"Oh." Mason nodded. He'd never met anyone in the Navy before. His grandfather on his father's side had supposedly been in the Army.

"I'm in the Navy, too," Jelly added, shrugging one shoulder as if it were no big deal.

"No, you're not."

"I am. I'm a Naval bounty hunter." She peeled back the papers on the desk to further reveal the packet of jelly and an open sleeve of dayglow orange crackers. She pulled a cracker from the cellophane and took a bite.

"It's a secret, though. Don't tell anyone," she added, orange crumbs raining from her lips.

He frowned and thought about his sneakers hanging from the telephone line. "I know how to keep a secret."

"Good. Not many people can. You must be special, too." She took another bite and held up the cracker. "Peanut butter."

"Why's your dad here?"

Jelly looked right and left before leaning in to whisper her answer. Something about her conspiratorial tone and the feel of her breath under his ear made him feel googly in his stomach.

"He's looking for a man who went AWOL. They have his partner in there," she said.

"What's AWOL?"

"Absent Without Leave. It means he owed the Navy

time, but he ran off instead. That's what Mick and I do. We find criminals and runaways for the Navy."

"Who's Mick?"

"My *dad*."

"You call your old man by his first name?"

Jelly nodded, and Mason realized his new self *did* feel some things. Right now, he felt *impressed*. He'd get slapped into the next county if he called his father Perry.

He looked at the door and realized what Jelly had asked.

Had his father been in the Navy?

"Is the man with the beard the AWOL fella?" he asked.

"No. That's his partner." Jelly popped the rest of the cracker in her mouth. "When Mick caught up with *his* man, the sailor said he'd tell Mick everything if he let him go. Said they robbed a jewelry store full of diamonds and hid a body in a swamp."

"A *body*?"

She nodded. "A lady."

Mason's skin grew clammy.

Jelly stopped chewing. Her head cocked. "When did your mom leave?"

"Two days ago." His tongue felt dry.

The girl swallowed and lowered her hand to rest on top of the one he had on the desk. He stared at her hand on his, tremors running through his body. He wanted to jerk away, but he couldn't.

Something about her touch reminded him of Momma.

Jelly looked at him, biting her lip, and then suddenly threw her arms around his neck.

Shocked, he clung to her, the strange girl he didn't know.

"It'll be okay, Peanut Butter," she said in his ear. "Mick fixes everything."

As if she'd invoked him, the man in the white uniform appeared behind Jelly, looking concerned.

"What's going on, Siofra?" he asked.

Mason released her and wiped his eyes.

Shee-fra. Is that her real name?

She sounded like some kind of superhero. Like He-Man's lady, She-Ra.

She pointed at the room where her father had been. "The man with the beard is his father."

She lowered her voice, but not enough so Mason couldn't hear.

"His mother is *missing*."

The officer couldn't disguise the horror rippling across his expression. He looked at Mason with softer eyes, confirming his deepest fears.

Momma's dead. Daddy killed her.

"His name is Peanut Butter," added the girl.

"*Mason*." Mason thrust out a hand, and the Navy man shook it, his grip as strong as he imagined it would be.

"Nice to meet you, Peanut Butter Mason."

He winked, and Mason offered a tight smile.

"I see you met my daughter."

"Yes, sir."

"Ever think about joining the Navy?"

Mason shook his head. "No."

"Hm. Well, if you ever do, look me up."

The officer pulled a business card from his pocket and handed it to him. Mason glanced down to read the name on it, *Commander Shea McQueen.*

Commander.

Mason marveled at the title.

He must be in charge of the whole Navy.

"My friends call me Mick. You can call me Mick until you're a sailor. Then you'll have to call me *sir*. Deal?"

Mason nodded. "Yes, sir. I mean, Mick."

Mick laughed and tussled Mason's hair with his strong paw.

"Commander? If you could come this way."

A police officer poked around the corner, beckoning. Commander McQueen winked and turned to leave, guiding Jelly by the shoulder to follow alongside him.

She looked over her opposite shoulder as she left, smiling. "See ya, Peanut Butter."

Mason nodded once.

"See ya, Jelly," he said, too quietly for her to hear.

CHAPTER ELEVEN

Present Day

Shee scooped sand into a bright yellow scallop shell and poured it on her big toe as if the shell were a little excavator. The strip of dry land where she sat shrank another inch as the surf pounded in, driven by a strong north-easterly wind. A winter squall had the temperature hovering at a nippy sixty degrees, and Shee zipped her hoodie to protect herself against the chill.

Where did Florida go?

A man walked by, holding both his skinny arms in the air as if he'd won a marathon. He wore nothing but ragged-edged jeans shorts and a Russian fur cap complete with ear flaps, his exposed nipples pointed into the wind like rocket nosecones.

Ah. There it is.

She didn't need to worry about Florida.

Shee rested her forehead on her knees.

This is it. I'm going home.

Mick had been too still. She couldn't remember when she'd seen her father lie so still in the middle of the day.

Something's wrong.

The way she saw it, she had two options. She could keep sneaking around, filling the Loggerhead Inn's airspace with spy drones.

Or...

She could sack up and walk through the door.

Angelina was probably the only person from the Inn's original staff still working there—the only person who could make her. Maybe no one would recognize her. She could get a room like a tourist.

Will it be safe?

If the people after her were in Jupiter Beach, they would have killed her already. *Right?* She'd been a ghost for fifteen years. Certainly, they hadn't been surveilling her father's hotel all that time, waiting for her to appear...

Shee stood and brushed the sand from her butt. A tourist couple walked by, holding hands. She could tell they were tourists because only shorts and tank tops covered their fish-belly-white skin. At sixty-five degrees, the locals were digging out their parkas. Visitors gritted through wearing their summer togs, chanting, *I will be on vacation, dammit.*

Shee shivered. It seemed she still had Floridian blood.

Okay. You can do this.

As the sun dipped to the west, she returned to her car and drove to The Loggerhead Inn, grateful the short trip had left little time to rethink her decision.

She pulled into the hotel's lot and parked across from the front door. A flock of white ibis strutted nearby, poking their curved beaks into a patch of thick green grass, plucking worms and millipedes.

Eleven.

Eleven birds, ten white and one mostly white with gray speckles. The number *eleven* hovered over the image of the birds in her mind, like the watermark on a copyrighted photo. The tiniest glimpse at a flock of birds and she knew how many were there, but ask her twenty-two percent of sixty-four dollars, and she'd spend twenty years, a redwood's worth of paper, and a thousand number two pencils working out the answer.

She hated math.

I like birds, though. Does a flock of birds become a herd of birds when walking?

Good question.

Here's a better one.

Can I think of any other stupid ways to delay getting out of this car?

Shee cut the engine, closed her eyes, and took a deep breath.

Here goes nothing.

She left the vehicle and pointed herself toward the inn's porch. The enormous man she'd seen guarding the front door during a previous drive-by had left his post.

She scanned the area, searching for the doorman. She liked to keep track of people capable of breaking her in half with their bare hands, especially after her current track record with giants, but she didn't see him.

Good. Maybe I won't be tempted to tackle him.

She opened the door and entered the lobby, the air conditioning chilling her bare arms.

"Hello?"

The white granite top of the unmanned check-in desk gleamed beneath a string of modern pendant lights. Another small wooden desk, one Shee guessed belonged to a concierge, also sat empty, but for a small pile of papers, a few clear containers of local attraction brochures, and a fuzzy black, bedazzled disk about the size of a dinner plate. The disc looked like Sunset Boulevard's aging movie queen

Norma Desmond had left a hat behind.

Shee took another cleansing breath and exhaled.

You're in. No one is watching you. This is good. You can go to Mick without having to go through anyone else.

If only all infiltrations were this easy.

She walked to the elevator, the slap of sandals against her feet deafening in the silence of the empty room.

Her attention pulled toward the ceiling, and she realized she'd been searching for speakers. The hotel needed lobby music to make guests feel welcome. Something mellow and Jimmy Buffett-y to confirm their expectations of Florida.

Heck with the music. Stationing a warm *human being* somewhere in the lobby would be a good start. As it was, the hotel had an after-the-apocalypse vibe. Empty. Abandoned *suddenly*, if the glowing iPhone on the check-in counter was any indication.

Strange.

If a zombie had come shuffling down the hall toward her, it wouldn't have felt out of place.

Shut up. Go to Mick.

Shee suffered a flash of dread.

Maybe everyone else *had* gone running to Mick.

Maybe something happened. Maybe his condition, whatever it may be, had worsened.

She hit the elevator call, and as if the lift had been waiting for eons for her arrival, the doors slid open.

Shee found herself staring at a group of people and a tiny dog.

Well, hello there.

Four people were in the elevator, but only three sets of eyes were staring back at her if she didn't count the dog. All but one of the people opened their mouths a crack as if startled to see her.

One didn't register any surprise because he was probably *dead*—judging from the man's slippers dangling from the rolled carpet.

Dead, or enjoying a friendly game of *human burrito.*

It wasn't Mick in there. Not unless her father had both ankles replaced by a black donor.

Shee might not have noticed the dead guy, except when the doors opened, the youngest woman fumbled her side of the rolled carpet. Feet slid out, but the fast-thinking giant holding the opposite end bent his knees to reverse the plane and stop Dead Guy's slide.

The big man with the barrel chest and keg belly wore a tropical shirt and khaki shorts, making him look like a *friendly* giant. He easily supported three-quarters of the rug's considerable weight.

Doorman located. *Check.*

On the opposite side of the rug, the young woman recovered from her shock and propped her end. For letting her side slip, she flashed an apologetic glance at the giant and then focused on Shee.

Shee's attention moved to the last breathing human in the group—a woman clutching an impossibly small, black-and-rust-colored dog against her bosom.

The woman looked like an older, very surprised version of Angelina.

"Angelina?" Shee heard herself say, but the word had hardly left her lips before the doors slid shut and the elevator headed back up.

Shee wasn't sure what had kept her from thrusting her arm between the closing doors, but she'd made no effort to stop them. Her reluctance might have been caused by the shock of seeing Angelina again after so long.

It might have been the dead guy.

CHAPTER TWELVE

Shee remained in the same spot, nose nearly brushing the elevator doors until they slid open again to reveal only Angelina, her trademark four-thousand-watt smile outlined by blood-red lips.

A newcomer, who *hadn't* just witnessed Angelina supervising the removal of a body, would have found the woman composed and relaxed as if she'd been upstairs at a day spa.

Shee noted her old family friend had been crying. The woman's pulse pounded in her neck like an African djembe drum. She clocked a thin makeup smear, reaching toward Angelina's eyebrow, where she'd presumably swept her melting kohl-black eyeliner to avoid looking like a raccoon. The dark smudge on her index finger confirmed this. The sheen of sweat at her brow line suggested she'd deigned to help carry that human burrito after all. Maybe, in a rush to get him off the elevator.

"Shee?" Angelina flung out the arm unburdened by a dog and clamped it around Shee's shoulders like a toddler demanding to be picked up. Shee resisted the urge to carry her from the elevator but tugged her into the lobby as the elevator doors bounced off her shoulder and threatened to pinch them closer together.

"Hey, Angelina."

The dog placed its front paws on Shee's shoulder to lick her right cheek. Angelina planted what Shee suspected to be a smeary cherry lipstick kiss on her left.

Well. Both those things were unnecessarily wet.

Angelina gave her a bonus squeeze before stepping back, her pointy heel nearly slipping into the metal slot between the elevator and the lobby. She tip-toed safely from the makeshift bear trap as the doors slid shut.

"You came back," she said. Her eyes rimmed with tears, and she slid the already black-stained knuckle of her index finger upward to wipe them away.

Shee pointed at the elevator. "So that guy in the carpet—"

Angelina's shoulders relaxed, and the smile returned to her lips. Even her slow-blink stare said *nothing to see here.*

"Hm?"

Shee couldn't help but smile.

Angelina. Ever the poker player.

She decided to circle back to the dead guy later.

"Once you shot my drone with a tracker, I figured you wanted to see me," she said instead.

Angelina strode to the concierge desk and placed the dog into the black, sparkly disk.

Ah. Not Norma Desmond's hat. A dog bed.

Angelina spun and shook a finger as if scolding a child. "Putting the tracker on the gopher tortoise was *mean*. You had poor Croix stalking that thing to get her equipment back."

Shee scowled. "What's a Croy? Half crow, half boy?"

"*Croix*. Like the island of St. Croix. I think it's pretty."

Shee hooked a thumb toward the elevator. "The girl?"

Angelina nodded.

Shee moved to the dog that was now standing like a miniature soldier, all eyes and bird-chested attitude. As she neared, its butt wiggled, tongue lolling. The strain of telepathically begging Shee to *come pet me* had broken its little brain. Shee scratched the dog's neck as if it were made of furry china, amazed something so tiny could act like a real dog.

"This can't be Harley."

"It is. Harley Two."

"You named a new dog Harley?"

Angelina flicked her wrist as if batting away the question. "I didn't want to go through getting this one registered as a therapy dog, and I still have Harley One's paperwork. Plus, I had a lot of collars and whatnot with her name on them…"

"Strangely, that makes sense."

"Of course, it makes sense. Why wouldn't I make sense?"

Shee's gaze shifted to the elevator as Harley's tiny dagger teeth gnawed her thumb. She wanted to run up the stairs to see Mick, but the fact Angelina hadn't yet mentioned her father made her nervous.

She wasn't ready to hear he was dead or wrecked beyond repair in any way.

Speaking of dead guys…

"Is *now* when I ask about the body in the rug?"

Angelina pulled out her concierge desk chair and dropped into it. "Put a pin in that for a second. I think you have a more pressing question."

Here it comes. She's going to tell me about Dad.

Shee braced and stopped scratching the dog. Harley Two stomped her foot with annoyance.

Angelina leveled her stare. "I assume you saw him with the drone?"

"Yes."

"Good." Angelina stood and adjusted her blouse. "I have to go."

"What?"

"I have to help them. They can't do it without me." She waved a hand toward the front of the hotel. Out front, the giant stood staring through the glass front door like a hungry kid outside an ice cream shop.

"Who *is* that enormous man? It must have taken a whole bolt of fabric to make that shirt."

Angelina flashed a genuine smile, revealing her affection for the man. "Bracco. He has aphasia, but he makes a great doorman. Would you try to bum rush this hotel with him outside?"

Shee winced at the memory of the New Hampshire giant. "You'd be surprised," she mumbled.

"He'd do *anything* for your father."

Shee's head cocked. Angelina's sentence resonated in the very *present* tense.

"So, to confirm, Mick's not dead?"

Angelina laughed. "No, he's not *dead*. Why would we leave him dead in his bed?"

"Oh, I don't know. Why are you wrapping bodies in carpets?"

Angelina's mouth pulled to the side. "So you noticed him?"

"Uh, *yeah*. Your girl Croix almost dropped him to the floor."

"Croix graduated from the Naval Academy with honors. Mick *adores* her."

Shee recoiled as if Angelina had slapped her.

Ouch.

"You said that to hurt me."

Angelina shrugged. "I'll be honest. I'm a little angry at you."

"Fair enough." Shee began to see a pattern. A giant with aphasia, a girl with a promising Naval career, instead of working at a hotel...

"Sounds like Mick's creating his own little Island of Broken Toys."

The corner of Angelina's mouth curled into a smile. "Something like that."

"And the dead guy?"

"Captain Rupert. Retired Army. Mick found him living alone nearby, with no family, riddled with cancer. Gave him a room and, eventually, a morphine drip."

"So Dad's a doctor now, too?"

"He has people."

"And this guy was rolled in a carpet because..."

Angelina sighed. "Because we promised we'd bury him with his wife, but the cemetery said *no*. He sold his adjacent plot to cover bills, and they'd resold it."

"So you're going to add him to his wife's grave in the middle of the night?"

Angelina nodded. "And I have to go. I made a deal with the night guard to get us in."

"Can I go see Dad while you're gone?"

"No."

Shee scowled. "You can't stop me."

"Sure I can. You can't even get to his floor without the elevator key."

Angelina pulled the chain on her neck from beneath her blouse to reveal a dangling key.

Shee covered her eyes with one hand and then pulled her palm down her face. "Fine. I'll go."

"What?"

"I'll help dig. Unless you made a deal with a guy with a backhoe, too?"

"That would wake the whole subdivision next door."

Shee took a step toward the front door. Angelina grabbed her arm, her jaw set, her eyes threatening to overflow a third time. "We've been trying to find you for *years*, Shee."

Shee looked away. "I didn't want to endanger you."

"That's *bullshit*."

Angelina stormed away and then suddenly spun on her heel to return. Shee took a step back, certain the woman would hit her.

Harley's black eyes shot toward her agitated mommy, and she moved to the edge of the desk, whining. Angelina scooped her into her palm and pressed her against her chest.

Therapy dog, indeed.

"You make me so mad—you made me forget my dog."

Angelina's glare threatened to slice Shee in two. The dog hadn't succeeded in changing the subject. The concierge strode toward the door again, making it one extra step before spinning to reverse course again.

Shee's neck retracted an inch.

Here it comes. Now, she's going to hit me.

Angelina spat words as she approached. "I've missed you, and I'm going to hug you, whether you like it or not."

Shee relaxed a notch. "Go ahead," she said, trying to match Angelina's agitated tone. "I'm going to pretend I don't like it but secretly *enjoy* it."

Angelina wrapped her arms around her and squeezed hard while still being careful not to crush the Yorkie. The dog scrambled against Shee's chest, though she didn't know if it was from irritation or a desire to get involved in the hug.

Shee pressed back, letting her cheek rest on Angelina's shoulder.

It had been a long time since she hugged someone she loved.

It felt good.

It also made her feel a little *crazy*.

Maybe I should let go before I can't.

"I—" Shee started, unsure what she might say.

Angelina saved her the trouble and cut her short as she stepped back.

"There's no excuse. Now it's too late," she said, adjusting her blouse.

"What do you mean?"

Bracco knocked on the door, and Angelina turned and motioned she'd heard him. "We have to go. We have a small window—"

"Wait. What do you mean *it's too late*?"

Angelina's diamond-edged glare returned. "You waited this long. You can wait a little longer."

"But you said—"

"There's no hurry, Shee. He's in a coma."

Angelina strode toward the front door, Yorkie peering over her shoulder to see if Shee would follow.

CHAPTER THIRTEEN

Shee couldn't remember many car rides as awkward as this one.

Once, a boy tried to kiss her under the guise of teaching her how to drive. Surprised, she'd jerked the wheel to the left and popped both tires against a curb.

Awkward.

But the current trip hit a *ten* on the awkward scale. She couldn't have been more uncomfortable if she were bound and gagged in the trunk with the dead guy.

Angelina flanked her in the back seat of an aging black Cadillac sedan, simmering between sobbing and livid. She tapped her bright orange fingernails against the bangle dangling from her left wrist in a strange rhythmic pattern Shee suspected to be some profanity-laden Morse code.

The earbud-clad young woman riding shotgun wore *attitude* like a cloak of invisibility. Though, she didn't try to hide the scathing looks periodically thrown in Shee's direction.

What did I do to her?

A gibberish-speaking giant sat behind the wheel, seemingly unfazed by the cauldron of bubbling emotion in which they all boiled.

The dead guy in the trunk didn't have much to add.

Shee stretched her back and tried to identify the tinny tune leaking from Croix's earbuds. She didn't know it. It sounded like someone beating a guitar with a chicken.

"Well. This is fun," she said.

No one responded.

She looked at her watch, eager for their task to be over so she could see Mick.

"Why is he in a coma?"

Angelina didn't look at her. "Later."

"Why can't you tell me—"

"You made him wait. *You* can wait."

"Oh, that's mature."

"Right. *I'm* the immature one." Angelina had eyes on her now. She hissed the words.

Shee opened her mouth and then shut it, noticing Croix squinting at her.

"What are you looking at?" she asked, tired of being made to feel like a criminal.

Croix rolled her eyes and faced forward.

Shee turned to the window and watched the trees go by.

Kids. Can't live with them, can't sell them to the circus.

They drove for a long, silent time down an increasingly rural road until the headlights shone on a cemetery's wrought-iron gates. A man wearing dirt-streaked cargo pants and a faded Lynard Skynard t-shirt appeared from the darkness. He spat as Angelina rolled down her window and then reloaded his sinuses with bubbling nasal friction.

Shee grimaced. "Charon could use a tissue."

Angelina dangled herself from the window like bait, and Charon shuffled over, intrigued.

"Hey, A," he said, running the back of his hand across his nose.

Shee looked away.

Oh, come on with the snot.

Angelina raised a hand and presented him with a wad of money produced from thin air.

"Thanks, Biff, we appreciate it," she purred.

Shee cocked an eyebrow. "*Biff*? I did not see that coming."

Biff took the money and nodded. "Just be quick."

Angelina patted Shee's knee but directed her next comment to Biff. "Don't worry. We brought our best digger."

Biff leaned down to bless Shee with an unsettling stare before ambling to the gates to enable their passage to the underworld. Bracco eased the Cadillac through, rolling down a stone path deep into the cemetery. As he parked at an angle, marble headstones shone beneath his headlights, glowing like stars against the thick, dark grass.

Bracco popped the trunk as the rest of them clambered out of the car.

Croix plucked the buds from her ears and jerked two shovels from the trunk, handing one to Bracco and holding the other aloft in front of Shee. "We only brought two shovels. You can take the first shift."

Shee placed a hand on her chest. "No, *please*, you first. I wouldn't *dream* of it."

Croix frowned but kept the shovel and followed Bracco to a nearby grave.

Angelina sat on a white stone bench tucked beneath a gumbo limbo tree, known as a *tourist tree,* for the way its bark peels like a sunburned snowbird.

"I suppose I should officially introduce you all," said Angelina, sounding as enthusiastic as a coroner. "Bracco, Croix, this is Mick's daughter, Shee."

Bracco looked over his shoulder. "Oughta plaster hearts."

Shee's brow knit. "What?"

"Aphasia," Angelina reminded her.

Oh. Right.

Shee nodded to him. "Nice to meet you, too."

Croix either nodded or stretched her neck in Shee's general direction. "I've heard so much about you," she muttered. Before Shee could comment, the girl replaced her earbuds, slipped on leather gloves, and started digging.

Shee sat beside Angelina on the bench and bumped her with her shoulder. "They'll warm up to me."

Angelina grunted.

Time to get to business.

Shee took a deep breath. "Can you tell me now? When did he come back to the hotel?"

"About two years ago. He spent six months waiting for you and then found himself a new mission."

A tsunami of guilt crashed against Shee's heart, so real it hurt.

Move on. Nothing to see here.

"New mission?"

"Uh-huh. Helping people."

Shee scoffed. "He always did that."

"Not like this. He devised a grand plan to make up for his whole life."

"What does that mean?"

"You know. Save a life for every life he took in the service, blah blah blah."

"I see you were moved."

Angelina shrugged one shoulder. "I wanted him to *retire* and run the hotel like a normal person. Instead, he sat still for about five minutes before some guy came looking for his lost son."

"He thought he was in the hotel?"

"No, he wanted to *hire* Mick. Lord knows how he knew Mick the Savior was open for business."

"Did Dad find the kid?"

"He did. Kid was fine. Just irresponsible and cruel. Sixteen years old." Angelina chuckled. "He tried to fight your father."

"I'm sure that went over well."

"Oh yeah. Mick delivered him to his father in a golf travel bag."

They laughed. Croix paused to glance at them, her scowl

deepening.

"And then there are the vets," added Angelina, nodding toward the diggers. "The hotel is staffed with them. Part of your father's grand plan to save the world, save his soul, save them..."

"He used to talk about doing something like that with the hotel."

Angelina nodded. "They show up with his handwritten invites, and we give them a home. Then he puts them to work helping his clients."

Shee leaned toward Angelina and whispered. "Why does the curly-headed one hate me?"

Angelina lowered her voice. "Mick treats her *like* a daughter."

"Ah. And I'm the real deal. She feels threatened?"

Angelina shrugged one shoulder.

Shee watched Croix dig, remembering when her father's approval meant *everything.* She wondered how she'd stayed away so long. "So, what happened? Something during one of his good Samaritan missions? Did he have a stroke?"

Angelina shook her head. "A month ago, someone shot him in the head. Not during a tussle, either. It was a hit. A sniper."

Shee gasped. "What? Who?"

"I don't know. You and Mick are the trackers, and *you* were nowhere to be found."

Shee ignored the accusation in Angelina's voice and stared at the ground, doing the math.

So close. Where was I four weeks ago?

She swallowed and fought to keep from slipping into a quagmire of regret.

"What do you know? Was it *here*?" she asked.

"No. He went to help a friend. It was a setup."

"What friend?"

Angelina's tone grew icy. "I don't know. Mick wasn't big on leaving trails. Called him *Thor,* but I doubt that's his real name."

"Viggo," said Shee, picturing her father's enormous friend.

Suddenly, my whole world revolves around giants.

"You know him?" asked Angelina.

"He was on Dad's team back in the day."

Angelina released a shaky sigh. "Okay. That's something we can work with."

"Big ole Viking—from Minnesota, I think."

Angelina slapped a hand on Shee's thigh. "*Yes.* That tracks. Someone sent an anonymous email from an untraceable IP." She waggled a finger in Croix's direction. "Whatever that means. That's her end of things. The email told us Mick was in an Airbnb in Minneapolis."

Shee gaped. "They left him lying in a coma in an Airbnb?"

"Yes."

"That's *insane.*"

"Yes. But it means someone wanted to help."

"Viggo?"

"Maybe. I had Croix try to track down who rented the house. The owner could only say it was a woman's voice on the phone."

Shee nodded. "I need *all* the information. Everything you've got."

"Naturally."

"Why'd you bring him *here*? He's not safe—"

"Yes, he is."

"How can you know—"

"He's dead."

Shee caught her breath, and sensing her horror, Angelina spoke quickly.

"Not *really*. We declared him dead and brought him back on the sly."

Shee realized she'd tensed and rolled her shoulders to keep from twisting into a pretzel. "What's the diagnosis?"

Angelina's voice dropped to match the softness of her own. "He could come out of it. His brain is active. Doc says he finds it odd he *hasn't* woken yet, but the *brain is a mystery* and all that medical jibberish."

"Can you trust the doctor?"

She nodded. "He was on Mick's shortlist of people to call if anything ever happened to him."

Shee picked at the bark of the gumbo limbo, removing a peel and snapping it into smaller pieces.

Mick told her to come home two years ago. Said he'd handled everything.

Why didn't I come back?

"Did Mick ever tell you who'd been after me and why he thought it was okay to come home?"

"No." Angelina scowled.

Shee raised a hand over her eye as if creating a makeshift eyepatch. "He might have been wrong. The person after me might have been who shot him."

Croix stopped digging and pulled the buds from her ears. "That's not it."

Shee realized she hadn't been hearing the tinny sound of Croix's music. The girl had been eavesdropping.

"What's not?" she asked.

"The stuff that drips out of your nose, but that's not important right now," said Croix. She giggled and looked at Bracco, who snorted a laugh without slowing his digging.

"Don't get them started with the movie quotes," grumbled Angelina. "They're totally stupid together."

"Make your point," said Shee to Croix.

The girl stabbed her shovel into the ground. "You said it might be the same person, the one after you and the one who shot Mick, but that's a negative, Ghost Rider."

Bracco chuckled.

"Cut it out," warned Angelina.

"Why do you think that?" asked Shee.

Croix sniffed. "Because he took care of your guy."

"How? Who was it?"

Croix took a deep breath and then released it as if the

world's weight had settled on her shoulders. "*He* wanted to tell you."

Shee stood. "That's all fine and dandy, but circumstances have changed."

Croix sniggered. "Fine and dandy—?"

"Just *tell me*." Shee stepped toward the girl to snatch the handle of the shovel from her. "This person hunted me for almost twenty years. He *ruined my life.* Tell me, or I *swear* I'll bury you with the old man in this grave."

Croix stepped back, rising from the shallow ditch she'd dug herself. Shee thought she'd seen a flash of fear in the girl's expression, but it shifted now to a smirk.

"If you finish digging, I'll tell you," she said, motioning to the hole.

Shee thought about swinging the shovel at the girl. Instead, she thrust out a hand. "Give me the gloves."

Croix handed them over.

Shee jerked them on, her gaze never leaving Croix's. "Tell me *while* I dig."

Croix sat beside Angelina, who patted her leg.

"Tell her. This isn't funny."

Croix shrugged. "I don't know."

Shee stabbed the shovel into the ground. "I swear to—"

Croix held up her palms. "Seriously, I don't know. He didn't tell me. I just wanted a break."

Shee looked at Angelina. Her friend's expression was empathetic, but she seemed resigned. She believed the girl.

Smirky Croix slid a hand across her hair, flattening her kinky curls. She'd made the same motion several times during the car ride and half a dozen times since they arrived at the cemetery.

She's self-conscious about her frizz.

Shee banked the information in case she decided to go full-high-school-mean-girl on Croix later. The girl had her feeling like an angry teen.

Angelina slapped the top of the girl's leg in what felt like an attempt to break the tension. "Hey, Shee, tell Croix how we met."

"I don't give a shit how you met," muttered Croix.

Shee hefted a clump of dirt behind her.

"Do you remember?' prompted Angelina.

Shee wiped her brow and sighed. "Of course, I remember."

"Tell them."

"Ding dong," said Bracco, pausing to wipe his forehead.

Shee glanced at Croix. The girl had slipped the earbuds back into her ears, refusing to look in Shee's direction, but no tinny music filled the warm night air.

Shee stabbed the shovel into the dirt again.

"Fine."

CHAPTER FOURTEEN

Twenty-Five Years Ago

"You going out?" asked Mick from the bathroom, where he stood shaving in front of the cracked mirror of his crappy motel room.

Shee moved to sit and then thought better of it. The chairs were so threadbare and greasy from wear they looked more like flesh than fabric. Her room, three doors down, wasn't much better, but if pressed, she'd guess more people had been murdered in Mick's room.

"We need to upgrade our hotels," she said.

"That would mean less stipend money for things more fun than sleeping." Mick bent closer to the mirror to clean the tip of his chin.

She chuckled. "You're going to wash out of flight school."

"What?"

"You lean closer to that mirror every year. Your eyesight is going."

He scoffed. "I'm still twenty-twenty."

"Uh-huh. But not *twenty*, old man."

"Who would want to be? That's *your* cross to bear. And don't think I didn't notice you didn't answer my question."

Shee grimaced.

So much for distraction tactics.

"*No*, I'm not going out. I'm running a cockfight out of my bathroom."

"The place isn't that bad."

Shee grunted. "More like a cock*roach* fight."

Mick moved to the bathroom's doorway, toweling his face. "You need to find some people your age."

"We're *working*."

"Doesn't mean you can't unwind."

"Like you did last night? *Ew*." She'd seen him canoodling with a dark-haired woman.

Mick's cheeks flushed even darker than they'd already grown from his hot shave. He turned back to the mirror for the last inspection. "She's a nice lady. I'm seeing her again tonight."

Shee dropped it. She'd learned years ago her father felt comfortable meeting ladies *anywhere*. She always booked a room a few doors down from his during their road trips. The only thing worse than waking to the rhythmic thumping of the couple next door was knowing one of them was her father.

So gross.

She placed a hand on the doorknob to leave. "I'll see you tomorrow, Romeo."

Her father called after her. "Go out and have some fun."

She shut the door.

Right.

In the parking lot, a couple argued beside a Ford Thunderbird, the color of baby vomit. From what she could glean through the scattered array of f-bombs, the woman didn't appreciate the man coming home from work half-drunk. On the other hand, *he was up to here* (about eight inches above his head) with her nagging. The blue-swaddled baby in the woman's arms didn't care either way. He giggled as his mother swung him back and forth. Mommy was like a rollercoaster when she argued with Daddy.

Ah, the glamorous life.

Shee smiled and then realized she'd fixated on the gurgling

baby that swung like a powder-blue clock pendulum.

Her mood darkened.

Stop it.

She knew where this rabbit hole led. Self-pity never got anyone anywhere. She wanted a life. She wanted her career.

Mason was better off without her.

They could have ended up being just like the couple arguing outside the motel about diapers.

Though she would never have bought *that* car.

Shee let herself into her room, flicked on a dim yellow bulb, and stood in front of the stack of papers piled on the dresser.

Time to take you down.

She'd started a side project, searching for a rich kid named Scotty Carson, last seen near their current location.

Ole Scotty's proximity was no coincidence. Shee had picked their target and suggested the motel next to the bar. It hadn't been hard to talk Mick into it. The job and the motel put her within driving distance of her side project.

She hoped.

A legacy candidate at the United States Naval Academy, Scotty Carson's Rear Admiral father ensured his son's acceptance. All Scotty wanted to do was party. He'd nearly gotten himself kicked out for grades twice before accusations of rape surfaced. Rather than face the music, he'd run.

Shee and Mick had been at the USNA in Annapolis, Maryland, when some female plebes let her in on the Scotty situation. She'd talked to several of Scotty's accusers, including a few who'd been too scared to report officially. The girls had been beaten, raped, and emotionally shattered. The women had been strong enough to enter the man's world of the Naval Academy, only to have hard-fought and well-deserved careers hobbled by the actions of one evil, entitled bastard.

It didn't take long for Shee to uncover Scotty's unsavory past. A trail of abused girlfriends led as far back as high school. One ex had gone missing, presumed a runaway, but with Scotty as the last man to see her alive...

How could I not help?

She might have talked Mick into hunting Scotty, but the Navy hadn't officially asked him to track the Rear Admiral's son. He wasn't authorized to moonlight, so she went through every possible case until she found someone near where she thought Scotty would be.

Shee hoisted the papers into her arms and carted them outside to take advantage of the fresh air and dying sunlight. She'd learned years ago spending time beneath the flickering lights of cheap motel rooms was the fastest way to ruin her mood.

Pulling a plastic chair to her portion of the shared patio, she plopped the pile on a matching white table.

Scotty's father swore he wasn't supporting his monstrous son during the boy's time on the lam. Maybe he wasn't. Rumor had it Rear Admiral Carson was planning to run for Senator. His rapey kid was embarrassment enough—let it be known he *helped* his son escape, and his political career would be scuttled.

Scotty's most probable support system lived nearby. Without Daddy, Scotty needed *someone*, and after poring through the old yearbook and Academy photos, Shee had noticed a boy named William Kay often appeared grinning by Scotty's side. Another entitled USNA legacy kid, William Kay had made it through clean and was currently training at the Naval Aviation Schools Command in Pensacola, Florida. He had a parent-funded apartment near Middleburg, Virginia, though. A home base.

An *empty* home base.

William Kay's apartment would be Shee's first stop. She looked at her watch. She wanted to be on the road before sundown, but her father was taking *forever* primping for his date.

Someone yanked open a sticky door, and she peered down the long porch to spot her father, looking dapper and hopelessly military, even in his street clothes. He spotted her pile of homework and frowned.

"What is that?"

"Just notes for the next case."

"You already picked a new one?"

She nodded.

"All work and no play makes Shee a dull girl," he warned.

She shrugged. "Someone has to balance us out."

He bobbed his head in the direction of the honkytonk. "I'll be over there a while. You're welcome to join us if you get bored."

"At the Donkey Tonk? Thanks, but no thanks."

"Oh, come on. It'll be fun."

She shook her head. "You just want to use me as bait."

"Bait?"

"Women love a man with a baby."

He laughed. "You're twenty-one."

"But I'm *adorable*."

Mick walked away, chuckling.

When he reached the halfway point between the hotel and the bar next door, Shee moved inside to drop her paper pile back on the dresser. She grabbed her oversized purse and the spare car key and headed to their Jeep. William Kay's house was twenty minutes away. If her hunch was right, she could have Scotty in custody in less than an hour, her first solo capture completed.

Running through scenarios in her mind, Shee nearly missed the turn into Kay's apartment complex. She circled the lot and parked one building down from his second-floor entrance. Nothing about any of the cars parked outside, screamed *Scotty*. He'd skipped in a hand-me-down BMW, but he'd have traded that car by now if he were smart. No doubt his father had some pretty talented gumshoes on his trail.

Shee looked up. The apartment's only front-facing window was dark.

Feeling her pepper spray inside her purse, she left the Jeep and went up the stairs to knock on Kay's door.

No answer.

No problem.

She retrieved her lock-picking pack and jimmied the door to slip inside.

So far, so good.

The small apartment was neat. It didn't feel as though anyone had lived there recently. Stale air filled her nostrils as disappointment slumped her shoulders.

Might have called this one wrong.

She moved from room to room. Bed made. No toiletries were displayed. Everything was clean, the way someone might leave a home if they knew they'd be out of town for a long time.

Hope dwindled until she spotted an envelope in an otherwise empty trashcan and plucked it out. Plain, white, empty. Reusable but trashed instead.

Hm.

Had William left something for Scotty to pick up? Something that fits in an envelope. Cash? Instructions? A key?

She moved to the kitchen trash and slid it from its hidden spot behind a lower cabinet. Like the other trashcan, it proved empty but for one thing, this time, an empty wine bottle.

Shee pulled out the bottle. She didn't know much about wine, but it looked expensive. Scotty had a *thing* for pricey wines if the photos she'd seen of him holding up glasses and bottles were any indication.

She turned over the bottle. Not a drop. It smelled like vinegar. He hadn't been drinking here lately.

Shee wandered to the sofa and sat, trying to imagine where Scotty had enjoyed his wine. Probably *here*, on the sofa, in front of the television.

On top of a coffee-table book about the history of military planes—no doubt a Christmas present from William Kay's proud parents to their son—sat a local *Pennywise* magazine. A classified ad circular was the sort of thing a local rich young man would *never* grab from the magazine stand outside a food store. No label, it hadn't come through the mail, and Kay wouldn't have left it out after otherwise meticulously cleaning his apartment.

She picked up the flyer and flipped through it.

What were you looking for, Scotty? What do you need? New car?

Maybe. And if his father wasn't supporting him, he needed *money*. He wouldn't make it far without Daddy paying the bills, not with his taste in wine.

Shee glanced at the envelope again. William and Scotty looked a lot alike. What if the envelope had contained an old I.D.? Using his buddy's I.D. to skip the country would be risky, but to get a job somewhere, figure out his next step...

Shee stopped flipping as her gaze settled on a classified ad for a local vineyard looking for store help.

That would be a way to keep Scotty's habit fed *and* earn cash.

Worth a shot.

Shee locked the apartment behind her and drove ten minutes to Fine Oaks Vineyard. Trying to look as cute and aimless as possible, she rolled up her shorts and tied the bottom of her shirt to reveal her midriff.

She'd be bait tonight, after all.

The sign on the door said the shop closed at six, but she found the entrance unlocked. Behind a large wooden counter, a middle-aged man busied himself wiping down a tasting station.

"We're closed," he said, glancing up from his work.

"Is Billy working tonight?" She wasn't sure why she'd asked for Billy and not William. Just an instinct, Scotty might alter the name. The town wasn't so large someone might not recognize the name William Kay, and as a grown man going by *Scotty*, *Billy* wasn't a stretch.

"Billy Kay or Billy Hightower?"

Shee fought to hide her excitement.

"Kay."

The man jerked a thumb behind him. "He's stocking. You can go back."

She smiled and headed through swinging doors into a small warehouse.

A young man turned as she entered. A boy she'd seen in a dozen photos.

Hello, Scotty Carson.

Scotty did a double-take before offering a guileless grin. He'd slipped into his *nice guy* persona as easily as donning a cap.

"Hello. Can I help you?" he asked, his gaze sweeping down to her toes and back up.

This might be easier than I thought.

He hadn't wasted a moment telegraphing his interest.

Scotty wasn't a handsome guy—only his youth and exaggerated air of masculinity provided him with an appeal. A well-practiced sheepish smile leaped to hide the wolf inside. *I'm safe,* it said. *I'm big and strong, but only here to protect you.*

Shee smiled. "I was going to buy my Daddy some wine for his birthday, but I don't know what to get. The man out front said you know a *lot*."

She batted her eyes, feeling ridiculous.

Too much?

She didn't think of herself as a bombshell, but she'd watched men's reactions to her raven hair, big green eyes, and generous bosom for years. In civilian life, she was out of Scotty's league. If she seemed too eager, he might get suspicious.

Scotty moved in as if she were magnetic. "He's right. I know a *lot*."

Scotty had no confidence issues.

"Aren't I lucky I bumped into you?" Shee bit her bottom lip.

He held out a hand. "Shall we?"

She forced a giggle and placed her hand in his. His touch was revolting.

He led her to a long rack of red wines and motioned to a bottle.

"This is my favorite, though if you're having steak, you might want something a little bolder."

"Ah… just want something *nice*." She noticed somewhere along the way, she'd picked up a southern accent.

Scotty slid a bottle from the rack. "This is a bargain for the money. Does nineteen dollars fit in your range?"

She grimaced. "Nineteen?"

He touched her shoulder and leaned in until his lips nearly brushed her ear.

"Tell you what. I get off in ten minutes. Why don't you wait outside and let me see if I can find you a *real* bargain?"

She struggled not to recoil. "Sure. Ah'll wait for ya."

With a final hair flip and a flirty smirk, Shee walked away, shaking her tush as best she could until she was outside. She leaned against the building wall, fingering the cuffs in her purse.

When can I slap them on? He was bigger than she'd imagined. His size and strength made his cowardly attacks on women even more despicable and made his capture dicier. She hadn't wanted to pepper-spray him in the store. The counterman might have come to his rescue and complicated everything.

Maybe I should call Dad—

Too late. Scotty appeared, a backpack over his shoulder. He looked around and sidled up against her, his hip touching hers.

Guy's about as subtle as a heart attack.

He unzipped the backpack to reveal two bottles inside. The way he glanced at the door to be sure no one was watching told her he hadn't bought them.

At least he's a thief, too.

"Two?" she asked.

He winked. "One for you and me."

She opened her eyes wide to appear impressed and grateful, stalling as she tried to formulate a plan.

She couldn't be alone with Scotty Carson. Alone was a rapist's favorite place. If only Dad—

That was it.

Take him to Dad.

Mick was at the bar. Surely, she could talk Scotty to a bar?

"Aren't you sweet?" she gushed. "But ah gotta stop at work real quick-like. Can we stop at the Donkey Tonk?"

"That boot-scootin' place? You work there?"

"Just started."

He nodded. He seemed unsure—he didn't want to be seen with her. *Smart.* Always best not to strut around town with your potential rape victim.

She rushed to offer the urging he needed.

"My roommate's out of town." She blinked at him, again feeling like a cartoon seductress. "Ah just gotta make that stop for a *sec*."

The confident grin returned to his face, and he shrugged.

"Sure."

She jogged to the Jeep with another forced grin, trying to bounce as much as possible. He got into an old pickup truck he must have bought for a song and followed her toward the Donkey Tonk. She checked the rearview often to be sure he didn't peel away with a change of heart.

Shee's nerves jangled as the bar's neon donkey came into view.

Now, she just had to hope her charming father hadn't sealed the deal too early.

She parked and approached Scotty's truck as he pulled in beside her.

"Come inside with me?" she asked.

He shook his head. "I'll wait."

Damn.

She'd guessed right. He didn't want to be seen with a potential victim.

She glanced at the bar with the most worried look she could manufacture. "Um…"

"What is it?" he asked.

"Nothing. There's a bartender in there giving me a hard time. If he saw you…"

She reached through the window to feel his bicep, hard and bulgy.

He watched her hand on his arm and looked up at her from beneath a lowered brow. Her request for protection had ignited something primal in him.

"I can hang in the back and look scary if you think that'll do it?" His tone implied he'd do much more if needed.

She squealed with delight as he cut the engine and joined her.

"Yer like a knight in shiny armor."

His chest puffed as they walked to the entrance. Shee chanted in her head.

Please be there. Please be there…

Inside, she scanned the staff. All the bartenders were women dressed in Daisy Dukes and red-checkered midriff-tied shirts made from what looked like picnic blankets.

All-female staff. Figures.

Scotty's dubious expression telegraphed that he'd noticed the same thing.

"You got a dyke hitting on you?" he asked.

"No. He's probably in the back. He's more like a *bouncer*."

She continued scanning until she spotted her father in a booth to the left.

Thank God.

In the mirror on the wall behind him, she clocked the reflection of his boothmate. Female, of course.

She motioned in Mick's general direction. "I have to grab my check. I'll be right back."

"Okay."

She walked toward Mick's booth slowly, willing him to look at her.

Look at me and recognize him. Look. Look, look, look—

She was nearly on him before Mick pulled his gaze off his ladyfriend and noticed her.

"Shee? What are you—?"

He was going to say *wearing*, of that she was sure. Hopefully, he'd surmise by her attire something was up. She didn't usually expose her belly and roll up her shorts until the curve of her butt cheeks saw the sun.

"Grab my wrist," she said, letting her arm swing wide and flashing her eyes to show she meant it.

"What?" Mick scowled, emotions passing over his expression like clouds — confusion, embarrassment, concern— but his hand whipped out and caught her arm. They'd been working together for too long. Like a well-seasoned improv group, they knew how to read each other. How to *listen*.

"*Jack*," she whined, pretending to pull away but grabbing his arm with her opposite hand to keep him from letting go.

She looked toward Scotty, pretending to panic. He saw. After a scan of the room to see if anyone else was watching, he strode toward her.

"Recognize him?" she said to her father, bouncing her eyes in Scotty's direction.

Mick watched Scotty approach. She saw the moment the boy's face clicked in his brain.

"That kid you wanted to—"

"Is this the guy?" asked Scotty, bumping into the back of Shee in his eagerness to show strength.

A rapist was trying to protect her from her father.

Score one for irony.

Mick released her arm and stood.

Scotty poked his shoulder. "Back off, old man."

The dark-haired woman in the booth couldn't have widened her eyes any farther without them dropping to the table like dice. Mick's puffing chest apparently aroused her.

Ew.

Shee took a step back to position herself at Scotty's side. She motioned to the angry young man threatening to hit her father.

"Remember Scotty Carson?" she asked.

Scotty's focus swiveled to her. "Wha—"

Fear flashed in his eyes.

He turned to bolt, but she'd expected it and thrust out a leg. With little room to maneuver between the row of booths and the tables, he couldn't avoid the trip. He stumbled, slowing his retreat long enough for Mick to grab his shirt and horse-collar him backward.

Shee whipped the cuffs from her purse and handed them to Mick. He clamped them on Scotty's right wrist. Scotty twisted, swinging with his left. Shee saw it coming too late, and her jaw shifted hard to the right.

He screamed.

"Bitch!"

Shee caught her balance against a lacquer-covered table, her jaw already aching. She refused to raise a hand to it. She didn't want her mark to know he'd hurt her.

Scotty's eyes grew white and wild. He seemed oblivious to Mick cuffing him, so intent was he to reach *her*. Mick had to kick his knees out to stop him from pulling toward her.

Shee smirked as he dropped to his knees. "Those grade-school girls must have been *merciless* for you to hate women this much."

She'd practiced the line in her head for days.

Her father's raven-haired date barked a laugh. She'd slid from the booth and taken a place behind Mick against the wall, safe but close enough to watch the action.

Shee eyed her. A calm aura of confidence and intelligence surrounded her. She didn't seem like her father's usual passing conquest.

Give them five more minutes alone, and he'll be in love.

Shee looked away to find Scotty's angry stare bearing down on her. Being duped by a woman seemed to infuriate him more than being captured. The photos of the black-eyed, bloodied-lipped women he'd abused at the Academy made sense now. It wasn't enough to rape them. He wanted to *hurt* them. He'd probably *loved* that they'd fought so hard.

"Call the cops." Mick tapped her arm and snapped her from her murderous thoughts.

Shee looked at him, her mind slow to shift gears.

"Cops?" she echoed.

"We need a place to keep him until the master-at-arms can get here. He wasn't scheduled to come until tomorrow for our other case."

Shee heard the annoyance in her father's voice. She sensed it was all he could do to keep from scolding her on the spot. There would be a reckoning for her freelancing.

It didn't matter.

I got him.

His date's attention had shifted from Mick to Shee.

"You're his daughter?" she asked as Mick jerked Scotty to his feet.

Shee nodded, and the woman turned her gaze back to Mick.

"So you *are* a bounty hunter?"

Mick's eyebrows arched. "Yes. You thought I was lying?"

The woman shrugged. "You have to admit. *Bounty hunter* makes for a sexy pickup line."

She reached into her purse and withdrew a man's black leather wallet. Shee recognized it.

It was Mick's.

Mick risked taking one hand off Scotty to snatch it from her hand.

"That's *mine*," he said, slipping it back into his back pocket. "You lifted it?"

She smiled, all teeth and ruby lips. "That's what liars get."

"But I wasn't lying."

She pointed a finger at him and clucked her tongue as if her hand was a tiny gun. "That's why you get it back."

Mick grinned, noticed Shee watching, and cleared his throat, wiping away any lingering trace of amusement.

Already in rapture from her victory, Shee fell in love with the woman playing her father like a fiddle.

"Who are you?" she asked.

The woman held out a hand to shake. "Angelina. Nice to meet you."

"Shee." Shee shook her hand before sensing the weight of her father's stare.

"Can you go make the phone call, *please*?" he asked, pressing a writhing Scotty to the wall as Angelina skittered out of the way.

"Oh, right. Sorry."

Shee bounced toward the bar, unable to control her giddiness.

CHAPTER FIFTEEN

Present Day

Bracco dragged Captain Rupert's rug-wrapped body from the Cadillac's trunk and hefted it over his shoulder before walking it to the grave's edge. The body bent neatly, the rigor mortis having worn off.

As Bracco lowered him to the grass, the rug slipped from his tired fingers. The body's weight spilled over the edge of the freshly dug grave, unfurling the carpet like a flag. The old soldier's body dropped on top of his wife's exposed coffin with a hollow *thud* and a collective gasp from the crowd.

Angelina and Croix rose from the bench and scurried over. The four peered down at the dead man lying akimbo on his wife's coffin, jaws slack.

Captain Rupert had landed face down. His skinny butt arched toward the moon as if he'd died in the act of making love to his wife's corpse.

"We can't leave him like *that*," said Angelina.

"It's a far cry from a twenty-one-gun salute," agreed Shee.

Bracco grunted and lowered himself into the hole. With some difficulty and a collection of tools shepherded from the Cadillac by Croix, he opened the coffin and slipped Captain Rupert in with his wife's bones, face-up, like a gentleman.

The lid refused to reseal on the double-stuffed casket. Bracco pushed and groaned for over ten minutes until it snapped into place. Finished, he looked up, triumphant, only to realize he couldn't climb back out of the grave.

"Pole isn't sky," he said in his gibberish, sounding defeated.

Croix picked up Bracco's shovel and handed it to Shee.

"We'll have to fill it in so he can climb out."

Shee glowered at Angelina, who smiled before settling back on the bench.

"Isn't it nice to be back?"

Croix started tossing dirt into the hole. Shee matched her shovel by shovel. Some primal part of her wanted to prove to the snot-nosed brat she wasn't old.

Croix picked up speed.

Shee paralleled her effort.

The girl's a machine.

By the time she'd finished, muscles screaming and soaked in sweat, Shee knew her pride had been a *grave* mistake.

Ha.

Not even her silent pun offered any joy.

They gathered to say a prayer and then shuffled back to the car. Lifting her shovel into the trunk, Shee groaned and then tried to cover it by coughing.

She stared at the passenger-side back door as Croix and Angelina entered on the opposite side, unsure she could lift her arm to open the door.

Bracco opened it for her.

"Thank you," she said, unsure of the last time she'd felt that grateful.

"Noodles," he said.

Sliding into the car, Shee closed her eyes and fell back on the one thing that could distract her from her pain.

From obsessing over her father's condition.

She'd left for years to *protect* him. In the end, it hadn't mattered.

She couldn't help feeling *she* was the reason he'd been shot.

An endless loop of regret and worry filled her stomach with sour acid until she could taste it rising toward her tongue. A clammy, prickly sensation broadcasted across her cheeks and forehead. It took her a moment to recognize the sensation.

Oh no.

"Pull over."

"What?" asked Angelina.

"Pull over."

Angelina looked at her before leaning forward to tap Bracco's shoulder and echo her order.

"Pull over."

Bracco guided his tank toward the shoulder of the road, and Shee opened the door, spilling out before the car stopped.

She dropped to her hands and knees.

Back arching, she threw up.

Her gagging sounded like a jet engine in the silence of the night. Mortified, she fought a second wave.

Don't do it. Don't you do it—

Footsteps on the gravel approached.

Heels.

"Are you okay?" asked Angelina.

She nodded and spat. "I'm sorry."

"You should have let Croix finish the grave."

"Yup."

"I saw you trying to beat her. You're not twenty."

"Nope."

Shee wiped her mouth and stood, waving away Angelina's offer to help her to her feet. She closed her eyes.

Think about the work, not the worry. Think about what you can change, what you can do. Think about—shit, my arms hurt.

Her eyes opened again.

"Are you okay?" asked Angelina.

Shee nodded and clambered back into the car. Angelina rounded the vehicle and reentered on her side.

Bracco pulled back onto the road. They rode in silence for another twenty minutes until they pulled into the Inn's parking lot.

Angelina put a hand on Shee's leg.

"Come with me."

Shee followed. She had to—she couldn't open doors without help. Her shoulders throbbed, a muscle against her right rib felt detached, and somehow, her hand had blistered, even through borrowed gloves. She felt less like she'd dug a grave and more like she'd clawed out of one.

Croix bolted through the front door before anyone else could reach the stairs and disappeared inside. She didn't seem sore.

Bitch.

Angelina watched the girl go and then looked at Shee. "This has been hard on her."

Shee grunted.

Angelina opened the screen door. "Having her here was a little like having you back—"

"*I got it.*"

She walked inside before she had to touch the door. All she wanted to do was go to sleep for a week.

Outside, Bracco pulled away. Bouncing, Harley appeared, yapping and twirling, clearly thrilled to see Mommy had returned. Angelina scooped her up.

She kissed the dog and looked at Shee. "Follow me."

Shee trailed into the elevator. Angelina pulled a key on a long silver chain from between her bosom, took a moment to untangle the squiggling dog from it, and unlocked the penthouse button on the elevator's panel.

The elevator lurched upward. Thirty seconds later, the metal doors split, revealing a long left-right hallway and a door directly across from them. Angelina knocked on the door and opened it with another key from the same chain.

Shee's mind flooded with memories at seeing her father's

apartment. As she'd suspected from what she'd seen through the drone camera, little had changed. Dark leather furniture crowded around a television *almost* big enough to mount in Times Square. The TV was a new addition. Televisions didn't come bigger than a barn wall back when she last visited.

The walls were repainted a neutral gray, a modern twist on the neutral cream they'd been fifteen-odd years ago. Nothing had frills, soft edges, or pastels.

Shee was surprised to find no sign Angelina had moved in. Clearly, her father had remained a bachelor. She could tick off forty reasons why their relationship would have ended with one or both of them dead or incarcerated—their on-again, off-again was the stuff of legends. But still, with them both getting older, she'd thought maybe...

The dark-skinned woman she'd seen with the drone sat in the same spot, her back to the window, a Kindle reader in her lap and bag of knitting beside her.

She awoke as the two entered.

"Still here?" asked Angelina.

The woman nodded and gathered her things. "Mi fall asleep," she said with a deep Jamaican accent.

Angelina motioned from the nurse to Shee and back. "Martisha, this is Mick's daughter, Siofra."

Shee nodded. "You can call me Shee."

The woman grinned. "Nice fi meet yuh."

Angelina tugged Shee's arm toward the next room and, with an apologetic smile to the nurse, moved into her father's bedroom.

The room smelled of antiseptic. Shee recoiled at the memory of every hospital she'd ever had the misfortune of visiting.

Her father occupied a metal-trimmed adjustable bed, lying in the same supine position she'd noted through the drone. From what she could tell, he hadn't moved a finger.

"You can talk to him," said Angelina, urging her forward.

Shee fought against Angelina's prodding. "Can he hear me?"

"I don't know. Maybe. I talk to him as if he can. I read somewhere it helps. I dunno."

Shee took another step and stopped again, her gaze tracing the white sheets outlining her father's body.

"I assume you're staying here tonight?" asked Angelina.

Shee pointed to the floor. "*Here*?"

"In the *hotel*."

Shee thought about the suitcase in her car. She'd packed and checked out of her hotel room before coming to the Loggerhead, though at the time, she wasn't sure if she'd been planning on staying or running.

She nodded. "Yes. If you have room?"

Angelina laughed. "Mick doesn't advertise just so he always has rooms free for his pet projects. I swear he gives himself bad reviews online to keep us empty." She sat in a chair against the wall. "Your room down the hall is ready to go." She paused and then added, "It has been for years."

Shee returned her attention to her father.

Mick looked ashen and frail, nothing like the larger-than-life creature she'd left. She touched his hand and found it cool, his skin thin.

Her eye traveled to his neck. She pulled down the collar of his pajamas.

"Does it look like his throat is bruised to you?"

Angelina stood and flipped on the overhead lights before joining her bedside. Shee pushed the collar of her father's pajamas aside to get a better look.

"Almost looks like finger marks," said Angelina, peering over her shoulder.

"It does, doesn't it?" Shee pulled down the blankets and unbuttoned the pajama top. There were no other marks on his upper torso.

She lifted his arm and pulled up his sleeves.

"Here." She pointed to scratch marks on the back of his arm. "These look fresh."

Angelina's brow knitted. "Maybe he fell out of bed?"

"In a coma?"

"Maybe she dropped him trying to change the sheets?"

Shee frowned. "Does that happen?"

"I don't know. He's a big guy. I'll ask her."

Shee started rebuttoning her father's shirt, and Angelina nudged her out of the way.

"I'll do that. Go to the other side. Look at his head."

Shee moved to the opposite side of the bed.

Now, with a better view than the drone had provided, she saw the large scar marring the side of her father's shaved skull. She ran her finger across it.

"How did he survive a bullet to the head?" she asked aloud, not expecting an answer.

"It's simple," said Angelina, patting his pajamas smooth.

"Yeah?"

"Yeah. He refused to die until he saw you again."

Shee dropped her gaze to the scar. The man in the bed didn't feel like her father. Nothing felt real.

"Find out who did it," said Angelina.

Shee nodded.

"I will."

CHAPTER SIXTEEN

Shee?

Mick called out, but something felt wrong. The shadowy figures around him didn't respond or *look*, no matter how loudly he yelled.

Can't they hear me?

He tried breathing harder. He could hear the sound of his panting and feel the breath in his nostrils.

The shadows moved in.

They could hear him breathing.

Maybe Shee can, too?

He had to warn her. He had to—

I'm asleep.

Awareness melted over his brain like chocolate syrup oozing across a sundae.

Syrup. Never hot fudge. Shee doesn't like hot fudge.

Bits of the room appeared before him, seen through a slit as if he were peering through blinds. He knew then he was asleep but trapped in a dream, unable to wake, his lids too heavy to lift.

Is Shee here? I have to wake up.

How many days had it been? He'd lost count. He'd tried to clock how many times light turned to darkness, but he didn't know when he'd started or if days had passed without him knowing.

Shee *had* to be a dream. One of the better ones. Sometimes

he dreamt about his time as a SEAL, fighting enemies and talking to his men. Sometimes he saw faces. Dead friends. Pets he'd had as a boy. Old classmates. Shee's mother. Sometimes he talked to them, fought them, and loved them. Other times he felt helpless, his limbs frozen. Trapped.

There was one constant. The Shadow. Cloaked in the smell of cinnamon and something else, something *earthy*. It spoke to him, told him he would be trapped for his sins. Asked where Shee was.

It wanted Shee.

No.

It had to be a nightmare. He'd made it safe for Shee to come home. But she hadn't. Did she know it was too dangerous?

How did she know?

She's always been smarter than me.

Still breathing hard, the darkness collapsed around him.

The scent of cinnamon filled the air.

It's back.

Two heads this time. One dark, one light. Two voices. Mocking him.

I won't die like this.

Mick threw a punch. Struck out again. His fists connected like pillows, puffs of air.

Are my arms even moving?

He heard a crash.

Glass?

Someone swore.

Did my knuckle hit something?

He tried to swing again, but nothing happened.

Hands fell on him, dragging him under. The fog rolled in. The world grew darker still.

Maybe I'm a ghost.

Maybe this is hell.

It feels like hell.

CHAPTER SEVENTEEN

Shee sat up in bed.

What was that?

Pain shot through her shoulder, and she hugged herself, squinting into the darkness.

My body is killing me.

Something had woken her.

Pain?

She frowned. No. A *sound*.

Some kind of animal?

She sat still, cradling her aching arms, in a silence so deep she could hear it reverberating in her ears. She didn't work well with *sound*. Silence was even worse. She needed to *see* things to process them.

She tried to *see* what she'd heard.

A feeling of *beige* came over her. The lighter shade meant a lighter sound, higher, and less bass.

Sharp.

Not a bark. Maybe a sharp shriek, like a fox?

Like glass breaking?

Slipping out of bed, Shee padded to the window on bare feet, happy to find the warm hardwood floors beneath her toes after spending the last few months in New England. She peered through the room's only window. She hadn't lowered the blinds, though. Maybe she should have—she'd heard the area was rife with drones.

Her gaze bounced from one point of light to the next. A string of party lights, someone's glowing window, a porch lamp on the opposite bank of the ICW. Pressing her cheek against the window, she spied a green light glowing like the beacon at the end of Daisy's dock.

How Gatsby. Does it represent my hopes and dreams? Everything I want, glowing upriver, too far to reach?

Real-life metaphors were never that simple.

In the distance, she heard a train whistle and snorted a laugh.

There's a better metaphor for my life. A train wreck.

Shee heard another sound. This one was low. More like a *moan.*

Had the sound come from *inside* the Inn?

Shee spun on the ball of her foot and moved to the door.

Even my hips hurt.

The hinges on her door whined, floorboards creaking beneath her weight as she moved into the hall. She cringed. She hated making noise. Noise never did anything for anyone in her line of work—whatever that was. She wasn't sure unlicensed detective-slash-bounty hunter-slash-skip-tracer was a line of work per se, but crashing around making noise didn't help in any case.

She froze again to listen.

Nothing.

Continuing down the hall, she reached her father's door and tried the knob.

Locked.

She recalled the key around Angelina's neck.

I'm going to need a copy of that.

She raised her hand to knock and then rolled her eyes.

Sure. That's all he needs—someone to *knock on his door.* Then he'd just pop out of bed and answer, coma cured.

What about Martisha? Where does she sleep?

She glanced to the opposite end of the hall.

Another door. Probably there.

They probably had monitors on him. They'd need to keep watch on his BP and—

She shook her head.

Now she was an unlicensed detective-slash-bounty-hunter-slash-skip-tracer-slash-*doctor*.

If I'm going to be unlicensed, I might as well be unlicensed at everything.

Shee pressed her ear against the door and listened, hearing only the steady thrum of what she guessed was her father's refrigerator. She returned to her room and crawled back into bed.

Different place. Different noises.

Maybe the moan had come from outside. She could ask Angelina. She probably knew all the local sounds.

Did Croix live in the hotel, too?

Are there any rooms left for guests?

In the hall, a floorboard creaked.

I know that noise.

Shee threw back her thin sheet, grunting in pain. She slid from the bed and flung open her door.

In the hall, Martisha turned to look at her as the hinges' whine announced Shee's arrival. The nurse wore a long black t-shirt hanging to her knees.

"Wah mek yuh awake at dis time of night?"

"You were checking on my father?"

She nodded, looking concerned. "Yea, mi hear a sound."

"Me too. Like a moan?"

She nodded.

"Does he make noises?"

"Sometimes." She tapped the side of her skull with her index finger. "Him brain there."

"You think he can hear us?"

Martisha spread out her hands, palms up. "Maybe. Come chat wid him inna mawnin."

"I will. Sure. Hey—" Shee took a step forward. "I noticed some bruising on his neck and some scratches on his arm. Do you know where those came from?"

Martisha nodded, looking grim. "Mi turn him fi di bed sores. Sometimes it's hard—him a big man."

Shee nodded. "We guessed as much. But you just checked on him? He's good?"

"Yea. Him fine, girl. Now wid yuh here, he'll probably wake up any day now."

Shee chuckled. "I hope so. Thank you, Martisha."

The nurse waved with her opposite hand as she disappeared into her room.

Shee shut her door and returned to her bed, her mind on her father.

If he could make noise, it *could* mean he was close to waking. Couldn't it?

The moan had sounded *pained.*

Was Mick having a nightmare?

The idea of it made her shiver.

Trapped in his head, unable to wake, alone with his thoughts…

Shee pulled the extra blanket over her.

The next morning, Shee awoke to the sun. She looked at her watch to find it was nearly seven o'clock.

Shameful.

She'd slept in after spending the evening creeping around. Maybe it didn't hurt that she'd slept in a bed that felt like home for the first time in as long as she could remember.

She swung her legs over the edge, her shoulder aching as

she pushed to her feet. Even her butt muscles hurt.

Note to self: no more grave digging.

Forty-five-year-old bodies didn't spring back from unusual physical tasks like *dewy-fresh Shee* used to.

She showered beneath scalding water, hoping the heat would ease her discomfort, and then dug through her bathroom kit to find a pain reliever when it didn't.

Stepping out of the steamy bathroom, she found a woman in her room straining across her stripped bed and tucking a new bottom sheet. The housekeeper wore a light blue uniform dress, the hem riding high on her thigh as she reached, revealing a garter with several small throwing knives tucked inside.

"Whoa."

The woman continued working as Shee ducked back into the bathroom. She shut the door and leaned her back against it.

Why is the housekeeper strapped?

On the upside, the woman hadn't acknowledged her presence, so she doubted she was a target.

"Hello?" she called.

"Hullo," came the answer.

"Is it, uh, safe to come out?"

"Yah."

Shee frowned. *It's safe to come out because the lady with the knives says it is?*

Shee cracked open the door. The woman stood on the opposite side of the bed, bouncing a pillow into a new case. She stared at Shee without expression.

"I, uh, wasn't quite ready for you," said Shee.

The woman chucked the pillow back on the bed. "I'll be done in a second."

Shee re-emerged from the bathroom with a towel wrapped around her body.

Okaaaay... Excellent at bed-making—crappy at taking a hint.

She grabbed clothes from her suitcase and slipped back into the bathroom.

Locking the door, she towel-dried her long dark hair before pulling it into a ponytail. Lifting her arms to put on her shirt, she groaned and considered the pros and cons of spending the rest of the day topless.

Ow. Ow, ow, ow.

Gritting through the pain, she finished dressing. By the time she reentered the main room, the housekeeper had left, the bed left crisp, a square of chocolate on her pillow.

Nice. I could get used to this.

She unwrapped the chocolate and popped it into her mouth as she moved into the hall.

Twisting her father's bedroom doorknob, she found it still locked.

Shee sighed. If the idea of keeping the entry locked was to protect him, they'd have to do better than a cheap lockset. She returned to her room, found her lock-picking kit, and returned to jimmy the door.

She eased the door shut behind her and tiptoed into her father's room.

She took his hand in hers.

"Hey, Dad."

He lay in the bed much as before, breathing slow and easy.

"We'll figure this out. Everything's going to be okay," she murmured. "I'm home."

Her lip quivered, and she squeezed his hand, dropping her gaze to the floor.

All those years avoiding his eyes, and now I'd do anything for him to—

"Gud mawnin."

Shee turned to find Martisha entering the room, dressed in colorful nurse scrubs. Her cheeks grew warm. "Good morning, Martisha. Sorry."

The nurse stood, hands folded in front of her, seemingly waiting.

I'm in the way.

Shee sniffed. "Just saying good morning before I go downstairs. Do you need any help with him?"

Martisha smiled and waved her away. "No, mi an Mister Mick 'ave fi wi mawnin' dance."

She lowered her father's hand back to the bed, running a finger down each of his to flatten them neatly against the thin cotton blanket.

"I'll get out of your way."

With a nod, Shee left the room, avoiding the nurse's eyes as if the woman could see her sins.

The elevator doors slid open to reveal Croix occupying the spot behind the check-in desk as she scrolled through her phone, head bobbing to a tune Shee couldn't hear.

"You start early," said Shee.

The girl didn't respond, and Shee frowned, remembering when she could talk to young people without their eyes locked on a glowing rectangle.

Those were the days.

Shee stepped toward the desk and waved to catch Croix's attention.

"Hey." Croix pulled an earbud from beneath her mat of curls, and Shee heard a faraway beat, like music from a passing boat echoing over the water.

"I said, *you're up early*."

Croix shrugged. "Not really."

Shee glimpsed a blister on the pad of the girl's right ring finger.

"Blisters," she said, pointing at her own. "I know how you feel. And my shoulders are *killing* me." She rubbed her arm because that's what people did in awkward conversations—they pantomimed perfectly simple ideas.

Croix's withering expression suggested Shee's comment was the source of *her* pain. She recorked her ear with the bud and returned to scrolling.

Shee grimaced. Apparently, kicking in with more than her share of the digging had not won the girl over.

Outside, Bracco stood sentry in his tropical doorman's uniform, his head slightly turned in her direction, watching her interaction with Croix.

Protecting her.

"You're not going to get anything out of her," said a voice behind Shee. She turned to find Angelina wearing her trademark black tights with a coral and gray long-sleeve blouse. Tucked in her arm, Harley squirmed, and Angelina lowered the dog to the ground.

Shee squatted and put out her hands to create a runway for hugs. Harley bounced over, rearing to place her front paws on Shee's knees. They exchanged a flurry of kisses before the dog took off around the counter to do the same with Croix.

"Coffee," said Angelina, heading for a room to the left of the elevator. It wasn't a question—it was a quest.

Shee followed through the opened French doors.

"Did Mick—"

Angelina raised a hand. "First, coffee." She pulled a mug with Harley's face on it from a cabinet. "Croix got this for me for Christmas. Do you want it or a plain-old lime green one?"

"I'll take the lime green. I wouldn't come between you and any of your Harleys."

Angelina handed her the lime mug and poured coffee. Neither helped themselves to the bowl of apples, the lone spotty banana, or the croissant piled beneath a glass cloche.

Shee motioned to the food.

"Does this mean there are guests here? Besides the ones you bury in the middle of the night?"

Without answering, Angelina left the room and walked down a hall leading through another set of French doors to the back porch. Shee shadowed her.

Angelina lowered herself into a turquoise Adirondack chair and set her coffee on the wide arm. Shee did the same in the chair's twin.

"We have a few guests," said Angelina with only a touch of pique. "Croix did some online marketing stuff for us, and business *exploded* for a while. We pulled back after Mick's thing."

"Does she live in the hotel?" asked Shee, nodding toward the front desk.

"Croix? Yes."

Shee recalled Bracco driving away after their graveyard visit. "But not Bracco?"

"No. He has a place over the bridge."

"And the housekeeper strapped with throwing knives?"

Angelina tittered. "Yeah. You're not going to want to complain about the turndown service."

"Duly noted."

"Beatriz was a *find*. She's a clean freak, which makes her a meticulous assassin. Now she keeps the hotel spotless."

"Anyone else I shouldn't piss off while I'm here? The cook? Maybe a luggage guy?"

"Did you meet William? Blond, goatee?"

Shee shook her head.

"He's been a lot of help picking up the management duties Mick can't do now. He's sort of me when I'm not here. The cook was in the hundred and first airborne. I have my suspicions the gardener was MI6."

"Yikes. Is that why Dad was so sure I'd be safe coming home? Because he's staffed the hotel with assassins?"

"I'm sure that's part of it."

"Speaking of Mick, let's start from the top."

Angelina sighed. "It started with a call from that guy you knew the name of."

"Viggo."

The image of Viggo Nilsson popped into Shee's head. She'd met him before, several times when she was young. She remembered him as bigger than Paul Bunyan, serious but kind, coifed with reddish-blond hair. Mostly, she remembered he shared the chocolate-covered oatmeal crisp cookies his Swedish mother sent him.

"Right. Mick goes to see Viggo. That's all I know until we get the anonymous email asking us to come get him."

"At an Airbnb."

"Yes."

Shee rubbed her forehead, wondering if her father's coma would have *stuck* if he'd received proper medical care instead of being left in some random person's bedroom.

"But if Viggo set Dad up, why would he half-ass save him?"

"I don't know. Maybe he shot him and then had a change of heart. Long story short, *someone* wanted Mick dead."

"That could be a long list." Shee leaned back in her chair. "Why draw him to Minneapolis? Why not shoot him here?"

Angelina shrugged. "Too close to the hotel, maybe?"

"And Mick's collection of killers?"

Angelina nodded. "You wouldn't want to poke this hornet's nest."

Shee sipped her coffee as a pair of black vultures landed on the end of the pier.

"We had a funeral, y'know," said Angelina, her dark thoughts no doubt inspired by the ugly leather-headed birds.

"For Dad?"

Angelina nodded, and Shee picked an imaginary piece of lint from her shorts. "I didn't know."

"I *know* you didn't know. You weren't *here*."

Croix poked her head out the back door, and for once, Shee was happy to see her.

"There's a guy out here for you," she said.

Angelina glared with dismay at her cooling coffee. "About what?"

Croix shook her head and pointed at Shee. "Not you. *Her.*"

Shee placed her hand on her chest. "*Me?* No one knows I'm here."

"*He* does." Croix's lips twitched as if she were fighting a grin.

With some effort, Shee stood from the low-slung Adirondack. "Did you get a name?"

"No."

"Why not?" asked Angelina, sounding annoyed.

Croix huffed. "*Sorry.* I got distracted. He was super nice and—" The girl's pupils floated up and to the right, a tiny smile on her lips as if she remembered something.

"And *what*?" asked Shee.

"He's kind of smokin' for an old guy."

"Old? How old?" Shee wondered if Viggo had come to them.

Croix shrugged. "Your age."

Shee looked at Angelina. "Charming."

Angelina chuckled. "Cheer up. If you're *old*, imagine what that makes me."

Shee motioned to Croix. "Go distract him. I'm going to go around the front to take a peek." Croix started to move, and Shee snapped her fingers to catch her attention. "Be *careful.*"

Croix flashed a bemused smile and slipped back inside.

Didn't listen to a word I said.

Angelina stood. "I'll go help her."

"Do you have a weapon handy?"

"Croix has a gun behind the desk. I have one in my room. And if you're going out front, Bracco has a Walther tucked in the back of his waistband."

Shee nodded. "Okay. I'll take a peek and let you know the threat level, if any."

Angelina sighed. "Things were so *calm* before you got here."

"Right. Nothing but headshots, comas, and carting around dead guys."

Shee jogged off the porch and headed left around the building. Reaching the front, she jumped to grab the front porch railing and hoist herself up. Bracco's head snapped in her direction. She put her finger to her lips, and he shifted his gaze forward to avoid drawing attention.

Maybe the big man didn't trust her yet, but the guy in the lobby was a *stranger* stranger.

The sound of Croix giggling echoed from inside.

Maybe I should have been more specific about how to distract him.

Angelina's low voice reverberated. More giggles. This time from Angelina.

What the hell?

Shee neared Bracco, and the doorman lifted the back of his shirt to flash a Walther PK380 semiautomatic centerfire pistol tucked in the waistband of his khakis.

She nodded her thanks and peered around Bracco to see inside.

Croix's description hadn't been wrong. The stranger stood a good six-foot-three, with broad shoulders, a strong jaw, and dimples flashing as he joked with the two women working hard to distract him.

Working really hard.

The man turned, affording her a better look at his face, and Shee froze.

Oh my God.

He looked the same.

Older, sure. *Bigger*, his biceps and chest straining against his polo shirt. But other than that...

Shee swallowed.

Bracco bumped her, looking for instruction, and she flinched, having forgotten he was there.

Oh. Right.

She straightened and patted Bracco's arm to let him know all was well. His hulking form dropped a notch as he stood down.

Shee opened the front door, surprised to find her hands still working. Attention turned to her as she entered. The man leveled his gaze on her, his eyes burning a turquoise blue that appeared lit from the inside.

"Hey, Jelly," he said.

Shee held up her index finger.

"Just a second."

She walked briskly past him, down the hall, past the breakfast room, and into the public bathroom. She hit the first stall's door so hard it bounced off her shoulder.

Dropping to her knees, she gripped the side of the bowl to throw up.

CHAPTER EIGHTEEN

Twenty-seven years ago, Navy Special Warfare Center, Coronado, California

Shee slapped her hand against her thigh. "But I want to at *least* do the legwork and then—"

Hefting the stack of papers she'd been attempting to commandeer from his arms, Mick took a step back. "*No,* Shee, you're not tracking anyone without me. Give you an inch, and you'll take a mile."

"What does that even mean?"

Mick pushed up his reading glasses, looking like a professor on his first day in class. The Navy had diverted him from hunting fugitives to cover for a missing instructor at Coronado Navy Special Warfare Center.

Shee's world was coming to an end.

Her father held her glare with trademark patience. "It means if I let you skip-trace these dirtballs, the next thing I know, you'll be off trying to *capture* them."

"No, I won't."

"Yes, you will. I'm not an idiot. I do learn from my mistakes."

Shee threw her head back so hard it hurt her neck. "That was, like, *one time.* You can't stop me now. I'm like a tracking *machine.*"

He sighed. "Why don't you take some college courses while we're here?"

"*Yawn.* Look. They'll never know—"

"It's not about the Navy *knowing.* I gave you an order, and I expect—"

"I'm not one of your sailors!"

Shee pouted. She hadn't meant for her voice to go *shrieky* and make her sound like the teenager she was, but Mick was *destroying her life.*

The heads of students passing Turner Field swiveled their way. She watched her father's face color and knew she'd crossed a line.

"Not *here,*" he hissed through gritted teeth. He spun on his heel and strode away from her.

Shee pursued in the hopes of continuing negotiations in a less embarrassing tone, pulling up short as a young man in tan camouflage jogged to intercept her father. The boy saluted before shaking hands.

She cocked her head.

Something about that sailor...

Shee never forgot a face, but something about this particular mug rang familiar and yet *not...*

She gasped.

Peanut Butter.

The young man standing before her father was the *boy* she'd met in Charleston as a little girl.

Mason.

She eyed him head to toe.

Oh my. Haven't we filled out?

Peanut Butter stood two inches taller than her father. He grinned, displaying a deep dimple on the cheek she could see.

If he was in Coronado looking that fit and wearing those fatigues...

Did he go SEAL? And make it?

That meant he'd already survived breakout, the beginning of Hell Week. He'd made it through the brutal boat Olympics known as Lyon's Lope and completed BUD/S—Basic Underwater Demolition training. He'd crawled beneath machine gun fire as a fog machine pumped smoke across the terrain. He'd run the O-course and climbed the pyramid of Hooyah Logs until his legs shook.

She knew what SEAL candidates endured. She'd researched the Warfare Center on their long drive from the East Coast.

It explained why he looked the way he did.

The baby SEAL's gaze shifted from Mick to her.

Shee stopped, only then aware she'd been shuffling toward the men as if caught in a tractor beam.

"Jelly?"

She smiled, fighting to look normal. Her lips felt *twitchy*.

"Peanut Butter? What are you doing here?"

His chest puffed a little more, something she hadn't imagined possible.

"Mason's a SEAL now, awaiting his assignment," said her father. He seemed happy to distract from her demands.

Nice try, old man.

She flashed her father a withering glance to inform him she wasn't finished and *hadn't* forgotten.

Mick shook his head in a way that said, *don't start.*

Fine. Temporary truce.

Shee turned her attention back to Mason.

"So, uh, you're *here*?"

Duh.

Mason chuckled, dimples now visible on both cheeks. "Yep. Your father helped me get into the Special Warfare Prep—"

Mick cut him short. "I didn't do anything. It was all you."

Shee's gaze floated back to her father.

You've been in contact with Mason behind my back? I swear I don't even know you anymore.

Mick shook Mason's hand again. "I've got to get going. Good

job, son."

"Thank you, sir."

Mick waggled his fingers at them as he hurried off. "You two should go get a burger or something. My treat. Shee, you pay, and I'll get you back."

Shee watched him retreat.

Coward.

"So, I guess you came with your dad?" asked Mason, strolling toward her like the gorgeous distraction he was.

Fine. Dad can wait.

Shee's chin lifted to meet Peanut Butter's eyes, *way up there...*

"Are you a SEAL?" he asked.

Shee giggled and rolled her eyes.

Since when do I giggle?

"Siofra." He said her name. No question, just her name.

"You remember my name?" she asked.

He nodded. "It's pretty. Different."

"Pretty different," she mumbled, pulling at the neck of her t-shirt to let the heat radiating from her body escape.

What the hell? I must be getting the flu.

"So you're, uh, all done?" she asked.

"We're never *done*."

"No, I just meant—"

"Hey, what're you doin'?" He blurted the sentence as if it had been building in his chest.

Alarmed, Shee looked down, afraid she'd done something weird without knowing. She *seemed* to be just standing there. "What? Why?"

"I mean, are you busy? I don't have to be anywhere until thirteen hundred. Ya wanna grab a burger like your dad said?"

Shee's bottom lip unstuck from her top, but no sound emerged.

"That's one o'clock," he added.

She retracted her head as if he'd slapped her.

"*I know.* I've been Navy since I was *nine.*"

He laughed. "Oh, *excuse me.* You must be an Admiral by now."

She sniffed. "Honorary Captain." She *had* made her father bestow unofficial ranks on her through the years. She'd only made imaginary Captain a week earlier, right before he broke the news about their assignment in Coronado.

Probably to shut me up.

Mason saluted. "Ah stand corrected, Captain, ma'am. We can go to McP's over on Orange if that sounds good?"

She hadn't wanted him to stop talking. His southern accent was *adorable.* It took a moment for her to realize he was awaiting an answer.

"Oh, yeah. Okay."

They fell into step beside each other, heading downtown, Shee pumping Mason for information about his SEAL training experiences, trying hard not to blurt out *how'd you get so big?* Everything about him was crisp and clean and smooth and hard like a G.I. Joe doll come to life if old Joe had joined the Navy instead of the Army.

Which he should have. Obviously.

"What was the worst part?" she asked.

He chuckled. "It was *all* the worse part."

"But if you had to *pick* something?"

He shrugged. "Drownproofing, probably."

"Where they try to drown you in the pool?"

"More or less."

"I *thought* that sounded like the worst. I'm going to do it, you know."

"What?"

"I'm going to do SEAL training."

He laughed. "You can't. You're a girl."

She scowled. "I'm going to train *myself.*"

"I dunno if that's the same."

"Oh, it'll be *worse.* I'm very hard on myself. A real tyrant."

He laughed. "I bet."

He was still chuckling as they sat on the patio of McP's Irish Pub. He looked *happy*. She guessed she'd be happy, too, if people weren't demanding she crawl on her belly through the sand into the freezing ocean for the first time in a while.

"So, what have you been up to?" he asked.

She shrugged. "Same as when I met you. Skip tracing and bounty hunting for the Navy with my father."

He chuckled. "No, *really*."

"*Really*."

"You're telling me you're a bounty hunter for the Navy?"

"Yep."

The waitress arrived to take their order, and Shee realized she hadn't been reading the menu, just staring at it. The waitress blinked at her, waiting.

"I'll get a cheeseburger," she said.

The waitress scribbled on her pad.

"Same, but two," said Mason, holding up a peace sign. "And a beer."

"Me too," added Shee.

The waitress side-eyed her.

"You twenty-one?"

"Yep. Two days ago."

The waitress nodded and left as Mason leaned back, tapping the table with his fingers. "Cool."

"What?"

"I always wondered what bounty hunters eat."

"Funny. I always wondered what SEALs eat."

He leaned in, flashing his blue eyes and snarling like a hungry tiger.

"We eat enemies for breakfast."

The sinews of his neck bulged, and Shee's stomach fluttered.

"Enemies for breakfast and hamburgers for lunch?" she asked, trying to keep a poker face.

"Yup." He leaned back again, a tiger tamed. "Are you really twenty-one?"

She shook her head. "Eighteen."

They held each other's gazes in silence.

She didn't even mind.

The waitress returned with their food, killing the moment.

They fell to eating, and Shee's mind raced, searching for small talk.

"Your family must be prou—" Her face heated like a stovetop burner.

Stupid.

She'd nearly forgotten how they'd met.

"It's okay," he said, seeming to sense her horror. "Old man's still in jail. Momma gave me what I needed to move past what he did."

Shee perked. "She's alive?"

He shook his head. "No. He killed her like you thought."

"I'm sorry."

"Not your fault."

"Oh. She gave you her strength first?" she guessed.

Mason nodded from side to side, those sapphire eyes twinkling, smiling as if he had a secret.

"What?" she prompted.

He shrugged. "You wanna go to the beach after this? Ah can show you the best spots."

Shee nodded, smiling behind her hamburger.

Yes, please.

He still had that smirky, faraway look in his eyes.

Ever since I asked him about his mom.

"What are you thinking about?" she asked. "Something about your mom? Something about what she gave you?"

He seemed surprised she'd noticed.

"Kinda."

"What?"

He shrugged and smiled. "A bag of rocks."

CHAPTER NINETEEN

Thirty-four years ago—Charleston, South Carolina

Mason's Aunt Tildy had three children of her own and little interest in raising a fourth. After his mother's murder and his father's incarceration, she took Mason in out of shame, or guilt, or—to be honest, she didn't know *why* she'd bothered. On his first night, she pointed him toward a threadbare sofa in his cousin Ely's room with a vague, mumbled promise of a future, proper bed.

While his aunt made a half-hearted attempt to get him situated, his Cousin Ely glared at him from beneath a lowered brow until Mason thought his skin might catch fire. As a boy in a house full of girls, Ely was the only child in his own room.

Mason ruined *everything*.

Their weekly fistfights started the next day.

He didn't mind thrashing with his older cousin, though each time meant a good whooping. Ely had two years and fifty pounds on him.

Mason spent as little time as possible at his aunt's house. The first chance he got, he borrowed Ely's bike and returned to his old home. Without him to mow, the front yard's weedy grass had grown as tall as his knees.

He pulled his bike around the back of the house, stopping

as he rounded the corner.

The back door hung open.

Not just the screen, which had fallen victim to its weight after his father broke the upper hinge the night his mother went missing.

The solid door beyond it also gaped by four inches.

The last time he'd been in the house, he was with his aunt and the social services lady, gathering his clothes and personal belongings. They'd entered through the *front* door.

Mason lay the bike down and crept up the back stairs to push open the solid door.

"Hello?" he called into the house.

He'd heard about 'hobo houses' filled with addicts who stole little boys and sold them for drugs and sex stuff.

But how bad could that be?

He'd started to notice the girls in his school, and being sold to a lady for sex didn't sound like the *worst* thing that could happen to him. It would be gross if she was as old as Aunt Tildy. She had to be *thirty*.

He decided to brave the chance of being sold to a thirty-year-old. He had to risk it. Not only did he have a plan for moving out of his aunt's—but he also wanted the flowy robe his mother used to wear. It smelled like jasmine, and jasmine smelled like his mother. Though, he'd have to be careful. The attacks would be merciless if Ely found a flowered orange satin robe amongst his belongings.

"Hello?" He wrinkled his nose at the smell inside the kitchen.

No druggies or child nappers called back.

Mason stepped inside, the wooden floorboards creaking beneath his second-best pair of sneakers. He made a fist and braced himself. Thanks to the floor, the child-stealing hobos would hear him coming from a mile away. He had to be prepared.

He stopped and surveyed the mess. Someone had been in

the kitchen. Every pot and pan had been pulled from the cabinets, and every plate jerked to the ground and smashed. Even the refrigerator door hung open, the food inside fuzzy and green. A pile of dried animal droppings sat nearby. Mason guessed the scat belonged to a raccoon. Scat identification and shooting were the two skills his father had taught him during better times.

Mason covered his nose and shut the refrigerator door with his fingertips.

He moved into the living room. It looked as if a knife-wielding tornado had swept through. Deep slashes split the flowered cushions of the couch his mother had so loved. He touched the white stuffing and studied the edges of the cuts. No animal had torn apart the couch. The gashes were deep and clean.

Mason's anger rose.

Who did this?

And, more importantly, were they still in the house?

He called down the hall.

"Hello?"

Moving to his parent's room, he found their mattress crisscrossed with the same kind of slashes, stuffing strewn everywhere. The pottery lamps, once flanking the bed, had been smashed. The closet's contents were piled high on the bed, including his mother's orange robe. He pulled it from the heap and pressed it to his nose. Closing his eyes, he imagined his arms wrapped around his mother's hips.

The perfume made his eyes water. Slipping his backpack off his shoulder, he shoved the thin robe inside.

As he tiptoed back through the mess, he spotted an unbroken bottle of perfume and picked it up to smell.

Jasmine.

He'd found the *source* of the robe's scent. He added the bottle to the backpack.

Mason found his drawing books strewn to the four corners

of his room and tucked them into his bag. At least whoever seemed so angry at the furniture didn't hate art enough to destroy his books.

He found his air gun in the corner, unharmed. Someone had dumped the pellets to the ground, and he scooped them back into the box.

Something about his room made him even more uneasy.

"Not a thief," he mumbled to himself.

A thief would have taken his pellet gun. Ely, the only other person he knew *angry* enough to destroy a house, would have taken the gun, too.

Who would tear apart his home and not steal anything? *Why?*

He dropped the box of pellets into his backpack and slipped his arms back into the straps.

Grabbing the gun, he surveyed his room.

I have a lot of cleaning to do—

Something down the hall clattered loudly enough to make him jump.

Hobos!

Lowering his bag to the floor, Mason removed the box of pellets and retrieved a few for his gun. The barrel clicked shut, and he waited, expecting the sound of heavy boots in the hallway.

Nothing happened.

Mason took one slow step forward, easing his weight onto the wood. He took another and another until he reached the end of the hall, his gun raised and ready.

Movement flashed near the back door. He swung his barrel toward it. As his finger squeezed, he jerked the gun upward to avoid hitting the mark.

Midnight.

The neighbor's black cat shot through the opened back door and into the yard as the pellet embedded itself in the wall.

That was close. The neighbor girl would have *killed* him if he'd shot her nasty cat.

Mason lowered the gun and surveyed the mess.

I have to secure the house.

The place would be no good to anyone if animals kept walking through.

Tucking his gun under his arm, he searched the kitchen floor for the spare house key that once lived in the back of the silverware drawer. He found it beneath a green loaf of bread.

With a heavy sigh, he left, closing the door behind him and locking it. He could return the next day during Ely's baseball practice. Maybe he could borrow his cousin Livvy's Polaroid camera and take a photo of what it looked like now, so later, his aunt and the social services which could see how much work he'd done to clean it.

Maybe then they'd let him stay.

Mason walked the bike to the front of the house and found himself standing in the same spot on the sidewalk where he'd been when his mother—

He looked up. His sneakers still hung from the telephone lines.

My favorite sneakers.

His mother had told him not to tell his father those were *his* shoes. But his father was gone now. If his old man ever returned, he might recognize the sneakers hanging there.

It had rained a few times since he'd moved into his aunt's house, but the chances of him getting new shoes soon were slim.

He couldn't leave them hanging.

Mason laid down the bike and raised the barrel of his pellet gun. Closing one eye, he aimed for the laces.

Steadying, he fired.

The shoes remained hanging like fruit.

A little to the left...

He fired again. The laces whipped up as the shoes plummeted to the ground.

Giddy at his prowess, Mason ran to them.

He shoved one into his backpack and lifted the other to do the same. As he did, a plastic bag slid from the toe to the heel, hanging there as he stared at it.

Mason blinked at the bag, trying to remember what he'd stuffed into the toe of his shoes. Nothing came to mind.

The contents looked like a collection of cloudy pebbles.

He let the twist holding the bag shut unfurl and plucked out one of the rocks. It seemed unremarkable. He'd had a rock collection as a kid and knew what pretty rocks looked like.

These were not pretty.

Where'd they come from?

He looked up at the wires.

Could a bird have put them in the shoe? He'd read something somewhere about birds eating rocks for digestion. Crows maybe.

A bird wouldn't steal a whole *bag* of stones, would it?

Had his mother put the rocks in there? Did she do it for the weight, knowing she wanted to throw the shoes over the telephone wires?

Mason noticed a man watching him from a porch a few houses away. He couldn't risk the man reporting him as a trespasser.

He stuffed the shoes and the bag of rocks into his backpack and jogged back to the bike.

Pointing away from the man, he pedaled.

CHAPTER TWENTY

Twenty-seven years ago, Navy Special Warfare Center—Coronado, California

Shee gaped at Mason, her last bite of hamburger hovering near her lips.

"*And?*"

"And what?" he asked.

"Did you ever find out why she put rocks in your shoes?"

"I guess to give them the weight to throw them up there," Mason shrugged to underscore his supposed confusion, but his expression suggested he was still hiding something.

She pressed. "But why would your mother throw your shoes up there?"

"Dunno."

Shee looked away, thinking. "Maybe your dad bought them for you, and she wanted to piss him off?"

"If so, it was a bad idea," he muttered, his expression darkening.

Shee frowned. She hadn't meant to imply his mother was at fault for her own murder. She reached out and put her hand on his.

"I didn't mean—"

He covered her hand with his own, stroking the back of it

with his thumb.

"I know. No problem."

Shee watched his movement.

Even his thumb is sexy.

They sat that way for a moment, both of them staring at their hands.

"So, beach?" he asked, glancing at his watch. "Ah can't dally, but ah've got a little time."

"*Dally.*" She giggled and pulled her hand out from under his, suddenly self-conscious.

"What's wrong with *dally*?"

"Just a funny word." She looked away, feeling like an idiot. It was like Mason was kryptonite that made her *dumb* instead of weak.

Mason pointed to a balding, potbellied man Shee guessed to be in his forties, waddling by in red shorts one size too small. "Maybe we should skip trace that guy. He looks suspicious."

"You can't skip trace someone if you already know where they are." Shee squelched a grin, doing her best to scowl with great portent. He *does* look like he's up to no good, though."

Mason nodded. "Definitely. Looks like the type who puts ketchup on a hot dog to me."

Shee lost her fight to remain serious and giggled.

Giggled.

Again.

They had their first kiss on that beach.

By then, Shee had realized *Mason* had caused the strange heatwave engulfing her body whenever he was near.

It wasn't the flu.

She almost forgot about skip tracing. She had other things to think about, like how the lines of Mason's neck led to the v-notch at the base of his throat and the way the rippling muscles of his stomach felt beneath her fingertips.

"Isn't being in love *amazing*?" he'd asked one day as they

perched on the rocks south of Avda De Las Arenas.

He'd leaned his forehead against hers, their noses touching.

"It's pretty great," she'd answered.

One day rolled into the next, her mind trapped in a fog that only cleared when he appeared.

All her investigative skills turned to Mason. She knew his schedule before he did. She'd uncovered the meaning of every micro-expression on his face.

The look he had now was new, but she had a feeling what it meant.

Lying beside him, she traced a finger from his hairline, down his nose, to his chin. He didn't try to playfully bite her finger as she bumped over his lips like usual.

No, this serious expression was different.

It wasn't *good*.

She pulled closer to his naked body and scanned the room around her.

This is it.

Everything was burned into her memory forever. The ugly lamp. Her wooden jewelry box. The pile of clothes with the damp blue bikini on top.

"Say it," she said, her voice a whisper. His chest rose and fell beneath her palm, and she closed her eyes, listening to the beat of his heart.

"I got my assignment."

She'd known this news was coming today, but her stomach still twisted. The end had come. She'd taken an allergy pill to dull her nerves and make what she needed to do easier.

"When do you ship out?"

She already knew that, too.

Two days.

Monday. Every morning she awoke to the color *red*. Monday was red. Monday was the end. Monday was the day that haunted her sleep and colored the world around her.

Not even the NSA could have kept her from finding out when Mason got his orders. He'd known for weeks. He'd started acting differently around that time, more distant one second, needier the next. She'd caught him watching her, staring as if he were trying to capture her image in a bottle in his mind.

"Two days," he said.

He turned on his side to stare into her eyes.

"I'll write you. We—"

Shee shook her head. "No. *Don't.*"

"I'm serious, Shee. I will." He reached for his shorts that lay on the ground beside the bed.

He's running. You're doing the right thing.

"No. I'm saying *don't*," she said.

Shorts in hand, he sat up and touched her cheek with his knuckles.

"Don't *what*?"

She pulled away.

Great. Now, I'll remember that touch, too. The feel of him tucking my hair behind my ear every time I do it myself...

"Shee—"

She slipped out of bed and got dressed.

"Don't write me. You need to be frosty."

"What?" He laughed.

"You heard me."

"You're worried ah won't be *sharp* if ah *write* you?"

She busied herself, plucking her damp towel from the floor and dropping it in her hamper. "I don't want you thinking about me. I want you thinking about whatever it is you need to do to stay alive."

Mason pulled his shorts on. "You're being ridiculous."

"I'm not. You better go. My dad will be back soon."

She stole a glimpse at him to find his bemused smile replaced by something like building anger.

"But—" he began.

"Go."

"Go? Just like that?"

His volume rose. She nearly lost her resolve and heard herself flounder.

"Look, I—"

"Thinking about you gives me an *extra* reason to stay alive."

She shook her head. "Dad and I are getting back on the road soon anyway. He hates being a professor."

"You didn't tell me—"

"There was no point. I knew you'd be gone by the time we left."

Mason stood, dipping to snatch his shirt from the ground. Something about how he kept his left hand in his shorts pocket seemed odd.

"So all this meant nothing to you?" He removed his hand from his pocket to pull on his shirt.

She eyed his hip. Nothing unusual. No lump.

So weird.

She sniffed. "I didn't say it didn't mean anything. But this is for the best. A clean break."

He moved to her and put a hand on each of her arms. Angry heat radiated from his body. She held his gaze. Her jaw clenched to keep her lip from quivering.

Don't give in now. Let him go.

"I *love* you," he said. His eyes looked glassy, his sapphire irises stormier than usual.

A dull gray blanket of allergy medicine made it possible to keep her face expressionless.

"You'll get over it."

She looked away. She'd found the words but couldn't look at him.

He glared. She could feel his thoughts—one word repeated over and over, as clearly as if he'd spat them at her.

Traitor.

"Go," she whispered.

He released her and strode from the room without another word.

She heard the front screen door bang and counted down from ten.

Two...One...

The clock's ticking in the kitchen sounded like a hammer in the silence.

He isn't coming back.

She sobbed one loud hiccup and slapped her hand across her mouth. Her chest felt as if it would crack open to spill her heart to the ground.

I can't do it. I can't live—

The screen door banged again, and she gasped beneath her palm.

"Shee?"

Not Mason.

Dad.

Home early.

She ran into her bathroom and shut the door.

"I'm in the bathroom," she called.

Hands over her face, she sat on the tub's edge, willing herself to stop crying. Through her fingers, she stared at the unfeeling objects around her. They looked the same as they had a day earlier but weren't. Everything had changed.

Her toothbrush.

Her hairdryer.

Her trash can, and in it, the white tip of the pregnancy test poking from beneath the wad of tissues she'd used to hide it.

CHAPTER TWENTY-ONE

Present Day

Shee stared into the bathroom mirror, her arms braced on either side of The Loggerhead Inn's guest bathroom sink, her breathing heavy. The taste of bile encased her tongue.

What's wrong with me?

Twice in twenty-four hours?

I haven't thrown up since that syrupy batch of hurricanes in New Orleans ten years ago.

She plucked a tissue from a shell-covered box and blew her nose.

I know they heard me heaving.

At least she'd made it to the bathroom. For a second, she thought she'd spew croissant across Mason's loafers.

She scowled.

They were nice loafers.

What SEAL wears Italian loafers? Was he deployed in Italy?

She shook her head.

Stop it. Who cares.

She didn't need to get all *skip tracer* on his ass.

She had bigger problems.

Is he really here?

This scene had played out so many times in her dreams,

though he'd never been at The Loggerhead. She didn't remember ever throwing up in her dreams. But she'd pictured seeing him again in so many different configurations…

He's older.

That was her proof.

She'd aged, but Peanut Butter had remained trapped, forever twenty years old, flying around her memories like the world's hottest Peter Pan.

There was something else…

Could he be *better*-looking?

The general shape of his body had remained the same. Tall, muscular, trim, as if he'd never received the memo about how age makes you soft. The lines that Time had etched on his face had somehow *enhanced* his masculinity. A bumpy scar peeked from beneath the polo sleeve on his right arm, evidence of a horrific wound… and yet somehow *sexy*. The crow's feet beside his piercing blue eyes, accentuating as he'd grinned at her, only made him look more adorable.

I want to kiss those crow's feet.

How was any of that *fair*?

He got sexier, and *she* bought a new night cream every month to fight back time.

She opened her eyes and found her attention floating to the silver tray of complementary products, specifically the bottle of mouthwash. She'd always wondered what crazy people used public mouthwash. A stack of waxed-paper shot glasses sat on the tray, but surely *some* idiot had swigged straight from the bottle, right?

She'd never used public mouthwash.

Now she understood. Some situations called for community mouthwash.

Shee poured herself a shot, swished, and spat. After a moment's consideration, she took another hit.

Rack 'em and stack 'em, bartender. Listerine for all my friends.

Shee squatted on her heels and rested her head on the counter's edge.

I have to go back out there.

Maybe it was a dream. Maybe he'd be gone.

The sting of minty alcohol in her mouth said *it was real.*

This is happening.

She straightened, feeling wobbly, closed her eyes again, and took a deep breath, willing herself into a trance of tranquility.

Breathe in...one, two, three, four...breathe out...one, two, three, four...

In her mind's eye, Mason waded from the Mediterranean sea, a shirtless, sexy Neptune, leading a team of men to the beaches, the rising sun glinting off the polished leather of his soggy Italian loafers...

She opened her eyes and stared at herself in the mirror.

"You have issues."

The image agreed, echoing her sentiment, and she nodded.

"Fair enough. Let's do this."

She took one strong step toward the exit and threw herself back to avoid the door as Beatriz entered, bucket in hand.

"Which toilet?" asked the housekeeper.

Stunned into obedience by the command in the woman's voice, she pointed to the first.

"There wasn't much. Coffee. Mostly dry heaves—"

Why am I sharing all this detail?

Beatriz ignored her and pushed into the stall.

Okay. Good talk.

Shee bared her teeth in the mirror one last time, searching for flakes of soggy croissant, and then strode into the hallway.

Here we go.

All eyes locked on her as she entered the lobby.

Everyone remained in the spots they'd occupied when she'd left, and she flashed a smile she feared that appeared more like pain than joy. "Sorry. Hi, Mason. It's good to see you."

His arms remained at his sides this time, having learned his lesson—*hugs equal barf.*

"I heard about your Dad. I'm so sorry," he said.

"He heard your dad *died*," said Angelina turning her face away from Mason to give Shee a hard stare.

Dad's dead to the world. Right.

"Thanks. Yeah, it was, uh, sudden."

Shee watched Mason nod.

If I held a block of cheese beneath that jawline, he'd slice it into neat squares.

Mason seemed lost in his thoughts, oblivious to her gawking. "He was the inspiration for everything that's mattered in my life."

He looked at her with the same sort of portent Angelina had shared.

Is he talking about me being something that matters?

Croix watched their silent exchange.

"Awwww…" The girl's voice lilted upward as if she'd found a lost kitten behind the desk. Plunking her elbow on the counter, she rested her chin on her fist and blinked, wide-eyed. She looked back and forth between Shee and Mason until Shee could bear it no longer.

"Let's go somewhere," she said, motioning for him to follow her.

Dodging a bemused-looking Angelina, she walked down the short hallway to the back door, strode onto the porch, jogged down the stairs, and didn't stop until she reached the end of the pier. She considered taking a few more steps into the Intracoastal Waterway and splashing around until an alligator found her. Maybe an affectionate manatee could wrap its flippers around her and accidentally drag her to the depths.

She heard the nubs of Mason's loafers on the composite decking behind her.

Uneven.

A limp?

She turned and watched him approach.

"You're limping," she said.

He smiled using only the right side of his face, one dimple dropping like a tiny, adorable sinkhole.

That's a wistful smile. Regret?

"Limps happen when you forget to bring your other leg," he said, jerking up his pant. His metal right ankle glinted in the sun.

She gasped. "When? How?"

"About two months ago. Mission."

"You were still out there? You're nearly *fifty*."

He chuckled. "Well, I'm retired *now*. Just one mission too late."

"What are you now? A Captain?"

"Commander."

"Hm. Congratulations," she said, but her mind wandered elsewhere, flickering images of Mason jogging with her on the beach at eighteen, his tan legs pumping, his feet hitting the sand.

He tapped his leg. "I wish the rest of me was built out of titanium. I'd hurt less in the mornings."

"I know what you mean. Aging sucks, doesn't it?"

They both fell silent with frozen smiles on their faces.

Nah. This isn't awkward at all.

"You disappeared," he said after the longest twenty seconds of her life.

Her gaze dropped to the dock. "I had to."

"For twenty-seven years?"

Shee toed a hunk of broken shell off the edge and into the water.

Seventeen, officially.

Before that, she'd only been hiding from *him*.

"No, I, uh..."

"I looked for you."

"I know."

She hadn't meant to admit she'd known. She'd heard he was looking for her and hid all the deeper. That was before she had to drop off the grid—before *everything* changed.

"That's all you have to say?" he asked.

He sounded angry. It was like reliving the day they parted all over again. In her mind's eye, she saw her room again.

The ugly lamp. The wooden jewelry box. The pile of clothes with the damp blue bikini on top...

No allergy medicine in sight this time to calm her nerves. Just three decades of raw disappointment and loss.

She looked up at him, realizing she hadn't answered.

"I'm sorry, what?"

He wore his exasperation like a heavy winter coat, the weight of it threatening to drag him to the ground. "I finally find you, and your response is, 'Hey, hope all's well with you, say *hi* to the family, see you in another thirty years?'"

She noted his southern accent had faded over the years—

Wait. Did he say family?

She sniffed. "You have a family?"

"What if I did? Would you *care*?"

 Shee found herself muted by the question.

Yes.

The idea of him with a family *hurt*.

How selfish can I be?

He had the right to be happy. Right?

Let's pretend I feel that way.

"No. I'm *glad* you have a family—"

"I don't."

Her shoulders unbunched.

"Ohthankgod."

He laughed.

"You?" he asked, his tone and the wrinkle between his eyebrow telegraphing he didn't want to hear she was happy without him. He looked like a man preparing to be slapped across the face.

"No," she said.

The news made the corner of his mouth curl up another millimeter.

"Never?"

"No." Without meaning to, she glanced up at Mick's window. She wanted to tell him Mick was still alive, but it had been a *friend* who lured her father to his assassination attempt.

What if Mason is next in a long line of traitors?

It was a thought. Why would he show up now after all these years? *Had* someone sent him? Who'd know he'd be the perfect weapon to wield against her?

She rubbed at her nose, obscuring her expression to keep him from seeing her every thought. She felt transparent.

"I, uh, have some things I need to do. Are you staying here?" she said.

I need to keep him close until I figure him out.

He turned his palms to the sky. "I'd planned to. I mean, it is a hotel, but—"

She nodded. "Right, yes, *stay.* I'll be back in a bit."

He ran a hand through his short dark hair and turned enough for her to glimpse the gray peppering on the sides above his ears.

Sexy.

Not fair.

"We'll have dinner or something," she added.

He nodded. "Sure. I'll check in."

"Great. Great." Shee opened her arms and took a step forward to embrace him. "It is good to see you. It is."

He squeezed her to him until she wondered if he'd ever let go.

Don't. Don't let go.

He released her and took a step back.

"See you in a bit?"

She nodded. "Definitely."

"You're not going to run?"

She snorted a laugh. "No. I promise."

"Sounds good."

He didn't move, and Shee wondered if it would be odd for her to hop into one of the little boats bobbing beside the pier and roar off into the sunset.

"I'll walk you back?" she asked, skinning past him and turning.

"I might stay out here a second." Mason moved to the end of the pier with his back turned to her. The hands he'd thrust into his pockets stretched his khakis across his butt *tight,* accentuating the curve—

Cut it out. Go.

"Okay. See you soon."

She headed for the hotel, trying hard not to bolt. As she approached the back door, she saw Angelina and Croix scatter toward the lobby.

Voyeurs.

By the time she entered, the two women had bunched around the reception desk, pretending to be deep in conversation.

"Oh, there you are. We wondered where you two went," said Angelina.

Shee scowled. "Nice try."

"Where's Romeo?" asked Croix.

"He'll be here to check in soon. I need to know *everything* about him. Run every search, pick through his suitcase, *everything.*"

Angelina's head cocked, and in her arms, Harley's did as well, as if they were both run by the same puppeteer. "Why? Who is he?"

"He's someone Dad and I used to know."

"And this is how you treat old friends? Poking through their luggage?"

"I'm not poking. You are. I have to go."

"Where?"

Good question.

Shee searched the walls for an answer. "Out. Important stuff."

Angelina frowned. "Uh-huh."

Croix poked Angelina's shoulder to get her attention. "I think Romeo has Miss Know-It-All flustered."

Angelina nodded. "Me, too."

"Shut up." Shee glanced behind her to find Mason framed by the screen door, still standing at the end of the dock. Still, she lowered her voice. "It was an old friend who tricked Mick. Remember?"

Croix's eyes widened. "You think he—"

"I don't *know*. That's the point."

"Classic honeytrap," murmured Angelina, staring out the back door.

Shee turned her attention to Croix. "His real name is Mason Connelly. Write that down in case it isn't what his I.D. says."

"Like I can't remember one name," Croix mumbled. "Like I use *pens*."

Shee glanced out the back again and saw Mason heading toward the hotel, his limp more pronounced.

When he doesn't think I'm looking.

Her heart filled with empathy as she pushed herself toward the front door.

"I have to go."

Bracco opened the door, and she hustled out, stopping at the top of the stairs.

A black pick-up truck with California license plates sat idling beside Angelina's Land Rover.

He didn't turn off his truck?

She looked at Bracco.

"Is that his? The guy who just came in?"

Bracco nodded. "Chilly sat."

She walked to the truck. As she grew close, a moppy, floppy-eared face popped up to watch her approach.

She put her hand on the window, and the pup licked her palms from the opposite side, leaving long, wet smears on the glass.

He has a puppy?

Shee frowned.

This has got to be a trap.

CHAPTER TWENTY-TWO

Angelina moved to her desk, dropped Harley onto the fuzzy black bed, and tried to look as casual as possible. The back screen door creaked open.

"Hello again," said Mason, entering the lobby.

"Hello!" chimed Angelina and Croix in unison. They glanced at each other, and Angelina could tell they'd shared the same thought.

Take it down a notch.

Croix cleared her throat. "Can I help you with anything, sir?"

Angelina fought an eye roll by glancing down at her phone as it chimed the arrival of a message from Shee:

Put him on a lower floor. Away from Mick.

The phone dinged again.

He has a freaking puppy.

"Do you have a room available?" asked Mason, moving to the reception desk. "And do you accept pets?"

Croix frowned. "No, we—"

"Sure we do," said Angelina.

Croix continued. "Like I was saying. *No,* we don't just take pets. We *love* pets. You have an alpaca?"

Mason laughed. "Dog. Pretty boring."

Croix typed something into the system. "Okay. Predictable

but... Let's see. How about the seventh floor with a nice view of—"

Angelina cleared her throat, and Croix glanced at her without moving her head from its lowered angle. Angelina raised her hand to the center of her chest and pointed down.

The girl paused, seemingly confused.

Grimacing, Angelina tapped out a text message.

Lower floor.

A dinosaur roared on Croix's phone, and she glanced at it before moving it to the shelf beneath the desk, far from Mason's view.

"I'm sorry. I thought that room was open. Will the third floor do? Still has a nice view of the Intracoastal Waterway..."

Angelina gave her a thumbs-up behind Mason's back.

He nodded. "Sure. That's fine."

Angelina's phone dinged. Shee again.

A room you can ransack.

Angelina scowled. *Who does she think I am?*

Another ding.

Check his safe. His luggage. Check unusual places like the heels of his shoes for hidden compartments.

Angelina snorted a laugh.

Drawn by the snort, Mason turned.

Angelina sniffed. "Sorry. Allergies."

Her phone dinged again.

Check hiding places in the room, too, under drawers, etc.

She'd barely finished reading before it dinged again.

Check—

Angelina stopped reading, turned the sound off on her phone, and dropped it into her purse. It vibrated a few more times and then stopped.

Mason handed Croix a credit card. "I'm going to grab Archie while you run that."

Croix nodded, and Mason headed out the front door. She watched him disappear and then looked at Angelina.

"Why the lower floor?" she asked.

"To keep him far away from Mick. Orders from the heir apparent."

The girl nodded and ran Mason's card for authorization.

"Well, his credit's good for the price of a room," she reported.

Mason returned a minute later with a harnessed puppy on the end of a black nylon leash. Harley jumped to her feet, yapping the alarm, and Angelina scooped her up before she could leap from the desk like an attacking howler monkey.

"She thinks she's terrifying," she said.

Mason told Archie to sit. The puppy did, but he didn't like any part of it. His butt wiggled on the floor, tail wagging. He wanted to say *hi* to Harley as much as Harley wanted to chew off his toes.

Mason took his room key from Croix and lifted his small duffle bag.

"Can I help you to your room?" asked Croix.

"I've got it. Thanks."

He moved to the elevator and pressed the button. Before the doors opened, he turned to glance back at the two women as if he could feel their gaze on the back of his neck.

They smiled.

The elevator doors parted, and Mason and his furry companion stepped inside to disappear behind a wall of silver, the ladies still grinning their goodbyes.

The moment the doors shut, Angelina plucked her phone from her purse and stood, Harley still dangling in her other palm, her glossy black eyes riveted on the elevator.

"That was a good idea, not to let him too close to Mick. I didn't think of that," said Croix.

"Shee sent us a detailed plan." Angelina handed the girl her phone, and Croix scrolled through the messages.

"Why do I feel like she's done this before?"

Angelina rolled her eyes. "The insulting part is she's acting like *I* haven't."

"So what do we do now?"

"We wait until he goes out."

"What if he doesn't?"

"He can't sit in his room all day. I should have given him the *Things to See and Do* list. Dammit." Angelina pounded the counter lightly with the side of her fist.

"You think he's going to climb to the top of the lighthouse or watch rescued turtles swim around a tank?"

"He might. Who knows?"

Croix smacked her lips, her gaze locked on the elevator. "I'll tell you what, for an old guy he—"

Angelina snapped her fingers in front of the girl's face. "*Hey.* We've got a job to do. Leave your daddy issues for the stripper pole. *Focus.* He's the enemy until he isn't."

Croix smirked. "You're telling me you don't think he's hot?"

Angelina pursed her lips. "Oh, I'd ride him hard and put him away wet."

They burst into giggles.

The elevator dinged, and the two women turned laughter into matching frozen grins. Archie trotted through the sliding doors, followed by his owner.

"We have to stop meeting like this," said Angelina, struggling to keep a wriggling Harley quiet.

Mason jingled his car keys in his hand. "Seems I have some time to kill. Do you have some sort of tourist guide or—"

"*Absolutely.*" Angelina hustled to her desk and pulled the *Things to See and Do* list from her drawer to the sound of Harley's staccato barking. "Here you go."

Mason glanced at it. "You have a lighthouse here? Hm. Ooh, turtles..."

Angelina flashed Croix a smug smile.

"I'll see you later." With a quick nod at each of them, Mason left.

Angelina moved to the window to watch Mason's truck

leave the parking lot before returning to the reception desk, palm outstretched. "Give me the key to his room."

"Way ahead of you." Croix circled the desk and headed for the elevator.

"Where are you going? Go start your black web searches."

"It's the *dark* web, and I think plain old Google will suffice unless he's selling weapons for Bitcoin. Anyway, that won't take long. I want to help search his room. I've never seen a heel safe before."

"You're too young. That was an old *Get Smart* reference. I need you to stay here and keep an eye out for him."

Croix hit the elevator call button and motioned to the door. "Tell Bracco."

Angelina sighed. "Fine. Bracco?"

The big man poked his head through the door.

"Ping my phone if he comes back."

Bracco nodded. "Whalefish."

Angelina followed Croix onto the elevator. "Just once, I wish you'd listen to me."

Croix smirked. "Stop it. You're ruining your Christmas gift."

The two rode the elevator in silence to the third floor.

"This is exciting," said Croix as she opened Mason's door. "It's been a while since we had some intrigue around here."

"You spent last night burying a body."

"That doesn't count."

"How does that not count?"

They pushed into the room, and Angelina lowered Harley to the floor, where the terrier ran scattershot like a berserker, smelling every place Archie's paws had touched.

"Archie will be able to smell her, too," said Croix.

"Shit." Angelina snatched the dog from the floor.

Croix rolled her eyes, clearly to be sure Angelina knew how much smarter she was than her.

Young people.

"Let's do it by sectors," suggested Croix. "We search one square area at a time until we're sure there's nothing, and then move to the next sector."

"You go sectoring. I'm doing things my way."

Frowning, Croix moved to the bathroom.

Angelina found the bureau drawers empty, but for one with a pair of shorts, running trunks, a pair of ankle socks, and two boxer briefs. Mr. Connolly hadn't been planning to stay long.

She moved to the small walk-in closet. The room safe remained open and unused. Three pressed polos hung from the silver bar inside. She checked under the spare pillow and blankets before noticing Mason's running shoes on the ground beneath the shirts.

I can't believe I'm going to do this...

She picked up a shoe and pushed and pulled on the heel.

Nothing.

"Stupid," she muttered, checking the mate.

"Anything?" asked Croix as Angelina moved back into the room.

"No. Though, apparently, there are two kinds of military men. Neat ones and *Mick*." She knew the comment wasn't quite fair. Mick *was* orderly, if not clean, but something about him always made her feel as if everything around him was about to explode into chaos. She supposed that was her attraction to him.

Angelina smiled at the thought of Mick and then changed the subject lest she becomes maudlin. "Anything in the bathroom?"

Croix shook her head. "Sector One, clear."

Angelina spotted Mason's bag on the ground and stooped to unzip it. She slipped a hand into each pocket, finding nothing but a small black box.

She opened it.

"What's that?" asked Croix, peering over her shoulder.

"Box of photos."

Angelina straightened, and they looked through the pictures together. Most featured a young man and a woman, all faded and muddy.

"Are these from nineteen thirty?" asked Croix.

"More like the eighties."

"So everyone was blurry then?" Croix plucked a photo of a woman in a bikini from Angelina's hand. "Is that Shee?"

"Yes. And that's *him.*"

Croix whistled. "She was hot."

"She's still hot."

Croix handed back the photo. "I guess. *Mom* hot."

Angelina's annoyance level climbed. "*Mom* hot? Shee's *gorgeous.* You should be so lucky to look like that at her age. Age makes people *hotter* because they're *wiser.*"

Croix laughed. "That's what old people say to make themselves feel better."

"Yeah, well, young people are *assholes.*" Angelina snatched the photo from the girl's fingers and returned it to the black box. She slipped it back into the side pocket and then jerked her hand from the bag.

"*Ow!*" She popped her index finger into her mouth.

"What is it?"

"Something cut me." She reached back into the pocket, moving slowly, until she felt something hard. Gripping it, she slid it out to reveal a shining strip of metal in a faux leather sheath.

"Is that a *scalpel*?" asked Croix.

"Yes." She scowled at the girl. "Could he be hot *and* a surgeon?"

"Maybe. Or a serial killer."

Angelina slid the scalpel back into the suitcase and inspected the tiny slice on her fingertip. "Hopefully, it was sterile."

Croix rolled her eyes. "It was in a suitcase. It isn't sterile."

Angelina zipped the case and stood to survey the room.

Fresh out of places to search, she headed into the hall with Croix on her heels.

"No smoking guns," she mumbled.

Croix hit the elevator call button, and the doors slid open. "Maybe he keeps them in his car."

"We'll check when he gets back."

The elevator dumped them back in the lobby. Croix returned to reception, Harley curled up in her bed, and Angelina sat at her desk, staring out the front door, chewing her lip.

"He's up to *something*," she said.

At her station, Croix nodded.

"Yep."

CHAPTER TWENTY-THREE

Shee made it to A1A before she realized she had nowhere to go.

I just can't be there. With him. Not yet.

Jerking the wheel right, she parked in the public beach parking lot and rested her forehead on the steering wheel.

None of her imagined coming home would be easy, but this was *ridiculous.*

I should have stolen his dog.

Curling up somewhere with her arms wrapped around a fluffy mutt sounded perfect. Maybe a cocktail. A citrusy Bahama Mama, a dog...*what else?* The sound of the sea lapping against the shore...

She looked up.

Well, at least I have the ocean.

Shee exited the car and made her way to the sand, already dotted with seasonal tourists.

She walked along the water's edge to the fishing pier. The stroll seemed like a good idea until the clouds burned off, and she felt her flesh baking like a tray of cookie dough.

Retreat.

Shee wiped her beaded brow and started back. Little girls in bikinis ran giggling into the sea as she basted. The only good thing about slowly evaporating into a cloud of steam was it made concentrating on her problems difficult.

I have to tell him.

Do I? Why tell him now?

I am melting.

I've avoided telling him for nearly thirty years.

How can it be this hot?

Why tell him now?

Because he deserves to know.

My hair is going to catch fire.

Her thoughts shifted to ripping off her clothes and swimming to England.

She *could* rip off her clothes. It *was* Florida. No one would even blink.

A yellow Labrador retriever ran after its ball, and she stopped short to avoid a collision. Jupiter Beach was the only dog beach for miles.

Maybe I could steal that dog...

She found it odd Mason had a dog. Having a dog meant having a whole *life*. In her mind, when she allowed herself to think of Mason at all, he'd always been twenty, humping through faraway lands in full gear. Now, her mind flooded with new images—Mason eating breakfast, brushing his teeth, food-shopping...

Thinking of him as a young, hot, two-dimensional soldier was less painful.

A small, pointy-eared mutt trotted toward her, and Shee squatted for some loving. She told herself the dog wanted kisses, but he probably just wanted the salt off her cheeks.

Good enough. I'm not picky.

Half a gallon of sweat and two dog pets later, she returned to the car. Blasting the air conditioning, she drove slowly back to The Loggerhead Inn.

Mason's truck was gone.

A strange mixture of relief and disappointment settled over her. She parked and nodded to Bracco as he opened the door for her to enter.

"Sponge," he said, grinning.

She squinted at him. "I look sweaty?"

He nodded.

Hm. Maybe his word choices aren't entirely random.

"Princess is back," said Croix as she entered.

Shee stopped and turned. "Why am I *Princess*?"

"Oh, you know, everyone around here's always waiting on you. Mick, Angelina, now the old hunk..."

"*Right.* I have it *so* easy. What are you? *Twelve*? My bad. I forgot you know *everything.*"

Croix sneered. "You don't know anything about me."

Shee leaned in. "I know if you don't lose this attitude, I will kick your perky little ass."

Croix scoffed. "Good luck with that, old lady."

"Did you find anything in Mason's room?"

"No. A scalpel. In his bag."

"A scalpel?" Shee scowled. "He's a surgeon?"

"I don't know. He's *your* boyfriend."

"He's not my..." Shee took a deep breath and wiped away a bead of sweat rolling down her cheek. "Where'd Angelina go?"

"I dunno."

"Where's Mason now?"

The girl shrugged. "Whoring. Said something about you being an old hag and left."

"He take the dog?"

"Yep. Threesome."

Shee sighed. She didn't have the energy to go to war with Croix. She needed to restart their relationship before she ended up arrested for child abuse.

"Look, we got off on the wrong foot—"

Croix grunted without looking up from her phone. Shee continued.

"I want Mick back as much as you do."

That caught the girl's attention. She glanced up.

"Sweat much?" she asked.

Shee wiped her brow again. She wasn't surprised to see more anger coming from the girl, but before she changed the subject, she saw clear evidence of *pain* in the kid's eyes.

Mick's the key. We both love Mick.

Shee swallowed her irritation and tried a new approach, one she liked to call the *We're in this Together.*

"Please, Croix, tell me what he was working on. I want to help."

The girl seemed thrown off-guard by her softened tone. It lasted four seconds. Then her expression clouded. "Oh, *now* you want to help—"

"Yes, I do."

Croix's lip curled. "You know, he never even *talked* about you. Except—"

She looked away.

"Except what?"

The girl ran her tongue over her front teeth, stalling. When she spoke again, her voice felt softer, although still caustic. "Sometimes he'd get this far-off look in his eye and kinda laugh in this sad way." She met Shee's gaze. "That's when I knew that he was thinking about you. The daughter who broke his heart."

Shee sucked in a breath as Croix's words slid like a blade between her third and fourth rib to pierce her heart.

She fought to keep her composure, speaking low and measured. "Just tell me *anything* that could be a lead. Angelina said he was helping people?"

Croix stared, clearly hoping she'd earn more of a reaction. Deprived, she huffed. "Yeah."

"What was he working on, *specifically*?"

"About a week before he went to Minnesota, he broke up a local massage parlor full of prostitutes."

Shee's eyes popped wide. Thanks to some of the high-profile johns involved, she'd seen a report about that bust on the national news—she'd taken it as one of the omens calling her home.

"That was Mick?"

Croix nodded. "Afterwards, somebody sent suits, asking Mick to scuttle evidence."

"Which he refused?"

"Duh."

"Do you know who sent them?"

"No. One of the rich dirtballs, I assume. Mick might've known."

"But all that's trapped in his head," mumbled Shee. Now she had two things to look into, Viggo and the massage parlor bust. "Thank you. That's a lead. See what we can accomplish when we work together?"

Croix returned her attention to her phone. "Whatever."

Shee plucked at the shirt sticking to her chest. Even the hotel's relentless air conditioning couldn't dent her body's need to purge liquid.

"I have to go change before I melt."

Croix nodded. "Thanks for the update."

Shee rode the elevator to her room, took the world's quickest shower, and then caught herself spending extra time on her makeup. She pulled back from her hunched position in front of the mirror.

What am I doing?

Staring at her image, she tried to remember what she'd looked like during her delirious summer with Mason so many years ago.

Younger.

She leaned in again.

Ah, what the heck. A little extra blush to hide that sun damage...

She grabbed a pair of shorts but eyed the cute skort she'd purchased on her way to Florida. Skirt said *flirty*, but the sewn-in tights beneath said *all business.*

Perfect.

Before heading to her father's room, she donned the skirt

and a v-neck tee. Upon knocking on the door, Martisha let her in with a smile.

"Miss Shee?"

"I'm just stopping by to say *hi*."

The woman motioned to the bedroom and returned to her sofa seat.

Shee entered to stand beside the hospital bed. She rubbed the top of her father's head.

"Your hair's getting long," she teased. "Another week, and you'll look like a hippie."

She smiled.

If that doesn't get him moving, I don't know what will.

"So Mason's here. Weird, huh? I'll bring him up to see you. I guess. I suppose he's still here. I sort of freaked out and left for a while..." She ran her fingers along the smooth chrome guard bar, imagining her father's side of the conversation.

She nodded. "Yeah. I know. I will. Don't worry about me. You worry about getting better. I want you up and at 'em by..."

What seemed like a reasonable request?

She saw green. *Wednesday*. Today was yellow.

"...*tomorrow*, or I'm going to get an Admiral in here to order you to your feet, Captain."

She leaned to attempt a hug.

"Okay. Good talk. See you in a bit."

Shee turned away, waved goodbye to Martisha, and returned to the lobby. She needed to make arrangements to go to Minneapolis, find out who sent men to threaten her father and deal with Mason—at least a little.

Keep it light. No need to—

The doors opened, and Shee saw the ladies in their positions, including Harley, curled in her bed. Both Angelina and Croix glanced her way, but neither acknowledged her.

She expected snubs from Croix, but Angelina?

Something's up.

Angelina caught her eye and bounced her orbs to the left.

Shee followed the motion.

Someone in the sitting room?

She took another step forward and, with her new angle, spotted a young man reading a newspaper in the room to the right of the entrance. She didn't recognize him.

First Mason, now this guy.

Judging from the reaction of the two lobby-dwellers, this new man was a wildcard. Probably here for her.

I'm Prom Queen today.

Shee walked toward the front door, pausing just past the entrance to the sitting room, where the visitor couldn't see her. Bracco stared at her from his post, trapped in doorman's purgatory.

Shee looked at Croix, who shrugged with her right shoulder ever so slightly. The man could see her from his vantage point.

She had no information.

Okay. Let's see what's up.

Shee took another step toward the door so Bracco could act. He opened the portal, and she said, "Thank you," loud enough for the man in the sitting room to hear. Without leaving, she sat on a dark wood Bahamian-style bench against the wall and motioned for Bracco to shut the door. He did.

Shee caught Croix's attention and bounced her gaze toward the sitting room and back.

Croix nodded as if she had a tune in her head and busied herself at the desk.

We have his attention.

Shee smiled. Making a tiny motion and having people understand her meaning felt good. It reminded her of the shorthand she'd shared with her father during their working years.

As she waited, a list of bullet points gathered in her brain, rolling out like a yellowed copy of the Constitution.

Why doesn't he have a drink? Wouldn't a relaxed person who likes to enjoy his paper have some coffee?

And why is he reading a newspaper? He's Croix's age. If I asked Croix if she reads physical newspapers, she'd laugh for a week.

He's trying to hide his face. Maybe he's watched too many old detective movies with private dicks hiding behind newspapers. Maybe so many movies inspired him to become a detective...

Shee heard the paper wrinkle, followed by footsteps on the wooden floorboards leading away from the entrance to the room.

He's looking out the front window. Looking for me.

A moment later, the young man hustled around the corner. He hadn't seen her at her car, panicked, and rushed out to find her.

His stride suffered a hiccup as he spotted her waiting on the bench. If his bouncing pupils were any indication, his brain was spinning, struggling to decide. Should he keep walking forward with this sense of purpose? Stop? Return to the sitting room?

Let's let him off the hook.

Shee sprang to her feet and cut in front of him before he could reach her. She pushed on the door, and Bracco jerked it open.

"Jerrytail."

"Thank you," she said, wondering what the connection might be between 'Jerrytail' and the game of cat and—

Mouse. Jerry? Tom and Jerry?

Shee tripped, her brain so distracted by the puzzle of Bracco's mind she forgot to pick up her feet. Catching herself on the railing post, she continued to her car and sat inside.

Okay, Young Sherlock, let's see—

She felt the sweat ooze from the pores on her forehead.

Oh, for crying out loud. Not again. I can't get another shower...

She started the car, turned up the air, and *sat*. In her rearview mirror, she watched the young man get into *his* car, a late-model Toyota sedan.

He, too, *sat.*

He didn't start the car. *That would be weird, right?* To sit in a car, idling? But isn't it weirder to sit in a car melting like griddle butter?

Shee sniggered. *Poor kid.* She needed to stop messing with him and find out why he was following her.

Give him a minute more?

Thirty seconds ticked by. The young man's car rumbled.

There it is. Air conditioning.

But he didn't pull out.

He's waiting for me. I'm sure of it now.

Shee turned off her car, got out, and *bolted* back into the hotel. Not *oh, I forgot something* bolted, more like *I'm being chased by wolves* bolted.

Bracco held the door open.

"What's going on?" asked Croix.

"Quick, I've only got a second. What do you know about that kid?"

"Kid? He was like twenty-seven."

"Everyone under thirty-five's a kid when you're my age. *Quick.* Is he checked in?"

"No. He said he was waiting for a friend."

"Did he say who?"

"No."

"Okay. When he comes in here, keep him busy. Don't let him know we're on to him."

Croix scowled. "How—never mind. I got it."

"I'm going out the back and around. Don't let him get back to his car too fast."

"Got it."

Shee ran out the back of the hotel and around the side. She peeked around the corner in time to see the young man get out of his car and stride toward the hotel.

He seemed agitated.

As soon as he entered, she crept into the parking lot.

His car was still idling.

Yay.

She scooted to the Toyota and opened the passenger door.

Clean. Rental. Ah, Bingo.

The man's wallet sat propped against the emergency brake. She didn't find that odd. Men didn't like to drive with their wallets in their back pockets. The lump threw their spines out of alignment and made their backs hurt.

Shee grabbed the wallet and shuffled through it. Nothing unusual. Driver's license, Florida-issued. *Logan Sandoval.* The name didn't ring any bells.

A flash of motion caught her eye, and Shee ducked down. The kid was on the porch looking around. He saw her car hadn't moved and re-entered the hotel.

He'll probably go look out back now.

Shee replaced the wallet sans license. She slid out of the car, gingerly closed the door and—

...and there he is again. Crap.

The young man appeared on the porch looking flustered. He tried very hard not to look at her as she approached. Pretending to scratch her leg, Shee slid the license under the tights of her skort. Damn thing didn't have pockets.

What is it with women's clothes not having pockets? Probably, men want us to carry purses so we can tote their shit around.

She started walking again, calm, cool—as if it wasn't odd that she'd run into the hotel and magically appeared in the front parking lot.

The man stretched, trying to appear equally casual.

She had another five strides to the first step leading to the porch.

That's when something shifted against her leg.

The license is sliding.

The skort tights weren't as tight as she thought.

She took an awkward step forward, and the license slid

another millimeter.

Shit.

Locking her knee, she hobbled, peg-legged toward the stairs.

I look ridiculous.

Logan Sandoval, boy detective, couldn't help but look at her now. How could he not when she looked like a pirate creeping up on him?

"Hey," she said.

Arrrrg, me matey.

"You okay?" he asked, brow knitting.

She smiled. "I'm fine. I forgot my—" The word *wallet* bounced through her brain because she'd been staring at one, but she rejected it. "—*phone*, and might have tweaked my knee." She offered a goofy smile to demonstrate how silly she felt.

You know us girls, always forgetting things...

"Do you need help up the stairs?"

She flashed him her most disarming smile. He was a little young for her charm to hit with full effect, but it was worth a shot. Maybe he had a thing for cougars.

"That's so sweet of you..." Shee glanced at the stairs.

Hm.

If she bent her leg and straightened it again to mount that stair, there was an excellent chance of the license fluttering between them.

That would be awkward.

But she couldn't say *no* and then loiter at the bottom of the stairs, whistling. Hell, even if it wasn't *weird*, she had no pockets to thrust her hands into. You couldn't loiter without pockets. Women never loiter. There's too much to do.

"Would you mind?" she asked.

He walked down the steps and steadied her, her left leg jutting to the side like a branch.

Walk this way...

Step. *Clump.* Step. *Clump.*

Shee reached the top of the stairs, and Logan released her hand.

She batted her eyelashes. "Thank you, I *so* appreciate it. I didn't catch your name?"

"Bill."

"Bill. Thanks. I'm Hunter. I appreciate your help."

His face twitched.

He knew she was supposed to be *Shee*.

They shook hands, and she clomped inside with Bracco's assistance.

"Blackbeard," he muttered as he opened the door.

She threw him a side-eye.

Now, he's a funny guy.

Shee limped to the front desk and glanced outside. The young man had left, no doubt, to turn off his car. Or maybe sit in there in case she tried to leave again.

Shee pulled the license from her skort tights and set it on the counter.

"Got your phone?" she asked.

Croix stared at her.

"Okay. Stupid question. Take a picture of this and see what you can find on this guy."

"I'm not the DMV."

"Just do it."

Croix took a photo of the license.

"I'm going to go out the back again. When he comes in looking for me, stall him while I drive away."

"I already did that once. He's going to think I have a crush on him."

"So?" Shee pushed the license toward her. "Tell him you found his license on the ground."

Shee jogged toward the back door. She made her way around the building and, peering through a Clusia hedge, watched Logan wander back inside. She bolted to her car and pulled out of her spot.

In the rearview, she spotted Bracco blocking the door, pretending he didn't notice the young man trying to get out as she peeled from the parking lot.

She grinned.

I like that Bracco.

CHAPTER TWENTY-FOUR

"There you are," mumbled Shee, spotting Mason on the beach.

Croix said Mason had taken his dog, so there were only so many places he could go. Shee surmised he'd go to the lighthouse, discover the park there wasn't dog friendly, and then head for the beach.

She drove along A1A until she spotted his truck with the California license plates. She parked beside a plumbing van, whose driver had picked the public lot for a napping spot, plucked a small set of binoculars from her glove compartment, and walked to the beach to search for Mason like a proper creeper.

Totally healthy behavior.

She found him tossing a piece of driftwood to his rambunctious pup. He'd throw and then jog away as the dog sprinted in the opposite direction, clearly practicing with his new prosthesis. Somewhere along the way, he'd changed into shorts and a t-shirt. The sun glinted off his hardware.

The dog was adorable, wiping out seemingly on purpose when it dove to grab the stick, rolling in the sand, bouncing back to its feet, and bolting back like a self-returning bowling ball.

So cute. I'm spying. He brought bait. All's fair.

The breeze picked up, but it remained hot even close to the ocean. As long as she didn't exert herself more than raising the spyglasses to her face, she'd be okay, but Mason jogging...soon he'd be all sweaty and sparkly...

Mason crisscrossed his arms and reached toward his waist to grab the hem of his tee.

That's right. Take it off for Momma...

He lifted his shirt, his muscular torso flooding her with memories of their time together in Coronado. Her visions blinded her until she had to lower the binoculars and catch her breath.

Why'd he show up now? When I'm already overwhelmed with Dad...

By the time she raised the spyglasses again, a new player had joined the scene. A well-groomed woman around her age, wearing a neon pink bikini. A puffy white dog danced at her feet. She stood near Mason, laughing.

Open-mouth laughing, all tits and teeth. She touched his arm. *Leaned in.*

"Oh, you're so *funny*," murmured Shee, providing the woman a voiceover soundtrack. "I'm so *vulnerable*. I need to lean on you to stay upright..."

The woman crossed her arms beneath her chest, a practiced move devised to press together her breasts as she listened to Mason in rapt attention while the dogs played a rousing game of butt-sniff.

Shee knew the move. She'd used it plenty of times.

Back off, Tits McGee...

Her watch buzzed with a call.

Cursing, she answered.

"What?"

"Excuse *me*," said Angelina's voice. "Did I catch you at a bad time? Are you with Superman?"

"No." It was only a half-lie. "Sorry. What do you need?"

"I thought you'd like an update on your other admirer."

"He's still there?"

"No. He left after he lost you, looking pretty defeated, I

might add."

Shee felt bad for the kid.

Poor Logan, P.I., there he was thinking he was Philip Marlowe, and he turns out to be Inspector Clouseau.

"I think he's a freshly minted P.I. Did Croix find anything on him?"

"You guessed right. He's a private investigator out of Ft. Lauderdale, licensed a year ago. Nothing special."

"Not military?"

"No."

Shee considered this. One of the rich guys caught with their braided belts around their ankles at the massage parlor might have hired a private investigator.

But a greenhorn? Not one of the more powerful ones. They'd hire a pro.

"Have Croix get me a list of the men charged with soliciting at that massage parlor. See if they're from the Ft. Lauderdale area or connected to Baby Gumshoe's family."

Angelina grunted. "Oh, sure. She lives to serve. She'll love that."

"It's not for me. It's for Mick."

"Got it. Don't you want to know if Mason's back?"

Shee sighed.

If you're going to make me lie...

"Is he?"

"No."

"Okay. Oh, hey, can you find an address for Mick's friend Viggo? Last name Nilsson. N-I-L-S-S-O-N. And book me the next flight to Minneapolis. I'll pay you back."

Angelina paused. "I'm sorry, when did I become your secretary?"

"It's for—"

"*Mick.* Right. I remember. What about Captain Hard Buns?"

Shee snickered. "He's actually *Commander* Hard Buns. What about him?"

"Do you want to tell me why you're running away from him?"

"I'm not—"

Shee turned to find Mason standing behind her, staring down, his dog at his side, happily panting and covered in sand.

"I gotta go." She ended the call.

Mason smiled. "Hello. I can't find you for decades, and now you're everywhere."

His eye dropped to the binoculars in her hand, and she tucked them a little farther behind her leg.

"I was looking for you. I need to fly to Minnesota."

She winced.

I shouldn't have been so specific.

He'd know exactly why she was going if he had anything to do with Mick.

His expression twisted with what appeared to be genuine confusion. "Minnesota? *Now?*"

"Yes."

"It's *winter*."

Ugh. She hadn't thought about that. "It's a work thing—"

"You're still skip tracing?"

"No. Yes. Sort of."

"How long are you staying?"

"I'm not sure."

His annoyance radiated off the t-shirt he'd slipped back on.

Spoilsport. Maybe he'd tired of being eye-raped by that neon hooker—

"I'll wait," he said.

"Hm?"

"I'll wait for you to get back."

Shee's chest tightened again. "It could be a while…"

He shrugged. "Whatever. Maybe when you get back, you can spare five minutes."

Sensing the end of their exchange, the dog stood, and Mason turned to leave.

Shee reached out and grabbed his arm.

"Wait."

He stopped.

"Do you want to come with me?"

She sucked in a breath. She'd had no idea that sentence was about to shoot out her mouth.

He cocked an eyebrow. "To Minnesota?"

"No. You're right. It was a stupid idea—"

"No, I'll go." His body was untensed, and he looked down at the dog. "I'll have to find a babysitter."

"The hotel can look after him," she offered, ever helpful.

What am I doing?

She used the dog to avoid Mason's eyes and squatted to pet it. The muppet raised his head, searching for chin scratches.

"What's his name?"

"Archie. A parting gift from my team."

"Your team? He's fluffy for a K9."

He chuckled. "Long story."

"Hello, Archie." Shee gave the dog another good scratching and then straightened, wiping the wet sand from her hands. She motioned to the parking lot across the street. "Are you parked over there?"

He looked at her as if she were an icing-covered kid claiming she hadn't eaten the birthday cake.

"You know I am," he said.

She nodded. "Yup."

He leaned against the steps' railing, grinning. "You might be the tracker, but that doesn't mean the rest of us are idiots."

"Sorry. I keep forgetting that."

"Speaking of which, let me try a Sherlock trick of my own. Minneapolis is about Mick, isn't it?"

"Yes." She stopped there. "We should go."

They started back, stopping at the A1A crosswalk as a biker pumped by in his sausage-casing-tight, Day-Glo racing jersey, looking as if he'd been wrapped in a giant, festive Mardi Gras condom.

"I heard he was shot," said Mason as they crossed.

"Who told you that?"

"My team. SEAL news travels fast."

She grunted.

"Was he?"

"Yes."

"In Minneapolis?"

"Yes."

Change the subject.

"So what have you been up to?" she asked.

He laughed. "Nice segue. *Smooth.* You ask like it's been a week since I saw you."

"We have to start somewhere."

He sighed. "Fair enough. I've been in the Navy. You?"

She rolled her eyes. "*Duh.* Could you give me a few highlights before we move to me?"

"No."

"No?"

"*No.* Because I don't think I will get much out of you, and *your* highlights aren't even classified."

"How do you know?"

They reached his truck and turned to face her, looking exhausted.

"Because I've been looking for you for *twenty-seven years*, Shee."

CHAPTER TWENTY-FIVE

Shee stared at the back of the airplane seat in front of her, eyes locked on the blue, pill-ravaged fabric. Beside her sat Mason, muscles spilling over the invisible boundaries of their seats, his attention captured by something at the front of the plane. She'd given him the aisle seat. It seemed cruel to make him sit next to the lady in the window seat. Cruel to the lady. At least if he couldn't help touching Shee's arm, they'd touched before.

My God, did we touch.

The flight to Minneapolis had Shee *longing* for the awkwardness of Bracco's Cadillac and their midnight cemetery trip. She couldn't work out where to start. She'd barely had time to process his presence. As much as she appeared to resent being used as a personal assistant, Croix had turned out to be *too* efficient in booking her flight. She'd easily snagged a second ticket for Mason.

The timing had been so tight she'd worried getting Mason's leg through security would make them late, but the TSA agent had taken one look at his chiseled jaw and scar-covered arms and filed him under *wounded vet*. The woman did everything but give him a quick back massage before letting him through.

What else could a slab of beef like Mason be but military? An accountant with a fight club addiction?

"I wonder if we'll get pretzels," mumbled Mason.

"Hungry?"

"Starving."

"When we land, we can go to your favorite restaurant."

Mason's brow knit.

She motioned to his leg. "IHOP."

He winced. "Oh, you're *hilarious.*"

Shee chuckled, pleased with her joke. She'd been waiting for a chance to hit him with it for an hour.

They fell into another uncomfortable silence.

"Maybe we could quid-pro-quo it," she suggested.

"Huh?"

"You ask a question, and then I ask a question until we're out of them."

He seemed amused. "I know what *quid pro quo* means. I saw *Silence of the Lambs,* Clarice. I'd just foolishly thought we could catch up like *normal* people."

She shrugged. "Just a thought—"

"Fine. I'll start. Have you *purposely* been hiding from me?"

Yikes. Right to the point.

Shee kept her eyes on the ground. "No."

"You're lying."

She looked at him as he pressed his lips together, glaring.

He smells like sandalwood. He'd smelled like nutmeg and cinnamon as a young man.

"Shee?"

"Hm?"

"I said you're lying."

"Why would you say that?"

"Because I *know* you."

She scoffed. "You don't *know* me. You *knew* me."

Ouch. That sounded harsh. She plowed on to bury that bit.

"Is that your next question? *Am I lying?* Oh, wait, no, it's *my* turn."

He seemed to have soured on the game. "Not if you're cheating."

"I'm not."

The elderly woman beside Shee grunted. She turned to find the biddy staring at her, oozing disapproval.

"I'm lying a *little*," she whispered to the woman, winking.

The woman frowned and turned to the window.

Shee returned her attention to Mason. "My turn. Why are you here?"

He rested his skull on the headrest. "I told you. I heard about Mick and wanted to come to pay my respects. And yes, so you don't have to waste another question. I *was* hoping to bump into you."

"What—"

"It's my turn."

Shee lifted her hands and let them drop to slap her thighs. "Fine. Screw this game. Let's talk like adults."

"Gosh, I don't know. Do you think we can handle it?"

"Honestly, I'm not sure."

He rubbed his hands on his pant legs. "So tell me what happened to Mick. I still don't know the details."

Shee studied his expression.

Open. Honest. Curious. Concerned...

Either he'd become a top-notch liar or knew nothing about what happened to Mick. She couldn't be one hundred percent sure, but her gut shifted another step toward Team Mason when it came to his possible involvement in Mick's *assassination.*

"He was visiting a friend in Minnesota. I think someone lured him there."

"Who?"

"A guy named Viggo."

"Viggo *Nilsson*?"

She gaped. "You know him?"

"I've met him. SEAL world is small."

Shee hung her head.

So much for keeping things from him.

"What do you know about him?" she asked.

"Nothing. Big guy. Gets the job done. What do *you* know about him?"

"All I know is Dad went to see him and didn't come back in one piece."

"But what did Viggo say happened?"

"Nothing."

Mason scowled. "He doesn't know? I don't understand. Was he robbed—?"

"Viggo wasn't available for comment."

"How is that possible?"

Shee grimaced. She wasn't sure how much longer she could dance around the odd way Angelina had been able to retrieve Mick. Certainly, not without admitting he was still alive.

"I don't know. Honestly. We have almost no details."

Mason huffed. "None of this makes any sense. Where did they find his body?"

"In an Airbnb."

"He'd been staying there?"

"I don't *know*." She barked the words, and the people in the aisles around them turned to look.

"Sorry," she said, holding up a hand.

She didn't bother to look at the woman beside her. She already felt the weight of her glare.

Shee took a deep breath. "What about you? Don't you have a life to get back to?"

"You're changing the subject," mumbled Mason.

"I am. Because I've told you everything I know. Why else would I be headed to Minneapolis? I'm looking for answers, too."

"Fine." Mason shifted in his undersized seat. "As for me, my schedule's pretty open. I'm retired because I don't have any interest in a desk or teaching job, and they don't let you get wet with one leg."

Shee made a wave motion with her hand. "You couldn't just swim mermaid-style?"

He looked at her. "Would you like to get all these jokes out *now,* or can I look forward to more in the future?"

She sniffed. "I think I'll just pepper them in, here and there."

"Great. So what have you been doing for the last twenty-seven years? Just exclusively writing cripple jokes or...?"

She laughed. "I'm boring. I've been doing the same things I always have, only not for Dad. Freelance skip tracing, more or less. Have you been overseas the whole—"

"Why did you leave me?" He blurted the words.

The question caught Shee off guard. She turned to the woman beside her as if maybe Mason were addressing *her.*

The old woman stared at Mason, mouth agape, before piercing Shee with a narrow glare.

Great. She thinks she's watching a soap opera and I'm the villain.

Shee returned her attention to Mason. "I told you. I didn't want you worrying about me."

"But you *disappeared off the planet.*"

"Not because of you."

"Then why?"

Shee pulled at a thread hanging from the bottom of her shirt. She couldn't tell him she'd been unable to face him for so long, and then...

That's it. I'll skip to later.

"Someone was trying to kill me. I had to hide for my safety and everyone else's."

"From whom?"

"I don't know." She sighed. "There's a chance Mick found out, and that's what got him shot."

Mason rubbed his hand over his mouth.

"I'm sorry."

She nodded.

"But you're still not telling me everything," he added.

"I am—"

He held up a palm as if he were stopping traffic, his entire aura seeming to harden. "It's fine. Let's concentrate on the mission. What's the plan?"

Shee's shoulders relaxed a notch.

Yes. Mission. Good.

"The plan is to find Viggo and ask him what he knows."

She reached into her purse to retrieve Croix's printed sheets, bearing Viggo's home address, family info, where his grandkids went to school, and his standing in the local bowling league.

"She's good," she muttered, reading the top sheet.

"Who?"

"Croix, the front desk girl. I had her gather intel on Viggo."

Mason's brow knit. "You had *reception* investigate Viggo?"

"She's ex-Navy. Everyone at the hotel is."

"Everyone?"

"Not Angelina; she's a con artist."

"What? Am I missing something here?"

Shee stopped reading and sighed. "Mick's creating a squad of avenging angels."

"*Creating?*"

"*Was* creating. Creat*ed*."

"Why?"

"I dunno. He used to talk about helping people who couldn't find help elsewhere. His way of gaining a ticket to heaven, I guess."

"Hm." Mason took the wad of papers from her and flipped through. He scowled. "What's this?" He pulled out a sheet and held it up for her to see.

Shee looked at the candid photo of a man's butt as he bent to pick up his luggage.

Mason.

She snatched the sheet from him. "She thinks she's funny."

He smirked. "She's not that good. My *left* is my better side."

CHAPTER TWENTY-SIX

Locating an aging Viking storm giant in Minneapolis was more of a needle-in-a-haystack situation than Tyler had ever dreamed. Just walking through the Minneapolis-St. Paul Airport, he spotted five old dudes over six feet tall sporting blond beards.

Ruminating on his spectacular failure at Miami airport, he remembered seeing his target and his enormous friend *twice* during his previous trip to Minneapolis. At the start of the job, he'd arrived early to case the parking lot where he'd been told to find them and popped into the attached mall to use the bathroom. On his way out, he spotted two old guys talking to a young man at the host stand of a restaurant. They matched the descriptions of his target and the friend. Later, he recognized them returning to their vehicle, this time through a rifle scope.

The way the big guy and the kid maître d' had been laughing, he suspected they knew each other. He had to be a *regular*.

All he had to do was find the maître d', get him to identify the big guy, find the big guy, get him to identify the target, and then find the target.

Easy peasy.

Then he could get his half-Cuban, Miami-born ass out of this arctic hellscape.

Tyler sat on a bench outside the mall restaurant, pleased to see the same young man at the host station. The kid was easy to clock—his wide eyes and easy grin said Boy Scout and the skull-heavy arrangement of tattoos poking from his crisp white shirt suggested a *desire to rebel.*

Tyler sniggered.

The boys in Miami would eat this kid and his boyish rebellion alive.

He'd worked as a busboy as a kid. Never made it up the ladder to *the guy who hands out menus.* The memory of his time working in restaurants made him shiver. He'd *hated* it and joined the Army the day after his seventeenth birthday. His mother signed the consent form, happy to find someone else to feed him. He didn't tell her he'd joined to shoot people.

Not that she would have cared.

"Come here. Mommy needs to sit a second."

Tyler turned as a woman surrounded by a whirlwind of kids and shopping bags sat beside him on his bench.

"I want to go *home,*" whined a girl with candy stains on her cheeks.

Another kid stared at Tyler, fingers in his mouth, a string of snot oozing from his right nostril.

Tyler tilted backward to look past the woman.

An unoccupied bench sat ten feet away.

You've got to be kidding me.

He took a deep breath.

Calm down. Don't draw attention to yourself.

He stood and walked to the restaurant.

"Can I help you?" asked the Rebel Boy Scout. His nametag read *Jody.*

What the hell kind of name is Jody?

Tyler nodded to a booth just inside the entrance. "Yeah. Can I get that table right there?"

"Table for one?"

He nodded.

The kid hesitated, probably because the table was what Tyler remembered from his glorious stint as a busboy as a *six-top*—seating for six—but it was three in the afternoon, and the place was nearly empty.

"Sure. Follow me."

Tyler caught a whiff of cigarette smoke as he followed Jody five paces to the right and sat in the booth.

Oh, Jody. You rebel.

"Your server will be with you in a minute." The kid placed a menu on the table.

"Thanks."

When the waitress came, bored and underwhelmed by her party of one, Tyler ordered a coffee. Her mood dropped another rung on the enthusiasm ladder.

Two sludgy refills later, a blonde girl with big blue eyes and a heart-shaped ass arrived to tuck her purse behind Jody's station.

The evening crew had arrived.

Jody chatted for a few minutes, fingering the pack of cigarettes in his pocket.

Here we go.

Jody excused himself and headed for the back.

That's my cue.

Tyler rose and followed the boy.

Jody pushed through a swinging door into the kitchen. Tyler loitered outside the bathroom and then pushed into the kitchen. The staff glanced up and, but for a couple of double-takes, ignored him.

He headed out the back door, icy wind slicing through his striped, short-sleeved guayabera shirt.

Sweet Jesus. Why didn't I bring a coat?

He'd lived in Miami so long he'd *forgotten* the weather could be so cold—he thought the weather app had been joking.

I'm going to die out here.

He scanned the parking lot to find it empty, but for what

he guessed were employee vehicles.

No sign of Jody.

He tried the door to get back inside.

Locked.

Tyler growled.

Hopefully, the kid was still on his way. Tyler decided to wait five more minutes. He set himself up behind the door and stood, shivering, his arms wrapped around his core like nervous pythons.

Three minutes later, the door opened, and Jody, wearing a heavy jacket, strode out, fumbling with his pack of cigarettes. He tucked a napkin in the lock to keep the door from sealing and then turned, jumping when he spotted Tyler beside him.

"Jeeze, you scared me," he said, slapping his hand to his chest.

"Sorry, man," said Tyler.

Jody laughed. "Are you locked out? Aren't you freezing?"

Tyler fought to stop his teeth from chattering long enough to speak. He nodded to the cigarette. "Could I bum one?"

Jody shrugged and reached for the pack he'd slipped into his jacket pocket.

"Sure—"

Tyler pounced. He wrapped his arm around the kid's throat and locked him in a chokehold. The warmth of the boy's body against his own felt *wonderful*. He twisted to use his victim as a windshield.

"Tell me what I need to know, and you'll be fine. Got me?" he hissed.

Jody nodded.

"I need the name of a big guy. Blond, beard. He was here with another tough old bird about a month ago. I saw you talking to him like you knew him."

Tyler released the pressure on the boy's throat to let him answer.

Jody coughed. "Mr. Nilsson?"

"What's his first name?"

"I don't know."

"Think."

"I don't know—"

He jerked Jody back into the corner of the building.

"Think."

The kid tapped his arm, and Tyler eased again.

"Wait—I remember. It's like that actor with the weird name," he said.

"Who?"

"He plays tough guys. He was in *Lord of the Rings*."

Tyler rolled his eyes. "I don't watch that magic shit. What's the *name*?"

"It starts with a V—*Viggo*, Viggo Mortensen."

"The guy's name is Viggo Mortensen?"

"*No*. The guy you're looking for is Viggo *Nilsson*."

"Make up your mind." Tyler tightened his grip. "Jody. Viggo. Don't you people have anyone named *David* in this godforsaken place?"

Jody put his hands on Tyler's arm, struggling. Tyler eased again.

"You got something else?"

The kid shook his head. "That's all I know."

Tyler raised his left hand behind Jody's head and clucked his tongue.

"That's too bad."

Curling the fingers on his right hand, Tyler whipped his arm back, catching Jody's chin in his palm, his left hand applying pressure on the back of the boy's skull.

The *snap!* of the kid's spine filled him with pleasure.

Like popping a zit.

Body limp in his arms, Tyler pushed the kid behind the brown bushes lining the mall's outer wall. A million tiny icicles stabbed his cheeks, making his eyes water.

He broke into a jog and, rounding the mall, headed for the

entrance. He needed to buy a damn jacket.

Minneapolis was as close to hell as he could imagine.

He chuckled as he ran.

Hell, I did the kid a favor.

Tyler scored on his first attempt. Minneapolis had a thousand Vikings, but the Internet promised only four of them were named Viggo Nilsson.

Four. Unbelievable.

Only *one* of those had an address close to the mall, though. No one becomes a regular at a restaurant on the far side of town.

Pulling to the curb a few hundred feet down the street from Viggo's address, Tyler pulled binoculars from his pack and scanned the house. He could see the giant through the sheer drapes covering his front window, sitting, fiddling with something on a table.

That's the guy.

"Looks like ole' Jody didn't lie," he muttered, exchanging the binoculars for his gun. He couldn't fly with his favorite weapon, a Dan Wesson Elite Series Havoc, but he'd done a job in Minneapolis before and had known where to get a gun quickly. The Berretta 92 cost him fifteen hundred dollars he wouldn't be able to expense to the client, but it was a small price to pay to regain his honor.

Snug in his new jacket, Tyler walked between the neighbors' houses and approached Viggo's back door, hoping to get lucky. Peering through the window, he could see straight through the small kitchen to a man beyond, sitting at the dining room table—

Something about the shape of the things on the table before him looked very familiar.

Is that a pile of guns?

Tyler chewed on his lip.

Who is this guy?

Probably a bad idea to burst in there. By the time he recovered from shouldering the door, the old man might have lit him up. He had a policy against sneaking up on a guy surrounded by weaponry. His target looked like Tony Montana lording over his mountain of cocaine, except Viggo's cocaine was guns.

As if he could hear the call of Tyler's thoughts, Viggo stood. Tyler tucked back against the house and then took a second peek.

The giant had moved to his front door.

Someone there. Nice timing.

Tyler tried the knob.

Open.

He slipped inside and quietly shut the door behind him, hoping Viggo's visitor wasn't another giant bringing a pile of hardware.

He crept toward the dining room, listening to a voice he assumed to be Viggo talking to someone else.

A woman.

Viggo invited her in.

Tyler slipped inside the bathroom off the kitchen, closing the door enough to hide his presence but not so tight it appeared someone was inside.

Time to make a decision.

He could swing around the corner, pop the woman and hold a gun on Viggo until he extracted the information he needed, or he could wait until she left and then take care of Viggo without distractions.

Tyler tapped the muzzle of his pistol against his lips.

Decisions, decisions...

CHAPTER TWENTY-SEVEN

Shee and Mason pulled up to a suburban home on the outskirts of Minneapolis in a rental car ill-equipped for icy roads. Shee missed the nosey lady beside her on the plane. Alone in the car, their secrets felt like a churning moat of sea monsters.

"We should have ponied up a little extra cash for a better car," said Mason as they slid to the curb.

"Sorry. Freelancing skip tracing isn't exactly the fast track to riches. I'm used to automatically choosing the cheapest option."

He put the car in park. "Remind me not to eat shellfish with you."

Shee studied Viggo's home. The previous night's snow had melted from his roof but not his neighbor's. That meant Viggo's house was heated, so he was probably home and didn't have sufficient insulation in his attic. She'd have to tip him to the money he could save on his heating bill right after she beat out of him why he tried to kill her father.

"What now?" asked Mason.

"I'm going to knock on the door. No need for subterfuge."

Mason's eyebrows raised. "Well, except that he killed your father. Maybe he'd like you dead, too."

She shook her head. "I don't think so. I think he's the one who left him in the rental for us to find."

"Then, *gosh*. He's practically Santa Claus." Mason touched the door handle and moved as if about to exit the car.

"What are you doing?" she asked.

"I'm going with you."

"No. Stay here."

Mason frowned. "Again—you don't know anything about this guy."

"But he might recognize you and see you as a threat. I need him talking, and you parked around the block."

Mason set his jaw, his blue eyes lasering his determination into her brain. "I'm *coming*."

"Did you forget the part where I stayed alive my whole life without your help?"

His body recoiled. Shee grimaced.

That sounded crueler than I meant...

"I just mean—"

"Fine. Go get yourself killed." Mason lifted his hand from the door and flicked his wrist as if he were tossing his fingers into the back seat.

She nodded. "Thank you."

"But I'm staying here where I can see the door."

"But he—"

"I'm staying here."

Shee felt the urge to continue arguing leave her. She wanted to get to Viggo. "Fine. Stay here and ruin everything."

"Still bullheaded," she heard him mutter as she left the car.

A frigid blast ate through Shee's hastily packed puffy vest as if she were wrapped in nothing but cheesecloth. Shuffling across the icy road, she rang Viggo's camera doorbell, noting it had a less obvious cousin nestled in a tree and another mounted on the eaves.

Someone's a little paranoid.

The door opened, and an enormous blond man peered down at her. His graying beard and his wrinkled plaid shirt gave him the feel of a Swedish hobo-lumberjack.

"Who are you?" he asked without taking his eyes off the idling rental car. He'd already clocked Mason.

"I'm Mick McQueen's daughter."

The man's attention returned to her, his once ruddy cheeks paling.

"Little Shee?"

"Not so little anymore, but yeah."

He looked back to the car. "He here to kill me?" Viggo's flat tone said he didn't care much if Mason loaded a gun as they spoke.

"No. I want to talk. Can we do that?"

He stepped back. "Come in. Bring him if you like."

She shook her head. "This is between you and me."

Shee moved into the warmth of the small home and stamped her shoes on the mat. Viggo lumbered toward a dining room table and pulled out a chair for her before dropping into his seat as if standing had been a strain. His home was neat but not *clean* and badly in need of a remodel. There were signs a woman once lived there—a small Hummel collection and pillows on the sofa with frilly edges—but something about the pile of guns on the dining room table suggested she hadn't been around in a while.

"Ignore them," he said, motioning to the weapons. "I have a little business cleaning and repairing. They're spare parts."

Shee eyed the pile.

Spare parts. For making untraceable guns.

"You make ghost guns."

His eyes shifted in her direction. *"Cleaning and repairing."*

"It's okay. I'm not here with ATF. I want to talk about what happened."

The fact that he didn't ask *about what?* told her he had answers. Instead, he glanced at a half-empty tumbler of golden liquid on the table.

"Sit. You want a drink?"

She shook her head and sat.

"I was hoping someone would come," he said. "Never dreamed it would be you."

"Someone might have come sooner if you'd copped to your involvement."

He shook his head. "It's complicated. How is he?"

"In a coma."

"Still? Damn."

Viggo seemed regretful. She needed to push before he changed his mind.

"Tell me what happened."

He leaned back in his chair and twirled a spare barrel on the table as if he were playing spin the bottle. "There isn't much to tell. They had my grandson. I didn't have a choice."

"Who's *they*?"

"I don't know."

"Why you?"

"Huh?"

"Why did they have *you* lure him *here*."

Viggo slapped the spinning barrel to stop it. "First off, you should know they never said they would shoot him."

"No? You thought the people who snatched your grandson just wanted to chat?"

His expression darkened. "That's what they said. Next thing I know, there's a shot, and he drops."

"Someone walked up or—"

"Sniper. From somewhere in the back of the parking lot."

"Fine. But, again, why *you*? It had to be someone who knew you'd been on his team, right?"

Viggo shrugged his rounded shoulders. "I guess."

"Who would know that?"

He stared at her, dumb, so she prompted for answers. "People you ran up against?"

He laughed. "Everyone we ran up against is dead."

"Their families aren't."

"No. But I was by his side on almost every mission. They'd

want me dead, too, wouldn't they?"

"What about other SEALs? Who's still alive?"

"Other—" He rubbed a large paw across his bulbous red nose, brittle fingernails scratching his cheek. "That doesn't make any sense."

She jumped as he reached out and clapped her hand between his own with unexpected speed. "I beat myself up every day for what happened. When I saw he was alive—I did everything I could."

"*You* left him in the rental? Made the call?" She asked, sliding her hand from his grasp. She didn't like the feeling that he could twist her arm from her body if the spirit moved him.

He leaned back. "They left him in the parking lot. No cleanup, thank God." Viggo cocked his head as if he'd had a new thought. "Why *did* they leave him? To pin it on me? Make it look like I lost my mind and killed my friend?"

"Maybe. Maybe that's why they had *you* draw him out in the first place."

"Yeah. Maybe." Viggo's gaze drifted past Shee. "Hey, let me show you something."

He stood, and she followed him into the kitchen. Two doors led elsewhere from there. The windowed one revealed a frozen tundra the locals called a back yard. The other hung nearly closed, but she spotted the edge of a toilet through the crack.

Viggo motioned to a familiar news clipping framed on the wall beside the bathroom. In it, young Viggo and Mick stood in full uniform beside the then-U.S. President.

"Did Mick ever show you this?" he asked, his shoulders straightening.

She nodded. "He has a copy."

The titan looked at her, his eyes watery and tired. "Yeah?"

He returned to his seat, avoiding her eyes, his face pointed toward the front window even after he sat.

"I'm sorry," he mumbled. "For everything. Tell him for me.

Please."

"I hope I get the chance." Shee sat and put her elbow on the table, lowering her head into her hand, thinking.

"Could you write down your team's names for me?" she asked.

Viggo shook his head. "We all loved him. We'd run through hell for him. Hell, we *did*."

"They used *you*. Maybe they approached one of them, too?"

Viggo growled and jerked a yellow legal pad from beneath a pile of gun magazines. "I hate this shit." He flipped to a clean page before scribbling a list of names.

"Some of them are dead." He said, putting an X beside a name.

"Understood."

He looked at the ceiling and cricked his neck before ripping off the page and handing it to her.

"Here. This is everyone I can think of."

Shee scanned the sheet. One name caught her eye.

"What does this say?" she said, pointing to his child-like scrawl.

He squinted at the page. "Bracco?"

Shee swallowed. "What's he look like?"

"Big kid. He was the last to join the team before Mick left."

"He have any problems with Mick?"

"Not that I remember."

Shee folded the sheet in half and pulled a card from her jacket to hand to him as she stood.

He took it, folding himself out of his chair. "This says *Hunter Byrne*."

"Alias I was using. Number still works." She pulled out her phone. "Give me your number in case I have more questions."

He rattled off the digits.

He grabbed her arm in his powerful paw as she turned to go. "You are *Shee*, aren't you?"

She smelled the whiskey on his breath as he thrust his

sallow face toward hers.

"I am. I used to eat your mother's cookies."

He smiled and released her, but his grin dropped as quickly as it had appeared.

"They can't find out he's still alive," he warned.

"Your grandson. Understood."

She moved to the exit, and he let her go without following. With a final nod, she left, closing the door behind her.

Striding to the idling rental, she fumbled with her phone and threw herself into the passenger seat.

"How'd it go?" asked Mason.

"He's drinking himself to death. But I might have something."

Angelina answered the opposite end of her call.

"Don't let Bracco anywhere near Dad," she said.

"Why?"

"Did you know he was on Mick's team? That he knows Viggo?"

"Yes and no. He didn't mention knowing anyone from Minnesota, but he's not chatty, either. You found him?"

"Yes. I'll fill you in when I get back. Just keep an eye on Bracco. He might know more than he's letting on."

"He *loves* your father. And if he wanted him dead, he could have done it years ago."

"They took Viggo's grandson to make him help."

"Who's *they*?"

"He doesn't know. Does Bracco have a family?"

Angelina hesitated for a moment. "I'm not sure."

"Keep an eye on him."

Shee hung up and pointed forward. "Back to the airport."

Mason threw the car into gear. "Yes, Ma'am."

Two pops echoed outside, and Shee slapped her left hand on Mason's arm.

"Wait."

Mason looked at her.

"That sounded like gunshots."

CHAPTER TWENTY-EIGHT

Mason twisted to reverse the car back into their previous parking spot as if the vehicle were pulled on a string. Shee scanned the street. The shots had been *close*.

"He might have killed himself. He had a ton of guns in there," she said. "He's not a happy guy."

Mason shook his head. "I heard two shots. Suicides don't usually get a second chance."

Shee grimaced. *Good point.*

She opened her door, and Mason put a hand on her thigh.

"Hold on. We *don't* have guns, remember?"

"We can't just *leave*."

"No, but let me take point on this one."

She consented, and they left the vehicle to pick their way across the icy street, gazes sweeping the area for shooters.

Mason ignored the front door in favor of heading around the side of the saltbox home. Pausing, he pointed at a set of footprints leading his own. He hugged the building as Shee followed in his footsteps.

Someone's here.

Reaching the back, Mason glanced around the corner and whispered his findings to her. "Footprints to the door and heading across the yard, over the back fence. Hang back a sec."

He crept toward the back steps to peer inside before

opening the door and disappearing inside. Shee followed, staring at the tracks in the snow leading to Viggo's chain-link fence. The footprints continued beyond it, disappearing around the corner of the rear neighbor's house.

Whoever had been there had jumped the fence to get away rather than heading back out front.

Because we were out front.

Though Shee was tempted, it didn't make sense to try and follow. Whoever had been to Viggo's was probably both armed and long gone.

She entered the house. Mason crouched at the threshold between the kitchen and the dining room where she'd sat with Viggo. She saw a portion of the big man's body on the floor at his feet.

"Is he dead?" she asked.

Mason held up a finger and slipped around the corner into the living room. Shee headed for Viggo, squatting to feel for a pulse. The hole in his forehead didn't look promising.

Mason returned a moment later.

"House is clear."

Shee straightened. "He's dead. One to the head."

"Two shots," said Mason.

They both homed in on the gun near Viggo's hand.

"He got a shot off?" Shee backtracked to the kitchen to find a bullet hole marring the wall left of the back door. "Yep. It's here. He missed."

Her attention moved to a dark patch on the wall near the bathroom. Something square had protected the paint there.

She'd been staring at that very spot with Viggo.

"The picture is missing." She pointed at the square. "There was a framed news clipping of Viggo and my father getting a commendation from the President."

Mason scowled. "Why would someone kill a man for a news clipping?"

"I don't know. Maybe he had something in the frame?"

Mason moved toward the back door. "We should get out of here."

"Should we call nine-one-one?"

"Maybe from a safe distance. Did you touch anything during your visit?"

Shee glanced at the dining room. Viggo stared back at her with unblinking eyes.

"The chair. The doorknob."

She grabbed a kitchen towel from where it hung over the stove handle and wiped down the dining room chair and the front door knob.

After a final visual sweep of the house, she followed Mason out the back door, taking the towel with her and wiping down that knob as well.

"We have to get home," she said as they made their way back to the car.

"We should circle the block and see if anyone is walking around in this cold."

She nodded. "Why kill him now? They saw me talking to him?"

"I doubt they've been watching his house all this time. Coincidence, maybe. They're slowly tying up loose ends?"

Shee slid into the rental car and looked at Mason as he pulled away from the curb. The right corner of her mouth curled into a smile.

How could she not trust a man leaving the scene of a homicide with her?

A new thought pushed its way to the forefront, and her sprouting smile wilted.

Unless that man was the one person who knew I'd be talking to Viggo.

CHAPTER TWENTY-NINE

Angelina headed over the bridge to the address she'd found on Bracco's 1099s. His first name was Robert.

Who knew?

She'd never called him anything but Bracco.

Did he have a wife? For some reason, she'd always assumed he did. Shee's suspicions made her realize how little she knew about the man.

I saw a picture of her at some point, didn't I?

Did he have children? Grandkids?

Any loved ones could be used against him.

She needed to get information before Shee returned. She didn't trust the girl to handle the situation with *finesse.* Bracco was a friend. Innocent until proven guilty.

She *needed* him to watch that door until Mick woke up.

Angelina found a parking spot at Bracco's apartment complex and cut her engine. Dim shadows played on the walls of the pale buildings, palms dancing in the yellow glow of ancient landscape floodlights. The building's plaster had split in several places, cracks racing up the walls, edges peeling to reveal cinderblock bones beneath. An orange glow caught her eye—a couple smoking on a balcony one building over. The man wore boxers, the woman only an oversized tee.

"Why do you live *here*, Bracco?" Angelina muttered aloud.

She knew Mick paid him well. He overpaid everyone. She felt certain the hotel hadn't made a dime since he opened it, but the paychecks kept coming. Soon she'd have to investigate, gain access to Mick's account and unravel the place. She hoped Mick would wake up before it came to that.

Angelina opened her glove compartment to retrieve a can of pepper spray and dropped it into her purse. Once she found Bracco, she'd feel safe. No one in their right mind would step to that mountain of a man. But on the way there...

Locking her car, she headed up the open-air stairs to the second floor, where she guessed apartment two-oh-nine would be. She found it at the back of the building overlooking yet another parking lot. Below, a pair of raccoons worked at chewing through a dumpster lid.

Angelina's lip curled.

I wonder if he pays extra for the view.

Angelina knocked on the door. The peephole darkened, and she heard Bracco say something that sounded like *cakewalk*. He opened the door wearing an old Ozzy Osbourne t-shirt and a paint-splattered pair of cargo shorts.

She pointed. "I didn't peg you for an Ozzy fan."

He smiled and shrugged, but his brow remained knit.

"I suppose you're wondering why I'm here?"

Bracco pointed in the direction of the ocean, looking concerned. Angelina guessed his meaning.

"Everything's fine at the hotel. Can I come in?"

He grimaced and looked behind him.

"Please?"

He opened the door wide enough for her to enter. It didn't take long for her to surmise why he'd been reluctant. A torn, black leather recliner and what Angelina guessed to be a thirty-two-inch television propped on a pair of plastic bins, served as his only furniture.

"I love what you've done to the place," she said, too late to stop herself. She poked her head into the kitchen. It was clean but equally old and sparse. A frozen pizza box poked from a trash can against the wall.

"Did you just move?" she asked.

Bracco shook his head. He motioned to the only chair.

"No, I'll stand." Angelina frowned. "Where's your wife?"

Bracco's expression darkened, and his shoulders snapped downward as if he'd given up trying to remain tall. He disappeared through a door at the back left corner of the room. Angelina saw a made bed inside, but nothing else. He returned with the largest shoebox Angelina had ever seen.

"You know what they say about guys with big feet," she said, waggling her eyebrows. "Big shoeboxes."

He chuckled and opened the lid to reveal piled papers and photos. From it, he pulled some bundled documents and handed them to her. She rolled them open to read the blue cover.

Divorce Decree.

Ah. Ex-wife.

She looked around the apartment. "Looks like she cleaned you out pretty good."

He plucked a photo from the box and handed it to her. In it, a woman sat smiling with a dark-haired boy on her lap.

"You have a son?"

He nodded.

Angelina relaxed her expression, but she saw more than a boy in the photo. She saw *leverage.*

Angelina handed him back the papers. "Kids do complicate things. You've been living here ever since?"

He nodded.

"Why didn't you say something?"

He hooked his mouth to the side and gave her a withering glance.

"You know what I mean. Are you going to therapy? I mean, I assumed you had a support system at home—"

Bracco pulled a therapy pamphlet from the box and thrust it at her.

"Broca Aphasia," she read the title aloud. "So you *do* go to therapy."

He nodded.

"Bracco has Broca," she murmured. "Maybe I should call you Robert from now on. Calling you a name so close to your condition feels a little like calling a dwarf *shorty*."

He laughed one loud bark and then touched her hand to make her look at him.

"Here?" he asked. The effort it took him pained her to watch.

Angelina gaped. She'd never heard him utter an appropriate comment before. "You're asking why I'm here?"

He nodded.

"You're getting better?"

He held up pinched fingers.

"Do you play it up a little at work?"

Grinning, he shrugged, seeming embarrassed.

"Because it makes us laugh?"

He nodded.

Angelina sighed as Bracco scowled and pointed to the ground several times.

"Oh. I'm here because we *do* have a little problem at the hotel."

Bracco straightened, and Angelina put a hand on his arm.

"Nothing urgent. But I have to ask you a question."

Bracco pressed his lips together, waiting. Angelina hesitated. She didn't like doubting the man's loyalty.

"Has anyone approached you about Mick? About hurting Mick or helping them get to him?"

Bracco's eyes flashed with what looked like anger.

"*No,*" he said.

"Maybe they threatened your kid?"

"*No.*"

Angelina believed him. His fist clenched, but she didn't feel threatened. He seemed *frustrated*.

"I'll tell you why I ask," she said, saving him the need to speak again. "Shee talked to Viggo Nilsson—"

Bracco's eyes widened.

"One of Mick's team, we know."

Agitated, he tapped his chest.

"Right. Part of your team, too. Well, someone threatened his grandkid and forced him to set Mick up. That's what got him shot. He was the person in Minneapolis."

Anger flared anew across Bracco's expression, and he continued to pound his chest, now with a flat hand.

"I know you think you'd never do that, but they threatened his grandkid, and you—"

She motioned to the box, the picture of the boy still lying on top of the pile inside.

"No," he said.

"Okay. I wanted to talk to you before Shee came back. She can't help being suspicious of everyone."

He grabbed Angelina's hand, staring deep into her eyes as if trying to telegraph a thousand emotions.

None felt like *betrayal*.

She patted his top hand.

"It's okay. I believe you. Shee doesn't want you near Mick for a bit, though, okay?"

He straightened, looking like a sentry, his lips working to find the word. "Door?"

"You can still work the door."

He nodded.

"Banana pie."

She laughed and pointed at him. "But I'm not falling for that nonsense anymore."

CHAPTER THIRTY

Tyler watched the man and the woman leave the Viking's house, get in their car, and drive away.

Did they not see the dead man?

He'd seen them enter the back door from his vantage point a block away. Then one of the neighbors appeared to shovel his walk, build a snowman, or do whatever insane *Snowpeople* did on negative ninety-two days, and he started moving.

By the time he came around the block, the woman and the man were getting back in their car and driving away.

They had to have seen the body, but they *left*. Didn't wait. He heard no approaching sirens.

What are they up to?

Tyler looked down at the framed newspaper clipping in his hand. The guy in the photo was his missed target, younger, but *him*. The other dude next to the President was the man he'd just snuffed.

That guy...

The giant had nearly clipped him before he got off his shot. Tyler had eased open the bathroom door after the woman left, feeling confident he had the drop on the old guy, and the next thing he knew, a bullet was screaming past his skull.

The near-miss left him a bit shaken. He hadn't screwed up so many times in a row since...he didn't know when.

He glanced down at the picture.

SEALs.

All the guns on the Viking's table made sense now. Tyler had been gawking at them, cursing that he'd had to kill Viggo before he could get the name of his buddy out of him, when the conversation between the man and the visiting woman returned to his memory. They'd been talking about the framed newspaper clipping on the wall. It felt important, so he'd snatched it from the wall on his way out.

Staring at the photo now, even with his brain half-numb from the ridiculous cold, everything fell into place.

Shea McQueen and Viggo Nilsson.

The woman had to have been talking about his target. She'd mentioned *Mick*, but his real name had to be *Shea*. *Mick* for *Mc*Queen.

Tyler felt like a *genius* for putting together the pieces. He grinned as best he could with his frozen cheeks.

I guess I still got it.

He twisted the cheap plastic frame until the back popped off. No need to carry around the whole frame.

How many Shea McQueens could there be? He knew the dude was a SEAL, probably retired now. He knew—

Tyler was about to toss the frame to the curb and head back to the airport when something behind the newspaper article caught his eye.

He slid out a handwritten letter on light green stationery. The top sported a sea turtle logo for The Loggerhead Inn and a date from two years earlier.

Dear Viggo,

Consider this your official invite to come to join us. I'm starting something. I think you'll like it. Swing by and let me tell you about it. I understand if you've got your own shit going on, but if you don't, I'm here. If you're looking for something, like so many of us, come see me. Anytime, buddy.

Mick

Tyler's attention dropped to the bottom of the letterhead to read one small additional line of text.

An address, phone number, and email.

You've got to be kidding me.

Tyler dropped the frame, pulled out his phone, and dialed the number on the letterhead.

"Loggerhead Inn, this is Croix. How can I help you?"

He clicked the phone dead.

The place still exists.

If *Mick* McQueen was still alive, The Loggerhead Inn in Jupiter Beach, Florida, would be the place to start looking for him.

Florida.

Tyler smiled and got into his rental.

Thank God.

CHAPTER THIRTY-ONE

Shee and Mason circled Viggo's block looking for the shooter, but Shee's mind kept returning to the man beside her. She questioned his motives until she couldn't stay silent any longer.

"You knew I'd be here," she said as he rolled down a new street.

"Hm?" Mason seemed to pull his thoughts back from somewhere far away. "What?"

"You said Viggo's death was a coincidence. I don't like coincidences."

He looked at her and then did a double-take when he saw her glaring at him.

"Wait—you think *I* set this up?" he asked.

"Who else knew I was here?"

"Why would I let you talk to him and *then* have someone kill him?"

"Maybe your man got here late?"

Mason hit the brakes so suddenly that they slid another two feet. Shee slapped her hand to the side of the car and stomped her feet, pumping imaginary brakes. When the car's tires finally found purchase on exposed asphalt, Mason left them idling in the middle of the snowy neighborhood street.

"What the hell are you *doing*?" she asked.

He shrugged. "Oh, I dunno. I thought maybe you'd want to get out of the car. You know, rather than drive around with a *traitor*."

She rolled her eyes. "Oh come on. You don't see how I could find this odd? You showing up now?"

"I showed up because I heard your father was *dead*."

"What about Viggo's? How did someone know we'd be there?"

"I don't know, Shee. Ever think maybe someone is watching *you*? Following *you*?"

She sat glaring at him, struck speechless.

Shit. The kid.

There *was* someone following her—Logan Sandoval. Maybe he was better at his job than she'd thought. Maybe *he'd* discovered she was headed to Minneapolis. Made a call. Warned someone.

Damn.

"Why do you have a scalpel?" She spat the words to distract him, and herself, from her failings.

His attention snapped to her as if she'd poked him in the side of the face. "How—?"

Someone honked behind them, and Mason glanced at the rearview. With a huff, he put them in drive, and they rolled forward as he continued, "Look, you don't have to tell me all your secrets, but if you don't even trust that I had nothing to do with *killing your father*, tell me *now*."

"I—it's just weird—"

"If you think for a *second* I could ever..."

He faded even as Shee let the air run out of her lungs. Everything in her gut told her he had nothing to do with it. She just wasn't sure if her gut could be trusted regarding Mason.

On the other hand...

He has a point.

It didn't have to be *him* who sent a killer to Viggo's. Logan could have ratted her out. Or it *could* have been a coincidence.

And Mason *did* seem to believe Mick was dead. If he was involved, there'd be no reason for him to show up at the hotel. His job would have been done.

"Fine," she said.

"Fine?"

"Fine. I *trust* you."

He looked at her. "You do? You're sure?"

"Yes. I'm sure." She lifted her phone. "I'm going to call the airline and see if we can get out of here any earlier."

He sighed. *"Fine.* I'm going to make one more sweep."

"Fine."

Mason drove around the block again, his jaw clenched. Shee had no luck finding a flight earlier than their redeye. She lowered the phone and tried to think of ways she could make it back to Florida without him peppering her with an endless stream of questions she didn't know how to answer.

I could stuff something in his mouth...

"We've got six hours to kill. Let's grab a steak," she suggested.

"A steak?"

"Isn't that what people eat in the Midwest?"

He shrugged. "You'll get no argument from me."

She did a quick search for a spot and directed him downtown.

She regretted the decision once they walked into the restaurant. The place felt a little celebratory for how they'd spent the day. Scanning the other diners, she felt underdressed in her jeans.

"I'm not sure my appetite is up to the challenge," she said.

Hearing no response, she glanced at Mason to find his gaze tracking the path of a sizzling steak on a waiter's tray as it navigated through the restaurant.

He didn't seem to share her misgivings.

She gave in and followed the maître d' to a small, white-clothed table. Mason sat and stared at her.

"What?" she asked.

He took a sip of his water. "You're tense."

"You *think*? I can't imagine why."

"We did everything we could."

She frowned. "Did we? What if—"

He slid a hand forward to rest his fingers on hers. "No one followed us to Viggo's. Calling it in won't bring him back to life. It would only get us wrapped into the investigation." He sighed. "We should agree not to talk shop during dinner."

Five minutes previous, she would have been thrilled to hear him say that. Now all she wanted to do was go over everything that had happened at Viggo's again and again.

She closed her eyes and tilted back her head. "I want a drink. A really, really *big* drink."

"That's your best idea yet." Mason pulled his napkin to his lap and winked at her. "Not that you're not always full of good ideas."

"Shut up," she mumbled, smirking. Drumming her fingers on the table, she craned her neck, searching for the server. "What's a girl have to do to get a drink around here?"

Mason leaned forward and peered at her from beneath a lowered brow. "Am I allowed to offer suggestions?"

Shee felt herself blush. "Stop that."

"Stop what?"

"You know what you're doing. You're giving me *the look*."

Mason sniffed. "Ah'm sure ah don't know what you're talking about."

"And cut the southern accent. You know I love that."

"Cut the—? Why, Miss Jelly, ah'll have you know ah grew up in the great state of South Carolina—"

She giggled. "You're the *worst*."

She refused to look at him.

The tall, skinny twenty-something server arrived and introduced himself as Chaz.

Shee smiled. "Great. Hi, Chaz. Do you have a wine menu?"

"Sure." Chaz bolted from the table before she could say another word.

Shee looked at Mason, embarrassed. "Sorry. I didn't mean to chase him off. I don't even know if you like wine."

He smiled as the table's candlelight danced in and out of his dimples. "I'm more of a bourbon kind of man. I'm surprised *you're* a wine drinker. Last time I saw you, it was strictly wine *coolers*."

Shee snorted a laugh and covered her mouth with her hand, shocked by the noise. "Oh God, I forgot about those horrible things."

"I guess my girl's all growed up now."

"Don't bet on it," she murmured. "This is a special occasion. I'm celebrating the complete unraveling of my entire life."

She looked at him, only to find him peering at her through those piercing blue eyes.

"Miss, do ah make you nervous?"

She froze, momentarily mesmerized.

My God. That face. How I loved that face.

Shee thrust herself forward until her nose almost touched his. "I don't know. It's kind of dark in here. Who *are* you?"

They laughed, and she heard her voice crack.

His grin dropped. "Are you okay?"

Shee realized her eyes had teared. The candlelight splintered into wavy prisms. She wiped her eyes.

"Sorry. I don't know where that came from."

He shrugged. "Long day."

Chaz returned to hand Shee the wine menu. She scanned it as he rattled off the specials.

"We'll take a bottle of the house cab," she said when he finished.

Mason held up a peace sign. "Two glasses with that, and I'll start with a bourbon, neat."

She mimicked his gesture. "Make that two bourbons, but I'd like mine with ice."

Chaz nodded. "Would you like the wine now or with the—"

"*Now*," said Shee.

"Of course."

She turned her attention back to Mason. He seemed amused.

"Don't laugh at me," she said. "You said it. It's been a tough day."

"I'm not laughing at you. But if you start snatching drinks off the other tables, I'm going to have to draw the line."

"Understood. I'll be good."

They fell into an awkward silence. Mason watched a man walk past their table, and she turned away to wipe her eyes, worried her mascara had run.

Get a hold of yourself, Shee.

Chaz returned with two bourbons, a bottle, and a wine key. They waited as he opened the Cabernet and poured. He wandered off, promising a hasty return.

Mason held up his bourbon glass. "To Mick."

She smiled and tapped his glass with her own.

"To Mick."

They sipped. Mason set down his drink, and Shee did too, worried if, given a chance, she'd mainline it.

A second later, she raised the glass to her lips again.

Excellent restraint.

"So. Archie's cute," she said, figuring the dog would be safe ground.

Mason nodded. "He's a good kid. We got to know each other on the ride from Coronado."

"I bet. Long drive."

"Very."

Silence again. Shee tried not to stare at Mason, but every time he looked away, she let her gaze molest every molecule of his body.

"So are you going to tell me how you ended up with him?" she asked.

"Oh. He saved my life."

"How?"

Mason finished his bourbon. "He was at my last mission. I turned to grab him. If I hadn't..." He popped out his fingers and made an explosion noise.

"Is that when you lost your leg?"

He nodded. "Without Archie, it would have been a lot worse."

"He doesn't look like a military dog. Too fluffy."

"He's not. He belonged to the target."

Shee arched an eyebrow. "Were you infiltrating the suburbs?"

Mason tipped an invisible cap. "I'm afraid that's classified, Ma'am."

Shee rolled her eyes and finished her bourbon. When she looked up, she caught Mason staring at her. His gaze dropped, and he slid away his empty tumbler to move his wine glass to a position of prominence.

"Any thoughts on that missing picture?" he asked.

"At Viggo's?" She shook her head, not minding he'd gone back to talking shop. "No. It's weird. If it's the same guy who shot Dad, why does he need a picture of him?"

"For his trophy case?"

"That's warped."

Mason shrugged. "Do you know many well-adjusted assassins?"

Shee's head cocked as a thought knocked it out of plumb. "Maybe he didn't want someone seeing a picture of Viggo and Mick together and start making connections?"

"It's a solid theory."

Sipping on her wine, Shee scanned the menu. "Is it wrong to order New York strips in Minneapolis?"

"I hope not. Hey, what about Angelina? Do you trust her?"

"Angelina goes waaay back with Dad. Smooth as silk and tough as nails. She could con the Pope out of his pointy hat."

Mason nodded, looking as if his mind had drifted elsewhere.

"Hey, remember that floppy blue hat you loved so much?" he asked.

"The one with the sunrise on it?"

He nodded. "I think about that hat a *lot*," he said, his voice suddenly soft and low.

An image of herself wearing nothing *but* the floppy blue hat, her body reflected in a bureau mirror, flashed through Shee's mind. Mason lay beside her on her twin bed, his naked hip visible behind her own—

Chaz appeared. "Can I take your order?"

Neither of them spoke. Mason's gaze locked on Shee.

She'd seen the look before.

"Um..." Her mind had gone blank.

Chaz's expression changed as if he'd suddenly recognized them. "Or did you want us to send it upstairs?"

Shee straightened. "Upstairs?"

"To your room. You're staying in the hotel?"

"There's a hotel upstairs?" Shee looked at Mason. "There's a hotel upstairs."

He nodded. "I heard that."

They fell quiet again, staring at each other.

Chaz cleared his throat. "I could take your order and then have them deliver it to—"

"I think we need it to go." Shee's gaze never left Mason's. "And maybe another bottle of wine?" She swiveled her attention to Chaz as if he were Santa, about to grant her every Christmas wish.

He grimaced. "I can't sell you an unopened bottle, but I could *un*cork and then *re*cork one for you to take upstairs."

"You're a genius, Chaz," said Mason. "Two New York strips? Medium rare?"

Shee nodded. "Perfect."

Chaz pulled out a pad and pen. "No problem. And your

room number?"

Mason stood, reaching for his wallet.

"I'll tell you that as soon as I get one."

CHAPTER THIRTY-TWO

Shee and Mason didn't so much *walk* down the hall from the elevator to their hotel room as they *rolled* along the wall like a pair of gravity-defying vampires, exchanging hungry nibbles.

"I think this is it," mumbled Mason, too busy to annunciate.

He fumbled with the key card. She snatched it from his hand. On her third try, Mason moved his lips to her neck, and suddenly she had a better view of what she was doing.

Another attempt, and the lock's green light lit.

Victory is mine.

The door popped open, and they fell into the room, the handle on their oversized wine doggy bag tearing. The bottles clanked together and tipped. Mason made a last-minute, one-legged dip to grab them both in one hand and hefted the corked bottles to safety.

"That was impressive," said Shee.

He set the bottles on the dresser and grinned. "You ain't seen nothin' yet."

He pretended to tackle her onto the bed, and she giggled. No, *squealed. Squealed with delight.* She didn't remember hearing that noise come out of her mouth before.

Maybe once. A long time ago. Somewhere in Coronado.

She wanted to pull him inside of her—directly through her

chest. She wanted to envelop him, *melt* into him like two candy bars left out on a summer's day. One big pile of sweet oozy goodness, impossible to tell the Hershey from the Godiva.

"What?"

Shee opened her eyes. "Hm?"

"It sounded like you just said *Godiva*."

She shook her head and tussled with her shirt. "I don't know what you're talking about."

He used the pause as a chance to rid himself of his shirt.

She grabbed onto him and twisted until he was beneath her, her palms splayed across his chest. She took a moment to drink in the vision of him, and her reoccurring dream turned real. She ran her hands across his massive chest, a man's chest now, not a boy's. The bump of the scar on his arm caught her attention, and she stroked it with her fingertips, feeling its rugged topography. Something hard sat beneath the surface.

"What happened there?" she asked.

He put a hand on either side of her hips and gazed at her like a hungry wolf. "Bullet."

His arms were bigger, too, darkened by a perma-tan. He had a few more scars, but beneath the new aftershave, he smelled the same. If she closed her eyes, she was eighteen again—

"What's that?"

She opened her eyes to find him pointing at her lower abdomen. She looked down to see the five-inch-wide scar smiling above the waist of her unzipped jeans.

Her mouth went dry.

Oh no. How could I forget?

"Uh—" She wanted to spit out the name of an organ found in that general area, but her mind offered no ideas.

"Did you have an operation?" he asked.

She nodded. "It's, um, from a long time ago." The words barely burbled over her lips. She couldn't push them out. She felt too weak.

Shee rocked back. The moment was over. He was staring at her, his mouth ajar.

He knows.

Her most horrible secret, stuffed so long in the darkest places of her heart, had finally clawed its way to the light. She struggled to find a way to brace for the impending storm.

"It looks like a C-section scar," he said.

She wanted to laugh, roll her eyes, slap his chest, and call him silly, but she couldn't do it. She couldn't lie to him.

Not again.

"You had a kid?" he asked. His voice sounded weak now, too.

Her once-flushed cheeks felt clammy.

She nodded. Something roiled in her stomach.

"You did?" he asked.

She could see he was struggling with a way to process the information.

He had no idea how much worse it was about to get.

No puppy to save you from this bombshell.

She cleared her throat, her hand shaking where it rested on her thigh. She dug her nails into her flesh to hold her fingers still.

"*We* did," she said.

"We—?"

"Excuse me."

Shee rolled sideways off the bed and ran for the bathroom, slinging the door shut behind her.

I am not going to throw up a third time—

She lost half a bottle of a bold, oaky Cabernet Sauvignon into the toilet, chased by a touch of aged bourbon.

She sat against the cool tile wall when she was done, staring at the closed bathroom door. The room outside was eerily quiet.

She pulled herself to her feet, rinsed, spat a few times, and dabbed her mouth dry.

"You have to come out sometime," said Mason's voice from the other room. It was a different voice than the one murmuring what he wanted to do to her when they got to the room. This one sounded...

Scared.

She opened the door.

He sat on the edge of the bed, his shirt back on, gripping the sides with curled fingers as if he feared the mattress would try to throw him off.

She closed the bathroom door behind her and leaned against it.

"That's why you ran away?" he asked.

She nodded.

His lip quivered. "Why didn't you tell me?"

She rolled her fingers into fists. "We were too young. You'd fought so hard to get where you were. I wasn't ready—"

He motioned to the scar. "But you had the child?"

"Yes."

Mason's expression twisted into something too complicated to read. Some strange combination of pain, horror, anger—

"You're telling me I have a son? Daughter?"

"Daughter. Charlotte."

The tears leaped to his eyes, so suddenly that Shee raised a hand to cover her mouth, her own eyes welling.

"That was my mother's name," he said.

"I know."

"Where is she?"

"West Coast. Near Tampa."

He wiped his eyes on the back of his hand. "How could you raise—"

"I didn't. I gave her to my sister. It was Mick's idea. She wanted a baby, and I wanted—" All the possible words to finish her sentence sounded awful to her now, and she let her thoughts die there.

"You have a sister?"

"Half."

"And *she* raised our daughter?"

"Until Charlotte was eleven."

"What happened then?"

"My sister died. Charlotte went to live with her grandmother."

"With her—" Mason stood, wobbling a little as he adjusted to his leg. "And you *knew*? You let that happen?"

Shee shook her head as if it could help her dodge the questions. "It's complicated. I couldn't take her. I couldn't risk anyone finding out—"

Mason clenched his fists. *"Why?"*

"Because it was *my fault*," Shee said, her voice rising to match his urgent tone. "I wanted so much—"

Mason's hand moved to the lumpy scar on his arm. He stood there staring at her, rubbing his fingers around its rough surface until he finally held up his palm and closed his eyes.

"I can't do this now."

"What?"

"I—" He felt his pocket for his wallet and looked around the room as if he'd lost something. "I have to go."

"Where?"

He strode toward the door. "I don't know. I can't be near you right now."

Shee drew a ragged breath as he jerked the door open and disappeared into the hall.

She slid down the door to the floor, sobbing.

CHAPTER THIRTY-THREE

Twenty-six years ago. Somewhere off the west coast of Africa.

Mason entered the cruiser's medical bay, gripping his arm. Blood oozed between his fingers.

Doc looked up from his magazine. He looked about fifty, with spikey gray hair echoing the steel tufts poking from his ears and nose.

"You're back already?" he asked.

Mason nodded. "Cakewalk."

Doc laughed. "I can see that. Sit down. Take off your gear."

Mason wasn't feeling chatty. This was his first mission, and he'd managed to get shot. The task had been easy, and he'd just messed up. A branch had snagged the locket around his neck and pulled it free. He'd doubled back to retrieve it and taken one in the arm before he could take out the shooter.

Stupid.

As Doc inspected his wound, Mason stared at the locket in his hand. It held one of the diamonds his mother had died for. This one had Shee's name all over it. He planned to ask her to marry him when he returned, but if the damn locket caught on everything, he'd lose it—or his life—*long* before returning to Coronado.

"Through and through. We'll be able to stitch you up both

sides," murmured Doc.

Mason nodded. "Hey, ah have a question for you. If ah gave you a little rock, could you drop it in and stitch it?"

Doc's expression twisted as if he smelled something awful. "You got a headwound, too?"

Mason shook his head and held his orb-shaped locket aloft. "Ah've got a diamond ah'm keeping for my girl. Gonna lose it if ah don't put it somewhere safe."

Doc's face didn't change. "You know they have these things called *banks*. Safety deposit boxes? Maybe you've heard of them?"

"That woulda been a good idea a couple of months ago, but there ain't much ah can do now that ah'm here."

Doc motioned to the locket. "You want *that* thing in your arm?"

"Just the diamond inside. It twists open."

The doctor took the locket and opened it. He spilled the diamond into his palm and let it roll around his palm.

"This is the ugliest damn diamond I've ever seen."

"It's rough. Uncut."

"Where'd you get it? Rob a jewelry store?"

Mason chuckled. "Something like that."

Doc sighed. "I guess I can tuck it in there for you, for *now*, but it's going to work its way out sooner or later."

"That's fine. Ah just need it safe 'til ah get back."

"I'll have to sterilize it. There's going to be a lump. The scarring will be worse—"

"That's fine."

Doc shook his head. "I can't believe I'm even considering this."

"Come on. Help me out."

Doc huffed a sigh. "Fine." He tapped beside the wound with his finger. "You want me to numb you up, or are you one of those SEALs who don't feel pain?"

Mason settled back. "Pain don't hurt."

Doc barked a laugh, reaching for his stitching needle. "You guys and your *Roadhouse* quotes. I swear."

CHAPTER THIRTY-FOUR

The flight back was *fun*.

Shee sat in the waiting area, her knee bouncing, certain she'd never see Mason again. She looked up to find a tan, fit, middle-aged man wearing a guayabera shirt staring at her. He looked away.

Not in the mood, buddy.

He seemed out of place wearing his Cuban-style short-sleeve shirt, but the plane *was* headed to Florida.

Maybe he had the right idea.

She removed her puffy vest and folded it in her lap.

Think warm thoughts.

It was hard to think of anything except the pain she'd caused Mason. There was no reason he should ever forgive her. She knew that. But he had to go back to Jupiter Beach, right? Had to pick up his dog, his truck... It would be crazy for him to take a later flight just to avoid her, wouldn't it?

She was shuffling up the boarding line one step at a time when he appeared. He slid into the queue beside her without a word. Both nerves and relief flooded her body.

Hi. Good morning. You almost missed it—

Every line sounded wrong. She remained silent.

As did he.

Shee handed her boarding pass to the check-in attendant

and picked a middle seat on the plane. She could feel Mason's presence behind her.

Please sit on the aisle beside me. Please sit—

He sat beside her.

More relief. More nerves.

He remained quiet as the rest of the passengers found their seats. The plane taxied and took off.

Still nothing.

Her heartbeat thrummed in her temple, though she knew that was more about the wine than her nerves. The steaks had shown up not long after Mason left the room, but she hadn't been able to eat. Instead, she sipped the spare bottle of wine until she found it empty.

Drinking on an empty stomach had *always* been a punishable offense.

She let the silence brew until she couldn't stand it any longer.

"You're here," she said.

"My stuff, my dog, and my truck are in Florida," he said flatly.

Yep. I've been clinging to that fact for hours.

Silence fell again like a heavy cloak around her shoulders.

"I'm surprised you sat—"

She winced. *Dumb thing to say.*

She was *begging* him to get up and move with lines like that.

He looked at her, deadpan. "I'm not five years old. I'm not going to pretend I don't know you just because I'm—"

Angry? Furious? Livid?

He didn't finish.

She nodded. "Right. No. Of course not." She traced a figure eight on her leg with her index finger for several minutes before looking at him again.

"Do you want to talk about it?"

The muscle in his jaw bulged. His head dropped, and he

stared at his lap.

"There are some things I want to know," he said.

"Great. Go. Ask me anything."

Another stupid thing to say.

He looked at her. "Is she safe?"

Shee perked.

That's an easy one.

"Yes. The safest place on earth."

"Disney World?"

"That's the *Happiest Place on Earth*. No, she's at a fifty-five-plus community called Pineapple Port outside of Tampa."

"Fifty—?" Mason's brow knit. "If she's over fifty-five, I hate to tell you, but she's not our daughter."

"She went there after my sister died. It's a long story."

"Isn't everything?" Mason squinted and looked away. She could tell he couldn't decide if he wanted to hear more.

After a moment, he started again. "Does she know about us at *all*?"

She frowned. "I thought it would only mess her up if she knew. And it was too dangerous—"

He dismissed her with a wave. "Right, right. You were on the run from the one-armed man or whatever."

"I *was*."

He stared at his lap again.

"I mean, not from a one-armed man. But *someone*," she added, quietly.

"Someone only Mick knows."

"Maybe."

The plane took off, and they fell silent again as the roar of the engines grew louder.

"We could go visit her," she offered after the plane leveled off and the captain announced cruising altitude or read a poem by Shelley—the voice was so garbled Shee couldn't tell.

Mason looked at her. Taking it as a hopeful sign, she continued, "I mean, when we're done with the current mess..."

Mason sighed. "You understand you stole any chance of me knowing my daughter from me, right?"

She nodded. "I know."

He paused, chewing on his lip. "I don't know how to forgive you for that."

Shee's eyes teared, and she sucked in a breath.

"I know."

Mason stared at the pocket of reading material in front of him while she tried to avoid melting to the floor in a puddle of tears and regret.

It seemed he'd finished talking.

Even through her stuffed nose, she could smell on his skin the same soap she'd used that morning. She guessed after he'd left the night before, he'd gone downstairs and booked another room. She'd imagined him sleeping in the lobby or walking the streets all night. That seemed silly now that she thought about it.

Shee felt eyes on her. She turned to find the thin, older man in the window seat beside her, staring.

She wiped her eyes again and faced forward.

The airlines should pay us for entertainment.

An hour into the flight, Mason shifted from his position, staring holes through the seat before him. Though busy mentally torturing herself, on some subconscious level, Shee registered her seat shift as he moved and looked at her.

"You said it was a long story," he said. "How your sister died, and Charlotte ended up in a retirement community."

"Yes."

Mason took a beat. "We have time."

Shee offered a tight-lipped smile.

The highs, the lows...

She took a deep breath.

He wasn't going to like this story, either.

CHAPTER THIRTY-FIVE

Sixteen Years Ago. Cocoa Beach, Florida.

"Knock, knock." Shee peered through the screen as her sister, Grace, turned to look from her reading spot at the kitchen table.

"Hey, come in."

To the sound of creaking hinges, Shee entered the colorful cottage outside Cocoa Beach and submitted to a hug from her half-sister. She'd met her half a dozen times, but visiting the woman raising her child never felt less awkward. The familiar, strange mixture of resentment and gratitude churned inside her—each taking turns ebbing and flowing as the visit played out.

Charlotte walked around the corner and stopped.

Shee gasped.

The girl was gorgeous, long dark hair and big eyes—granted, the teeth were pretty funky at this stage, but still—

"I swear, she looks a foot taller every time I see her," she said, aware she sounded like some corny old grandmother.

Grace shrugged, looking morose. "That's probably true."

Shee grimaced. She only stopped by when she and Mick were in the area. Everyone had wanted it that way. Grace didn't want the girl to know she was adopted because she wasn't *officially*. She and her husband moved with the baby, and new neighbors had no reason to question whether the child was theirs. It wasn't like it was hard for Mick to get his hands on a forged birth certificate.

"You remember your Aunt Shee, don't you?" asked Grace.

Charlotte offered a half-nod, half-shrug that said, *maybe, I don't know, it doesn't matter.*

"Hi," said Shee.

Charlotte paused and then disappeared back into the house like a shy cat.

Okay. There's the visit.

Shee smiled. The girl had always reminded her of Mason, but maybe now she could see her own features in that face. She and grace didn't look anything alike, but now that Grace's husband was dead, people would assume the girl favored her missing father.

Speaking of which...

"Sorry to hear about Luke. It was a work accident?" Shee remembered he'd been in some kind of construction.

Grace nodded.

"You doing okay? Is she?"

"Well, yes, as can be expected. She's been really strong."

Pride washed over Shee.

Just like her daddy.

Grace glanced toward the back of the house, stood, and brushed past Shee to step outside on the porch. Shee followed.

"She hears *everything*," said Grace, shutting the door behind them.

"Kids." Shee wasn't sure why she said it. She didn't know *kids* from iguanas. "Do you need anything? Are you getting the checks?"

Grace leaned her butt against the front porch railing, arms crossed against her chest. "I work. Between that and Luke's insurance—what you send is more than generous. Charlotte doesn't want for anything if that's what you're wondering."

Grace's tone took a shift toward snotty.

Shee frowned. "Why do you sound angry?"

Grace picked a piece of lint off her arm. "I don't know. I guess I sort of resent it when you show up."

Shee's eyes widened. "You do?" She'd thought she was the seething one.

"Yes. Every time you stop by, it reminds me I'm not her mother by blood. It reminds me Luke and I were never able to have our own child."

"I didn't know you felt that way."

Grace put a hand on Shee's arm. "It's not that I'm not grateful. Everything you went through with Charlotte's birth...I'm more grateful than I could ever—"

Somewhere behind Shee, a sharp *pop!* echoed. Something moved past her cheek, so close and hot it burned. She raised a hand and recoiled, thinking a wasp had stung her, even as her mind screamed that wasn't the case.

Grace's expression froze, her eyes wide and her jaw slack as if someone had ripped the batteries from her back. Her sister's knees buckled, and she collapsed to the ground, clipping the back of her head on the porch railing as she fell.

A red mist hung in the air.

Sniper.

"Grace!"

Shee dropped to a squat to feel her sister's throat for a pulse, but Grace was dead. There was no question. She'd seen the back of her sister's head explode into a halo of blood. She shifted the body aside and scrambled into the house as another explosion sent a sliver of wood spinning from the porch railing.

The bullets weren't meant for Grace.

"Charlotte!" Shee called as she closed and locked the front door.

Whoever shot her sister would be arriving soon to finish his botched job. She had to find the girl and get her to safety.

"Charlotte?" Shee ran from room to room, poking her head in each before moving to the next. She opened the back door and scanned the yard as best she could without sticking her noggin out like a shooting gallery duck.

The girl was gone.

Down the street, she heard the sound of kids calling to each other, playing.

There she is.

She had to be playing with the other kids.

Did the assassin know about Charlotte? Would he hunt her down?

She heard the front door rattle and reached for a gun that wasn't there.

Shit.

She'd left it in the car. Grace had scolded her once before for bringing it into the house.

She slid her phone out of her pocket and called Mick, pleased to hear him answer. She hadn't been sure he would. He hadn't warmed up to cell phones yet.

"Hey, you done already?" Mick sounded relaxed. She guessed he'd stopped at some tiki bar to wait for her. Voices chatted and laughed in the background.

"Someone shot Grace."

"What?"

"Someone shot her. I think they were aiming at me." She touched her cheek, remembering the heat of the bullet tearing past. She looked at her fingertips and found them red with blood. The bullet had grazed her.

"I'm on my way."

Shee dropped the phone as the glass in the front door shattered.

The assassin would be in the house any second.

I should have grabbed a knife.

She'd run right past a butcher block of knives and hadn't taken one.

Why bring a knife to a gunfight? Mick liked to say.

Now she had an answer.

Because you left your frickin' gun in the car.

No time to go back.

She hovered at the back door and then thought better of escaping. There could be another shooter waiting to pick her off. And she didn't want to endanger the kids playing down the street with Charlotte.

Footsteps creaked in the kitchen and Shee dove for the primary bedroom. She'd lose any chance of surprising the shooter if she barricaded herself. She left the door open behind her.

Slipping into the en-suite bathroom, she scanned the small, beige-tiled room for a weapon, settling upon a toilet bowl brush and a spray bottle of tile cleaner. As she weighed the pros and cons of swapping the toilet brush for the oversized hairdryer, the floorboards in the hall outside the bedroom creaked.

She threw her back against the hall closet door between the bath and bedroom entrance. She took deeper breaths, hoping to slow her pounding heart.

She heard steady footsteps move past the room.

Heavy. Probably a man.

Statistically, the odds favored the assassin being a man. She didn't subscribe to Assassin Stats Weekly but knew assassins were often retired military. The male-to-female soldier ratio heavily favored men, and it hadn't taken the shooter long to reach the front door, so it probably wasn't an oversized woman—

Stop it. Assume it's a man. Avoid contests of strength.

She searched for some reflective surface to glimpse the bedroom entrance but found nothing.

Is he coming with a rifle, or did he switch out for a handgun?

She hoped he'd stuck with the rifle. In close quarters it would be less effective.

The back door creaked and then slammed.

Charlotte.

Shee didn't know how much the gunman knew. Had he

followed her to Grace's house? Had he been to Grace's before? Did he know to grab Charlotte and use her as leverage to draw her out of her hiding?

She was about to reel from the closet in the bedroom when a floorboard creaked.

Still here.

He'd *pretended* to leave out the back to see if she'd pop from her hiding place.

It had almost worked.

Hopefully, that meant he didn't know about Charlotte.

Footsteps moved toward the bedroom until she could feel his presence. She heard him take another cautious step forward.

Holding the tile cleaner high, she reached around the corner and sprayed where she thought his eyes would be.

He roared.

Shee cracked the toilet brush across the hand, holding what she could now see was a pistol. He'd come prepared for close quarters.

The gun went off as it fell from his hand, the bullet embedding in the floorboards not far from Shee's feet. He smacked the spray bottle from her hand. She kicked him hard against the side of his knee.

Another yelp. He grabbed at her shirt as he started to topple, his leg collapsing under his weight.

Shee jerked forward and fell on top of him. He grappled to hold her there.

"Shee!"

A voice called her name from somewhere in the house.

Mick.

The assassin heard, too. Shee grabbed for the gun lying on the floor by the nightstand. He scrambled to escape from beneath her and flee the bedroom. Springing to his feet, he bolted for the hall. She fired as he turned the corner toward the back door. Blood splattered against the white wall. The bullet continued into the dining room to strike a lamp. She heard Mick swear.

"Shit, Shee, you almost shot *me*."

"Sorry." She raised a hand of apology and leaped to her feet to give chase.

Wherever she'd hit her foe, her bullet didn't slow him down. Shee pursued as far as the back porch, choosing not to fire as she watched the man limping, gripping his upper arm, and running in the opposite direction to the children playing down the street.

She'd be lucky if the neighbors hadn't already called the police.

Mick appeared behind her.

"He got away?"

She nodded. "I think I caught him through the arm."

"Yeah, I know. You almost caught me through the head."

"Sorry about that." She looked back into the house. "Grace is—"

"Dead."

She nodded, finding it hard to look him in the eye.

Mick moved into the bedroom to yank a pile of blankets from the top of Grace's closet.

"Help me get her to the car."

"Charlotte?"

"No, *Grace*. I can't leave her here."

Shee gaped. "You can't just drive off with her."

"If they find her with a bullet in her head, there will be questions."

"The kind of questions that might find her killer?"

"No, the kind of questions that don't end well for Charlotte. Grace's death will be in the paper. The people after you will find out about her."

"The people...?" Shee's head felt as if it might spin off her neck. "Who's after me? How could they know Charlotte is mine?"

"I don't know. But normal people don't have snipers

shooting at them. Someone wants *you*. We have to assume they know everything."

Shee glanced toward the back door.

"What about Charlotte? She can't come with us if it's as dangerous as you say. What are we going to tell her about Grace?"

Mick spoke through gritted teeth. "I don't know yet. Come on. Help me get Grace wrapped up."

Mick pulled Grace inside the house, and they wrapped her in the blankets. He hoisted her to his shoulder, and when he felt comfortable with the weight, he nodded down the hall.

"Clean the blood off there and the front porch."

She shook her head. None of this felt right. "The neighbors must have heard the gunshots."

"We'd have heard sirens by now. It's a nice neighborhood. They don't think gunshots are gunshots."

"What about *Charlotte*?"

"I'll call her grandmother. She'll come to get her."

"Luke's mom?"

"Grace's mom." He shifted the body on his shoulder. "Estelle's never going to forgive me for this." He moved to leave and then paused. "I saw him this morning."

It took Shee a moment to register the topic shift.

"Who?"

"I saw a maroon minivan this morning at the hotel with a man sitting inside. I saw the same van parked down the street on my way here."

"Then we should go—"

"It's long gone by now."

Shee huffed. "If he followed me from there, it means he probably hasn't been watching Grace. He probably doesn't know about Charlotte."

"That's why we have to get her out of here *now*."

Mick headed outside as Shee held open the door. Her mind raced.

Who wants me dead?

Down the street, a boy yelled for his friend. The call snapped Shee from her trance.

"Are you okay?" asked Mick, returning empty-handed. "I'm going to grab Charlotte and go. Are you good with the cleanup?"

She looked down at the blood pooled on the porch. Grace's body was gone, tucked away in Mick's trunk.

She nodded. "I'll get the hose."

CHAPTER THIRTY-SIX

"If it makes you feel any better, Charlotte thinks my sister died of cancer," said Shee as the plane circled Palm Beach International Airport.

Mason tilted his head and stared at the ceiling. "Wow. Yeah. That makes me feel a *lot* better."

"Sarcasm isn't going to—"

"Wait. How'd you pull that off?" Mason stared at her. "Charlotte believed her mother went from fine to dead in an hour? From cancer?"

Shee shrugged. "She was eleven. I guess Mick and her grandmother sold the story." She stretched her back. It felt as though her butt had fallen asleep. "Please understand the whole arrangement was supposed to be temporary, but then Mick found out there was a bounty on my head and—"

"And you hit the road."

"Yes. For what I thought would be a month. It turned out to be fifteen years."

"Mick kept an eye on her in the meantime?"

Shee cringed. "Um..."

"*No?*"

"Not exactly." She held up her palms, trying to calm him as if he were an angry buffalo preparing to charge. His expression didn't look dissimilar. "He was busy looking for who killed

Grace and who was after me, and we didn't know if maybe *he* was a target..."

Mason's blue eyes lit like natural gas flames. Shee worried if she dropped one more unpleasant fact, his training might kick in, and he'd snap her neck with his pinky or something.

He closed his lids and took a deep breath.

"So Charlotte grew up with Estelle?" he asked without opening his eyes.

Shit.

"Estelle died not long after Charlotte showed up." She mumbled the words, hoping they were inaudible.

Mason lowered his shoulders. His fury seemed to have shifted to resignation.

Shee worried she'd broken his brain.

"You've got to be kidding me."

Somehow, his new calm felt scarier than all the muscle tightening and teeth-gritting.

"Well..." She searched for a shred of good news. "She was safe. She remained in Estelle's house, and from what I understand, the neighborhood brought her up—"

"Like a stray *cat*?" His tone hit a crescendo. He jerked it back to earth by *hissing* the word *cat*.

Shee swallowed.

Now that you mention it...

"I only just found out about that bit," she added.

He nodded. "Of course. You were running around the country, saving everyone but your daughter."

Shee flinched.

Ouch.

She reminded herself she didn't have the right to be offended. "I guess that's fair. But..."

"But what?"

She paused.

I've never said these words out loud before.

Her bottom lip trembled, and she pressed it against the top

one to stop it as she stared at her lap. "I thought I was a *curse*. I didn't want to get her killed—the way I'd gotten Grace killed. The way Mick looked at me—"

No. Too much. She couldn't go there again and tried to start over.

"You have to understand—"

"I don't *have* to understand any of this." Mason ran a hand over his hair.

He fell silent, and as the speakers crackled and the captain announced their arrival, she felt herself morphing back into a persona non grata.

Where I deserve to be.

Shee wanted off the plane. She wanted to grab Mason, shake him, and beg him to forgive her. She couldn't sit, trapped, staring at the pain and betrayal in his eyes any longer. No more than she'd been able to watch it in her father's eyes.

When the plane landed, they marched to the overnight parking garage without exchanging another word. Mason's icy silence gnawed at Shee, but some tiny part of her felt freed. The worst thing she could imagine, telling Mason about Charlotte, had *happened*. The thing that had given her anxiety dreams for twenty-seven years was *over*. Now, whatever he decided—

"Wait." Shee's hand shot out to grab Mason's arm.

He stopped. "What?"

She pulled him to face her. "Pretend we're talking."

"We *are* talking."

"There's a car parked across from our aisle, four down, at your seven. It belongs to a private investigator who stopped by the hotel yesterday."

"What? When?"

"When you were at the beach with Archie."

He looked daggers at her. "Do you tell me *anything*?"

"I wasn't sure I could trust you yet."

"Right. Because *I'm* the one with a history of lies and subterfuge."

"Can we not do this now?"

Mason tapped his closed fist against his forehead. "Is he dangerous?"

"No. He's a shiny new P.I. and seems pretty useless, but I want to find out who he's working for. He could have been the one to send someone to Viggo's." As she spoke, her anger grew.

Screw this day.

"You know what? I'm going to confront this joker right now."

She dropped her bag on the cement.

"Shee, wait—"

She dodged to avoid Mason's attempt to stop her and strode across the parking lot toward Logan Sandoval's car. His engine started, and she broke into a sprint.

No, you don't, you sunova—

Shee threw herself across his trunk, trying to sound as much like a *collision* as possible. He slammed on his brakes. Rolling to the driver's side, she found her feet and pounded on his window.

"Open this window, you little shit!"

Logan peered through the glass at her, grimacing. He put the car in park.

The window lowered.

"Can I help you?" he asked, entirely too smugly for a boy about to have a hurricane of frustration released on his ass.

"Cut the bullshit, Logan. Why are you following me?"

Logan's eyes bulged at the sound of his name as if someone had tweaked them from behind like a clown horn. He grimaced, shoulders slumping. "You know I can't tell you that."

Shee reached inside and grabbed the young man by his shirt collar, jerking him toward the open window.

"I am *not* in the mood—"

"Get off me!" The young man slapped at her face, and Shee jerked back to avoid contact. She struggled to hold his collar as he wrestled to pry away her fingers.

"Get off me, you crazy b—"

"Hey!" Mason's roar sounded an inch from Shee's head.

Logan stopped wrestling and went pie-eyed at the sight of the SEAL.

"Cut it out. *Both* of you."

Shee and Logan remained entangled, still but straining, gazes locked.

Mason tapped Shee's arm.

"Shee, I swear to—"

"Fine." She released the kid.

"She started it," said Logan, adjusting his stretched collar.

Shee slapped her chest with a flat palm. "*I* started it? You're *following me.*"

Shee didn't want to calm down. Logan was such a welcome distraction she wanted to beat the snot out of him and hug him at the same time.

"Who are you?" asked Mason.

"Logan Sandoval, teenage detective," spat Shee.

Mason shot her a warning glance, and she crossed her arms against her chest.

Fine.

Logan found his wallet and held it open for them to see. I'm a detective. Licensed. Just doing my job."

"Someone hired you to follow me."

He offered a withering stare. *"Duh."*

Sonova—

Shee reached for the kid again, and Mason blocked her with his elbow.

"*Just* follow?" he asked Logan.

Logan rolled his eyes. "Yes, just *follow*. What do you think? I'm an assassin?"

Shee snorted a laugh. "You're not even a detective."

"Who hired you?" asked Mason.

"I can't tell you that."

"Did you arrange Minneapolis?" asked Shee.

Logan's expression twisted. "Minneapolis?" He looked at Mason, appearing genuinely confused. "Did she get hit in the head or something?"

Shee leaned into Mason. "Give me five minutes with him."

"Easy." Mason pushed her back from the car, inserting himself between her and the detective, resting his massive forearms against the side of Logan's window. "I get it, Logan. You're just doing your job."

Logan sat up and adjusted his shirt. "*Exactly*. Thank you, man. I—"

Before he could say another word, Mason grabbed him by the hair and yanked his head toward him. He pressed the young man's throat against the edge of the lowered window.

Logan struggled, gagging, and then slapped on his steering wheel as if trying to tap out. That hand found the horn and laid on it.

Mason snatched the boy's wrist and jerked his horn-pressing hand out of the car. The parking garage went quiet again, but for the sound of Logan gagging.

"Feel that pressure on your windpipe?" asked Mason.

Logan nodded as best he could.

Mason continued. "Windpipes are pretty fragile. Tell us who hired you." He eased the pressure.

"You can't just kill me in the parking lot," croaked Logan.

"I can't?" Mason looked at Shee. "Did you see any signs about that?"

"Don't leave your luggage unattended. Stay to the right— no, you know what, nothing about killing detective wannabes."

"Spit it out," growled Mason.

Logan coughed, straining to keep his throat from the edge of the glass. "I don't *know*."

Mason pressed down.

"I swear! I don't know!"

"How did they contact you?"

"She called."

"*She*? Could you tell anything about her? Old, young?" asked Shee over Mason's shoulder.

"Accent."

The kid's eyes flashed white like those of a frightened horse, and Shee could tell the bulk of the boy's discomfort had shifted from his Adam's apple to the wad of hair twisted in the SEAL's grip.

"What kind of accent?"

"Like, *islandy*."

"*Islandy?*"

"Like Jamaican or something."

Shee felt the blood drain from her cheeks. She slapped Mason on the back.

"We have to go."

He turned. "That's all you need?"

Shee found her bag behind Logan's car, grabbed it, and headed for Mason's truck. She stood at the locked door as Mason released Logan and followed.

Logan pulled out of his space and left.

She motioned to the door with the hand, not speed-dialing Angelina. "Open. Let's go."

"Where are we going?"

"Back to the hotel as fast as you can drive."

Mason's Ford beeped, and Shee hopped inside.

He joined her. "What's going on?"

"We have—"

Shee stopped.

Crap.

She looked at Mason as he reversed from the parking space.

He's going to kill me.

"What is it?" he prompted.

"There's something else I didn't tell you," she said.

Shee's head bounced on the headrest as he hit the brakes to glare at her.

"Are you kidding me?"

She shook her head.

"Did you just remember we had *twins*?" he asked through gritted teeth.

"*No...*"

Shee heard Angelina answer her side of the line as she met Mason's stare.

"...but the rumors of Mick's death have been greatly exaggerated."

CHAPTER THIRTY-SEVEN

Something's different.

Mick opened his eyes.

This dream world is new. This isn't a memory.

Through slit eyes, he scanned what he recognized as his room, but everything felt *off*.

Wrong, but somehow, more *real*.

He tried to sit up.

So weak.

When did I get so weak?

He tried to swing a leg out of bed but couldn't move them.

Am I paralyzed?

A memory flashed through his mind. A crack, pain exploding in his head—

I was shot.

He strained to remember more details.

Viggo. His friend Viggo was there. He'd gone to see him—

"Ooh, mi suh late."

That voice.

He'd heard it in his nightmares.

Rustling in the other room. The sound of his front door closing.

Mick looked around his bed for a weapon. *Anything.* On the table beside him sat a box of tissues and a ceramic mug. Silver metal tubing surrounded him like a fancy little fence.

This isn't my bed.

He willed his left arm to move toward the mug. His hand rose and floated in that direction.

I am seeing this. This is real.

Fingers shaking, he tried to loop his index finger through the mug's handle. He felt it slide through. He felt the smooth ceramic.

Success.

He took a few breaths and jerked the mug toward him. The mug clanged against the side of the bed. The liquid inside splashed to the floor.

He winced.

He dragged the mug toward him with as much speed as possible and hid it beneath his sheets. Its cool surface rolled against his leg.

I feel it.

That had to be a good sign.

Something entered the room. He caught a blurry flash before closing his eyes to play possum. His brain processed the image.

Panic swelled in his chest.

The Shadow and the Sun.

His tormenter had arrived, bigger, split into light and dark.

Maybe I'm still dreaming?

Decades of SEAL training rushed forward to squelch his fear.

He didn't have time to be afraid.

Even if I'm dreaming, I'm going to kill this thing this time.

Mick cracked open one eye and saw something move toward a large cabinet.

Not a shadow.

A *woman*.

Dark skin. Hair piled in coils on her head. Heavyset. Tall. Nurse's scrubs.

Familiar.

He tried to log every nuance that might be useful down the road.

I know you.

The woman fiddled with keys, letting herself into the cabinet. She pulled out an IV bag, muttering to herself as she waddled toward him.

She changed his infusion and then cocked her head, her eye casting downward like a bird spotting the movement of a worm in the grass.

The spilled liquid. She's seen it.

She bent lower.

"Waah dis now...?"

This is it. My chance.

Mick jerked his arm from beneath the sheet. The sheet slid away. The mug appeared. He swung, straining to arc his weapon over the metal guard rail.

He lowered the mug as hard as he could against the nurse's head.

Yes!

The ceramic bounced on her thick coils, never touching her skull. The mug slipped from his fingers and hit the floor, shattering.

The woman jerked upward, eyes blazing with anger.

Left with no other option, he rolled at her, swinging with his untested right fist.

"No!" she barked, easily blocking his punch.

She grabbed his throat with her other hand. He tried to fight her off, every movement feeling as if he were underwater.

So slow. So weak.

Sharp nails dug into his wrist. She smacked him in the face with the back of his hand. Pressure on his throat gagged him. She lowered her face to his, coffee on her breath. Her skin smelled of cinnamon. He recognized the scent from his nightmares.

She hissed in his ear.

"You can't wake up yet, Mister Mick. Nuh, for a year and a half. You suffer the way he did, just the same. That's the rules."

He? Rules?

He gasped for breath.

Who is she talking about?

He couldn't fight her. Instead, he'd take her words deep into his brain and *think*. He'd find something that made sense. Come up with a new plan.

The nurse dropped the silver sidebar and raised a knee to hold down his arm closest to her, a surprisingly agile move for a woman so large. One hand still on his throat, she used her other to start the new IV.

"Your daughter's here, Mister Mick. She'll be next."

Mick gasped, half in shock, half for the air her meaty paw denied him.

Shee's here?

It hadn't been a dream.

No! Shee!—

Even as he fought, the fog rolled over his eyes.

CHAPTER THIRTY-EIGHT

"Mick is alive, and he has a Jamaican nurse?" asked Mason as they roared north up I-95 from the airport to the Loggerhead. "Is there anything else you'd like to drop on me?"

Shee took a moment to think about his question.

Is there?

She'd almost forgotten he didn't know about Mick being alive. What else was she forgetting?

While she thought, Mason ticked off her bombshells.

"Secret baby, sister assassinated, daughter raised by wolves—"

"*Retirees,*" she corrected.

"Oh, excuse me, *old wolves*. Mick's alive—is the Loggerhead the lost city of Atlantis?"

"*No.* And, for your information, Charlotte is very well adjusted—"

She winced.

Whoops. There's another thing.

The light ahead turned red, and Mason slammed on the brakes. Shee slapped the dashboard to keep from breaking her nose.

"Will you cut that out?" she snapped.

"You've *talked* to her?"

"Who?" She knew the answer but felt she needed a few more seconds to get her thoughts together.

"Charlotte."

"Oh. Yes."

"When?"

"Last week," she mumbled.

"For the first time?"

She nodded. "Since that day at Grace's."

"What did she say?"

She shrugged. "Nothing. I mean—"

"She had *nothing* to say to the mother who abandoned her? Didn't try to kill you, for instance? Come to think of it—maybe *she's* the one who put a hit out on you."

Shee scowled. "Come on—"

The light changed, and Mason stomped on the gas, throwing Shee back against her seat.

She sighed. "She found some things at Estelle's house and came looking. But it was before I went to the hotel. I just sort of bumped into her while I was working on a case. I didn't tell her who I was. I think she still thinks I'm her aunt."

"Which means she doesn't know anything about me yet?"

"No. I mean, *yes*, she doesn't."

"You were working a case? You came back for that? Not to see your father?"

Shee chewed her lip. "I didn't know he—"

Mason held up a hand to silence her.

"All I know is, if Charlotte is well-adjusted, that makes *one* of you."

He fell silent again.

Shee's mood darkened. It felt like they were *talking* again for a little while. How could she explain to him why she hadn't come home sooner when she wasn't entirely sure herself? Why she'd made the decisions she did?

Maybe his silence was the best she could hope for.

You reap what you sow.

They drove in silence until Mason pulled into the driveway of the Loggerhead Inn. Bracco stood at the door as usual, like

Anubis guarding the tomb of her past life.

Mason parked and cut the engine, his gaze locked on Bracco. "I thought you told Angelina to get rid of him until you got back."

"I told her not to let him near Dad."

Shee opened her door and was about to exit when Mason touched her back.

"Hey—"

She turned.

"Slow down," he said, looking serious.

"What?"

"Slow *down*. You can't go running in there pointing fingers at everyone."

"The hell I can't."

"You can't base every move you make on some kid talking about an *islandy* accent."

She settled back into her seat and pulled the door closed. "It *has* to be her. The accent is too much of a coincidence."

"She's not the only Jamaican in the world."

"But—"

"And he's a *kid*. New at his job. It could have been a *Russian* accent, and he probably wouldn't know the difference."

She considered this. He had a point.

Mason continued. "Shee, *think*. If you go up there screaming for her to get out—"

"I'm not going to *scream*—"

"—she's going to know she's burned. You'll blow any chance we have of figuring out what's going on."

Shee looked at him. "We?"

He took a deep breath and released it. "I'm not going to leave you alone with all this."

Shee looked away, fighting back grateful tears.

"Thank you."

His voice grew soft. "You're welcome. It doesn't mean I don't want to choke you."

"Understood. You can choke me later." She wiped her eyes under the guise of wiping her brow. He'd cut the air, and the atmosphere in the cab grew thicker by the second.

"It's getting hot in here," she mumbled.

She dropped out of the truck and headed for the hotel, hearing Mason's trademark limp falling in line behind her.

Bracco moved from his spot at the door to the top of the stairs.

She stopped, staring up at him.

What is this?

"Shee," he said. His expression belied the strain it cost him to formulate the word. He put a closed fist over his heart. "M-M-*Mick.*"

Shee stared at him, unsure what to say. Tears gathered in the man's eyes. Already on the verge of crying herself, she felt her cheeks grow hot. She was one sentimental dog commercial away from dissolving into a permanent puddle.

"You love Mick?" she asked.

Bracco nodded so violently that Shee worried he'd shake his brain to jelly. He pointed at her, his lip quivering. "You."

This guy is killing me.

The waterworks pressed harder against Shee's eyes, and she pinched her expression to try and hold them back in her head. She barely knew the man, and she only wanted to hug him.

Screw it.

She threw her arms around his waist, and Bracco wrapped his meaty arms around her, squeezing her to him.

"You are a straight-up train wreck," she heard Mason mumble behind her.

She released Bracco and turned, sniffling. "Shut *up.*"

He held his palms up to her. "Just saying. Maybe we should go find Crazy-Eyes and come up with a plan."

"Crazy eyes?"

"Angelina's always got her eyeballs on me—"

"Ol' Crazy-Eyes is right here," said a voice behind the blubbering Bracco.

Bracco stepped aside to reveal Angelina standing behind the screen door.

Shee took the last step to the porch and entered the hotel. Archie bolted for Mason, butt waggling. From the crook of Angelina's arm, Harley yapped, furious about everything.

Shee dropped her bag to the ground. "Is Martisha upstairs?" she asked, squatting on the ground. She tried to sneak a hug from Archie, but in his unbridled joy, the dog refused to hold still long enough for her to get in a good one. She straightened.

"He's not a great therapy dog."

Angelina studied Shee's teary face with concern before her attention shot to Mason.

He shrugged. "Long day."

"I'm fine," said Shee wiping her cheeks dry. "Where's Martisha? We need to check on Mick."

Angelina's attention shifted to Mason.

"It's okay. He knows," said Shee.

"Really? Did we make that decision all on our own?" Angelina huffed. "She's still out. And, of course, I checked on Mick the second you called. He looks normal."

Shee nodded. "Good. We can't let her back in."

"No. It *had* to be her who called the detective. Too much of a coincidence," said Angelina.

Shee looked at Mason. "See?" She stuck out her tongue.

He rolled his eyes.

Harley continued her staccato bark at Archie as the furry mutt earned more attention from Mason.
Angelina put her hand over her dog's face to quiet her.

"The thing I don't understand... If Martisha wanted Mick dead, she could have killed him weeks ago."

"What do we know about her?" asked Shee.

Angelina shrugged. "Nothing. Mick had hired her to take care of the Captain."

"Who's the Captain?" asked Mason.

Shee rubbed her hand across her face.

I didn't tell him about burying the Captain...

She dismissed him with a wave. "No one important."

She refocused on Angelina. "I assume Martisha has an elevator key?"

"Of course."

"Can you re-key it?"

"I don't know."

"Find out. When she gets back, tell her I want to spend more time with Dad and give her a week off."

"Don't do it alone," said Mason.

Angelina shifted Harley to her other arm. "And what happens in a week?"

"We'll look into her. We'll give her another week off if we haven't cleared her in a week. We should change Dad's bedroom lock, too." She turned to Mason. "What do you know about changing locks?"

He crossed his arms against his chest. "It's mostly what I did in Iraq."

"Really?"

He smirked. "*No.* But it isn't rocket science."

CHAPTER THIRTY-NINE

Martisha sat in her car, watching her hand shake. She covered it with her opposite hand and kneaded the back of it.

She wasn't sure how much more she could take.

Miss Angelina was too smart. When Miss Angelina looked at her, it felt like the woman could see into her heart. All the people in the hotel were canny. They were killers, she was sure. If they found out what she was doing to Mister Mick...

What have I become?

Twenty-two years as a nurse, and now...

She swallowed and looked in the rearview at Bracco. He was standing at the door, watching her.

Me haffi move.

It made her smile to hear her mother's voice in her head. Her mother had moved her to the States as a child. She had no real Jamaican accent of her own left, but she'd been channeling her mother's much heavier patois since arriving at The Loggerhead. It kept people from starting conversations with her.

Another glance at Bracco. He seemed more on edge than usual.

Are they on to me?

The old Captain, her first patient at the Inn, had disappeared. No ambulance had come for him. What had they done with him? Were they having him autopsied?

She glanced at her watch, though it felt like checking a wall clock to see how much longer she had on her prison sentence.

The girl had come for her daddy. It was the girl he wanted. Maybe she wouldn't have to stay.

At least she wouldn't have to try and pry the girl's location out of Mister Mick anymore.

Martisha hung her head, using her thoughts to practice her accent before heading back inside.

Wha mek me did tell him?

Why had she told him about her children? He'd been so weak and sweet. She never dreamed he'd turn out to be such a monster.

She could feel the weight of Bracco's stare.

Me haffi move.

Martisha grabbed her purse and stepped out of her car. She felt light on her feet. She'd lost nearly twenty pounds since arriving at The Loggerhead. She found it hard to eat.

Suh stupid.

How could she have been so stupid? She'd let him get into her head. Ruined by greed. She'd never be a real nurse again. She'd end up in jail.

Bracco's watchfulness draped like chains on her body. She wanted to scream.

Martisha unlocked the car again. She sat inside and opened the glove compartment to retrieve her gun, an old snub-nosed thirty-eight, a gift from her brother. Slipping it in to her bag, she locked the door once more and started toward the hotel.

"Gud afternoon, Mister Bracco," she said, nodding at the big man.

He nodded in return. He didn't talk. Something was wrong with the man's brain. She'd overheard a little gibberish between him and Miss Angelina and guessed he had some sort of aphasia. She could help him with that, but she never offered—too dangerous to spend more time with him.

It made her sad.

Was it her imagination, or was he looking at her differently today?

No. No. Stop.

She couldn't let herself panic. Not here. She had to get to Mister Mick's room, and maybe she could take a minute to come up with an escape plan just in case—

"Martisha, there you are."

Miss Angelina met her just inside the door, looking happy and calm.

Very calm.

She's hiding sup'm.

The new dog ran toward her, and she took a step back.

"Don't be afraid. He's sweet," said Angelina as her rat of a dog barked from its place on the desk.

The new dog stared up at her with one brown eye and one blue, *still,* as if he were considering what to do with her.

Martisha swallowed.

He sees the real me with that blue eye.

"Martisha?"

Martisha pulled her attention from the dog and looked at Miss Angelina.

"Hm?"

She scanned the room.

Nothing felt right.

The girl, Croix, stood behind the reception desk, staring at *her* instead of her phone. The new man with the blond goatee, the one they called William, appeared from the hall and took a place in front of the elevator, crossing his hands in front of him. He leveled his gaze on her.

The woman spoke, but Martisha only heard a smattering of words. Something about Mister Mick's girl wanting to spend time with him. Something about how they didn't need her for a while. Fear gripped Martisha's chest as if Miss Angelina had reached through her ribs and snatched away her breath.

They're firing me.

She couldn't look at the man in front of the elevator. He wouldn't let her upstairs. She knew that. She glanced behind her. Bracco had turned, his attention locked on her.

He's going to grab me.

"Are you okay?"

Miss Angelina was talking again.

"Yeah, yeah. I—bathroom," Martisha pointed down the hall.

Her accent had disappeared. Her mother's voice had left her head.

Come back, Mama.

She tried again.

"Mi guh—" The words caught in her throat.

Best not to talk at all.

Her mother had taken back her voice to punish her wicked daughter.

They know. They know.

She'd disappear like Captain Rupert. Her kids would never know what happened to her.

"Um..."

Angelina didn't look happy about her bathroom plans, but Martisha moved past her. She couldn't go out the front door. Bracco would grab her. She gave the man guarding the elevator a wide berth, nearly missing the hallway and walking directly into the wall.

She slipped into the bathroom and leaned against the door, breathing heavily but feeling as if no oxygen had entered her lungs. Her hand slid into her purse, and she felt the gun.

She could tell them it wasn't her fault. That he'd made her do it—

They won't care.

Even if she reached the front door, she'd never get to her car before Bracco stopped her. Or William shot her. Or Beatriz—that little woman might be the scariest of all. Where was she?

Hiding? Waiting for her?

The back. The boats.

If she could sneak out the back... They left the keys in the hotel's runabouts.

Martisha cracked open the bathroom door far enough to peer down the hall. She saw the back of Angelina's heel. She was still out there but turned away.

She slipped out and crept through the back door, careful to close the screen without letting it bang. She eased down the stairs, holding her breath.

Once on the ground, she ran for the boats with her purse clutched against her chest.

CHAPTER FORTY

With Angelina and Shee beside him, Mason stared at Mick's doorknob. Angelina handed him a new lock sealed in plastic, and he took it, happy to have a project. It would keep his mind off Shee's bombshells for five minutes. Keep him from *killing* her.

"Think you can swap it out?" Shee asked.

He nodded. "Yes, but I need tools. I'm retired Navy, not Swiss Army."

Shee chuckled and turned to Angelina. "Where do you keep tools?"

Angelina's mouth hooked to the left. "I generally marry them."

"I mean, like, *screwdrivers*."

"Oh." Angelina hit the elevator call button. "There's some downstairs. I'll get them."

The silver doors opened, and Mason found himself alone with Shee in the hall. She stared at him, and he sensed her brain searching for words.

"I don't want to talk about anything right now. Just the current mission," he said.

She nodded and chewed on her lip. After a moment, she perked.

"You want to see Mick?" she asked.

He nodded. "Sure."

Shee pushed through Mick's unlocked door and led him inside. The main area of Mick's apartment looked like a typical living room but smelled like a hospital. The smell only grew stronger as they entered Mick's bedroom.

Mason had to keep himself from gasping out loud. It had been years since he'd seen Mick, but the man in the bed looked nothing like the one he remembered. Pale, thin, his cheeks sunken...

Mason hung his fingers on the silver roll guards, watching his old leader's chest rise and fall beneath a thin blanket.

"I'm having trouble reconciling this man with the one I remember," he said.

"Tell me about it," mumbled Shee.

"What's the prognosis?"

"Angelina said his doctor said he *should* be awake."

"Shouldn't he be in a hospital?"

She shrugged. "Mick's guy is pretty high up the food chain. And if he was in a hospital—"

"The world would know he's alive."

"Exactly."

She motioned to Mick's head as her phone rang. "The gunshot wound is on the other side—"

She stepped aside to answer, and he rounded the bed to see where the sniper had left his mark.

"Where? Okay. We'll be right down," said Shee into her phone.

"What is it?" asked Mason, staring at Mick's scar. It made him smile—the first evidence that the man in the bed *was* Mick McQueen.

Leave it to Mick to survive a gunshot to the head.

Shee tucked her phone into her pocket and headed for the door. "Martisha's downstairs. We should go down."

Mason patted Mick on the arm and followed Shee into the hall. Before they could recall the elevator, a low rumbling filled the air.

"What's that?" asked Shee.

Mason cocked his head. "Sounds like a boat?"

Shee moved to the window overlooking the back of the hotel. Her jaw fell slack.

"It's Martisha."

Mason joined her at the window. Below, a heavyset black woman in nurse scrubs tossed the lines of a Boston Whaler Montauk to the pier. He recalled admiring the little boat the day before. Another identical craft remained tied to the opposite side of the pier.

"She looks in a hurry."

"I think she's running." Shee flung open the door to the stairs and started down.

Mason started after her and then stopped at the top of the stairs.

Shit.

He hadn't mastered *stairs* with the new leg.

Deciding it would be faster, he returned to the hall to find the elevator doors sliding shut. He threw his arm out to block them from closing and hopped inside, slapping at the ground floor button.

"Come on, come on, come on..."

By the time the elevator spat him out and he pushed through the hotel's back door, Shee had dropped into the remaining Boston Whaler. Croix, Angelina, and Bracco stood on the pier.

He moved as fast as he could as Shee barked orders at the others.

"Stay here. Lock the place down. I want men on doors front and back."

Mason pushed past Bracco, whose bulk practically blocked the entire pier.

"I'm coming," he said, eyeing the ladder. He couldn't circumvent it the way he had the stairs.

"I'm starting to think the world wasn't made for a one-legged man," he grumbled.

"What?" asked Shee.

"Nothing." He made his way down, using his upper body strength to do most of the work, before dropping himself into the boat.

Shee started the engine.

"Let me drive," he said, moving to the center console and hipping her out of the way.

Shee glared at him, unsure.

"Boats are kind of my thing," he added.

She relented.

"Good point."

CHAPTER FORTY-ONE

Mason slammed the boat into reverse as Shee threw out a hand to catch her balance against the bench seating. She braced as Mason maneuvered back and shifted forward.

Martisha's craft had already disappeared around the river's bend.

"We're going to lose her," Shee screamed over the engine's roar.

"Not many places for her to go."

Shee found her sea legs, the wind whipping her hair behind her like a flag. She was thrilled Mason had made it to the boat. He looked at home behind the wheel. Unlike him, boats weren't *her thing.*

They passed a small fishing craft. Shee turned to see its operator shaking a fist at them as they passed.

"I think we're going too fast," she said.

Mason maneuvered around a larger boat, sending docked crafts rocking in their slips. "She isn't following the speed limit."

Shee spotted Martisha's boat, wondering what they'd do if they caught her. As far as she knew, the woman hadn't done anything except tend to her father. An *islandy* accent on the opposite side of a phone wouldn't hold up in court. Only the nurse's panicked escape helped to confirm their suspicion she was somehow involved in *something*.

An idea occurred to her. There was *one* thing they could prove.

They could have her arrested for stealing the boat.

Shee squatted in front of the console and tapped Mason's leg to get him to move out of the way. She hit metal.

Whoops.

Somehow, he still recognized her request and shifted to the right, enabling her to open the compartment beneath the steering wheel.

"What are you doing?" he asked as she rooted.

"Looking for a gun."

"You think they keep guns in the guest boats?"

She shut the compartment and stood. "It's Florida. Worth a shot. You don't have a gun, do you?"

"Sure, it's taped between my butt cheeks if you want to grab it."

Shee sighed. They maybe should have taken a second to grab weapons.

"She's headed for open water." Mason jerked the wheel right to point toward Jupiter Inlet, the treacherous stretch of water leading to the ocean.

"Are those whitecaps?" Shee pointed at rows of churning white lines in the distance.

Mason nodded. "She might wreck the boat getting through there."

"*We* might wreck ours getting through there."

He seemed unconcerned.

Mason whipped around a large sightseeing boat pulling from a pier. Shee grabbed the windshield to keep from being thrown off the side.

Martisha's boat hit the whitecaps, and the gap between them closed.

Shee held her breath, watching Martisha's small craft bob and dip. A moment later, the nurse successfully cleared the churning inlet and streaked to the right, heading south down the coast.

Damn.

Mason used one hand to push her back onto the bench. "Hold on."

He dropped their speed and hit the first wave at an angle, the boat rolling so hard to the right Shee feared it might flip. Her fingers strained to keep a grip on the underside of the seat.

She remembered why she never spent a lot of time on boats.

Mason motored away from the rocks. In the park at the edge of the inlet, she spotted onlookers pointing, no doubt wondering who the crazy people broaching the inlet in tiny boats were.

Another rolling wave slammed into the side of the boat, and Mason fought through it, righting the craft and moving into the open ocean. Compared to the protected waters of the Intracoastal Waterway, the wind and chop increased here tenfold. Shee's ears whistled no matter which way she turned her head. Her hair whirled like a storm.

"Where is she *going*?" she asked aloud, knowing the chances Mason could hear her were slim.

Does the woman have an escape plan? Or has she simply panicked?

Shee heard a *pop!* loud enough to surmount the thunder of their roaring engine. Martisha had turned toward them, one hand on the wheel and one pointed in their direction.

Shee squinted.

"Is she *shooting* at us?"

She stood. Another crack rang out, and Mason dropped the boat's speed. The shift in momentum, combined with Shee's rise from the bench, tossed her forward like a ragdoll.

Her fingers found no purchase grappling along the smooth sides of the console. Shee turned her head a second before smashing her face into the windshield, striking her temple above the hairline. The metal bit into her scalp. Her rib cracked against the port railing as she spun to the left. Her feet arched above her head.

She tumbled into the water.

The roar of the wind stopped.

Shee smiled.

The quiet was *lovely*.

Something whizzed by her like a little bottle rocket.

Neat.

But—

Why is it so cold?

She opened her eyes to find her hands floating above her, backlit by sunlight.

That's weird...

Her chin dropped as movement caught her attention.

Three small sea turtles hovered before her, floating like babies in embryonic fluid. She reached to touch them.

So beautiful...

A shaft of light illuminated their adorable black eyes, their tiny fins pumping through the water.

Look at how they swim...I want to swim...

Something caught in her hair, jerking her backward.

No!

Before she could escape, something clasped her upper arm, yanking her from her turtle friends.

They blinked at her, drifting farther away.

No, wait—

A fire lit in her lungs.

Oh my God. I can't breathe. I can't—

The wind returned, roaring in her ears. She gasped for breath. Soothing oxygen filled her lungs.

"Grab the boat!"

It was Mason's voice, demanding her attention. He slipped a hand beneath her armpit and hauled her into the Whaler like a landed tuna.

He hovered above her, and his expression twisted with concern.

"What happened?" she asked.

She liked it on the floor of the boat. The wind couldn't get to her, and the engine had stopped.

"Are you okay? Your head's bleeding."

She stared into his face, trying to piece together what had brought her to this place.

"Did you see the baby turtles?" she asked.

He shook his head. Instead of being enchanted, he seemed even more concerned.

He would have liked them if he'd seen them.

"They were so cute—"

"You hit your head."

His fingers moved through her hair as if he were searching for nits. He touched something sore, and she jerked away.

"Ow."

"You're cut. You might need a stitch or two."

She closed her eyes. "They just want to go home."

"Who?"

"The loggerheads."

Mason helped her sit up. He lifted the seat cushion and rummaged in a locker to retrieve a small white towel. He handed it to her.

"Press this against your head. Stay down here. Do *not* get up."

She took the towel as he started the engine.

"They just wanted to go home," she mumbled again, pressing the towel against the bit that hurt.

CHAPTER FORTY-TWO

Tyler rolled past The Loggerhead Inn in his rented dark red Hyundai sedan, noting the cars in the hotel's parking lot.

Looks like it's still in business—

He dropped his speed another notch.

Hold on. That's the couple's truck.

He squinted, straining to catch the license plate on the back of the black Ford F150.

What are the chances?

He was ninety percent positive the woman he spotted in the airport was half the couple he'd seen entering Viggo's place. His distant vantage point hadn't provided him with much detail, but the puffy navy vest and the long dark ponytail tracked.

When the big guy joined her in the boarding line, he knew it was them.

He'd followed them off the plane to the parking garage and watched as they fought with some guy in a sedan. The big guy roughed him up. He didn't know what all that was about. He hadn't felt comfortable getting close enough to hear every word. But when they finished with the schmuck in the car, they got into a black F150 and left. Tyler had noted the license plate and then rented his vehicle, thinking he'd probably never see them again.

And now, the truck was here, of all places, parked at The Loggerhead.

Could they be my competition? Is a new hit team tracing Shea McQueen's whereabouts the same as me?

Hiding in Viggo's bathroom, he hadn't heard the whole conversation between the woman and the old giant, but her tone had rung sad at times.

Could she be related to Shea?

The name *McQueen* had been itching his brain since he'd found the framed news clipping. At first, he'd chalked the familiarity to the famous actor Steve McQueen—

Wait—crap—

Tyler snapped from his thoughts to jerk his steering wheel left and make a U-turn at the end of the cul-de-sac. He'd nearly taken out a mailbox.

Jeeze, Tyler, pay attention.

He pulled to the side of the one-way street beside a tree-heavy empty lot and parked the car.

McQueen.

I remember now.

There'd been a contract on a *McQueen* years ago. A woman with a strange first name he couldn't recall. He'd put a little time into tracking her while freelancing, working toward establishing his reputation. What he thought would be an easy gig wasn't. He'd discovered tracking wasn't his thing. He hooked up with Brett to get more steady work. No hunting. Just killing.

Could that McQueen still be alive? Could this be her?

Tyler smiled to himself.

This could end up being a twofer.

Tyler eyed the empty lot beside the hotel.

Hm.

He exited the car to scope what vantage point existed in the postage-stamp-sized forest beside the hotel. The underbrush grabbed at his clothing.

I hate nature.

Tyler silently thanked Minneapolis for being the sort of hellhole to inspire him to wear jeans. Without them, he would have passed out from lack of blood before he got halfway into the forest.

The lot ended at a shallow beach, flanking a slow-moving river. To the left, the hotel's pier jutted into the water. Large Tuscan-style mansions lined the opposite bank.

He glanced upriver.

The smart way to show up might be by kayak.

He ducked back into the forest; thoughts lost in planning.

"Hey there."

Tyler's head jerked up. A bleach-blond man with a matching goatee stood between him and his vehicle, standing with hands on hips.

"Hey," said Tyler, a smile leaping to his lips.

Shit.

"This is private property," said the man.

"Is it?" Tyler looked around as if he were confused. "I'm sorry, man. I've been looking for a lot like this, and I thought maybe there was a *for-sale* sign on the riverside."

Good one. Nice.

The man shook his head. "Nope. Not for sale. Property of The Loggerhead." Blondie motioned to the hotel.

"Oh, gotcha. No problem, man."

"Everything okay, William?"

A woman dressed in housekeeping togs appeared at the boundary between the hotel and the forest.

Tyler's brow knitted even as his smile remained steady.

What's up with this place? Two staff on my ass that fast?

"We're all good," said the blond man, holding up a hand.

"I was just leaving," added Tyler, tromping toward his car.

His cheeks ached from smiling.

CHAPTER FORTY-THREE

"She shot at us. Shee fell and hit her head." Mason screamed his message into Shee's phone. He didn't dare slow the boat, but making himself heard over the engine was like trying to have a conversation in a wind tunnel. "She might need stitches."

Feeling he'd relayed the necessary information, Mason hung up, his nerves still jangling. When Shee hit the water—

There'd been a time he could have scooped her in his arms and *swum* her back to the hotel. He'd suffered a split second of piercing doubt when she fell, questioning if he could haul her back into the boat.

He'd never second-guessed himself in a moment of crisis before.

He didn't like it.

He'd pulled her out of the water. Soon, he'd have to get her out of the boat. New prosthetics and pier ladders weren't a marriage made in heaven.

He glanced down at Shee. She sat on the deck, her hand gripping the bench seating like he'd instructed her to do. Her eyes were open, and she seemed okay, but he didn't trust her to climb the ladder to the pier on her own. She'd been woozy when he plucked her from the sea—seemed more interested in talking to sea turtles than him. The white fishing rag in her hand had turned pink with a mixture of blood and seawater.

Roaring toward The Loggerhead's dock, Mason spotted Angelina, Bracco, and a dark-haired, spectacled man he didn't recognize, waiting.

His shoulders relaxed a notch.

The cavalry has gathered.

He dropped speed and slid the Whaler into its spot, sidling up to the ladder.

"Is she okay?" asked Angelina.

Mason leaned down and hefted Shee in his arms, taking an extra moment to be sure his leg didn't betray him.

"Put me down. I can *walk*," protested Shee.

She seemed a little more like herself now.

First-class pain in the ass.

"Just let us help you," he mumbled, pushing her onto the ladder. She gripped the rungs.

Crouching, Bracco grabbed her wrists to lift her to the pier.

"I can climb—"

She couldn't finish her sentence before Bracco collected her into *his* arms and carried her to the grass. The stranger followed and dropped to his knee beside her as Bracco lowered her to the ground.

"Put me *down*," she demanded.

"She's shot?" asked Angelina.

Mason scowled. "What? *No*."

No wonder Angelina looked so panicked.

He climbed out of the boat. "I said we were shot *at*. She hit her head and fell into the water." He thrust his chin in Shee's direction and increased his volume to be sure she could hear him. "Because she didn't stay seated like I *told* her to."

"That doesn't sound like her at *all*," said Angelina, looking relieved.

Shee glared at him. "You drive like a *lunatic*. You could have given me a heads up before you slammed on the brakes— *Ow*."

The man Mason didn't know inspected Shee's cut, and she jerked her head away from him.

"Don't *touch* it. I'm *fine*."

"He's Mick's doctor. Let him look and stop being such a baby," scolded Angelina.

Glowering, Shee submitted.

Mason swallowed a smile and jerked his attention from her.

"We're going to need more security," he said to Angelina.

"Yep. Already on it. Pulling staff from other duties."

Standing at Angelina's side, Bracco nodded.

The doctor straightened and offered his diagnosis. "Couple of stitches wouldn't hurt."

Shee grimaced. "Since when?"

Angelina motioned from Bracco to Shee. "Bring her inside."

"Whoa, whoa, whoa." Shee wobbled to her feet like a newborn calf. "I can *walk*."

She tilted to her right, and Bracco stepped forward to serve as a wall where she could steady herself.

"Thank you," she mumbled before squinting at the stranger.

The doctor held out his hand. "Hi. I'll be the one stitching your scalp back together. Cough, Retired Naval Surgeon."

Shee shook it. "Cough?"

He smiled. "Like *turn your head and...* Your dad gave me that nickname."

Shee glanced at Mason. "Sounds like Dad."

She smiled as if to assure him she was all right, and he offered a tight smile in return.

"Well, let's not operate on the lawn. We'll scare the guests," said Angelina, heading back up the path to the hotel.

Bracco walked beside Shee as they followed Angelina.

Mason lengthened his stride to catch up with them.

"You're feeling okay? Not hallucinating about sea turtles anymore?" he asked.

She side-eyed him, still holding the towel to her head with the arm not gripping Bracco's.

"I *did* see turtles."

"Sure."

She sighed, her face pointed toward the ground in front of her. "And I'm fine. Except I can feel my heartbeat in my scalp. I don't think that's normal." She looked at him. "She got away."

He nodded. "We'll find her."

She paused, and he stopped to meet her gaze.

"Thanks for saving my life if I didn't say it earlier," she said.

He shrugged. "I figured Mick would be pissed if I left you out there."

She chuckled and mounted the stairs.

Angelina held open the door and led Shee and Cough to her room to use it as an operating theatre.

Mason lowered himself onto the leather sofa in the lobby to wait.

A fiftyish-year-old man with a goatee and a middle-aged woman in a housekeeping uniform entered through the front door. The man eyed Mason and then turned to Croix.

"Where's Angelina?"

Croix pointed down the hall. "She's with Shee and Doc Cough—"

Angelina appeared where Croix pointed, scowling when she spotted the blond.

"What's up, William?" she asked.

"There was a guy in the woods."

Mason looked up. "Doing what?"

William scowled at him.

Angelina motioned to Mason. "It's okay. He's Shee's, uh...*friend*."

William directed his answer toward Angelina. "He said he was looking to buy a lot."

"Any reason to be worried?"

William shrugged. "Rental car. Didn't look like a guy who

could afford it, but who can tell nowadays?"

"I got his plate," said the housekeeper.

Mason studied the housekeeper with new eyes. Her squat, taut frame, her thick neck, the way she held herself... If she spent half her day cleaning rooms, it looked like she dedicated the other half to training for the local Ultimate Fighting Championship.

Angelina nodded. "You two come with me. We're going to mix things up a bit."

Angelina motioned for Bracco to join her, and the four moved into the breakfast room.

Mason turned his attention to Croix typing on her laptop at the reception desk.

"You're not part of the defense meeting?" he asked.

Croix's gaze didn't rise from the screen. "I'm doing more right now than they'll do all night."

"Yeah?"

"Yeah."

"Care to share?"

Croix huffed. "I'm *tech*. I run the cameras. I helped Mick set up the security system."

"Ah." Mason tapped his knee with his finger. All the extra walking had his stump aching. "What does your tech tell you about Martisha?"

She grunted. "Not much."

Mason chewed on the inside of his cheek, thinking. "I can tell you she didn't seem very *nurse-like* shooting at us."

Croix shrugged. "So weird. She always seemed so nice."

"Could she have set Mick up? Could she have wanted to be *his* nurse?"

Croix put her elbows on the counter and plopped her chin into her hands. "Like she hired someone to shoot him in the head but not kill him? Hoping we'd move her from Captain to Mick? That's crazy."

"How did Captain die?"

Croix's eyes widened. "He died after Mick showed up. Right when we were thinking about getting a second nurse... I wonder if—" She straightened. "We're going to have to dig him up again."

Mason scowled. *"Again?"*

Croix nodded. "We buried him with his wife the other night. Your girlfriend helped."

"My—" Mason gritted his teeth. "Funny, she didn't mention that."

Croix ignored him, still seemingly lost in her thoughts. "Thing I can't figure out is, why didn't she kill him weeks ago if that was her plan?" She slapped the counter. "We should check her room."

Mason stood. "Yep."

She squinted at him as she rounded the desk. "I meant *me*."

He followed her. "Many hands lighten the load."

"Many—?" She hit the elevator button and turned to face him. "Where do you old people get all these goofy phrases? Do you just buy them online, in bulk?"

"Mail order." He offered her a double-dimple grin, trying to look as harmless as possible. "Come on. Let me come with you. We'll make a game out of it."

Her rapier stare jerked back toward him as if he'd used a fish lure to hook it.

"What kind of game?" she asked.

The doors opened, and she stepped inside. Mason followed. She didn't stop him.

"The person who finds evidence first wins. Seasoned professional versus a snot-nosed kid."

Croix stared at him as if weighing the pros and cons of letting him to the upper level. He'd forgotten the key wasn't *being allowed on the elevator.* The key was the *key.*

Mason folded his hands in front of him and stared forward, chuckling.

"What's so funny?" she asked.

"Nothing. It's just I'm going to *crush* you."

Croix fit the key hanging off the squiggly pink plastic bracelet on her wrist into the control panel.

Mason smiled.

When the doors opened, he followed Croix to the bedroom at the end of the hall, where she used a key card to enter Martisha's room. The open door revealed a sparse but not particularly neat room. Mason was intrigued to see the unmade bed. If the nurse asked housekeeping to skip her room, maybe she did have something to hide.

"Okay, here's how we're going to do it," said Mason, clapping his hands together. "You pick the spot you want to search, and then I do. First one to find something helpful wins."

"I can go first?"

He scoffed. "Of course. It wouldn't be fair otherwise."

She grinned. "Oh, you're going down, old man. *Closet.*"

"The whole closet? Jeeze, I should have been more specific." Mason crossed his arms against his chest.

Croix opened the closet door and searched every inch, knocking on the walls, shaking out dirty laundry, and feeling inside pockets and shoes before tossing cleared items to one side. She dragged a chair from its table by the window and stood on it to check the upper shelf.

"Dammit," he heard her mutter.

"Looks like you struck out," said Mason.

She returned the chair to its place. "How can there be nothing in a whole closet?"

"Too obvious," said Mason, pretending to yawn.

She frowned. "Maybe."

"Rookie mistake."

"Shut up. Your turn."

He scanned the room. "I'll take the bed."

"Ha!" Croix pointed. "You could have had the dresser."

Mason ignored her and patted each pillow on the queen bed. He lifted the mattress to peer beneath it. He lowered himself to his knees to look underneath.

"Nothing but dust bunnies," he muttered.

Croix grinned. "I call dresser."

Mason used the bed to pull himself back to his feet as Croix rummaged through the dresser's drawers.

"Jeeze, you could wait until I said I was done," he said, peering over her shoulder.

That's weird.

Something about Martisha's underwear drawer looked different from its opposite mate. The stain at the bottom of the drawer was a darker shade of brown. He looked away so she wouldn't notice his interest.

Finding nothing, Croix closed the last drawer and turned, her gaze settling on the side tables flanking the bed.

"You only get one side table," she said.

"What? Side tables are a *pair*."

"Nope. Which do you want?"

He pointed behind her. "I pick the bureau."

Croix's jaw dropped. "But I just did that."

He slipped past her to open the underwear drawer with the darker bottom. Sliding it from its frame, he dumped the contents to the ground. As he turned it sideways, something *thunked*.

"What was *that*?" Croix tried to snatch the drawer, and they jerked it back and forth.

"*My* drawer," said Mason.

"The bureau was *mine*."

"Until you were done."

"I never actually said I was *done*."

"Ooh, you're such a cheater. How can you sleep at night, girl?"

Croix giggled as the door to the room swung open, and Shee appeared, her hair a dark explosion bunched around the white bandage stuck to her head.

"What are you two doing?" she asked.

She looked annoyed.

"We're checking Martisha's room," said Croix, breathless from their struggle over the drawer.

Mason released, and the girl stumbled back onto the bed, starting her laughter anew. She knocked on the bottom of the drawer.

It sounded hollow.

She glanced at Mason, smirking.

"Hey, now. That's *my* find," he said.

"Nope. *My* dresser."

She flipped the drawer and pushed against the bottom until it slid away to reveal a hidden compartment and, in it, a cell phone.

"False bottom," she said, looking at Mason. "How'd you know?"

He thrust his hands into his pockets. "Um, I'm *awesome*?"

"Don't touch it," said Shee, pointing at the cell. "We might need prints."

"They're probably all over her underwear," said Mason, pointing to the pile on the floor.

Croix tittered.

Shee's expression suffered an extra twist of lemon. "Can you hack the phone?"

Croix shook her head. "No, but I know someone who maybe could. I can lift prints, though; want me to do that?"

Mason pinched a pair of granny underwear and dangled it near Croix's face. Snorting a laugh, she knocked it away.

"*Ew.* Cut it out."

Shee jerked a t-shirt from an open bureau drawer and handed it to the girl. "Take the phone downstairs. See what you can do."

Croix wrapped her hand in the tee and picked up the phone.

Mason took a step forward to block the girl's path, bumping her as she tried to leave.

"Oh, excuse me. I didn't see you," he said.

"You're an idiot," she said, snickering.

Croix left, and Mason looked at Shee to find her scowling at him.

"Head hurt?" he asked.

"It's fine. He numbed it."

"For a couple of stitches? What a *wuss*." He thought his expression made it clear he was teasing her, but she continued to frown at him.

"Why are you looking at me like that?" he asked.

She nodded toward the open door. "What did you do to her?"

"Huh?"

"*Croix*. You two were laughing your asses off when I came in here."

"So?"

"So she's been staring daggers at me since I darkened her door."

"You're jealous?" He shrugged, amused. "I guess I'm just charming."

Shee frowned more deeply as she reached to touch her dressing.

"Don't play with them."

"I'm *not*."

"I know they can itch—"

"They *don't*. The bandage is ripping out my hair."

She yawned.

"Tired?" he asked. "Maybe you should lie down?"

She thrust a hand into her pocket and pulled out a folded envelope, holding it up for him to see. "No time."

"What's that?"

"Angelina found Martisha's address *before* she moved into the hotel."

"I guess that's where we're headed?"

She nodded and headed into the hall. "Yep."

He followed.

"Hey," he said as they stood waiting for the elevator doors to open. "Tell me about the guy you buried the other night."

Shee's chin dropped to her chest.

"Shit."

CHAPTER FORTY-FOUR

Martisha saw the black pickup truck pull to the curb in front of her house. She recognized the big man at the steering wheel.

How did they find me so fast?

Didn't matter. Too late now.

"Mom?" said a voice on the phone at her ear. "Are you still there?"

She smiled. "I'm here. Gotta go. Me luv ya."

Her daughter finished with the family sign-off and hung up. They both knew when the other was too distracted to chat.

Martisha sighed. She shouldn't have packed. She should have grabbed her passport and run. But as she stuffed clothes into her overnight bag, she realized she *couldn't* run.

She couldn't pack her daughter and her family into her bag.

They'd still be out there.

He would come.

I'm so tired.

The couple dropped out of the truck and headed for her door.

Mister Mick's girl.

Martisha had seen her fall into the water. She thought she'd shot her, though she'd only been trying to scare them away.

She thought the darkness in her life had claimed another

victim.

But *no*. Shee's alive, walking to her door with the big man.

That's something.

She wondered if she could warn them.

No. Best not.

She didn't want to give that vengeful demon of a man any more reason to go after her daughter.

I'll snip my thread clean.

The couple mounted her front stairs. Mick's girl saw her through the big front window. They locked gazes, and Martisha tried to will all the knowledge in her head into the girl's brain as she raised her gun.

I'm sorry.

Shee grabbed the man's arm to warn him.

Martisha pressed the nose of the gun to the soft flesh beneath her jaw and pulled the trigger.

CHAPTER FORTY-FIVE

Now I understand why they had me pop the old man in Minneapolis.

Tyler spat on the ground and peered through his rifle sight again. He couldn't shake the feeling The Loggerhead Inn was more than it seemed.

First, it sat nestled at the end of a one-way road, surrounded by water and nature preserves. If you were on the Inn's street, you were there for the hotel or the smattering of private houses.

Excellent defensive position.

For that reason, he'd decided to paddleboard to the clump of trees west of the hotel. He didn't want the staff to spot him again. Didn't want some army of housekeepers showing up.

On the upside, he felt even more confident that Shea "Mick" McQueen had holed up in the hotel.

He peered through the scope again. The barrel-chested doorman remained at his post.

The couple from the airport had left in the Ford F150. After watching the man rough up the guy in the parking garage, it had buoyed Tyler to see him *leave*.

He chewed on his options.

Maybe I'll just storm the place.

Mr. and Mrs. America would probably return. His odds might be better without them around.

But the damn cameras.

Red and green glowing eyes peeked from every crevice of the building.

And if that wasn't bad enough, the housekeeper he'd met earlier guarded the west perimeter.

Who asks their housekeepers to march back and forth outside?

Tyler lowered the scope and stared at the dirt.

Do they know I'm coming?

The place seemed on high alert. *Weird.* The client knew how to reach *him*—called him directly. *Weird.* The girl holed up with McQueen might be another old target. *Weird.*

His leg growing stiff, Tyler shifted, reconsidering the entire operation.

Everything about this job feels—

A twig snapped as he moved, and Tyler winced more out of habit than concern. The noise had been barely audible—

The housekeeper stopped her marching and turned toward the clump of trees.

Tyler froze.

You've got to be kidding me.

She remained still, head cocked.

What is she? Half bat? Some kind of Terminator robot?

Tyler glanced at his feet and looked up again. That quick. The time it took for his heart to beat.

The housekeeper was gone.

What the—

He raised the scope to his eye and leveled the crosshairs on the doorman. He still stood like an overfed statue. No one had alerted him. The little woman hadn't moved to the porch.

The patch of trees around Tyler felt darker. He glanced toward the edge of land flanking the Intercoastal Waterway where he'd landed his paddleboard.

At least delay...

He could push his plane ticket home a few more days. Give himself more time to run recon on Hotel Fort Knox.

Tyler straightened to full height and secured his rifle on his back. He didn't like moving without knowing where that crazy maid went but—

"Ow!"

Something bit his arm. Sharp pain exploded from shoulder to wrist. He slapped at the spot with his opposite hand, fingers touching metal. He whimpered as the object protruding from his flesh shifted.

Sonuva—

Tyler rolled behind a tree and heard another object strike the trunk behind him.

What the hell?

A throwing knife.

Possessing no knife-tossing talent of his own, he refrained a moment from removing the weapon. Peering around the tree, he spotted a small figure tucked behind another trunk fifteen feet from where he stood.

Even in the dim light, he recognized the outfit.

The housekeeper.

It had to be.

The sun took its last gasping breath and dipped below the horizon. Tyler slid his night vision monocular from his belt and scanned the trees.

The housekeeper had disappeared again.

Is she some kind of knife-throwing ghost?

Tyler pulled his silenced .22 Ruger from his waistline. Even silenced, it would be loud enough to catch the big guy's attention at the front door, but dropping the housekeeper would buy him time to paddleboard the hell out. *If he could paddle with the wound, which, if he took the knife out, would probably leave him bleeding like a stuck pig.*

I'd leave a trail. They'd know I came by water, so I couldn't do it again...maybe I should make a false trail...

Tyler caught a flash of movement in the trees. A crop of goosebumps ran along his arm.

This bitch is crazy...

He crouched, leveling his gun at what he felt certain was a *knee* poking from behind a tree.

He didn't want to waste noise on such an uncertain shot, but—

"Beatriz?"

The voice came from Tyler's left.

Shit. More of them.

He flicked his attention in that direction. The goateed man who'd confronted him earlier appeared at the forest's edge, backlit by the glow of the hotel's porch lights.

The woman spoke, her voice closer than Tyler ever imagined she could be.

"William, take cover—"

Tyler's attention returned to the tree he'd been watching. The housekeeper bounced from her cover, three trees closer to him.

It's now or never.

He squeezed his trigger.

The woman yelped and dropped.

Gunfire popped to his left, and Tyler rolled behind his tree, putting it between him and the man.

Great. This one has a gun.

The big guy would no doubt join in soon. They'd made enough noise to wake the whole neighborhood.

Tyler glanced in the direction of the water.

I have to make it to the paddleboard.

He could be halfway down the river before the blond with the gun figured him out.

Tyler glanced at the still body of the housekeeper, feeling confident he'd hit her in the chest, solid.

This was his chance.

Run.

Tyler sent a smattering of shots in William's direction and bolted for the water. Crashing through the tangle of underbrush like a panicked deer, he ignored the sting of the thorny weeds tearing at his legs. He stumbled. Something tightened around his ankle. It felt as though someone had *lassoed* his feet.

No—

Falling like a felled tree, he jerked his leg against the restraint and felt it snap...

Not a rope.

The vine tore away in time for him to find his feet. He was moving again.

He spotted the blue paddleboard as another pop of gunfire exploded behind him.

Too late, sucker—

Something struck his neck.

Tyler stopped. He raised his hand, fingers crawling across his collarbone.

Oh.

He inhaled. Air stuck in his throat. He tried again. Something bubbled and coughed like a coffee maker at the end of its brew cycle.

I'm drowning.

Tyler looked at the paddleboard, surprised to find he hadn't fallen in the water beside it.

But the water...?

His fingers felt a familiar shape protruding from his throat.

Metal.

He turned and shot as he fell to one knee.

Tyler jerked the knife from his throat. He gulped air.

Heaven.

Feeling renewed, he took another breath.

Nothing.

He was drowning again.

Tyler poked at the wound in his throat. He tried to stretch it open, searching for a way to clear his pipe for air.

Darkness bled from the edges of his eyes, closing in. He reached for the silver throwing knife on the ground before him.

Maybe I can cut a new hole—

The darkness closed in. The knife disappeared.

Blind, his fingers scrabbled across the earth, searching for the blade.

His face hit the mud.

CHAPTER FORTY-SIX

"Get back!"

Mason wrestled Shee from Martisha's front step as she struggled against him. She gripped the handrail.

"She shot *herself*!"

Mason eased but refused to release her. "What?"

She pushed him to arm's length, panting. "Martisha shot herself. No one's shooting at *us*."

"You saw?"

She nodded and pointed to the window where she'd been standing. Mason climbed the stairs and peered through. Shee slipped her hand past him to try the knob.

It turned. She pushed the door wide.

"Judas Priest," muttered Mason, his gaze rising to the mess of blood and grey matter on the ceiling above the woman on the sofa.

"Get inside before the neighbors see," said Shee, entering. He followed, and she shut the door.

"Give me a second to clear the house," said Mason.

He moved from room to room as Shee walked to the back of the sofa, ignoring his orders. If someone was in the house, she figured the gunshot would have brought them running.

The ragged-edged hole in the top of Martisha's skull left little room for interpretation.

"Definitely dead," she said as Mason returned.

He grimaced. "Hard to miss at that range."

Shee put her hands on her hips, her gaze sweeping the small cottage. The air smelled stale, as if the house had been sealed for some time. A thick coat of dust covered every surface.

"There's got to be something here. Something she came back for."

Mason nodded to Martisha. "I think we're looking at what she came back for."

Shee wandered into the bedroom, finding it crammed with oversized furniture. The woman had lived at the Loggerhead long enough that most of her clothing had migrated there.

Draping a shirt over her hand, she opened drawers, finding them, like the closet, largely empty. She found a brown file box on the floor of the closet and flipped through tabs with titles like "paystubs" and "taxes."

One of the 1099s from three years earlier caught her eye.

Mason walked into the bedroom as she stood, still scanning the document in her hand.

"She used to work at the Navy Consolidated Brig, Chesapeake," she said.

"As a nurse?"

"I guess so. Doesn't say."

"Does that mean something to you?"

She shook her head. "No. But it's interesting."

"Is it? Doesn't your dad have a habit of hiring vets? Maybe she's a vet, too."

"True." She folded the document and slipped it into her pocket. "Nothing out there?"

He shook his head. "Nothing except a dead woman. We should go."

"Leaving the scene of a death. We have to stop meeting like this." Shee pulled open the bedside table drawer and pushed around the contents. She plucked out a rolled piece of lined paper and unraveled it to reveal a pencil sketch of a middle-aged man with a goatee. Mangled holes edged the top as if it had been ripped from a larger notebook, and the ragged bottom implied the torn sheet had once been larger.

"That looks like William," said Mason.

"Who?"

"William. He works at the hotel. You haven't met him?"

Shee pushed the drawer shut with her thigh. "No. Great. I haven't even won Croix over yet, and now there are more people to meet."

"Maybe Martisha had a crush on him."

"Is he handsome?"

"Not my type."

Shee shrugged. "Either way, maybe he knows something. Let's go."

They returned to Mason's truck, Shee grateful the fallen night would cloak their exit. The last thing she needed was for neighbors to identify the truck to the cops when the body was found.

Shee's phone rang, and she glanced at the caller ID.

Angelina.

She answered. "We're on our way back—"

"Beatriz is dead," said Angelina. "We need you here. *Now.*"

CHAPTER FORTY-SEVEN

By the time Shee and Mason returned to the hotel, two bodies had been laid on a plastic paint drop cloth, side by side, on the king bed of Captain Rupert's old room.

Shee stared at the woman who'd been making her bed only a day before. Beatriz's long, honey-brown hair had been neatly displayed over each shoulder, partially covering the bloodstain on her shirt.

Shee motioned to the male body beside the housekeeper.

"Who's this?"

Angelina stood with her hand over her mouth as if it were the only thing keeping her from screaming. Her mascara pooled beneath her eyes. No attempt had been made to fix it.

She lowered her hand and licked her lips. "No idea—other than he killed Beatriz."

"She got him first?" asked Mason.

Angelina nodded and motioned to the man's neck.

Shee moved to get a better view of the wound. The stranger's skin appeared ashen, his camo gear covered in darkening blood. She spotted the tear in his neck the moment she rounded the bed. Her eyes widened. It looked as though an animal had tried to chew off his head.

"My God, what did she do to him?"

"Throwing knife. William thinks he was digging at the

wound, trying to breathe."

"William? He found them? Where is he?"

"He found them in the woods next door. He's checking for more now."

Shee pulled the small rolled sketch from her pocket.

"Is this him? We found it at Martisha's." She unrolled it for Angelina to see.

Angelina squinted at the sketch. "That's one of the Captain's."

"Mason thinks it looks like William."

"It does. You haven't met him?"

Shee set the picture on top of a corner bookshelf, and it rolled itself tight like a threatened armadillo. "Do you trust him?"

"He came with a personal invite from Mick. He tried to save Beatriz..." Angelina motioned to the bodies. Her head tilted.

"What is it?"

"I don't know. Captain liked copying his drawings out of books. I don't remember him ever doing a live portrait."

She opened a drawer in a small bureau against the wall to retrieve a pad of paper. The sheets were the same as William's portrait, boasting a similar tight crosshatching style. She flipped through a few pages, unveiling people and landscape sketches.

"Any idea why Martisha took this one? It was on her bedside table like it meant something to her."

Angelina ran her knuckle under her eye, but the mascara had re-dried, and she did little to erase her raccoon mask. "Maybe he gave it to her as a gift? She *was* his nurse. I guess she wasn't there to ask?"

"She was there," mumbled Shee.

"So you *did* talk to her?"

"She shot herself before we could."

Angelina gasped. "You found her dead?"

"Something like that." Shee's lips pressed into a tight knot.

Cough walked in, frowning at the bodies.

"Is that Beatriz?"

Angelina nodded.

He clucked his tongue. "I'm sorry to see that."

"I should head outside. Maybe get a bead on William," said Mason.

Shee looked at him and sighed, certain this had to be the worst vacation Mason had ever taken. "This isn't your war."

"It is now," he said without looking at her. Instead, he locked on Angelina. "Where's Archie?"

"The dogs are in my room. It's unlocked if you want to let him out. Down the hall, last door on the left—"

He shook his head. "He's safer there for now, if you don't mind."

Angelina shrugged and shook her head.

Mason turned and headed toward the lobby.

"Be careful," Shee called after him. She cringed. "I sound like his mom," she muttered, lowering herself into the cushioned chair in the corner of the room. She dropped her head into her hands. Her head throbbed in time with her heartbeat. Fatigue poked at her muscles and hung from her eyelids like monkeys, dragging them down.

She leaned back to address Angelina as the doctor inspected the stiffening remains.

"So we know whoever is after Dad, they're sending more people. They know he's alive."

Angelina nodded. "No doubt, thanks to Martisha. They could know almost anything."

Shee looked at Cough. "How's Mick?"

His attention pulled to the horrific wound on the stranger's neck, so the doctor was slow to answer. "Um...oh. He's fine. I changed out his IV. His medical cabinet was locked, but I had a spare. I'll give you guys a crash course on what to do until you can hire a new nurse."

Angelina shook her head. "How can I bring someone else into this death trap? I need you to stick around."

Cough turned, eyebrows lifted. "Because it's okay for *me* to stay in the deathtrap?"

"Just a couple of days? Until we figure things out?" Angelina took his hand and held it to her chest. "Please? For me?"

Cough glanced at Shee, his cheeks coloring.

"Fine." He pulled his hand back and returned his attention to the neck wound.

Angelina turned away and winked at Shee.

Shee smiled and stood. "Let's find out who this guy is, and then we have to find this William." She traded places with Cough as the doctor rounded the bed to inspect Beatriz.

"It looks like he stole Batman's utility belt," said Angelina, motioning to the collection of gadgets strapped around the dead stranger's middle.

Shee rifled through his pockets until she found a small, black leather wallet. Flipping it open, she pulled out a license.

"Roger Cooper," she read. Behind it sat another—the same man in the photo, different name. Shee frowned, imagining someone rummaging through her things post-mortem.

This feels familiar.

"He's got a second license. *Tyler Vale.* Both with Miami addresses. Either ring any bells?"

Angelina shook her head.

Shee tossed the wallet on the stranger's chest, noticing a folded paper tucked in his belt. She slipped it out and unwrapped it, catching a glimpse of a familiar newspaper clipping before it fluttered to the ground. A piece of Loggerhead stationery remained in her hand.

"That's the clipping we saw at Viggo's," she said, pointing as Angelina stooped to retrieve it. "It was missing when we went back."

"What's in your hand?"

Shee scanned the sheet. "It's a letter from Dad to Viggo, asking him to come here."

Angelina peered over her shoulder. "One of Mick's invites. It's how he builds his army of do-gooders."

"You mean his *Navy* of do-gooders."

"Beatriz was Army."

Shee grunted. "Oh. I didn't know Dad had gotten so *liberal* in his old age." Her gaze dropped to the bookshelf tucked in the corner. A tall, leather-bound book sat shuffled with others, unremarkable, but her skin still crawled at the sight of it.

Why does that look so familiar?

"Where's the other shooter?" asked Cough. He had his black bag open on the bed and stood with a pair of long tweezers in his hand. The tongs clamped on what looked like a crushed bullet.

Shee eased past Angelina, heading for the bookshelf.

"Hm?" She heard Angelina ask as she slid the red book from the shelf.

"Beatriz took one in the chest. Not enough to kill her, necessarily," said Cough.

"There's a second in her head," said Angelina.

"I saw that. The problem is, what blew out the back of her skull isn't the same thing I just pulled out of her chest."

Shee held the red book in her hands, staring at the cover. Her limbs felt cold.

"Where did he get this?" she asked.

"What?" Angelina sounded annoyed. "I can't talk to both of you at the same—"

Shee held up the tome. "It's a Naval Academy Lucky Bag Yearbook."

"So?"

"I need to know how it got here. It's *mine*."

"Oh excuse *me*." Angelina rolled her eyes. "I don't know. Your father probably gave it to him." She turned back to Cough and then, scowling, bounced back to Shee.

"Wait—you didn't go to the Naval Academy."

Shee flipped through the book, feeling as if her fingers knew where to go. The tome fell open to the spot she'd been seeking.

A tucked piece of torn sketch paper marked the page.

"It was research." Shee pointed to the photo of a brown-haired young man in a plebe first class uniform.

"You two are missing the importance of what I'm saying here," said Cough, still standing with the bullet in his tongs.

Shee plucked out the page marker. At first, she'd assumed it was her marker from long ago, but the lined paper was too familiar. She flipped it over to find a pencil sketch of the plebe she'd identified.

No.

Shee dropped the book into the cushioned chair and snatched Captain's portrait of William from the top of the bookshelf. Unfurling it, she raised the sketch of the plebe to the bottom.

The tear fit perfectly.

"Look." Shee held up the sheets so Angelina could see. "They're the same person."

"But that's William. And that's—" Angelina's gaze dropped to the opened yearbook on the chair.
She gaped. "You're saying William is—"

"Ladies!" Cough barked the word, shaking the bullet in his tongs. "Someone *else* killed Beatriz. The second shot is a different caliber."

Angelina blanched. "William found her."

Shee tossed the sketches on Tyler Vale's shins as she turned for the door.

"Mason's out looking for him."

CHAPTER FORTY-EIGHT

Two Years Ago

Scotty Carson sat in the hard wooden chair as the Master-at-Arms chained his wrists to the interview table. A familiar man sat on the opposite side of the desk, though Scotty couldn't place him. He wore civilian clothing, but his posture and choice of haircut smacked of the military. Retired, Scotty guessed, considering he appeared to be in his late sixties or early seventies.

"Who are you?" he asked.

The stranger stared at him as if he could set him ablaze with his eyes. "You're supposed to get out soon. I'm not going to let that happen."

Scotty forced a smile. "Oh yeah? Why's that?"

The stranger sniffed. "Because you killed my daughter."

Scotty looked away to hide the ripple of concern he felt running like seismic activity beneath his expression.

Is that where I know this guy from?

It didn't make sense. The high school slut's dad was a skinny guy with glasses. An accountant or lawyer or something. Scotty pictured him at the funeral—the funeral *he'd* attended as her grieving ex-boyfriend. It still gave him shivers of joy remembering all those mourning people and him, smack in the middle of the crowd, the only person who knew what happened to her.

He closed his eyes and fought his way from his daydream.

Stop it. Pay attention.

This man wasn't *her* father.

Are they trying to pin another murder on me?

Scotty returned his attention to his visitor and repeated the phrase he'd said many times before—at his trial and parole review boards…

"I never killed *anyone*."

The man pulled a photo from the chest pocket of his linen short-sleeve shirt, slapped it to the table, and slid it forward. "You killed that girl. We proved that. But you killed my daughter, too, same as if you pulled the trigger."

Scotty glanced down at the mugshot of his first cellmate, Jugger.

Wait.

That's who this is? But if his daughter is dead—

Nothing made any sense.

Jugger had been dead for years. He'd promised to be his right hand, and he'd failed. After Jugger, he'd hired one assassin after another. He'd spent over ten years hunting her, the one who rallied the whores from the Academy to claim rape, the one who pointed the police toward his missing ex-girlfriend. Orchestrating a hit from prison wasn't easy. Finding Siofra McQueen proved even harder.

Is this *her* father?

Is the old man saying she's dead?

Scotty leaned as far back in his chair as he could, his wrists chained to the table.

"I don't know what you're talking about."

The iron-haired man shifted in his chair. He seemed agitated, as if he were straining against invisible bindings. Scotty felt confident those hidden ropes kept the old man from pouncing on him like a tiger.

"I was there. Remember? I put the cuffs on you, you piece of shit. Name's Mick McQueen."

Scotty pictured the dark-haired girl in the honky-tonk and the man in the booth she'd pretended to struggle against. The man's image remained fuzzy. He'd only had eyes for Shee.

Mick continued. "You had your ex-cellmate try to kill my daughter. He missed."

I'm aware.

"He hit my other daughter."

Laughter exploded from Scotty as if he'd been holding it back since his incarceration, spittle atomizing into a cloud around him. A drop landed on his accuser's chin, and the man's scowl pinched deeper. He didn't wipe it away. He just *glared*.

"You're kidding?" Scotty glanced at the camera in the corner of the room. "I mean, not that *I* hired anyone, but that is some shitty luck, my friend."

A tornado of emotions gyrated inside Scotty. He'd thought for a moment the daughter that *should* be dead was. That didn't fit his new plan. He'd spent the last year thinking about her—not just fantasizing about what he'd like to do to her, but *planning*. He'd be out soon. He'd hire someone to find her, but *he'd* be the one to finish her.

He'd be the one to make sure she suffered for ruining his life.

Just a little longer.

Getting things done right when he was free would be a lot easier.

He smiled, anticipating the release of it.

She'd be older now, but he bet she still looked pretty good. He'd work her until she felt his whole damn prison sentence.

Mick McQueen stood, his fists squeezed tight at his sides. His movement snapped Scotty from his thoughts. It looked as though the guy might pounce on him, after all.

The old man ran his tongue over his front teeth. "Look for me at your parole hearing."

Scotty smirked, but his stomach soured.

Could this guy cause trouble? He knows about Jugger. Does he have proof, though? What else does he know?

This couldn't happen now. Not when he was so close to getting out.

Scotty lolled in his chair. "That it?"

"That's it. I just wanted to see your face. Make sure I was right. I am." Mick moved to the exit. Scotty waited for the sound of the door opening, but it didn't come. Instead, the man spoke again.

"Hey, Scotty, you like your new spot?"

Scotty twisted in his seat. He'd been recently transferred from Chesapeake to the Jacksonville, Florida brig.

He'd wondered why.

"Are you making friends?" asked McQueen.

Scotty scowled. He *wasn't* making friends. He'd already narrowly avoided an attack, and he'd only been there two days.

"No?" the man continued. "That's too bad. I guess you shouldn't have raped all those little girls."

Scotty sat up. "I never—"

A cold sweat beaded across the back of his neck.

Oh no.

That's what the other inmates had said to him. Something about him and little girls. At the time, he thought they'd been referring to the *women* he'd raped. But now—

McQueen shook his head, somehow looking regretful and *giddy* at the same time. "Shame how rumors get started. *Nobody* likes kiddie predators."

Scotty jerked on his chains. "I'm going to *kill* you."

"See you at your parole hearing." McQueen grinned and knocked on the door to be let out. "If you live that long."

Scotty's eyes fluttered open, the light above him blinding.

Someone gasped. He turned toward the noise. A dark-skinned woman peered over him, and her expression was broad with what looked like shock.

"You're awake," she said.

He licked his dry lips and chewed his tongue, trying to work up the spit to swallow.

"Where am I?" he asked, his voice barely above a whisper.

"You're in the brig's medical ward."

Scotty looked around the tiny room and tried to remember what had happened. Faces danced in his memory. *Angry* faces. A group of inmates, punching him, slamming his head into the cement floor...

"How long have I been out?" he asked.

"Almost a month."

A month? But I was two weeks away from—

He grabbed the woman's hand. "My parole—"

She patted his arm and smiled. She had kind eyes. *Dumb* eyes.

"I was just now getting you ready to go home," she said.

"I got it? I'm out?"

"I don't—" Her brow knit. "I heard your father made a case for taking you home. I don't know about parole."

Scotty nodded. During his run for senator, his father had distanced himself from his black sheep son.

Looked like the old man had finally come through for him.

The nurse held up a finger. "Hold tight. I have to get the doctor."

"Wait," Scotty clamped on her wrist to keep her from moving. "*Don't.* You can't. They might not let me go."

"But—"

Scotty's mind raced. He had to do something *quick*. He lowered his voice. "Listen. I'm *rich*. My family has *tons* of money. I'll make it worth your effort."

The woman bit her lip and looked at the door.

She's thinking about it.

She pulled against him a little. He held tight.

"You can't fake a vegetative state," she said.

"I won't have to fake it for long."

"But you *can't*—"

He snarled. "Then put me *back*."

Her eyes flashed white, and she pulled from his hold.

He closed his eyes and shook his head. "I'm so sorry. I didn't mean to scare you. This is all so confusing." He took a deep breath, thinking about flies and honey. "Please help me."

She chewed the inside of her cheek.

He bulldozed on.

"I'll pay off your house. Put your kids through college—you have any kids?"

She didn't answer, but he could see by her expression she did.

"Son?" He paused, seeing no reaction. "Daughter?"

Her cheek twitched.

There it is.

She remained silent.

"I'll hire you as my private nurse on a yearly salary, and you won't have to do a thing. We're talking life-changing money."

Her jaw creaked open. She looked terrified. She didn't like his proposal, but she couldn't seem to say *no*.

Just another little push. I need to give her a reason to do it beyond money.

"*Please*. If they throw me out there again, they'll kill me."

"Who? Why?"

Scotty grimaced, stalling for time to think. "Do you know why I'm here in the first place?"

She shook her head.

Excellent.

"I'm innocent. I know everyone says that, but I've been in jail for *decades* on a trumped-up charge because of what I know." He glanced at the open door and lowered his voice. "The man who put me here is trying to kill me."

The nurse stared at him with rapt attention. "Why?"

Remember, she has a daughter.

"Because he killed a girl, and I know it. If I get out, I'm going to prove it."

She gasped and raised her hand to cover her mouth.

Scotty clasped his own hands together as if he were about to pray. "If you help me get out of here, you'll be helping to put away a very bad man. Who knows who you'll be saving from him..."

"I *could* induce a coma..." The nurse's eyes drifted as she retreated into her thoughts. "I'd have to see if they have what I need—"

Scotty tilted his brows like an opening bridge, forcing his lower lip to tremble. Working up real tears seemed beyond his abilities, but he added a quiver to his voice. "You're an *angel*. A godsend." He reached out, and she gave him her hand. He clasped it gently between his own two hands. "What's your name, sweetheart?"

She smiled, her expression softening further. "Martisha."

CHAPTER FORTY-NINE

Shee ran into the lobby and headed for the front door. The elevator opened when she passed it as if it was motion-activated. Croix stepped out.

"What's going on?"

"I need a gun. *Now*." Shee threw out a palm as if the girl could manifest a weapon and drop it into her hand.

Croix brushed past her to get to the reception desk. Shee fell into line behind her, until the girl dropped to a squat behind the counter. Shee had to stop short to keep from falling over her.

"Where were you?" Shee asked.

"Angelina has me watching Mick, but I think he—"

"Don't let William anywhere up there."

"Why?" Croix slid two books from the shelf in front of her. Shee heard something click.

"Remember that story about my first capture? Scotty Carson?"

"Yeah?"

"I think we just figured out William *is* Scotty."

"What? That's *crazy*."

Croix looked as animated as Shee had ever seen the girl. It was almost as if she'd finally said something worthy of Croix's consideration. She felt honored.

The girl jerked on the bookshelf, and it slid away, revealing a lighted panel. Handguns hung from the blue felt-covered wall inside, several large knives interspersed to break up the monotony of the firearms. A row of grenades lined a low shelf-like portly armored soldiers awaiting their orders.

"What, no rocket launcher?" asked Shee.

"I think that's out in the shed." Croix waved her hand like a game show hostess. "Take your pick." She pulled open a drawer. Inside, clips and boxes of bullets sat neatly organized.

Shee leaned to snatch a Glock 19 9mm from the wall. By the time she straightened, Angelina had appeared breathless on the opposite side of the counter.

"What are you still doing here?" she asked.

"Needed weapons." Shee dipped to grab another. "One for Mason." Croix handed her two clips of bullets, and she shoved one in each pistol.

Stuffing one gun in her waistband, she moved for the door. "If you see William, don't let him know we're on to him, but protect yourselves. Don't let *anyone* upstairs." She paused, hand on the door. "Here's a thought. Are there *guests* here?"

Angelina shook her head. "No."

"*Yes,*" correct Croix. "Mr. Burrows in three-thirty-six refused to leave. I tried to—"

Angelina put her hands on either side of her head. "Croix—"

"I don't have time for this," said Shee. "Figure it out. I have to go warn Mason."

She pushed through the front door and then paused, realizing the door usually opened before she could touch it.

Where's Bracco?

Shee jogged to the end of the porch, crouching before peering around the corner. Bracco and Mason stood beside each other ten feet away as if talking.

She scanned the area.

No sign of Scotty.

She ran down the stairs to join them.

"Hey," she said, slapping on a frozen smile as she approached, in case Scotty was watching.

"Hey," said Mason. His brow knit. "What's wrong? You look crazy."

"We have a problem," she said, clenched teeth bared like a jackal.

"Inside? Out here, too. Bracco thinks he saw someone in the woods. We shouldn't stay here, exposed."

Mason turned toward the front of the hotel as Bracco and Shee followed. Shee tried to scan the woods without appearing to stare, but she didn't see anything. The hotel floodlights spilled as far as the trees but dissipated into the darkness beyond the frontline of leafy sentries.

"Could it be William? Do you know where he is?" Shee looked at the doorman. He shrugged.

"Why are you thinking *William*?" asked Mason without turning. "Because of the drawing?"

"We found the other half. William isn't William."

Mason's head swiveled. "What?"

"He's a guy I sent to jail twenty-five years ago. Scotty Carson. Rapist. Murderer. Beatriz has two different rounds in her. One from the dead guy—"

"And you think the other one's from him?"

"Makes sense. He found them. He could have been working with the dead guy and killed Beatriz when he had the chance."

"You're *sure* he's Scotty?"

Shee shrugged. "Maybe that's why Captain had to die. I haven't seen Scotty. I think he's been avoiding me on purpose."

"If Martisha was working with him, why would she keep evidence like that?"

Shee considered this. "Leverage? In case he double-crossed her? That sociopath can only pretend to be human for so long."

Mason mounted the stairs to the front porch. "You think he shot your dad?"

Shee gasped and gripped the stair railing as the world

around her spun on its axis. She'd been concentrating so hard on connecting William and Scotty, wrestling with guilt that Scotty had come for her and killed Beatriz instead, that she'd forgotten to tie everything to her father.

Mason turned and stared down at her.

"Are you okay?"

"He didn't get to Martisha *after* my father was shot. *He* shot him to draw me out." She remained white-knuckled as the pieces fell into place like a game of Tetris in her mind.

"You think—"

She looked up at Mason. "*He's* the one who's been trying to kill me all these years."

Shee's chest tightened. She turned to head back down the stairs, feeling as if a bomb had detonated in her brain.

Mason grabbed her shoulder.

"Where are you going?"

"I'm going to kill him."

"Shee, stop."

She jerked free only to have him capture her a second time.

"*Shee.*"

She spun to face him. "What?"

"Take a breath. We have to be smart about this. There are other people in danger here."

She shook her head. "We have to find him. *Now.*"

"I agree. But he's already come with one soldier. He had Martisha under your noses for months. Who's to say what he has planned? We could take him out right now and still end up with an army at the hotel."

Shee dropped her face into her hands and screamed, vibrating with frustration.

Mason continued. "If Bracco saw what he thinks he saw, there's someone in the woods. Maybe Scotty, maybe more assassins."

"And?"

"And, if we head toward those trees looking for him, he'll

see us coming from a mile away."

Shee hated Mason sounding so *reasonable*. All she wanted to do was run around the hotel, shooting like a video game character, until Scotty had so much lead in him he was declared a health hazard.

Mason continued, oblivious to the first-person shooter game playing in her head. "First, we have to lock the place down." He put out his hand. "Go inside. Give me your gun."

She obeyed. He seemed pleased with her response until she pulled the second weapon from behind her back. His shoulders slumped.

"I meant give me *all* of them. You go inside."

She loaded one in the chamber. "Not a chance."

"Shee, let me handle this. A trained SEAL against some guy who spent the last twenty-five years in prison? He doesn't stand a chance."

"He has two legs."

Mason scowled. "My missing leg doesn't level that particular playing field."

She looked at Bracco. "You have a gun?"

Bracco pulled up his shirt to reveal a Glock identical to her own.

"Good. Go inside and secure the place. Watch over Mick. Shut off the lights, indoors and out."

She took a quick breath hoping the momentary pause wouldn't give Mason a moment to butt in.

"They won't see us crossing the lot in the dark," she continued. "Here's a fun fact. No moon tonight, and Jupiter Beach restricts lights to keep the nesting turtles' lunar navigation on track. It's dark as a witch's armpit tonight."

Bracco put a hand on Shee's arm, his lips moving as he strained to find his words.

"Safe," he said.

She nodded, and he lumbered inside.

Mason hung his head. "Please go inside with him."

"Not a chance."

"You know we can't just march into the woods and shoot him, right?"

"No?"

"*No.* We're in *America.* Not a movie."

She shrugged. "Accidents happen."

He walked down the last step to join her on the ground. "Look, if you go inside—"

She grabbed his shirt with the hand not holding her gun. Curling her fingers into a fist, she pulled his face toward hers.

"Mason, I'll shoot *you* before I let you do this without me."

She released him.

He leaned back. "Hm. That would be the one thing you *haven't* done to me yet."

The hotel's lights shut off, plunging them into darkness.

Mason's fingers gently gripped Shee's jaw, holding her still as his lips brushed hers. He pressed, lingering there for a moment before pulling away.

"Thank you," she whispered. She wasn't sure why.

"You're insane," he said. His left hand slid down her arm to take her hand, his fingers entwining with hers.

"Let's roll."

CHAPTER FIFTY

With only the dimmest light glowing from the houses down the street, Shee and Mason sprinted across the short patch of grass to the adjacent woods. They secured a spot behind one of the larger trees, placing the trunk between themselves and the river several hundred yards away.

Shee slapped at her neck, using the tips of her fingers to avoid making noise.

"If Scotty doesn't get us, the no-see-ums will," she whispered to Mason. "All they'll find are our gnawed bones."

Mason cocked his head. *"Listen."*

Voices echoed from the opposite side of the forest, near the water. At least two. Maybe more.

"Not just Scotty," she said.

"No. Stay here. I'm going to move in."

He pecked her on her forehead and moved away, striding from tree to tree.

The spot where his lips touched her forehead warmed as if he'd branded her. She reached up to touch it.

Does that mean he forgives me?

The poisonous red fog enveloping her brain lifted. For a moment, he'd stunned the rage out of her.

Maybe that was the point.

She peered around the tree and caught a flash of

movement fifteen feet ahead. He'd gotten far, quietly, in a short time, with one good leg.

Almost like he does this for a living.

Tiptoeing her way in his wake, she squinted through the darkness, stepping over branches and other earthy bits she thought might be noisier than others, pleased with her stealthy approach.

She didn't reach the next tree before Mason's head swiveled, and he waved her back.

Shee tucked behind the tree.

So much for my career as a ninja.

The voices still chatted near the water's edge. Mason stood halfway between herself and them.

He might be close enough to hear them.

She moved to the next tree and then another. In her haste to get as close as possible before Mason caught her creeping again, she stepped on a twig.

It snapped.

She froze.

The voices stopped.

She'd been about to lean her shoulder against a tree before her misstep. At least she wasn't standing in the open. She held her breath.

The talking began again.

She released her air in a slow, steady stream.

"You *are* trying to get us killed," hissed a voice one tree to her left.

Mason had backtracked.

"Sorry," she whispered.

He moved to her tree, standing close to her, her back against the trunk.

"There's at least four of them. Looks like they're wearing body armor."

Shee frowned. Their clothes could stop bullets. Her attire couldn't even stop biting flies.

"I—" Mason raised his index finger to his lips. Shee had heard it, too. A sharp bark of noise, as if several voices had chanted a word in unison. She heard leaves crunching and swiveled her attention to the left to watch shadowy figures move toward the hotel.

She looked at Mason. She could tell he saw them, too. She slapped her pockets and groaned, realizing she'd left her phone in Mason's truck.

"Do you have your phone?" she asked. He shook his head.

"They left one behind," he said, motioning toward the water.

"They're headed to the hotel. I have to get back," said Shee.

He took her hand in his and held her gaze.

"Listen to me. They're going for the back. Go to the main entrance. Warn them. I'll be there in a second. I'm going to take out the straggler while the odds are in my favor."

She put a hand on his cheek and gave him a stare she hoped conveyed her thoughts.

If it's Scotty, and you kill him, I'll kill you.

The corner of his mouth curled into a smile, and she blinked.

Did he read my mind?

He pushed her toward the hotel, and she stumbled from behind the tree. Exposed, her options were to throw herself back at Mason or run for the hotel.

She ran.

CHAPTER FIFTY-ONE

The lights of The Loggerhead Inn went dark. All of them. The outdoor floodlights, the porch lights, the indoor lighting—even the landscape lighting blinked out.

Scotty Carson's mood also blackened from his spot in the small patch of forest beside the hotel.

They know something.

Scotty pulled on the vest brought to him by his team, eyeing the young men around him as they bounced from toe to toe, overcome by boundless energy. He expected a more seasoned group for the money he'd dropped on them. They looked as if they'd spent the afternoon in a frat house crushing beer cans on their heads. He had to remind himself he'd been that young once—younger even, at the Naval Academy—and he considered himself a *beast* then.

He'd laugh if the memory of his lost youth didn't make him feel so *murderous.*

He hadn't wanted to breach The Loggerhead this way, but everything was spinning out of control. That *stupid* P.I. was raising suspicions. Martisha was panicking. That big *friend* of Shee's showing up...

No surprise there.

Once a whore, always a whore.

But it had been the stranger in the woods that forced his

hand.

Who was that guy?

He'd hesitated to kill the stranger, thinking he might be part of his team arriving early.

That knife-throwing *trash* had noticed.

Hopefully, *that guy* was the reason the hotel had gone dark. There was no reason for them to suspect *him* yet.

Scotty pulled his work shirt on over his Kevlar. He still had the element of surprise but might not have it much longer. Not if they took a good look at Beatriz.

Scotty rubbed his eyes.

He planned to have his team enter the hotel and take Shee. He had a house rented and waiting out by Lake Okeechobee.

Remote.

It excited him just *thinking* about the fun they'd have there.

He'd done everything right. He thought Shee would come running as soon as she heard about her father. *Dead father* had been the original plan, but *dying* father worked just as well. It just meant more work for Martisha, keeping him quiet.

Who knew Shee hadn't been keeping in touch with the hotel? He and Martisha had tried to get her tough old man to reveal her location. Torturing a doped-up ex-soldier without leaving marks in the middle of the night in a hotel full of people hadn't been easy.

He'd almost given up hope when Shee arrived.

Then, somehow, everything had gotten *worse*.

Time to right the ship.

"Ready, sir?" asked the oldest team member. Traynor. Maybe thirty-two years old. He spoke the best English by far.

Scotty nodded. "Call me *Alpha Leader*."

Traynor nodded once. "Okay."

He sniffed. "Okay, team, we're going in. Everyone is expendable except Siofra McQueen. You all remember what she looks like?"

They nodded in unison.

"Give me an *affirmative, Alpha Leader*."

"Yes, Alpha Leader," they chimed. Scotty chalked their lackluster voices to stealth.

"Good." He pointed at the youngest face. "You stay here with the boat—"

Something snapped in the forest, and all heads turned. They froze, listening.

Nothing else moved.

Animal. Maybe.

Scotty pointed at the next soldier and lowered his voice another notch. "You—sweep the woods and then come meet us at the hotel. The rest of you, with me. We're going in the back."

He put out a hand.

"*Team*, on three."

They piled their paws on top of his.

"One, two, three—*team!*" They quietly chanted the final word with him.

With a final glance into the woods, Scotty used his index and middle fingers to point to the hotel and jogged his team toward the back entrance.

"Stay in formation behind me," he said over his shoulder.

He couldn't wipe the smile from his face.

"Ready or not, Shee, here I come."

CHAPTER FIFTY-TWO

Mason dashed toward the water, wobbled, and clipped a tree with his shoulder. He'd almost forgotten about his prosthetic. He grunted and put a Florida pine trunk between himself and the soldier at the water's edge.

Dammit.

So much for sneaking up like a SEAL. His attack needed more brain, less leg.

His stump throbbed. On the road with Archie, he'd ended his evenings early. By six p.m., they'd be holed up in a hotel, sharing takeout. He'd remove his cup and sock and let his residual limb rest.

But this day refused to end.

He peered around the tree. The soldier wore black, and his frame bulked with body armor.

Never a good sign when people show up at your door in body armor.

Average height, average size. Not good at his job if the sound of Mason slamming himself into a pine didn't catch his attention.

The soldier stared at The Loggerhead, his hands resting on the automatic rifle hanging around his neck, as Mason started his crawl forward again. It frustrated him to move so slowly. Old, one-hundred-percent-intact Mason could have sprinted and been on the scout in seconds. Nullified him. Moved to the next battle.

The battle about to erupt inside the Inn.

He needed to get to Shee and the others. Even if the hotel *was* staffed with retired military like Shee had said, they weren't prepared for an armed squad of—

A twig cracked beneath Mason's metal foot.

Shit.

He threw his back against a tree. He heard footsteps heading his way.

Here we go.

Crouching as best he could, Mason came out low and fired, aiming for center mass. He hit his target in the chest. A spray of bullets hit the trees above Mason's head as the man fell back.

The soldier's butt hit the ground as Mason moved forward, gun raised.

"Stay down," he said.

The young man lay on his back, struggling to breathe, fumbling with his rifle. The blow to the boy's chest armor knocked the wind out of him, and by the look of his panicked reaction, he hadn't been shot before. Mason guessed him to be in his early twenties.

Mason jerked the rifle off the boy, tossing it into the trees for later. An automatic weapon might come in handy. He plucked the kid's sidearm from his holster and tossed it into the river.

"What are you doing here? What's the plan?" he demanded.

The boy stared at him, his hand on his chest over what Mason guessed was a nasty bruise.

"How many of you are there?"

"*Дівчині. Нас десять.*"

Mason scowled. The kid didn't speak English. Ukrainian?

Mason kicked his foot. "Speak English."

"No English."

Great. If the kid was determined to play the *I no speak*

English game, he didn't have the time to change his mind. He needed to get to the hotel.

Mason moved toward the canoe resting on the shallow shoreline, his weapon still trained on the merc, hoping to find rope.

He noticed the Ukrainian's attention shifting past him a moment too late.

"Freeze," said a voice to his right.

Mason closed his eyes and silently swore.

He raised his hands.

"Don't shoot me," he said, trying to sound nervous. After all, he was just a guy in khakis and a polo shirt, out of his depth against trained soldiers.

"Drop the gun," said the second merc.

Mason turned to face his new foe. This one was older by ten years, his face ravaged by pockmarks. His accent suggested he, too, was Slavic. He wore the same black body armor but had no rifle. Mason guessed they'd left him on the far side of the lot to keep an eye out for nosey neighbors. He'd heard gunshots and come running. He pointed a nine-millimeter at Mason's face.

Mason held his weapon above his head. He waggled it, his eyes wide. "Hey, easy, man. I don't even know how to use this thing. Who are you guys?"

The kid on the ground said something, no doubt pointing out the American had known how to use his gun well enough to tag him in the chest.

Shut up, kid.

The new soldier barked something in Ukrainian, and the downed kid began clambering to his feet.

"Drop it," Pox said again, eying Mason's waggling gun. He took a step toward him.

Too close.

Mason smiled. "No problem. Sure, man."

He thought about how his leg would react and then tossed the gun toward the soldier like a spaz.

The guy's attention moved to the weapon. He couldn't *not* watch, as awkwardly as Mason had lobbed it to him.

Mason snatched the merc's gun from his hand. Clearly shocked, Pox lunged forward to retrieve his weapon, and Mason clocked him on the side of his head with the gun. The guy's knees buckled.

Mason felt pretty good about the entire exchange—until the bruised kid kicked out his leg.

Mason fell forward just as the second solder recovered from the blow to his noggin and straightened to full height. Mason tucked his head and slammed into him, using the man's body to catch his balance and drive Pox against a tree.

The soldier threw back a leg for leverage.

Showoff.

Pox swung his right, rabbit-punching Mason in the kidney. The air blasted out of him.

They wrestled for control of the gun. The soldier wrapped an arm around Mason's neck to put him in a headlock. Mason punched him in the stomach and then used both hands to keep the gun.

The kid moved in to help. Both soldiers worked at prying the gun from Mason's hand.

Fine. Nobody gets the gun.

With a roar, Mason twisted his arm free long enough to flick his wrist and toss the gun into the river.

The two men watched it fly. The pressure on Mason's body eased. Finding balance on his prosthesis, he kneed the smaller man in the crotch. The kid doubled over, and he kneed him again, this time in the face.

Pox hung on his shoulder. He felt the man's jaw against his collarbone.

At least I know where your nose is.

Mason back-punched him in the face, and the monkey on his back fell away. Attention still on the kid, he grabbed the top of his vest and jerked him up to plant his fist on his Ukrainian nose. He needed to nullify this one to concentrate on one foe at a time.

The young man's eyes rolled back into his head. Mason felt movement behind him. He spun, jerking the limp kid like a dancer swinging his partner.

Pox came knife-first, a large black combat blade.

Mason hefted the kid in front of him. Unable to stop, Pox fell into his partner.

The Kevlar couldn't help the kid this time.

Mason heard the first merc gasp from behind his human shield as the knife slipped through the vest fibers and penetrated his lower abdomen.

Pox's eyes widened. Mason reached around to chop at the hand holding the knife. He struck the wrist hard. Pox released the knife, leaving it in his partner, who raised his hands to it as he collapsed. Without Mason to hold him up, he fell face first.

He remained on the ground, still.

Mason took a step toward the other soldier.

"I don't have time for this."

The man took a fighting stance.

Come on...

They exchanged blows, a flurry of blocks and thrusts. Mason connected to the bridge of Pox's nose. Cartilage collapsed. A second later, the soldier's fist found his jaw. Mason felt his mandible shift uncomfortably to the right. Pox took the opportunity to kick. Mason blocked with his forearm. His leg faltered as his balance shifted.

Shit.

Mason felt as if he'd been attacked on two fronts, once by the soldier, once by his own body.

Let's even the playing field.

Mason blocked another kick and then dove forward, tackling the man to the ground.

They bounced, grappling, both rolling to gain the upper position. They hit the water. For a moment, Mason had top bunk—he pressed Pox's head into the water. Too shallow. All he did was soak the guy's hair. The soldier bucked, and they were rolling again, deeper into the river.

Weighed by his body armor, the man floundered. Mason took a breath and pulled him down. Beneath the water, they wrestled. Pox struck him in the head, tried to choke him, and strained against him to reach air. Mason took the blows and let him swing, using all his strength to hold him under.

The soldier stopped fighting. He pushed away, but Mason held tight, twisting in a death roll like an alligator.

Pox stopped thrashing just as Mason's lungs began to burn.

Apparently, the Ukrainian hadn't been drown-proofed.

CHAPTER FIFTY-THREE

'Alpha Leader' slapped Popov on his chest as they reached the top of the porch stairs.

"Stay here. Guard the back so we don't get flanked. Radio silence. I don't want them knowing we're coming."

Popov nodded and exchanged a glance with Rudenko on his left as he wrinkled his brow. His teammate's expression telegraphed that he'd had the same thought.

What an idiot.

Popov suppressed his bubbling laughter. How could he ensure they weren't *flanked* by guarding the *back*? And *radio silence?* The man spoke like a child playing soldier.

Who calls themselves Alpha leader, anyway?

He'd be worried if they hadn't been hired to attack a hotel.

Get in, get out, kidnap a woman. Easiest money we'll ever make.

He'd bet a hundred dollars the woman was the moron's ex-wife. Rudenko bet the woman was a cheating girlfriend. *Alpha Leader* told them a bullshit story about her being some 'bitter slut' who had tricked him into jail. He warned them the hotel was full of *trained assassins*. Popov and the team had laughed for *days* over the crazy rich man's fantasies.

Ah well. The crazy man paid well.

Popov slapped Rudenko on the back as his buddy and the

others entered the hotel.

Alpha Leader had a *key* to the back door.

That was a new one. *Handy.*

Strolling from one end of the porch to the other, Popov spun on his heel to squint into the darkness.

Something moved off the side of the hotel.

What the hell is that?

Over by a palm, it looked as though a very tall man beckoned to him.

Very tall.

Popov lifted his rifle and walked to the stairs. He peered into the night sky, cursing the lack of moon.

So damn dark.

Refocusing on the figure, he walked down the stairs to the grass.

No man could be that tall, but the *shape*...a head, outstretched arms...

He moved in. What looked like sticks protruded from the tall man's sleeves, and more poked from the neck of his dress shirt.

Popov chuckled, realizing his mistake. He lowered his rifle and released the breath he'd been holding.

A scarecrow.

He rotated to head back to the hotel.

Look at me. Jumpy outside a tourist hotel—

Movement flashed in his peripheral vision as he turned.

The scarecrow's right hand beckoned.

Popov spun back around, the smile fading from his lips as he slid his revolver from his holster. He turned his face to the left and right, eyes never leaving the scarecrow.

No breeze kissed his cheeks from any direction.

There was no wind.

Why was the scarecrow's hand moving?

He took a step toward the scarecrow. Clumps of plants gathered around the figure's feet. It looked like a garden...

This is crazy.

He stood two feet before the raggedy figure, staring up at the tilted hooded head. It smiled down at him with its painted U, black triangle eyes staring.

Popov shook his head.

I shouldn't have had that beer before we left.

He turned again, the gray image of the stuffed man still burning in his memory. Hay poked from its neck and sleeves, his burlap face and gloved hands. The hand that had moved— had it been holding something?

Something hard struck Popov's back. It felt as if a gorilla had pounced from a tree above him. A sharp pain exploded in his neck as he hit the ground. His wrist snapped against the uneven ground. He tried to catch himself as he fell.

Grass in his mouth, he flipped to his back and tried to scramble to his feet. His wrist screamed with pain. His arms felt too weak to push up. Collapsing back, he reached up and felt his throat. His gloved hand slid across his skin, lubricated by something.

He blinked, and the scarecrow stood over him, pruning shears in his hand. Popov recognized them now. His mother had a pair back in Kurhan, outside of Odessa. She loved to garden.

Popov reached for his gun but couldn't be sure his arms had even moved.

"Curiosity and the cat and all that nonsense," said the scarecrow as it wrestled with removing its head. British accent. The idea of a scarecrow with a British accent almost made Popov laugh. He felt giddy.

The burlap hood pulled away, revealing a red-haired man. The Brit grinned down at him, plucking the hay from his neck and sleeves.

"Now, time to see your friends."

The scarecrow took one step toward the hotel before a shot rang out.

The scarecrow crumpled at Popov's feet.

"Bugger."

Popov giggled.

Then everything went black.

CHAPTER FIFTY-FOUR

Shee reached the front door of the hotel and jerked open the screen. She wrapped her hand around the silver knob of a large wooden door she'd never seen closed before and turned.

It resisted.

Locked.

Shit.

Hands shaking with urgency, Shee studied the keypad lock above the knob. She thought about the postcard her father had sent her almost two years earlier. The one with the Loggerhead sea turtle on the front.

Stop by anytime, it said. *The key's enclosed.*

But, of course, nothing had been enclosed. It was a postcard.

There *had* been a strip of color blocks along the bottom, trimming the edge like a flattened rainbow.

That was what she pictured now, and her eyes squeezed tight.

Orange. Blue. Red. Red. Yellow. Purple.

She could see the boxes, colored in with permanent marker. She'd known then what it was. Her father knew about her synesthesia. He knew the colors of her days and the day that began the week in her mental calendar.

Orange. Thursday is orange and the fourth day of her week. *Four.*

Blue. Red. Red. Yellow. Purple.

Saturday. Monday. Monday. Tuesday. Friday.

She punched in the code.

Four. Six. One. One. Two. Five.

A green light blinked on.

She smiled.

Thanks, Dad.

The smile faded from her lips as she swung open the door to find two guns raised to greet her, a Glock and a shotgun.

She raised her hands. "It's me."

Bracco and Cough lowered their guns. Cough couldn't have looked more relieved if he'd just discovered a letter he thought was from the IRS was just a workplace OSHA poster.

"I'm going to destroy this place on TripAdvisor," said Shee, running a hand through her hair.

A radio clipped to Bracco's side crackled to life.

"Shee is at the front door. Let her in," said Croix's voice.

"Thanks, Croix, great timing," said Shee, locking the door behind her. "Where are they?"

"Angelina took Croix and the dogs to your father's room," said Cough.

Bracco pointed to the shuttered front window. Shee read the concern on his face.

"Mason stayed to take care of a guy in the woods. There are soldiers on their way—"

"Men at the kitchen door!" crackled Croix's voice.

Gunshots exploded in the distance.

Bracco turned toward the hall, his bulk blocking Shee as she tried to head that way. She bounced off his shoulder, spun, and came to a stop, pointing at Cough.

The doctor swallowed and tried to aim his weapon down the hall. His hands were shaking. Shee stepped forward to push the muzzle of the shotgun toward the floor for fear he'd aerate the retreating doorman.

"Are the stairs locked?" she asked.

Cough nodded. "Angelina gave me the key."

More gunfire. Different pitches, different weapons—it sounded as if a firefight had erupted. She could see Bracco still at the end of the hall, peeking into the kitchen.

The sweat on Cough's brow gave her pause. She guessed Angelina or Croix had chosen the shotgun for him *because* such a weapon made it difficult to *miss*, but the last thing she needed floating around the hotel was a jumpy man with a scattergun.

She motioned to the stairs. "*Go.* Lock the door behind you and guard the stairs. Don't let anyone up."

Cough thrust his hand into his pocket to retrieve the keys. He dropped them, stooped to pick them up, fumbled them a second time, and then tripped toward the stairs.

Shee ran down the hall after Bracco as the big man pushed through the kitchen's swinging door and fired.

CHAPTER FIFTY-FIVE

Scotty left a soldier to guard the back porch before opening the kitchen door with the key he'd made while at the hotel. He'd thought of everything.

Stepping back, he motioned his men ahead.

"Elevator and stairs are in the front lobby. Remember, *do not kill the woman*."

With a nod, his lead merc raised his gun and led the other three men inside as he held the door.

Scotty couldn't erase the grin on his face.

This is going to be a cakewalk.

He felt *powerful*. He'd walk through the hotel like a *god*, a true Alpha Leader, his team of assassins fanned in front of him, clearing the way.

Mick's gang of misfits had no idea what was about to hit them.

With two soldiers in front of him, Scotty stopped the third to take his place in line as they crept into the kitchen.

The gunfire started almost immediately.

Scotty turned to retreat, only to find the last soldier blocking his way. The merc put a hand on his shoulder and pushed Scotty down as he lowered to a squat.

The two front men sat on their heels. A man wearing what looked like striped pajamas popped up from behind the large granite island in the center of the room. Bullets sprayed in their direction.

Scotty raised his hands over his ears as the soldier behind him stood and fired. His head rang. The image of the shooter bouncing like a whack-a-mole flashed again in his brain.

The cook?

He hadn't talked to the cook much during his time at the hotel. The man seemed too fat to be a soldier. He certainly hadn't considered the possibility of tubby guarding the kitchen. Was he afraid they'd steal a steak on the way in?

The cook would slow them down and alert the rest of the hotel to their arrival. Scotty glanced at the black Luminox Navy SEAL Chronograph watch he'd bought especially for the mission. They needed to get moving. How many gunshots could ring out before the neighbors realized they weren't fireworks? *Even in Florida?*

Scotty gritted his teeth. "Kill him!" he barked. "What's taking so long?"

The front man rolled to the left and fired behind the island. Scotty heard a grunt.

No gunshots answered in turn.

Scotty nodded.

There. They just needed some direction.

He stood and clapped his hands together. "Okay, men, into the lobby."

He'd taken one step down the path between the island and the walk-in freezer before the door swung open, and a head popped in.

Bracco.

Scotty froze, realizing his mistake. He'd taken point. He raised his gun and released a wild shot. Bracco withdrew.

Scotty collapsed to his knees as Bracco's arm and weapon reappeared to fire twice. The bullets flew over Scotty's head. Air escaped the man behind him as one struck his chest.

Even hit, the merc returned fire over Scotty's head, and his ears rang anew. He clamped his hands on the sides of his head and swore.

Bracco ducked back into the hall. No doubt he'd be back.

Scotty's mind raced.

What am I doing?

Surely, Bracco had seen him on his knees. The next shot would be low.

I'm a sitting duck.

He stood and scrambled to push past the merc behind him.

"Go, go, get him!" he commanded, snarling. "Get out of my way!"

After the bullet's blow, the soldier was still winded, making it easy for Scotty to grab his vest by the armpits and spin him to the front of the line. The second soldier stared at Scotty, his hulking form blocking his escape.

"Get out of the—"

The second soldier raised his gun. Scotty thought he had a mutiny on his hands for a split second, but the guy fired past him.

Scotty threw himself flat against a wall of shelving. With his left hand, he pushed the lead soldier toward Bracco, and with the other, he jerked the walk-in freezer handle. Something wet sprayed the side of his face as he stumbled inside the metal box and shut the door.

Gunshots erupted again.

Scotty waited, panting. He touched his face. He could tell something slippery had splattered his cheek, even through his tactical gloves. Thankfully, the freezer was pitch black.

Footsteps shuffled outside. Scotty opened his eyes wide, trying to see.

Did Bracco see me slip in the freezer? Is there a back door out of here?

He reached out, feeling for an alternative escape hatch. His fingertips brushed shelves lined with what felt like frozen meat.

Gunfire again.

Scotty cocked his head.

Farther away. Out back?

Someone nearby made a strange, loud grunting noise.

"Okay, I got him—" said a female voice.

Scotty reasoned the grunting had to have been Bracco trying to communicate.

Big, brain-dead mother—

Footsteps again. More gunfire farther away to his left. It sounded as if the fight had moved to the yard.

"Where are you hit?" said the woman in the kitchen.

Scotty gasped.

Shee.

It had to be.

His men had fallen back. She was tending to the fallen cook.

This is my chance.

Scotty felt for the freezer's safety release and pulled it slowly, easing open the door. It wouldn't open further than the width of his head.

What the hell?

He saw a black boot on the floor. Bracco *had* shot his lead man. The soldier had collapsed in front of the freezer, his body wedged between the door and the island.

"Put pressure there. Good."

The woman was on the other side of the island.

Scotty took a deep breath.

Go out. Grab her. Take her out the front while the others are busy in the back.

Scotty pushed his head through, straining his shoulder against the door. His eyes adjusted to the dim light cast by the clock on the mounted microwave.

A face stared back at him.

Shee.

She stood behind the island, gun pointed at him.

Scotty didn't move.

Shee was something to behold.

He'd sneaked looks at her from afar since she arrived at the hotel, of course, but even in the dim light, she was *so much more* up close.

It was as if decades of prison dreams had *materialized* in front of him. His revenge. His fantasy. Almost within arm's reach.

"You look the same," he said, tucking back into the freezer a notch.

"You look like shit," she said. "But you never were a good-looking guy."

Something in Scotty's brain snapped.

He'd planned things better. He'd wanted to be cool, to slip his gun out, maybe wing her if he had to. Say something cool.

But that *mouth*.

That smart bitch *mouth*.

He couldn't help it. Fury boiled his blood, and he lifted his gun.

She fired.

Scotty jerked back into the freezer like a turtle sucking into its shell. Bullets struck the door. One went through and hit the wall across from him. He grimaced, curled tight in the corner like a standing fetus.

Then he heard it.

Click. Click. Click.

She was out of bullets.

Scotty's body exploded with elation.

You're mine now.

He pushed open the freezer door and thrust out his gun. He squeezed the trigger. Once. Twice.

No returning fire. No scream of pain.

He poked out his head.

Nothing.

Where did she go? Roaring with effort, he wrestled the door open far enough to push his bulky vested torso through.

Leading with his gun, he crept around the island.

Nothing.

Even the cook was gone.

Intermittent gunplay continued out back. He glanced out the back window into the darkness.

She wouldn't have run into that mess.

She would have gone to the lobby.

He turned that way. The swinging door still rocked.

Got you.

He leaped forward as something exploded beyond the door. He threw himself against the wall.

What the hell was that?

Had one of his men shot Shee as she ran away?

A woman's voice exclaimed something he couldn't make out.

Was Shee hit? Begging for her life?

Without me?

Scotty braced himself to push through the swinging door.

No, no, no, no...

CHAPTER FIFTY-SIX

Mason held the Ukrainian underwater for a few more seconds and then thrust himself to the surface with his good leg.

Sucking air, he swam for shore. The toes of his right foot struck sand. He'd lost his loafer somewhere.

He frowned. He'd liked those loafers. They'd been a big step toward trying to feel like a civilian.

He coughed, brackish water purging from his lungs. Somewhere on the opposite bank behind him, a gunshot echoed.

He spun.

Where..?

Stifling a second cough, Mason shuffled up the bank to find a position just inside the tree line. He scanned the opposite shore.

Another shot. The blast came from farther downriver, somewhere across from the hotel.

Sniper?

These guys thought of everything.

Mason retrieved his gun and threw the kid's rifle over his shoulder.

He moved as fast as he could toward The Loggerhead, hoping the darkness would be enough to hide him from the sniper. He was halfway across the grass separating the hotel from the forest when he heard another shot. Something flew past him.

Not dark enough.

He threw himself against the side of the Inn.

"Y'missed me again, ya git," said a voice from the back yard.

Mason scowled. Creeping along the side of the building, he peered around the corner.

A man lay flat behind a raised bed of flowers. A second man in black body armor lay nearby, face down as if he'd been asked to imitate the dead Ukrainian Mason had left on the river bank.

"Hey," called Mason.

The man tucked behind the bed stretched his neck to look behind him.

"Hullo there," he said. "You'll be wanting to stay put. Sniper."

"Got it. I assume you're one of ours?"

"Gardener," he called back. "Trimmer."

Mason wondered why the man called himself a trimmer. *Gardener* covered everything gardeners did.

As if he could read Mason's mind, the gardener continued. "Last bit's my name. Trimmer."

Ah.

"You okay?" Mason scanned the trees across the water, calculating his chances of successfully retrieving the fallen gardener. It was too dark to see much of anything. Sniper probably had a night scope. The odds weren't on his side.

"Took one in the leg. Not cricket, having a chap over there."

Mason motioned to the still body in black. "That guy's dead?"

"Have a look—you'll see he's got my shears sticking out of his neck."

So that's a yes.

Mason sighed. The sniper had Trimmer pinned. To run over and drag him to safety would be suicide. Probably end with both of them dead.

"You have a gun?" he asked.

"No. You?"

"Couple. How bad are you bleeding?"

"I tied it off. Ruined a perfectly good shirt doing it."

Gunfire blasted just inside the hotel.

Mason frowned. "Look, Trimmer, I gotta get inside. I'm going to toss you a rifle. You sit tight."

Trimmer's head nodded. "Cracking idea."

Mason rose from his crouched position long enough to toss the rifle. It landed two feet from Trimmer, who rolled to grab it before spinning back to his position against the raised bed. "I'd like to go in the back here," added Mason.

Trimmer waved once. "Cheers. I'll keep our friend across the water busy." He pointed the rifle over the bed and let off a shot.

Mason ran toward the back porch as more gunfire exploded inside. He rolled aside as two men burst onto the porch.

Men in black.

He fired, clipping one in the arm. The merc fell down the stairs and tumbled out of Mason's line of sight.

From his spot behind the plant bed, Trimmer twisted and sprayed the porch with bullets.

A second merc spilled out of the kitchen and fell directly on his back, a hole in the center of his forehead.

Bracco appeared in the doorway.

"Sniper!" warned Mason from his crouched position in the darkness behind the porch railings.

Too late.

The gun echoed. Mason heard Bracco's wind escape and the thud as the big man hit the ground.

"Bracco?"

Bracco grunted.

"Hold on, buddy. I gotta take care of some things." Mason turned his attention to Trimmer, who shot a staccato string of bullets toward the opposite end of the porch.

He must have missed that soldier. Now the merc sat in the perfect position to pick the Brit off.

Mason wanted to stay low and creep to the end of the porch, but he feared his leg wouldn't let him move like he wanted. He tucked his gun away.

Here goes nothing.

He tucked and rolled sideways past the open stairs. The sniper fired, the bullet striking the building.

Mason threw himself to his stomach and aimed. Alerted by the sniper's shot, the merc hiding on the side of the house popped up his head, looking for him between the spindles of the porch railing.

Mason fired.

The solder dropped.

"Cheers," called Trimmer from his hiding spot.

Mason belly-crawled to the end of the porch and peered over the edge. The body of the merc lay on the ground below. He flipped himself over the railing to join him to the sound of another gunshot. He saw the muzzle flash in the darkness as he fell.

Mason gritted his teeth.

I hate snipers.

He scanned the opposite shore. He'd never get a clean shot at the sniper in the dark.

His gaze dropped to what looked like a body on the ground an arm's length away. He stretched out to poke it.

Soft.

What is that?

Mason reached out and pulled the object toward him to find it was a giant doll made of straw pinned to a long stick.

Hm.

He poked his head around the side of the house.

"Hey, Trimmer."

"At your service."

"How you doing?"

"Brilliant."

"I've got some kind of straw doll here I'm going to throw to you."

Trimmer twisted to look. "Guy Fawkes? He's my scarecrow."

"Whatever. Heads up."

Mason popped up long enough to fling the doll at Trimmer, dropping back to his hands and knees as the sniper took another shot.

Mason saw the flash on the opposite shore again. He had a general idea of where the sniper lay.

"I'm coming next," he said as Trimmer pulled the scarecrow to him.

Mason spun like a rolling pin down the hill toward Trimmer, crawling at the last second to join the gardener behind the raised bed.

Mason slithered up beside him.

"How do you do?" said Trimmer.

"Give me the rifle. I need you to lift the doll when—"

"Scarecrow."

"*Whatever*. Lift it on my mark. Give me a second to set up."

Mason scrooched around until he found a comfortable position and pointed the rifle toward the spot on the opposite shore where he'd seen the flash.

"Up!"

From his supine position, Trimmer lifted the scarecrow. The sniper fired two quick shots, and Mason let a flurry of bullets go where he saw the muzzle flash.

He stopped and ducked back down, waiting.

"Try it again," he said.

Trimmer waved the scarecrow.

No shots.

"I think I got him," said Mason.

"Might be a trick," said Trimmer.

He nodded and glanced back at the hotel. "One way to find

out."

CHAPTER FIFTY-SEVEN

Shee ran into the lobby, grabbed the doorknob to the stairwell, and rattled it.

Locked.

Dammit, I—

A blast exploded that sent Shee rolling sideways. Splinters of wood peppered the side of her face as she ducked away.

She glanced back to see a hole as large as her head blasted through the stairwell door. Cough's head appeared in it, his eyes bugged.

"Jeezus, Cough!"

"I'm so sorry!"

"Get away from the door—go up, go somewhere. He's on my heels!"

Cough ran up the stairs.

"Wait—"

Too late.

She realized the stair door remained locked, the hole too high for her to use to reach through and open the door from the inside.

"Sunuva—"

She glanced back down the hall. No Scotty yet, but he'd burst through the swinging door any second. Hitting the elevator call button would do her no good. She'd be dead by the time it arrived.

She looked at the useless weapon in her hand.

How had she emptied an entire clip into the freezer?

I need another—

The elevator door slid open to reveal a portly, dark-haired man in pajama bottoms and a polo shirt.

"Are you people shooting fireworks?" he asked before his gaze dropped to the gun in her hand.

Before he could step out, Shee shoved him back and hit the highest floor button she could use without the key.

"What are you *doing*?" The man stumbled against the back of the car. He pushed her back and slapped the lobby button. The doors slid open again.

"Why would you do that?" Shee glanced down the hall as the door pushed open, and Scotty peered out.

Shit.

Shee shoved the man again and slapped the door shut button. She raised the gun in her other hand for the man to see.

"Touch another button, and I'll kill you."

The man's eyes grew wide, and Shee turned to point the gun out of the elevator as the doors closed. She heard Scotty slapping outside as the doors sealed. The elevator lurched upward.

Shee remembered to breathe again. She lowered the gun. With her eyes closed, chin against her chest, she felt movement behind her. She looked up in time to see her unwanted elevator-mate hit the *three* button.

She glared, gun rising again. "Is there something wrong with your *brain*?"

"It's my floor," he said. He looked as though his brain had flipped on autopilot.

The doors opened, and the man pushed past her.

"Get to your room. Don't come out," she called at him as he jogged down the hall.

He held up his middle finger.

Shee sighed.

Fair enough.

Another gun blast exploded to her left. The stairwell door swung open as if it had been kicked, slamming into the wall behind it.

Scotty.

Shee slapped the elevator door-close button. The doors slid shut at their own leisurely pace, her heart threatening to pound out of her chest.

She had to find a way to the penthouse before Scotty took the stairs. Maybe the tourist had done her a favor by detouring them to the third floor.

The elevator opened on the floor below the penthouse, and Shee ran out, only to stop dead, her hands outstretched on either side of her as if she were guarding a soccer net at the end of the hall.

What am I doing?

Even if the door to the stairwell was open, the door to the penthouse floor would be locked.

She was out of bullets. Scotty was headed up the stairs.

She straightened.

Cough.

He had to be in the stairwell.

She bolted to the door and flung it open.

Cough stood there with the shotgun pointed down the stairs.

"Oh thank God," he said. "I think someone's—"

"Give me your phone. Do you have a phone?"

"Yes—"

"Give it to me."

He fumbled his cell from his pocket, and Shee dialed Angelina as she dragged him toward the stairs leading to the penthouse.

"Shee! Where are you?" said Angelina on the line.

"I'm one floor down. Scotty's on his way up. I'm out of

bullets. I'm with Cough—he might have one shell left. We're coming up. Open the door!"

"We're coming!"

Shee shoved Cough in front of her and peered over the railing down the stairwell. She heard Scotty below, taking two steps at a time.

It would be tight.

She joined Cough behind the locked door to the penthouse level.

"Come on, come on..." Shee looked from the door to the stairs and back again. She heard keys, and the door opened.

Croix stood in front of her, gun in hand.

"I've never been so happy to see you," said Shee.

"I wish I could say the same." Croix pushed past her and shot twice down the stairwell.

Cough followed suit, leaning and blasting his shotgun over the railing.

Croix reeled back, her free hand on her ear. "You can't do that!"

Shee grimaced, pleased she'd taken a step into the hall before Cough made her ears bleed but disappointed to see him empty his last shot. "Do you have more shells?" she asked.

Cough shook his head. "They're in a bag on the reception desk."

Shee looked at Croix. The girl rolled her eyes.

"I'll hold him back. Go get loaded."

Shee looked down the hall to see Angelina's head sticking out of her father's apartment. She ran toward it. She needed a working weapon. Then she and Croix could work their way down to Scotty and end things.

"Get in, get in," said Angelina, motioning to her.

She slipped inside.

"I need a gun." She waved her weapon. "Or bullets for this one."

"Take mine," said Angelina, thrusting an enormous

Magnum .45 into her hand.

Shee gawked at it. "*This* is your gun?"

"I picked the big one. I like to know I can stop someone."

"You could stop Godzilla with this. The kick alone would send you back in time."

Angelina ignored her. "What's going on?"

"Scotty has a team. Bracco might have them tied up. Maybe Mason. I don't know. I only know Scotty's on his way—Croix has him pinned in the stairwell for now. I have to get back. Did you call the police?"

Angelina shook her head. "Mick said not to. He doesn't want to endanger them or get the staff in trouble—"

Shee huffed. "Well, I think he might feel differently today—"

Angelina shook her head. "No, Mick is—"

"I have to go."

Shee ran back into the hall. Croix stood at the end with the door propped open, watching her approach. Cough stood behind her.

"Where is he?" she asked as she ran.

"I don't know," Croix called back. "I haven't heard anything for a while."

Shee stopped.

The light.

She'd seen a *light* on the elevator panel as she ran out of her father's room.

The penthouse light.

She turned as the elevator doors slid open.

Scotty stepped out.

He turned and saw her.

He raised his gun.

Shee squeezed the trigger of her forty-five. The blast shook the walls and sent her stumbling back.

Scotty spun back into the elevator. A second later, gunshots echoed from inside.

What is he—?

Her father's door sat across from the elevator.

He's shooting the lock from the elevator.

A second later, Scotty bolted across the hall, smashing Mick's apartment door with his body.

He disappeared inside.

CHAPTER FIFTY-EIGHT

"Angelina!"

Shee and Croix sprinted down the hall, Cough somewhere behind them. Gunshots echoed from inside Mick's apartment.

Fear twisted around Shee's heart like an Everglades python. An invasive species that had made a home.

I took Angelina's gun. I left them defenseless.

Behind her, she heard Croix closing in, shouting warnings.

"You can't run right in there—"

The girl didn't understand.

It's all my fault.

She'd stolen Mason's baby. She'd hunted Scotty on her own, behind her father's back, full of foolish pride. She'd led assassins to her sister's house and stolen her own daughter's life a second time. Mick had taken a bullet because of *her*. In a moment, both he and Angelina would be dead.

I'm a curse.

She'd had years to decipher that Scotty Carson was the assassins' puppet master, and she'd blown it. She'd gotten lazy and settled into her role on the run, happy to be forgotten.

On the road, she didn't have to look into her father's eyes. Eyes that never looked at her the same after Grace died. She'd spent a lifetime searching for approval in those eyes.

The bullet was meant for her. Grace had paid the price.

Croix's fingertips brushed her back.

"Slow down—"

Shee jerked her shoulder away and found another gear, one last burst of speed to put distance between the girl and herself. Only the door frame stopped her momentum. She crashed into it, twisting to hit back-first as she raised her gun.

Inside the apartment, the gunfire had stopped.

They're dead.

She knew it.

A blur of motion hit the door at the same moment Shee did. It stepped on her toe and slammed into her shins.

Pulling up, Croix's gun snapped downward to meet the advancing threat.

Archie, racing in a blind panic.

Croix jerked up her weapon as the dog shot by, running full-tilt down the hall.

The girl swore. "That was close."

She looked at Shee, who stood frozen, back against the door jamb, gun raised but pointed low.

"You have him?" she asked.

Shee swallowed. The black-clad, still body of Scotty Carson lay on the ground in front of her, face down.

In the bedroom doorway, Mick stood, draped in a hospital gown, gun in his hand. Tiny Harley stood beside him, her bird-chest puffed, yapping at the dead man, daring him to rise.

Mick wobbled and slapped a hand against the jamb to steady himself.

"I'm going to fall now," he said, his knees beginning to buckle.

Shee tossed her gun onto the sofa as she lunged forward to catch her father. Croix followed inside.

"Get Cough," said Shee as, from the bedroom, Angelina pointed the way back to Mick's bed like a helpful crossing guard.

Croix nodded and ran back to the entrance, nearly crashing into Cough as he appeared.

Mick leaned against his bed, his bleary, blue eyes rising to meet Shee's.

"You're home."

Shee threw her arms around her father. He squeezed.

"I've missed you so much," he whispered in her ear.

"I'm so sorry," she said.

Cough moved in. "Lie down—"

With a sniff, Mick released Shee and wiped his eyes to better glower at the doctor. "Where the hell have *you* been?"

Cough slapped a hand to his chest. "Me?"

"Yeah, *you*. Where's Martisha?"

"Dead," said Shee.

Mick acknowledged the information with a glance and then returned to Cough. "Where were *you* while she was *poisoning* me?"

"Poisoning—?"

"She woke me up every day and then put me back under—" Mick waved his hand in the air as if motioning down the long road he'd traveled under Martisha's care.

Cough's attention swiveled to the I.V. hanging beside the bed. "I gave you one of my bags this time. She must have used something else to induce your coma. Thiopental, maybe. I'd have to—"

Mason burst into the room, and everyone jumped. Croix lifted her gun and then lowered it, looking relieved.

"Today's not the day to enter without knocking," she muttered.

Mason stood wide-eyed, weight shifting to his good leg. "*Mick?*"

Mick's forehead wrinkled. "Mason? What are you—" He looked at Shee. "Are you two—?"

Shee ignored him. "What's going on downstairs?" she asked Mason.

"They're all dead, but Bracco and Trimmer are hit."

"Trimmer?"

"The gardener."

Shee nodded and turned to Cough. "The cook, too. He's stable, hiding in the dining room behind the kitchen."

"I'm on it," said Cough.

"Trimmer's in the back yard. Bracco's in the kitchen," said Mason. "I'll go with you. Call an ambulance."

Cough glanced at Mick. "You good?"

"I'll be fine when somebody tells me what the hell is going on."

Shee put a hand on her father's shoulder. "We'll fill you in. Why don't you rest?"

He snorted a laugh. "You couldn't get me to lie back in this bed again with a gun to my head."

"That could be arranged," said Croix, waggling her weapon. She grinned at Mick. He grinned back.

Shee felt a tinge of jealousy.

Outside, sirens wailed. Mick frowned, struggling to his feet.

"Help me get dressed," he said to Angelina. "I need to keep whatever happened here out of the paper."

The next morning, Shee sat on the porch with her coffee, watching a pair of osprey circle over the river, searching for fish.

It had been a long night. The police had a *lot* of questions. Only Mick's pull with the sheriff kept them all from being dragged to jail until the authorities sorted out what happened.

"You're up," said Angelina, pushing through the screen door. She lowered herself into the Adirondack chair beside Shee and balanced her mug of java on the wide arm.

"Kind of," said Shee. "I feel like a crazy person."

"Three hours of sleep can do that to you."

"Yeah. I'm sure that's all it is. Lack of sleep."

Angelina took a sip of her coffee. "So how's it feel to be free?"

Shee took a deep breath and slowly released it through her nose. "That's what I was thinking about. You know, I'm not sure *free* is the word. I feel more...*untethered.*"

"A lot to process."

"Yep."

"But Mick's awake. Mason's here..."

Shee scoffed. "Not for long."

"I dunno..." Angelina bounced her head from left to right. "Mick asked him to stay."

"Here?" Shee stabbed a finger toward the ground as Angelina nodded.

"Yep. Mick says he needs to bulk the staff. We almost lost them all last night."

Shee laughed. "I'd like to think *that* isn't going to happen again."

Angelina shrugged. "I wouldn't bet on it."

One of the osprey dove, and the women fell silent, watching as the bird plucked its breakfast from the river.

"He didn't ask *me* to stay," mumbled Shee.

"Mason?"

"Dad."

Angelina rolled her eyes. "That's a *given.* Don't be a stupid mopey kid."

She sighed. "And Mason said he'd stay?"

"He did."

Shee chewed on her lip as Angelina watched her.

"You don't want him to?"

Shee shrugged. "I don't think he can forgive me."

Angelina reached out and placed her hand on Shee's.

"He's *staying.*"

"But—"

Angelina held her gaze. "You don't stay to *not* forgive someone."

Shee smiled, hot tears brimming in her tired eyes.

Something clattered in the kitchen behind them. Mick's voice roared.

"What the hell happened to my kitchen?"

~~ THE END ~~

Win a Kindle or a copy of another Shee McQueen Book on Amy Vansant's website!
https://amyvansant.com/giveaways/enter-to-win-kindle-shee-mcqueen-books

WANT SOME MORE? FREE PREVIEW!

If you liked this book, read on for a preview of the next Shee McQueen Mystery-Thriller Series AND the first Pineapple Port Mystery (which shares characters with Shee McQueen's world!)

THANK YOU!

Thank you for reading! If you enjoyed this book, please swing back to Amazon and leave me a review — even short reviews help authors like me find new fans!

FOLLOW AMY on AMAZON or BOOKBUB

ABOUT THE AUTHOR

Amy Vansant is a *Wall Street Journal* and *USA Today* best-selling author who writes with a unique blend of thrills, romance, and humor. She lives in Jupiter, Florida with her muse husband and a very strange Bordoodle, name Archer.

BOOKS BY AMY VANSANT

Pineapple Port Mysteries
Funny, clean & full of unforgettable characters

Shee McQueen Mystery-Thrillers
Action-packed, fun romantic mystery-thrillers

Kilty Urban Fantasy/Romantic Suspense
Action-packed romantic suspense/urban fantasy

Slightly Romantic Comedies
Classic romantic romps

The Magicatory
Middle-grade fantasy

FREE PREVIEW

THE GIRL WHO WAS FORGOTTEN

Shee McQueen Mystery-Thriller Two by Amy Vansant

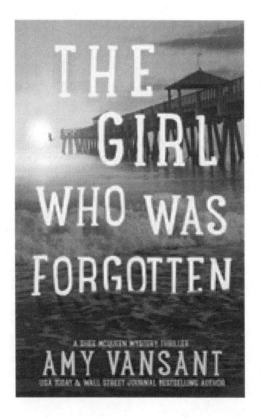

CHAPTER ONE

Five Years Ago

The night air clung to the inside of her lungs as she ran, a rattle burbling in her throat.

It's like breathing water.

Light from a half-moon provided illumination for dodging trees. It also kept the horrors lurking in the jungle draped in shadow. She heard animals scatter. Leaves rustled to her right. Something big moved. It was only a matter of time until she ran into something lacking the time to skitter from her path.

She kept running.

Something stabbed her foot and she yelped. Slapping her hand across her mouth, she stumbled on, ignoring the stinging pain in her arch until she couldn't bear it any longer. Panting, she threw her hip against a tree to lift her foot and pluck out a thorn.

Keep moving.

She'd been running for...*how long?* Five minutes? Ten? Would he chase her?

Run.

The jungle floor tore at her bare feet. A familiar tree appeared on her right.

Am I running in a circle?

It was hard to tell.

What if I'm circling back to him?

She shook away the thought and tore through a thorny tangle of vines. She'd passed the last few big trees to the *left*. Maybe she'd pass the next few on the *right* to make sure she wasn't looping back to the beginning.

Would that work? Does it make sense?

"Hey!"

The man's roar echoed through the dark trees.

Her throat tightened.

He's coming.

His voice sounded far away but *he* had shoes. He had a flashlight. He could run faster. He had all the things she *wished* she had. She pictured him running—bouncing off trees without slowing, like a charging boar.

She picked up her pace and clipped the trunk of a scrub pine with her shoulder. Pain throbbed. Knocked off balance, she spun, arms flailing to catch herself on another tree. Lights flickered in the distance, sparkling through the leaves like fairies.

Lights.

She stopped, watching.

A glimmer of white appeared on her left and moved to the right before turning red.

Cars.

A road.

"Stop!"

The world went gray again beneath soft moonlight. She listened for the sound of cars.

A flash.

There.

She broke through the edge of the forest before realizing she'd reached the road. Soft grass felt like her mother's sateen robe beneath her feet. The robe with the Japanese flowers on it. The one soaked in blood.

Closing her eyes, the girl shook her head.

Why think about that now?

She couldn't stop in time. She'd built too much momentum and the edge of the jungle had come too fast.

The lights closed in.

Grass turned to gravel and gravel to pavement.

Brakes screeched. The smell of burnt rubber assaulted her nostrils. Stumbling, she covered her head with her hands and collapsed in front of the vehicle.

All this way to be hit by a car.

It was almost funny.

"Ohmygod. No, no, no..."

A female voice.

The girl opened her eyes to find a woman squatting beside her. Long graceful fingers tipped with light pink nails fluttered against her throbbing shoulder.

"Are you okay?" asked the woman.

The girl blinked at the woman.

"Stop!"

The voice in the woods was faint.

The woman didn't react. The girl froze her expression, pretending not to hear.

He'll scare her. She won't help me.

"Are you okay?" the woman asked again.

Radio music played. The car door was open, a steady warning pinging like a robot's heartbeat.

"Hospital," said the girl, clambering to her swollen feet.

The woman stood up from her crouch, looking both confused and relieved, and the girl realized her mistake.

I look too good.

The woman might leave her behind.

She limped toward the open driver's side door.

"Um..." The woman followed. "Where are you—"

The girl ducked her head into the car.

"Are you okay? You ran out like someone was chasing—" The woman looked over the car into the trees, her eyes wide. "Wait—*is* someone chasing you?"

"Yes." The girl crawled into the car to take her place in the passenger seat. "Hurry. Get in. We have to *go*."

"Is someone coming?" The woman's voice rose to a squeak. She dropped into her seat and closed and locked the door, her hands shaking.

The steady chirp of crickets stopped. The radio played.

"Come on Eileen, oh I swear..."

The girl stared through her window into the jungle, expecting him to burst through the tree line the way she had.

She turned to find the woman gaping at her, slack-jawed, like a cow.

Pounding her thigh with the side of her fist, she yelled to shake the woman from her stupor.

"Go! Go! Hurry! Before he gets here!"

"Ohmygod..." The woman jumped and slammed the car into drive. She stomped on the gas, her fingers white on the steering wheel. "I'm sorry. I'm so sorry," she chanted, her gaze bouncing from the road to the rearview mirror to the road again as if she were watching a tennis match. "I couldn't see you. I *didn't* see you until it was almost too late. What happened? Is someone really after you?"

"Yes."

"A man? Was he trying to kidnap you?"

The girl twisted to peer through the back windshield. A shadowy figure, illuminated by gray moonlight, burst from the woods, stumbling forward, looking as she imagined she had earlier.

"Yes."

The woman gasped.

The man found his feet and, legs spread, took his place in the middle of the road. She couldn't see his face, but she knew he was staring at their red taillights, both he and the lights getting smaller and smaller in the distance from each other.

"I'll get you to the police—"

"*No.*" The girl's hand jumped to the door latch.

The woman slapped a hand to her leg, holding her in place. "Oh honey, don't be scared. They're on *your* side. You—" She swallowed. "Oh God, you're probably scared of men. I'll find you a lady officer, okay?"

The girl lowered her hand to her lap. "Okay."

"I can't imagine what you've been through—" The woman took a deep breath and released it. "I haven't even asked—what's your name?"

The name had been locked, screaming somewhere in the back of the girl's skull, so she set it free.

"June."

CHAPTER TWO

Shee McQueen blinked at the dimpled glass lamp on the nightstand beside her bed. The light seemed a little *classy* for the places she usually stayed.

Where am I?

She rolled onto her back, sinking into the soft luxury of the bed. Not a single spring ground into her spine.

Okay. Not a motel bed.

She scanned the room.

Oh. Right.

She was in her father's hotel, The Loggerhead Inn—her new home.

Through heavy morning brain fog, Shee's world emerged

like a tattered ghost ship.

What the hell did I do last night?

One squinted eye spotted two empty tumblers on the bureau next to the flat-screen television. Her thoughts were messy—stumbling around her head like a still-drunk, morning-after prom queen—mascara caked beneath each eye, a broken heel, and a half-empty bottle of tequila in one hand.

Ah. That was it.

I smell tequila.

Shee rubbed her eyes and sat up.

Bad idea.

The pressure in her skull shifted. The wailing, raccoon-eyed debutante in her brain dropped to her knees, struck down by the sudden onslaught of a throbbing headache.

Stop it. Shut up, you sloppy—

Something in the bed *moved*.

Startled, Shee recoiled, pulling her sheet against her chest.

A retired Navy-SEAL-shaped lump rolled to face her.

Mason.

Her ex-boyfriend, twenty-six years removed, licked his lips and groaned as if his head clanged, too. She doubted he was imagining himself as a ragged prom queen, but whatever the male equivalent might be...

Mason's eyes fluttered open, his hand rising to his forehead, muscles, and tendons flexing. A gnarled scar on his bicep glowed hot pink beneath the light peeping through the gauzy drapes of her room at The Loggerhead Inn.

He was in her room.

In her *bed*.

"It feels like a battalion is marching through my head," he muttered.

Shee chuckled.

There it is.

"I've got a pissed-off prom queen," she said.

"What?"

"In my head. I've got—"

He squinted at her, clearly confused.

"Nevermind." Shee relaxed her death grip on the sheets and rubbed her tongue against the back of her teeth. "Did we eat cotton balls last night?"

Mason expelled a soft snort of air and focused on her with bright blue irises floating in blurry pink seas. His expression remained inscrutable.

Did he mean to wake up in her bed? Was it a mistake he regretted?

Wait, did we...?

She looked beneath the covers to find herself fully dressed in jeans and a wrinkled top. She turned to glance at Mason. He, too, wore clothes from the evening before.

There'd been no great reconciliation.

Don't mistake his presence for forgiveness.

"Drinking doesn't feel the same in your forties," he mumbled.

"You noticed that, too?"

Catching a whiff of her breath, she rolled out of bed.

My mouth tastes like—

She glanced back at him and a memory from long ago fluttered through her mind. Mason, wearing only the sheet of her single bed, she tracing the v-notch at the base of his neck, the nerves beneath her skin tingling beneath his touch—

Stop.

Shee continued to the bathroom, more certain than ever nothing had happened between them the night before.

It's okay. I get it. He has every right to hate me.

He hadn't thought she was serious when she broke up with him days before his first tour of duty. By the time he'd returned, she'd disappeared. She'd run away, pregnant with his child. It would take him more than a day or two to forgive her for hiding their daughter's existence from him.

Maybe a year.

Maybe forever.

Shee shuffled into the bathroom and brushed her teeth, snippets of the previous evening flaring in her head like a flashbulb popping in a dark room.

She, Mason, and the Loggerhead's ragtag army of retired military had stopped the man who'd been hunting her for years. Her father had awakened from his coma. They'd spent the next day visiting their fallen comrades in the hospital and repairing the damaged hotel—*and then they'd celebrated.* They'd had a drink. Then two.

Then too many.

Commander Mason Connelly, ever the gentleman, had helped her to bed and—

Shee stopped brushing and stared in the mirror. She winced as another flashbulb blasted toward an ugly corner of her memory.

There'd been crying. Some mea culpas. He'd tried to leave and then—

Mason's voice rang from the bedroom.

"Where's my leg?"

Shee closed her eyes.

Right.

Spitting out a mouthful of minty foam, she rinsed and reentered the bedroom. Mason sat perched at the end of the bed, glaring at her as she emerged.

"Hm?" she asked.

He pointed to his knee. The one with no calf beneath it.

"My *leg*."

"Oh. Um...did you lose it?"

"Shee, I swear—"

"Okay, okay. Hold on. I'll remember in a second."

In truth, she already recalled too much of it. He'd removed his metal appendage to relieve an ache. She'd snatched it and hidden it to keep him from leaving. He'd been kind enough to let it go after she pretended to fall asleep.

No amount of shameless cajoling had inspired him to remove anything but the leg.

Shee's gaze settled on the closet.

That feels familiar.

She opened the door. Inside, a titanium stalk grew from an umbrella stand. She lifted it to find a foot at the opposite end.

"Is this it?" she asked, holding it up for him to see.

He held out a hand. "Give."

She handed it to him and watched him tuck his stump into it.

"Want to grab some breakfast?" she asked.

He stood and tested his weight on his prosthesis. "No. I want to get a shower and eat a jar of aspirin."

"Bacon helps—"

He shook his head and patted her upper arm a couple of times before leaving the room.

No further comment. No hesitation.

Gone.

She watched the door click shut.

Bastard.

He'd *patted* her. Dismissed her like a golden retriever.

Not a good sign.

Pinching her shirt, she plucked it out for a sniff.

I sort of smell *like a golden retriever.*

She retrieved and drank a sixteen-ounce water from her mini-fridge and took a shower. By the time she'd dressed, she felt almost human again.

She put her hand on the doorknob and took a deep breath.

I can do this.

Even with her lost love hobbling around the hotel, furious at her over his hidden daughter, life was better now than it was a week ago.

Isn't it?

She wasn't on the run, her father—ole Unbreakable Mick McQueen—had recovered, and she had a home at the hotel—all good stuff.

"All good stuff," she said aloud and marched down the hall to the door of her father's room. Raising a hand to knock, she glanced at her watch.

Seven a.m.

Hm.

Maybe she could let him sleep a little longer.

She made an about-face to punch the elevator call button as her phone buzzed in her pocket. Slipping it out as she entered the elevator, she paused at the site of the caller-ID.

Speak of the devil.

She glanced back at her father's door and answered. "Hello?"

Mick's voice sounded gruff and officious. "Hey. I need you and Mason down here in the meeting room."

"I don't know where he is."

"Uh-huh."

"What do you mean, *uh-huh*?"

"Just get down here." He hung up.

Shee glared at her phone until the elevator tried to close, ping-ponging her shoulders against the silver doors and rattling her skull anew.

Ow.

Jumping back into the hall, she stomped to Mason's door to knock. When no one answered, she pushed her ear against the wood to listen for a running shower.

Nothing.

She huffed.

Am I his keeper?

No.

She strode back to the elevator.

Dad can summon his own damn troops.

Get *The Girl Who Was Forgotten* on Amazon!

ANOTHER FREE PREVIEW!

PINEAPPLE LIES

A Pineapple Port Mystery: Book One – By Amy
Vansant

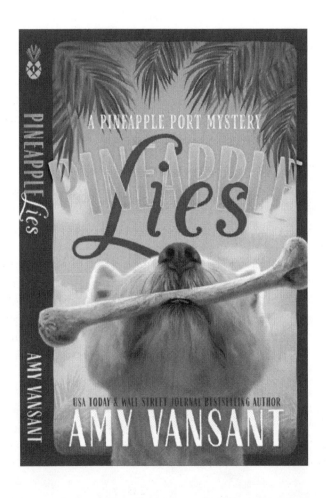

CHAPTER ONE

"Whachy'all doin'?"

Charlotte jumped, her paintbrush flinging a flurry of black paint droplets across her face. She shuddered and placed her free hand over her heart.

"Darla, you scared me to death."

"Sorry, Sweetpea, your door was open."

"Sorry," echoed Mariska, following close on Darla's heels.

Charlotte added another stroke of black to her wall and balanced her brush on the edge of the paint can. Standing, her knees cracked a twenty-one-gun salute. She was only twenty-six years old but had always suffered bad knees. She didn't mind. Growing up in a fifty-five-plus retirement community, her creaky joints provided something to complain about when the locals swapped war stories about pacemakers and hip replacements. Nobody liked to miss out on that kind of fun.

Charlotte wiped the paint from her forehead with the back of her hand.

"Unlocked and open are not the same thing, ladies. What if I had a gentleman caller?"

Darla burst into laughter, the gold chain dangling from her hot-pink-rimmed glasses swinging. She sobered beneath the weight of Charlotte's unamused glare. Another pair of plastic-rimmed glasses sat perched like a baby bird on her head, tucked into a nest of champagne-blonde curls.

"Did you lose your other glasses again?" asked Charlotte.

"I did. They'll turn up."

Charlotte nodded and tapped the top of her head. "I'm sure."

Darla's hand shot to her head.

"Oh, there you go. See? I told you they'd show up."

Mariska moved closer, nudging Darla out of the way. She threw out her arms, her breezy cotton tunic draping like aqua butterfly wings.

"Morning hug," she demanded.

Charlotte rolled her eyes and relented. Mariska wrapped her in a bear hug, and she sank into the woman's snuggly, Polish-grandmother's body. It was like sitting on a favorite old sofa, rife with missing springs, and then being eaten by it.

"Okay. Can't breathe," said Charlotte.

"I'm wearing the top you bought me for Christmas," Mariska mumbled in Charlotte's ear as she rocked her back and forth.

"I saw that."

"It's very comfortable."

"This isn't. *I can't breathe.* Did I mention that? We're good. Okay there..."

Mariska released Charlotte and stepped back, her face awash with satisfaction. She turned and looked at the wall, scratching her cheek with flowered, enameled nails as she studied Charlotte's painting project.

"What are you doing there? Painting your wall black? Are you depressed?"

Charlotte sighed. Darla and Mariska were inseparable; if one wasn't offering an opinion, the other was picking up the slack.

"You're not turning into one of those dopey Goth kids now, are you?" asked Darla.

"No, it has nothing to do with my mood. It's chalkboard paint. I'm making this strip of wall into a giant chalkboard."

"Why?" Darla asked, her thick, Kentucky accent adding

syllables to places the word *why* had never considered having them. Her mouth twisted and her brow lowered. Charlotte couldn't tell if she disapproved, was confused, or suffering a sharp gas pain. Not one guess was more likely than any other.

"Because I think I figured out my problem," she said.

Darla cackled. "Oh, this oughta be good. You have any coffee left?"

"In the kitchen."

Darla and Mariska lined up and waddled toward the kitchen like a pair of baby ducks following their mama. Mariska inspected several mugs in the cabinet above the coffee machine and, finding one, put it aside. She handed Darla another. Mariska's mug of choice was the one she'd given Charlotte after a trip to Colorado's Pikes Peak. She'd bought the mug for herself, but after Charlotte laughed and explained the double entendre of the slogan emblazoned on the side, *I Got High on Pikes Peak*, she'd thrust it at her, horrified. Mariska remained proud of her fourteen thousand foot spiraling drive to the peak, however, so she clandestinely drank from the offending mug whenever she visited.

Charlotte watched as she read the side of the mug, expelled a deep sigh, and poured her coffee. That heartbreaking look was why she hadn't broached the subject of Mariska's *I Got Baked in Florida* t-shirt.

The open-plan home allowed the two older women to watch Charlotte as she returned to painting the wall between her pantry door and living area.

"So are you pregnant?" Darla asked. "And after this, you're painting the nursery?"

"Ah, no. That's not even funny."

"You're the youngest woman in Pineapple Port. You're our only hope for a baby. How can you toss aside the hopes and dreams of three hundred enthusiastic, if rickety, babysitters?"

"I don't think I'm the youngest woman here anymore. I think Charlie Collins is taking his wife to the prom next week."

Darla laughed before punctuating her cackle with a grunt of disapproval.

"Stupid men," she muttered.

Charlotte whisked away the last spot of neutral cream paint with her brush, completing her wall. She turned to find Mariska staring, her thin, over-plucked eyebrows sitting high on her forehead as she awaited the answer to the mystery of the chalkboard wall.

"So you're going to keep your grocery list on the wall?" asked Mariska. "That's very clever."

"Not exactly. Lately, I've been asking myself, what's missing from my life?"

Darla tilted her head. "A man. *Duh.*"

"Yeah, yeah. Anyway, last week it hit me."

Darla paused, mug nearly to her lips, waiting for Charlotte to continue.

"What hit you? A chalkboard wall?" asked Mariska.

Charlotte shook her head. "No, a *purpose*. I need to figure out what I want to *be*. My life is missing *purpose*."

Darla rolled her eyes. "Oh, is that all? I think they had that on sale at Target last weekend. Probably still is."

Charlotte chuckled and busied herself resealing the paint can.

Mariska inspected Charlotte's handiwork. "So you're going to take up painting? I'll take a chalkboard wall. I can write Bob messages and make lists…"

"I'll paint your wall if you like, but starting a painting business isn't my *purpose*. The wall is so I can make a to-do list."

Darla sighed. "I have a to-do list, but it only has one thing on it: *Keep breathing*."

Mariska giggled.

"I'm going to make goals and write them here," said Charlotte, gesturing like a game show hostess to best display her wall. "When I accomplish something, I get to cross it off. See? I already completed one project; that's how I know it works."

There was a knock on the door and Charlotte's gaze swiveled to the front of the house. Her soft-coated wheaten terrier, Abby, burst out of the bedroom and stood behind the door, barking.

"You forgot to open your blinds this morning," said Mariska.

"Death Squad," mumbled Darla.

The Death Squad patrolled the Pineapple Port retirement community every morning. If the six-woman troop passed a home showing no activity by ten a.m., they knocked on the door and demanded proof of life. They pretended to visit about other business, asking if the homeowner would be attending this meeting or that bake sale, but everyone knew the Squad was there to check if someone died overnight. Odds were slim that Charlotte wouldn't make it through an evening, but the Squad didn't make exceptions.

Charlotte held Abby's collar and opened the door.

"Oh, hi, Charlotte," said a small woman in a purple t-shirt. "We were just—"

"I'm alive, Ginny. Have a good walk."

Charlotte closed the door. She opened her blinds and peeked out. Several of the Death Squad ladies waved to her as they resumed their march. Abby stood on the sofa and thrust her head through the blinds, her nub of a tail waving back at them at high speed.

Mariska turned and dumped her remaining coffee into the sink, rinsed the purple mug, and with one last longing glance at the Pikes Peak logo, put it in the dishwasher. She placed her hands on her ample hips and faced Charlotte.

"Do you have chalk?"

"No."

She'd been annoyed at herself all morning for forgetting chalk and resented having it brought to her attention. "I forgot it."

Darla motioned to the black wall. "Well, there's your first item. *Buy chalk.* Write that down."

"With what?"

"Oh. Good point."

"Anyhow, shopping lists don't count," said Charlotte.

Darla chuckled. "Oh, there are *rules*. The chalkboard has rules, Mariska."

Mariska pursed her lips and nodded. "Very serious."

"Well, I may not have a chalkboard, but I have a wonderful sense of purpose," said Darla putting her mug in the dishwasher.

"Oh yes? What's that?"

"I've got to pick up Frank's special ED pills."

She stepped over the plastic drop cloth beneath the painted wall and headed for the door.

"ED?" Charlotte blushed. "You mean for his—"

"Erectile Dysfunction. Pooped Peepee. Droopy D—"

"Got it," said Charlotte, cutting her short.

"Fine. But these pills are special. Want to know why?"

"Not in the least."

Mariska began to giggle and Darla grinned.

"She's horrible," Mariska whispered as she walked by Charlotte.

Darla reached into her pocketbook and pulled out a small plastic bottle. She handed it to Charlotte.

"Read the label."

Charlotte looked at the side of the pill bottle. The label held the usual array of medical information, but the date was two years past due.

"He only gets them once every two years?"

"Nope. He only got them *once*. Ever since then I've been refilling the bottle with little blue sleeping pills. Any time he gets the urge, he takes one, and an hour later, he's sound asleep. When he wakes up, I tell him everything was wonderful."

Charlotte's jaw dropped. "That's terrible."

Darla dismissed her with a wave and put the bottle back in her purse.

"Nah," she said, opening the front door. "I don't have time for that nonsense. If I'm in the mood, I give him one from the original prescription."

Darla and Mariska patted Abby on the head, waved goodbye, and stepped into the Florida sun.

Charlotte shut the door behind them and balled her drop cloth of sliced trash bags. She rinsed her brush and carried the paint can to the work shed in her backyard. On her way back to the house, she surveyed her neglected yard. A large pile of broken concrete sat in the corner awaiting pickup. As part of her new *life with purpose* policy, Charlotte had hired a company to jackhammer part of her concrete patio to provide room for a garden. The original paved yard left little room for plants. With the patio removed, Charlotte could add *grow a garden* to her chalkboard wall. Maybe she was supposed to be a gardener or work with the earth. She didn't feel particularly *earthy*, but who knew?

She huffed, mentally kicking herself again for forgetting to buy chalk.

Her rocky new patch of sand didn't inspire confidence. It in no way resembled the dark, healthy soil she saw in her neighbors' more successful gardens. Charlotte returned to the shed to grab a spade and cushion for her knees, before kneeling at the corner of her new strip of dirt. It was cool outside; the perfect time of day to pluck the stray bits of concrete from the ground before the Florida sun became unbearable. She knew she didn't like sweating, so gardening was probably not her calling. Still, she was determined to give everything a chance. She'd clean her new garden, shower, and then run out to buy topsoil, plants, and chalk.

"Tomatoes, cucumbers…" Charlotte mumbled to herself, mentally making a list of plants she needed to buy. *Or seeds? Should I buy seeds or plants?* Plants. Less chance of failure starting with mature plants; though if they died, that would be even *more* embarrassing.

Charlotte's spade struck a large stone and she removed it,

tossing it toward the pile of broken concrete. A scratching noise caught her attention and she looked up to find her neighbor's Cairn terrier, Katie, furiously digging beside her. Part of the fence had been broken or chewed, and stocky little Katie visited whenever life in her backyard became too tedious.

Charlotte watched the dirt fly: "Katie, you're making a mess. If you want to help, pick up stones and move them out of the garden."

Katie stopped digging long enough to stare with her large brown eyes. At least Charlotte *thought* the dog was staring at her. She had a lazy eye that made it difficult to tell.

"Move the rocks," Charlotte repeated, demonstrating the process with her spade. "Stop making a mess or I'll let Abby out and then you'll be in trouble."

Katie ignored her and resumed digging, sand arcing behind her, piling against the fence.

"You better watch it, missy, or the next item on the list will be to *fix the fence*."

Katie eyeballed her again, her crooked bottom teeth jutting from her mouth. She looked like a furry can opener.

"Fix your face."

Katie snorted a spray of snot and returned to digging.

Charlotte removed several bits of concrete and then shifted her kneepad a few feet closer to Katie. She saw a flash of white and felt something settle against her hand. Katie sat beside her, tail wagging, tongue lolling from the left side of her mouth. Between the dog and her hand sat the prize Katie had been so determined to unearth.

Charlotte froze, one word repeating in her mind, picking up the pace until it was an unintelligible crescendo of nonsense.

Skull. Skull skull skullskullskullskuuuuullll...

She blinked, certain that when she opened her eyes the object would have taken its proper shape as a rock or pile of sand.

Nope.

The eye sockets stared back at her.

Hi. Nice to meet you. I'm human skull. What's up, girl?

The lower jaw was missing. The cranium was nearly as large as Katie and had similar off-white color, though the skull had better teeth.

Charlotte realized the forehead of this boney intruder rested against her pinky. She whipped her hand away. The skull rocked toward her, as if in pursuit, and she scrambled back as it rolled in her direction, slow and relentless as a movie mummy. Katie ran after the skull and pounced on it, stopping its progress.

Charlotte put her hand on her chest, breathing heavily.

"Thank you."

Her brain raced to process the meaning of a human head in her backyard.

It has to be a joke... maybe some weird dog toy...

Charlotte gently tapped the skull with her shovel. It didn't feel like cloth or rawhide. It made a sharp-yet-thuddy noise, just the sort of sound she suspected a human skull might make. If she had to compare the tone to something, it would be the sound of a girl about to freak out, tapping a metal shovel on a human skull.

"Oh, Katie. What did you find?"

The question increased Katie's rate of tail wag. She yipped and ran back to the hole she'd dug, retrieving the lower jaw.

"Oh no... Stop that. You sick little—"

Katie stood, human jawbone clenched in her teeth, tail wagging so furiously that Charlotte thought she might lift off like a chubby little helicopter. The terrier spun and skittered through the fence back to her yard, dragging her prize in tow. The jawbone stuck in the fence for a moment, but Katie wrestled it through and disappeared into her yard.

"Katie no," said Charlotte, reaching toward the retreating dog. "Katie—I'm pretty sure that has to stay with the head."

She leaned forward and nearly touched the jawless skull before yanking away her hand.

Whose head is in my garden?

She felt her eyes grow wide like pancake batter poured into a pan.

Hold the phone.

Heads usually come attached to bodies.

Were there more bones?

What was worse? Finding a whole skeleton or finding *only* a head?

Charlotte hoped the rest of the body lay nearby and then shook her head at the oddity of the wish.

She glanced around her plot of dirt and realized she might be kneeling in a *whole graveyard*. More bones. More *heads*. She scrambled to her feet and dropped her shovel.

Charlotte glanced at her house, back to where her chalkboard wall waited patiently.

She *really* needed some chalk.

Made in the USA
Middletown, DE
29 July 2023